THE HIDDEN ONES

BOOK ONE OF
LEGACY OF THE WATCHERS

NANCY MADORE

Published in the United States

ISBN: 9781479321209 (paperback)

ISBN: 1479321206

ISBN: 9781624075148 (Epub)

ISBN: 9781624075155 (PDF)

ASIN: B009R4CJB8 (Kindle)

Edited by Mark Hackenberg

Cover Design by Gregory Rose

OTHER BOOKS IN THIS SERIES

For Jenny

"The Nephilim were on the earth in those days, and also after, when the sons of God came in to the daughters of man and they bore children to them. These were the mighty men who were of old, the men of renown."

— GENESIS 6:4

PROLOGUE

The car crept slowly down the deserted little street. It was just after midday, so everyone was still performing *salat*. The sun flooded through the car windows, lulling its silent occupants into an agreeable drowsiness. The driver hesitated in the unfamiliar neighborhood. Helene Trevelyan snapped out of her stupor to speak.

"It's the third one on the right," she said. A small twinge of excitement shot through her, taking her by surprise.

As the car turned into the driveway, the woman sitting in the front passenger seat turned to look at Helene. "Are you sure you'll be all right?" she asked.

"Of course," said Helene, reaching for the door handle. She heard the trunk pop and the driver stepped out of the car.

The woman frowned. "It doesn't feel right leaving you here by yourself," she said.

"I'll be fine," said Helene. She was impatient to leave but lingered a moment longer, so as not to appear rude. Like Helene, the woman was shrouded in the all-too-familiar black, leaving nothing exposed but her eyes. The eyes were all Helene noticed now anyway. It was surprising how telling that single feature could be when it was all you had to distinguish one person from another. These eyes were distracted and weary, but they were also touched with concern. "Really," insisted Helene, trying to keep the impatience out of her voice. "You've been kind enough already." And this was true. The woman and her husband had bent the rules to help Helene—a virtual stranger—and that was saying something in this part of the world. The woman's husband, meanwhile, had fetched Helene's bag out of the trunk and silently stood on her stoop, waiting for her to open the front door.

"You're sure someone's coming?" the woman asked, still uncertain.

"Yes. My friend will be here within the hour," Helene lied. "Thank you again. I don't want to keep your husband waiting." Helene got out of the car and self-consciously walked up to the house. Her heart had begun the strange fluttering, just as she knew that it would. With her eyes respectfully lowered she unlocked her front door and stepped to one side. The man went only far enough into the house to place her bag inside and then left without a word. Helene slipped inside and shut the door with a sigh of relief.

Home at last! Helene looked around. Something was different. The house was so quiet. How strange it seemed without everyone in it. When was the last time she'd been alone? Helene pondered this as she waited for her heart to resume its regular tempo, and she suddenly realized that she'd never been completely alone in this house before. A guilty thrill trickled through her. She wondered, a little bewildered, what she should do first. She was exhausted and knew that she should eat something but, of course, she would have a look in the garden before anything else.

Leaving her bag where it lay, Helene slowly made her way through the house to the courtyard Zaahid built for her. A small smile curved her lips at the thought of Zaahid. She would never forget the day she found out about her step-son—or Fa'izah, his mother. Nor would she forget the look on their faces when they found out about her! And yet, what a blessing they both had turned out to be. Of course, Helene hadn't been particularly thrilled at the time, and neither had poor Fa'izah, but the wide-eyed little boy, Zaahid, was delighted. From the very first day he followed Helene everywhere, like a benevolent little shadow; helping her, defending her and eventually becoming her biggest supporter—especially when it came to her garden.

It seemed a crazy idea, planting a flower garden in the desert, but Helene had needed something to take her mind off her troubles and the challenge kept her distracted. And she was determined. The garden was like a lifeline for her, representing the only link to her past. In some small way it helped bridge the enormous gap between her homeland and this, defying their most obvious contrasts. For the England of her memory was vigorous and alive. It was constantly changing and full of surprises, from its bright, jolly summers to its blustery, tempestuous winters. Saudi Arabia seemed stark by comparison, but Helene refused to yield to its limitations. All of her frustration for the whole of Arabia became concentrated on that little parcel of land she set out to tame. And tame it she did, with Zaahid by her side, planting, cultivating and weeding. He even recruited the others, working his way through their extended family until he finally roped every last one of them into helping her—some more begrudgingly than others—and the project became so enormous that it pervaded every aspect of their daily lives. Table scraps were religiously collected to be converted into compost, and buckets of used water were saved for watering. Gifts almost always came in the form of a plant. And now, all these years later, there was rarely a moment in Helene's garden when something wasn't in bloom.

Although it wasn't at its peak on this particular November afternoon, the garden's effect on Helene was as powerful as ever. There was just enough color to catch the eye, and the sweet, gentle scent of the foliage hung lightly in the air. It was a splendid afternoon, warm enough to linger outdoors. Helene picked up a pair of hand shears that were lying on a nearby bench and began absently deadheading the plants, creating a pouch in her *abaya* to collect the wilted flowers in. She noticed that the plants had been watered and her heart swelled in gratitude for Fa'izah. The intensity of her feelings for the woman she shared her husband with surprised her a little. Their relationship was unexpected, to say the least. But if nothing else, life had taught Helene to expect the unexpected. Would death be the same? As she meandered through the neat little rows of plants, chopping off the dried up flower heads, Helene wondered. She didn't feel like a woman who was dying, though she did feel weaker than usual and, too, there was that disturbing slowing and, alternately, racing of her heart. It wouldn't bother her so much, she decided, if not for the alarm it sometimes caused. Each time it happened she couldn't help wondering: would this be the moment when her heart stopped for good?

But at least she'd escaped that dreadful hospital. And she had to admit that the timing of it couldn't have been better. There was no one to make her stay. For once, there was no one to make her do anything. They'd all gone to Mecca for *Hajj*. And she would have been forced to go too, if not for the attack. Perhaps in the end Allah had decided to be merciful, granting her this small reprieve for a lifetime of going through the motions.

Allah. The old resentment automatically rose up in her and she closed her eyes, practicing the breathing exercises the nurses taught her. She reminded herself that her aversion was not really toward God, but the people who presumed to speak for him. How she fought them! But in the end they won, just as she supposed they always had throughout history. She no longer blamed Aabid. Her husband was as much a victim as she and Fa'izah were. Poor Zaahid and Rashad! They were destined to be just like their father. How could they be any other way? His way of thinking had been ingrained in them through every aspect of their lives, not just by Aabid but by their schools, their laws and their culture. It seemed to Helene that there was no way out for any of them.

Except Gisele. She got out. Unwanted tears came to Helene's eyes and she focused once again on breathing slowly and deeply. But this time the breathing didn't help, and the wild fluttering became more pronounced until Helene's heart was clamoring painfully in her chest. She felt a moment of fear. She was not ready to go yet! She crouched low, bringing her head down past her bent knees, and waited for the painful thudding to subside. A late-blooming crocus, peeking out from behind a cluster of dried-up blossoms caught her attention. The petals on the tardy little flower were a brilliant lavender that contrasted delightfully with its red and yellow center. Helene inhaled deeply, capturing the delicate scent of it and then, sufficiently calmed, stood up with an ironic laugh. There was a time when she'd prayed for death, though she never fostered any hopes of something better waiting for her in the afterlife. She envied the religious their absolute certainty of a heavenly reward, and yet she could never understand their willingness to sacrifice happiness in this life for a promise of it in the next. "A bird in the hand is worth two in the bush," was her philosophy. Yet her proverbial bird had long since flown, so she supposed the two in the bush were all she had left.

Gisele knew, and that was what frightened Helene. If there really was some kind of existence after death, wouldn't her daughter have finally made contact, after all her thwarted efforts to do so in life? For although Helene never actually received any of Gisele's letters she'd been made aware of each and every one. Aabid was not one to mete out retribution passively. Oh no, he'd taken great pleasure in sharing little tidbits from Gisele's letters—not enough to quench Helene's thirst for information about her firstborn child, but just enough to pique her interest or give her cause to worry. And to this day, Helene knew he believed he'd done it for her own good. To the bitter end he'd held his ground, never once wavering, not even when that last letter came.

"Your daughter is dead," was all he told her. "May Allah have mercy on her infidel soul."

As always, the garden soothed her. The stone benches, so deliciously warm, had a therapeutic effect. She thought again of the hospital, recalling how frightfully cold it had been. Her teeth had never once stopped chattering throughout her stay there. Each time she heard the air conditioning click on—a sound that could wake her out of a dead sleep once she'd been there a few days—she shuddered with dread. Although she knew it was crazy, she had the peculiar impression that they were trying to *keep* their patients, like meat, from spoiling. And yet she would always be grateful to the doctor for allowing her to check herself out of the hospital, which normally required the permission of a woman's *wali*. Letting her go without her husband's consent was one thing, but the doctor, a gentle, caring woman of perhaps forty-five years (judging from her eyes), had even arranged for one of the nurses to take Helene home at the closing of her shift. Such acts of kindness were rare, as they could bring terrible repercussions if challenged. Helene hoped this would not be the case for her doctor.

Helene dug out a clump of irises and began carefully separating the shoots with a sharp knife. She handled the large, bulbous roots carefully, taking her time. There was no reason to hurry. There was nothing pressing to be done. There was no one to disturb her. She let her mind wander as she worked, allowing it to lead her where it would while she remained under the comforting influence of her courtyard paradise. Her thoughts moved tentatively toward the memories that most profoundly touched her life and, for the first time in years, she thought about that fateful trip to Qumran. Breathing deeply, she brought forth the images of her father, Butch and Huxley. Her lips curved in an unconscious smile. They were like three little boys looking for a ghost in a haunted house. And damned if they didn't find it! How different things would have been if only they'd made it out of Qumran. Helene sighed. That 'what if' had been played out a long time ago. They didn't make it out. The image of her father lying dead in the road suddenly flashed through her mind and Helene was abruptly jerked out of her reverie.

It was a lifetime ago. And it involved something bigger than Helene, her father, Butch and Huxley—bigger even than the discovery they traveled so far to find, which itself was so big it would have set the entire science community, and the world, on its ear. Yes, it was even bigger than that! Helene couldn't comprehend the extent of it, but she knew it was too big for this world. And she knew that what happened with Lilith was at the center of it.

Lilith. Helene shuddered as she remembered the creature (there was no other way to describe it) that lured them—and her father's killer—to Qumran. Helene could still see her pointed teeth, sharp and menacing, which Lilith tried to hide behind her dark curtain of hair. And those terrible claws! There was no denying that—whatever Lilith had been in life—death had made her a monster.

Well, at least she'd been stopped. Helene had seen to that. No one would find her again.

Helene felt calmer, confident that she'd done the right thing. It was tempting to sympathize with Lilith. There was a time when Helene was in awe of her. She couldn't help admiring Lilith's strength and determination. Back then, Helene would have given anything to be more like her. In her darkest moments, she even considered turning to Lilith for help. Thank goodness she never succeeded! She knew now that it wasn't really Lilith she admired, but her independence. Independence was the only thing worth envying. In a way, heroes and villains were made—not by the gods or even themselves really, but by their fathers. Their very freedom to act was often the result of the careful planning of previous generations, passed down like a legacy. More often than not, the parents set the stage for the choices their children would ultimately have. This certainly had been true in Lilith's case—and in Helene's as well. They were both victims of circumstances far beyond their control. Their destinies had been set and unalterable.

And yet, perhaps Helene did not envy Lilith so much after all. She'd suffered a violent death, and then lost all independence in the afterlife. Helene's death would likely be gentler, though she couldn't say what would happen after that. She could only hope that the place she was going would be better than the terrible place Lilith had gone.

A lush peacefulness fell over Helene like a velvety blanket. She had a strong desire to sit for a moment, and did so, still clutching the iris in her hand. She looked at the thick, gnarly bulb with interest, and then her gaze moved to her hand, which looked strangely similar to the root it held. It was the hand of a much older woman. Her fingers were misshapen but still strong, with thick knuckles from years of hard work and fingernails that were permanently stained grayish yellow from handling the earth. She examined them indifferently for a long moment and then closed her eyes, lifting her face toward the sky. Her heart was fluttering riotously again, but it was happening so frequently now that it wasn't quite so alarming. She even, sometimes, welcomed the giddy lightheadedness that came along with it. But a sudden, sharp pain took her by surprise and her eyes flew open. *No, she cried inwardly. I haven't even finished separating the irises!*

But the pain kept increasing as a fierce heat tore through her chest. She tried to focus on her breathing, but the air didn't seem to be reaching her lungs.

The sun seemed inordinately bright—which was odd because Helene could have sworn it had long since slipped past the courtyard wall. She stared up at it in astonishment. It seemed to be getting bigger, taking up more and more of the sky. Helene had the dim realization that she was dying, but where were the loved ones who were supposed to rush forward to greet her?

May Allah have mercy on her infidel soul.

No! Helene cried inwardly, refusing to even contemplate what her daughter's absence in this critical moment might signify.

As the light grew even brighter, Helene had the sensation that she was being drawn upward. She searched the encroaching whiteness frantically for signs of life. *Please God,* she begged, *let me see her this one last time.* But in a hasty, final rebellion she shut her eyes tight, refusing to look, refusing to give Him this last opportunity to smite her. In her mind's eye she strove to conjure the image of Gisele for herself, just as she looked the last time Helene saw her. Gisele was only sixteen then, and her beautiful face, normally so amused and full of pride, had been distorted with grief. "*Ummi,*" she'd sobbed, squeezing Helene so tightly that it hurt. "*Ummi,* I won't leave you."

"You *will* leave!" Helene shouted, speaking more harshly to her daughter than she'd ever done before out of fear that she might suffer the same fate as her. At all costs, she must get her daughter out of Saudi Arabia. And she succeeded, though it meant that she would never see or hear from her daughter again.

Not liking this particular memory, Helene called to mind a different one. She recalled how brave Giselle had been the day she left them forever, assuring her mother confidently—"Don't worry *Ummi,* I'll make you proud!" Her eyes had sparkled with determination even as she struggled to hide her anxiety. "You'll see."

A small gasp—half sob, half laugh—escaped Helene's lips, and then her body went limp, falling backwards on the cool stone bench.

CHAPTER
1

Present day, Manhattan

She knew something was wrong the minute she set foot in the ladies' restroom. It was one of three bathrooms on her floor, shared among nearly two dozen offices, a small café and a nail salon. This one was situated about halfway between Nadia's office and the café, so a trip to the restroom always triggered a craving for a latte—a guilty pleasure at this time of day. But although she loved her work, Nadia's attention would wane in the afternoons, just about the time the sun came round to her window, warm and distracting, gently luring her away from whatever it was she was doing. The Europeans had it right, she thought, with their afternoon naps. And yet, sluggish as she sometimes felt, she knew she would never be able to sleep. A shot of caffeine seemed the next best thing. It would give her that second wind, even if it did leave her a little on edge and make it all the harder for her to sleep that night.

Aside from these two o'clock doldrums, as Nadia came to think of them, she had no complaints. Her career had progressed like a fairy tale, with everything falling magically into place. If only the rest of her life were this easy she might not be spending her vacation in her office. But it comforted her to be there, where everything made sense and her efforts were always met with success. And she was proud of each and every accomplishment, like a mother doting over her children. Why, just to get an office in this part of Manhattan was an achievement in itself. It was impossible to do without the right connections—in addition to enormous amounts of money. And even then, there were concessions. Her office, for example, was terribly small. But size had ceased to matter once she'd gotten her first glimpse out the only window and saw that it overlooked Bryant Park. It was mid-July, and the hollyhocks were coming into bloom. All up and down their imperious stalks were pastel-colored flowerets with furled edges, peeking out from the big, billowing leaves like cheeky girls in Easter bonnets. Nadia also spied an array of bright yellow and orange daylilies among clusters of purple foxglove. There were too many species for her sweeping gaze to identify, but she was delighted by the prospect of admiring each and every one from her new office window. Gardens were in short supply in the city, and she had killed enough house plants to give up on any dreams of someday creating one of her own. But now she could enjoy extensive gardens without chipping a nail. She imagined herself taking long, leisurely walks through the park in the mornings, or bringing her laptop outside to work on sunny afternoons (neither of which she ever actually did in the six years she'd been there). Yet she had a deep appreciation for flowers—almost a distant calling to be near them—and she knew that their mere presence would satisfy that primal urge. Cost hadn't been a factor—apart from the occasional twinges of guilt she felt about it—but in those moments she reminded herself that location played a huge part in the immense sums of money she was able to raise. Her success depended on her proximity to the most privileged, and Manhattan was where the most privileged were housed. Education and wealth afforded social consciousness. Compassion for the less fortunate was as much of a luxury as jewelry or fine wine—a sad fact but one which Nadia had been made aware of from a very young age. That awareness was what made her so good at what she did. She truly believed in what she was doing. She sometimes wondered who benefited the most—the relief victims she raised money for or the people making the contributions. The key was to make it personal for the donors. Nadia made sure her patrons knew exactly where the money was going, sparing them no detail. She made her charity events educational, and encouraged other forms of giving besides just the writing of a check. Her efforts accomplished much more than mere fund-raising. She'd brought multitudes of people together, improving the lives of more than just her relief victims. Those who had everything found a new satisfaction in such activities as fishing through disaster debris for a treasured child's toy or scrubbing mold from the walls of a flooded school house.

Although she was never satisfied that she'd done enough, Nadia loved every minute of it. Helping people in crisis gave her life a sense of meaning, and the fund-raising was the icing on the cake. It was exciting and effortless, and Nadia went about it 'first class all the way,' as her mother would have said.

Nadia supposed she had a little of her mother in her after all, although her father was the one she had consciously tried to emulate. She'd been influenced, one way or the other, by both parents; one the eternal philanthropist and the other the self-indulgent social butterfly. She couldn't help enjoying the lavish parties any more than she could resist the call to duty in any disaster. She could still see her mother, dark and glamorous, flirting shamelessly with a powerful senator or a wealthy CEO while her father spoke somberly of the issues at hand. Nadia liked being the center of attention too. But unlike her mother, she was interested in other people besides herself, and she liked to think that she would ultimately put their interests above her own. And she was able to find pleasure in little things, like gazing out her office window at the splendor of the park below, or enjoying an afternoon latte when she knew she really shouldn't. But on this particular September afternoon, these pleasures were tempered by an odd, creeping sense of doom.

To begin with, the restroom was empty. In a city like Manhattan, this is an odd thing. Being alone in Manhattan, truly alone, the kind of alone where none of the senses are infringed upon by another human being, can bring about an alarming sensation. There was always some sign of other people's presence. Smells and sounds wafted through windows and vents, bringing with them a vague but constant awareness of activity, from the shrill scream of a fire engine's siren to the gentle ping of an elevator. In Nadia's office building, there was always a steady flow of traffic making its way up to the fourth floor to conduct business with the various investment companies, publishers and accountants who kept offices there, not to mention the café and salon. There were times when Nadia had to wait in line to use the restroom, and she sometimes wondered if people weren't just wandering in off the street. But no one else seemed concerned by their presence, trusting, she supposed, in the abilities of the security people on the first floor.

But the minute Nadia entered the restroom on this particular afternoon, she knew she was alone. She could tell by the unusual silence that hung in the air. The restroom was actually a long, slightly curving hallway with an exit at either end. The bathroom stalls were lined up along one side, and the sinks and mirrors were located on the other. Nadia's sense of unease increased as she hurried to empty her bladder. It wasn't just that the bathroom was empty. Although unusual, this wasn't unheard of. But there was something in the silence itself that was disturbing; it had too strong a presence to ignore. At one point Nadia actually looked up, half expecting to see a face looking down at her from one of the adjacent stalls. She laughed at herself when she saw that, of course, nothing was looming overhead, but even the hollow sound of her laughter brought her up short. It was a Friday afternoon in September…in Manhattan. Where was everyone?

The odd sense of isolation was so strong that Nadia was actually relieved—though startled—when she stepped out of the stall and found a man standing there. He wore a janitor's uniform and was quietly moving a cloth around the sinks. He glanced up at her with a blank expression.

"Oh!" Nadia exclaimed, moving automatically toward one of the sinks to wash her hands. "I didn't hear you come in!"

The sense of strangeness increased. Everything was wrong, yet Nadia found herself oddly incapable of action. It was as if everything was happening in slow motion while her mind tried to piece the puzzle together. There had been no sign to indicate the janitor's presence when she came in, and yet neither had there been any warning calls to announce his arrival. In fact, there had been no sounds at all; no clanging of the cleaning cart, no footsteps, nothing.

"You must have slipped in after me," the janitor concluded offhandedly.

He was what was most wrong. He looked out of place in the ill-fitting janitor's overalls, which seemed to clash with the rest of him. He was too meticulously groomed; his chestnut brown hair too expertly cut and styled, his expensive shoes too finely polished. Even his hands seemed at odds with the cleaning cloth as his perfectly manicured fingers maneuvered it over the countertops with an almost disdainful air. His demeanor was what was most wrong. He was too superior. His blue eyes flashed over Nadia with cool disdain, almost as if she was the one who had trespassed on him! He certainly didn't act like the other janitors she'd encountered there. Yet for all intents and purposes, he appeared to be completely focused on the job at hand, meticulously circling the cloth over the countertop, moving it quickly and efficiently around the row of sinks.

These observations occurred in mere seconds—in the time it took Nadia to exit her bathroom stall and advance two or three steps to the sink. She acted out of habit, and there seemed no opportunity to alter her course before the man, who'd been circling his cleaning cloth nearer and nearer to the sink she was approaching, suddenly turned and was on her. In one fluid motion he pressed the cloth firmly and securely over her nose and mouth. It was saturated with a nauseatingly sweet-smelling substance that instantly jerked Nadia out of her stupor. She tried desperately to fight the man off, clawing at his hands and wrenching her head back and forth. Nadia was healthy and strong, but she might have been a sickly child for the all the effect she was having. From both sides of her peripheral vision she could see two more men entering the restroom from the exits at either end. They were wearing the same janitorial uniforms as her attacker. It was as if it was happening to someone else as she watched the events in the mirror. People always said she resembled her father, but the woman in the mirror looked more like her mother, which was odd, because Gisele had been as dark and exotic as Nadia was classic and fair. Yet there was something in her expression—perhaps it was the wild look in her eyes—that so resembled her dead mother that Nadia became momentarily confused. She felt a single, sharp thrill of terror just before everything went black.

CHAPTER
2

Nadia came to with a jolt. She was aware of extreme discomfort, but couldn't pinpoint where it was or what was causing it. Full consciousness eluded her, but something—a distant thought or memory—seemed to be knocking with some urgency upon her mind. She tried to ignore it, instinctively preferring blissful insensibility but, bit by bit, the intruding thought eventually wedged its way in. As her memory slowly returned, her discomfort turned to horror. She tried to cry out but her voice was muffled by something thick and heavy that had been packed firmly into her mouth and secured there, most likely with tape. All of her joints were aching. Her body was bent and compressed into the fetal position and restrained somehow to stay that way. She must be tied up. After a moment of ineffective struggling, Nadia realized she was confined in a very small space. And she was being transported in a vehicle. She could feel the steady, rumbling movement beneath her, punctuated by the occasional bump in the road. Her fear increased with each and every realization, making it harder and harder for her to breathe. The fear seemed to take hold of her internal organs and squeeze them in its vice-like grip. Adrenaline rushed through her, swift and severe. The rapidly rising panic seemed to be robbing her of what little breath she had. She felt a chilling certainty that she was going to die and every part of her recoiled at the thought. Yet she was utterly powerless to save herself.

Or was she? With great effort, Nadia corralled her scattered wits and reminded herself that she had been trained to respond in a crisis. At all costs she must keep from panicking. She struggled to gain control of her thoughts. She would need to stay focused if she were going to survive. She'd been able to breathe while unconscious and therefore it stood to reason that she could do so now. *Don't think about the gag*, she told herself. *Just breathe.*

Nadia turned her thoughts to the abduction, meticulously going over every detail. Each recollection brought stern recriminations. She should have listened to her instincts and fled the bathroom the minute she got that eerie feeling. When she saw the strange man at the counter—why hadn't she screamed? Or better yet, run? He'd been just far enough away that she might have actually escaped if she'd acted quickly enough. The other two men were covering the exits, she supposed, but she might have at least alerted someone on the floor that she needed help. She berated herself inwardly for each and every missed opportunity, coming up with one thing after another that she might have done, until she was even scolding herself for being at the office at all when she was supposed to be on vacation. But although these thoughts were distracting, they were definitely not helping. Her only hope was to accept the situation and assess her options.

There were at least three strong, healthy men involved. The first one appeared to be in his early to mid-thirties, well groomed, arrogant, and most definitely not a janitor. He was a white man with chestnut brown hair and blue eyes. She didn't get a good look at the other two, but she recalled that they were both dark skinned with brownish-black hair. She was pretty sure one of them was African American, but the other could have been Middle-Eastern or possibly Asian. The first man must have followed her into the restroom while the other two guarded the doors to prevent anyone else from entering. Yet they had managed all this without making a sound – the strange quiet had been the first thing she noticed.

In addition to the janitors' uniforms, the men had acquired a janitor's cart, stocked with the usual cleaning paraphernalia. She didn't know how difficult this might be. There were, of course, security personnel in the building, but Nadia had no idea what they did besides greeting her when she came in every morning. Somehow, the three men had gotten in. Attached to the janitor's cart, Nadia suddenly remembered, was an oversized barrel used to collect trash. Could that be where she was now—inside that barrel? Nadia strove to control the new surge of panic this realization brought. She turned her head upwards but was enveloped in darkness. She was covered with something soft—trash perhaps—but was there also a lid overhead? Or maybe she'd been placed in the barrel upside down? She tried to wriggle her body in either direction, but her limbs were too constricted to move and her efforts were making it harder to breathe. Working particularly hard to keep her breathing even and slow—it took a long moment for her to accomplish this—she forced her mind to continue its assessment of the situation.

She'd been kidnapped of course, but why? Possibilities came at her from all directions. A kidnapping was not so hard to conceive, given her position and her family. She was well connected politically and economically. Her mother had been notable, if not famous. Although nearly five years had passed since Gisele's death, the settlement of her estate had only recently been finalized. These details of her life had been duly noted by the media. As Nadia considered this she felt a small bit of relief. The kidnappers would be looking for money. And of course her father would pay anything to get her back. All she had to do was keep her head and cooperate.

But what if—even after getting the money—the kidnappers killed her anyway? Or what if this wasn't about money? The man in the bathroom didn't look like a desperate felon who kidnapped for money.

Nadia tried to keep her fear in check as other, even more terrifying possibilities, came to mind. She decided to take them one at a time, starting with the one that frightened her most. Terrorism. Given the business she was in, she had to consider it. Slowly and methodically she made a mental list of her most recent activities. Yet her mind balked at the idea that her abduction could have anything to do with BEACON. While it was true that organizations such as hers were sometimes the objects of protests—even violent protests, on rare occasions—she felt that BEACON fell way below the radar on controversial matters. It was extremely rare for any of the numerous special interest groups to find cause to protest her activities. She'd made it her policy to offer her services without taking sides or issuing judgments. It was the only way to gain trust enough to reach the people who were the most needy in a crisis—many of whom would otherwise be forgotten. There were officials who would refuse help for their constituents if they didn't care for your political position, preferring to let their own people suffer and even die, rather than to accept assistance from a source who would later use it to criticize or control them. By remaining neutral, Nadia was able to help the people who really needed it, many of whom were as much victims of their own government as they were of whatever disaster had just struck.

Then again, people were sometimes offended when you didn't take sides. Still, it was hard to imagine that Nadia's actions in helping disaster victims could somehow be related to this. For one thing, BEACON was much too small to warrant a protest of this kind. There were much larger organizations wielding a bigger impact on industry and human rights throughout the world. In the realm of political adversaries, there were definitely bigger fish to fry.

Thinking about BEACON had a soothing effect on Nadia, and she allowed her mind to linger on the thing she was most proud of in her life. BEACON had helped thousands of people—and it would help her now. She felt a surge of confidence that defied all negative thoughts. Sure, she'd used her parents' connections to get where she was, but then again, by the time she founded BEACON she'd established almost as many of her own. She'd attended charity events with her mother all her life, alternately working in the field alongside her father. Compounding her experience with an MBA, it seemed a natural progression for Nadia to go from volunteer to director. She had planned to only act as a broker at first, maintaining just enough control to ensure that the contributions reached their intended destinations. She'd intended to keep BEACON small, private and independent, but she was simply too good at what she did. The assistance she was able to bring to disaster victims impressed everyone who encountered her in the field, and after her work in the 2004 earthquake in India, she gained national acclaim. Money came pouring in and even the UN's disaster relief commission, UNDRO, wanted to add her to their call list. Community organizations like CERT—the first responders in most disasters—quickly followed suit, and with the extra funding and support these organizations brought, Nadia had no choice but to become an official nonprofit organization, with a plush office in Manhattan and several assistants to help her manage it all.

But along with the acclaim there were bound to be criticisms as well. In times of disaster, one often had to make concessions, many times choosing between the lesser of two evils. In her obsession to help the people of India, for instance—a passion of hers since her involvement in that catastrophic earthquake of 2004—Nadia joined forces with an organization that turned out to have some rather dubious connections to extremist groups out of Pakistan. She'd taken a considerable amount of heat for it too, even though BEACON was only one of several charities involved. It seemed unlikely that BEACON would be the one singled out for that incident.

These thoughts were interrupted by the sudden slowing of the vehicle, which jerked Nadia abruptly back to the present. And once again she became painfully aware of her too-small confinement and concluded that she was, in fact, inside the dreaded garbage container, where they could easily bury her alive if they wanted to. She recalled the unflinching determination of her captor. His cold, calculated method of subduing and removing her from her building sent chills down her spine.

These thoughts opened the door to a host of other thoughts that Nadia had been desperately trying to avoid. Now, distracted by the alternately slowing and turning of the vehicle—which gave her hope that they were nearing their destination even as it raised new fears about what would happen to her when they did—her thoughts became scattered, rushing, and quickly spinning out of control. One, in particular, kept pushing its way to the forefront of her mind, forceful and commanding, challenging her to deny that—regardless of their reasons for abducting her—the kidnappers were far too competent to show their faces if they intended to let her live. They were going to kill her.

And in that moment Nadia realized why she'd been so actively avoiding this thought, even as the panic rose up in her all over again. It spread quickly this time, too formidable to stop. Every breath was becoming a struggle. The pain of confinement was unbearable. She could feel her fingers and toes going numb. The space seemed to be getting even smaller. Each time the vehicle slowed she felt a spark of hope, but then all hope was dashed again when the car simply turned and slowly crept on. She was sure she would suffocate before they got her out. The garbage can would be her casket. Nadia burst into tears, giving in to her despair. But the release—muffled and constrained as it was—offered very little comfort before demanding its deadly price. She instantly stopped, realizing her mistake, but it was too late. Her nostrils were now congested, obstructing her only remaining passage-way for air. The realization that she really was going to die put her in a temporary state of shock.

Had the vehicle stopped? Yes—either Nadia was hallucinating from lack of oxygen or it really stopped this time. She could no longer hear the engine running. Hope sparked again.

Car doors opened and closed, but it was all happening much too slowly. Nadia heard the pop of a latch—like that of van door—but there was yet another pause before she felt the container she was in being hauled out of the vehicle. Each action seemed to be stretched out indefinitely. Nadia's lungs ached from the lack of oxygen, but some-how her heart kept up its frantic pace. She could feel it hammering in her temples, and wondered if it was possible for a heart to explode. Instinctively she kept trying to breathe. Her body jerked wildly against the walls of the container as the world seemed to spin all around her. She was vaguely conscious of being turned upside down.

Then suddenly—and quite unceremoniously—Nadia was dumped out onto the ground like so much garbage.

CHAPTER
3

The fading brilliance of the afternoon sun was blinding to Nadia's light-deprived eyes. She continued to struggle until someone finally tore the tape from her lips and removed the gag from her mouth. She gasped loudly, taking long, convulsive breaths in an effort to get as much oxygen into her lungs as possible. She tried to sit up, blinking frantically in order to regain her sight. Although she'd been released from the container her movements were still restricted, and she realized that her wrists were bound and her ankles connected by a chain. She managed, with effort, to sit up on her knees. As her vision gradually returned, she perceived three figures looming over her. A small, involuntary cry escaped her lips as they came into focus.

Her kidnappers' faces were now hidden behind dark, ominous-looking masks that fit over their heads like helmets. All three masks were the same. They had the formidable aspects of ancient warriors—possibly Greek, or Middle-Eastern. Small circles had been carved into each of their foreheads to give the impression of curls creeping out from beneath the helmets, and more of the circles were carved on their elongated chins to look like beards. The eyes were cut out, as were the nostrils beneath the long, imperious noses. There was a small hole in the center of each grim-looking mouth.

Nadia stared up at the masked men in bewilderment. Were the masks indicative of something or simply to hide their faces? The first option was too terrifying to contemplate, so Nadia focused on the latter, which suggested to her hopeful mind that they intended to keep her alive after all. Yet they had to realize that she'd already gotten a good look at them—especially the first one—back in the restroom. She was certain she could identify him in a line up. Did they think she wouldn't remember?

There was no point in conjecture. She looked around anxiously. They were in the middle of what appeared to be an abandoned field. Off in the distance she could see trees and even farther off, mountains. She had no idea how long she'd been unconscious in the car, but she didn't think they could have traveled very far from Manhattan. And yet there was no sign of the city in any direction. Her gaze returned to the men. They were all around the same height—somewhere between five-ten and six feet tall, she estimated. They were lean and healthy looking, and all of them had that same, superior manner as the first one. Or maybe it was the masks. Nadia recognized the man who attacked her by his cold, blue eyes, which were glaring at her from the holes in his mask. The other two were harder to distinguish between, as both had dark skin and brown eyes. They had removed the janitors' uniforms and now wore casual shirts and jeans.

The silence was disconcerting. Nadia had expected comments, taunts or perhaps even interrogations. They stood silent, staring at her, as if they were waiting for her to speak. She began to tremble as she searched for the right words.

"Please…," she began, coughing reflexively from the effort to talk after her ordeal. "I…have money," she choked out. "And I will cooperate."

"If you speak again, for any reason, your mouth will be filled and taped shut like before," said the man with the piercing blue eyes. His cold, matter of fact tone left no doubt in her mind that he would do exactly as he threatened.

Nadia stared at him, stunned. He merely stood there, indifferent, watching her. She looked at the others. From behind their masks they seemed just as indifferent. She wondered what she should do. This was unexpected and jarring. She had thought that once they reached their destination she would find out what was happening. Why all the mystery? And why were they waiting out here in this clearing? It was a struggle not to demand answers, but Nadia kept quiet, mentally cursing the tears of frustration that spontaneously slipped down her cheeks. At all costs she wanted to avoid having her mouth taped again. And too, she didn't want to give them the satisfaction of seeing her cry. She tried to maneuver her body into a more comfortable sitting position. She was trembling violently now. Though her hands and feet were bound, she was able to straighten her limbs enough to relieve some of the pressure in her aching joints. She was far from comfortable but she was afraid to move too much lest they put her back in the container, which had been tossed to one side and which was, in fact, the container used for garbage, just as she guessed.

She silently wept, keeping her head down and staring miserably at the ground. The men appeared to be waiting for something. She wondered what it was. Her trembling didn't let up, and though jarring it was also mildly distracting. She could feel herself slowly disconnecting, as if the vibrations were actually shaking her loose from herself.

Eventually there came a low rumbling from off in the distance. Nadia turned toward the sound but she knew before she spotted it that it was the sound of an airplane approaching. She watched in a kind of stupor, realizing that this was bigger than anything she had imagined. A small hope arose in her that surely they would not go to all this trouble if they intended to kill her. But where were they taking her?

The jet decelerated rapidly once it touched down, and then it seemed an eternity before it finally crept to a stop within a few yards of where they stood. It was a large private jet—much bigger than what was necessary for the four of them. A compartment beneath the cabin door popped open and a long, metal contraption emerged, slowly unfolding as it lowered itself to the ground. Within seconds it was transformed into a full set of stairs, complete with handrails on either side. The moment the stairs touched the ground the cabin door popped open and the kidnappers sprang into action. The first man stood at the bottom of the stairs while the other two approached Nadia, one on each side, and jerked her up by her arms. With her feet chained together, Nadia was obliged to take very small steps, but the two men held her steady and led her up the stairs. Nadia went along quietly until they reached the top, and then something inside her revolted. She stopped, surprising even herself with the force of her resistance, and twisted herself free from her two shocked captors. Turning, she now came up against the increasingly familiar icy blue stare of the man who seemed to her the most malevolent of the three. Somehow she stood her ground, glaring back at him with a mixture of terror and defiance as she actually considered kicking him down the steps. Some impulse was overriding her common sense, insisting that it would be better to die there in that field than to get on the jet and be taken even further from home. But the impulse passed almost as quickly as it occurred. Nadia didn't want to die. Besides, she couldn't kick with her feet tied together and the men on either side of her were already swinging her back around. They urged her forward more forcefully this time and, if that weren't enough, strong hands from behind suddenly grasped her by the waist and lifted her effortlessly over the threshold and into the craft. Even once they were inside, the men kept relentlessly ushering her on, practically dragging her to a seat in the front row. Before there was time for further resistance Nadia was firmly strapped in, and then the chain connecting her feet was bolted to the seat. The plane door slammed shut with the force of a gunshot. The utter hopelessness of her situation sunk in, and Nadia surrendered to the despair that had been stalking her since she first came to in their vehicle.

Her kidnappers, meanwhile, were taking their seats and buckling themselves in. The two darker men sat behind Nadia while 'blue eyes,'—as Nadia couldn't help thinking of him—sat in the same row as her, across the aisle. He sat sideways in his seat so he could watch her. He said something to the pilot and shortly afterwards the plane began to move, slowly at first, and then picking up speed until she felt the dizzying sensation of being lifted and carried off into the afternoon sky.

The disturbingly callous blue eyes never seemed to stray from her face. The ancient mask made them appear like something inhuman, a mystical force out of a science fiction horror film. Nadia had to remind herself that the man behind the mask was, in fact, human, regardless of how he appeared. He was just a man, with a man's limitations. It would help to remember this. 'Blue eyes' and his comrades also had weaknesses. Her life might depend on finding out what they were.

She realized now that this was not a simple kidnapping for a negotiated ransom. If that were the case, she would have been kept somewhere relatively close to home. This was something much bigger. But what, then, was happening, and why? And should she simply continue to acquiesce in silence? Yet what choice did she have? There hadn't been a single opportunity when she'd felt there was anything to gain by fighting them (other than when she was first accosted in the bathroom, but that was water under the bridge now and she had no desire to dredge it up again). She felt an overwhelming urge to do something—but what? At the moment, there was nothing she could do. She would simply have to wait. She couldn't afford to make another foolish mistake, and she didn't want to bring needless suffering onto herself either. Resistance would bring further restraint or, worse, injury or death. She was pretty sure they wanted her alive—for the moment—considering all the trouble they were going to, but they could easily hurt her if they wanted to. She would avoid that at all costs. And too, she didn't want to alert them to be on their guard with her. She would need the element of surprise when she finally found her moment.

Nadia wondered why they were so adamant about not letting her speak. In fact, she couldn't help noticing how alert and wary they had been ever since they released her from the container. She found it rather disconcerting—and odd, given her current state. What did *they* have to be wary of? She'd have to be the bionic woman to pose any threat to them. She recalled how quickly and cautiously Blue Eyes connected the chain to her seat and then immediately withdrew, almost as if he was afraid of her. It seemed impossible and yet, she was suddenly certain of it. What did it mean? She felt she was missing something important and sighed, frustrated.

Her only hope was to outwit them at some point. She was no bionic woman, but she was smart. She would watch them just as closely as they were watching her.

But this proved harder than it seemed. To look at them was to meet those hostile stares head on. Nadia had no mask to hide behind. Even *not* to look at them; she could still feel their eyes upon her, steady and oppressive, like heavy blankets on a stiflingly hot day. Why were they watching her so closely?

Stealing surreptitious glances in Blue Eyes' direction, Nadia was struck once again with the impression that he wasn't the typical kidnapper. She noticed that his hands, though strong and well defined, were smooth, and his fingernails were clean and neatly trimmed. This suggested that his strength came from working out, not from working. His clothing was simple and casual, but Nadia could tell that it was expensive. But it was his dark, disdainful gaze that was most disconcerting. Whenever her eyes met his, Nadia was always the first to look away.

The only opportunity Nadia had to observe Blue Eyes freely was when he turned, occasionally, to speak to the pilot in the cockpit. He spoke in a low voice, and though she strained to hear, Nadia couldn't make out what he was saying over the engines.

As the hours passed and the afternoon wore away, Nadia wondered if she was being taken out of the country. Her initial terror was spent, leaving her too weak to summon further feelings of panic. The trembling had subsided and she felt strangely detached. She was relatively comfortable for the moment, so she forced herself to rest in the peculiar calm before the storm and save her energy for whatever came next.

Nadia closed her eyes in order to block out the image of the harassing blue stare. She wished her kidnappers would speak to her. An interrogation would be preferable to the unending silence. She couldn't help acknowledging how proficient these men were at what they did. This was a well-planned venture. Even the timing couldn't have been better. Although it wasn't much of a feat to find Nadia in her office on a Friday afternoon, as far as everyone else was concerned the office was closed and she was on vacation for two weeks. She wouldn't be missed for a while. Everyone, including her father, thought she was spending a long weekend with Joe. But Joe was gone. The thought of Joe brought Nadia up short. Odd that this was the first time she thought of him, and yet it seemed to put things in perspective. She'd faced trauma and near death without giving him a passing thought. Weren't you supposed to think about the one you loved most in your final moments? Somehow Joe had ceased to matter, except in how he might affect the final outcome of her current situation. All their breakup meant now was that no one would miss Nadia. She had distanced herself from everyone in an effort to avoid telling them about the breakup, which would make it all the harder for anyone to become suspicious when she didn't answer her phone or turn up for any events.

Why, oh why, hadn't she at least told her father about Joe? If she had, he would have been checking in with her periodically. In fact, he probably would have talked her into spending the weekend with him instead of waiting until Tuesday to join him on the island. Nadia imagined her father, sitting on the porch of his house in the Hamptons, staring peacefully out at the ocean while sipping an extra dry martini packed with olives. She could have been there with him, instead of here on this plane. She was filled with regret, and suddenly angry with Joe. Thinking he might change his mind, she'd avoided telling her father about the incident, knowing that he would not be as forgiving as she was. And maybe she knew that her father was right. She tried to picture Joe's face in her mind but the effort exhausted her. She dozed restlessly in her seat. When she woke up, a new, more immediate problem arose. She had to use the bathroom.

Immediately upon opening her eyes Nadia was accosted by the dreaded blue stare. She looked out the window and saw that it was completely dark outside. How long had she slept?

She reluctantly turned back to Blue Eyes. Afraid to speak, she tentatively raised her bound hands to get his attention, but froze halfway through the gesture when she saw him flinch. Had she imagined it? She didn't think so. He suddenly seemed more alert too, eyeing her even more warily than before. Nadia stared at him, momentarily stunned by the odd reaction, but eventually necessity overcame everything else and she pointed in the direction of the lavatory.

He seemed to relax the tiniest bit, but he sighed heavily, clearly put out by her request. He signaled the men behind her and she heard them unbuckle their seat belts and stand up. The two stood guard from behind while Blue Eyes approached her and unfastened the chain connecting her to her seat. He drew back quickly and motioned for her to get up. She rose, wondering bleakly at their cautiousness. If they were this careful in midair, what chance would she have when they landed?

When she reached the tiny bathroom, Blue Eyes still didn't back off. He stood resolutely in the doorway facing her. Nadia forced herself to meet his gaze head on, aggravated by the unshakable resolve she saw there. His dark, slightly enlarged pupils seemed to punctuate the futility of him giving in. She gave him a pleading look, pointing to the door meaningfully with her hands.

"No," he said firmly.

She stared at him for a long moment before turning her head away in disgust. She looked miserably around the tiny bathroom as if it might provide an answer. What now? Would she not be allowed even this small privacy? Anger welled up in her. She met the awful stare again, infuriated by the lack of feeling there. She glared at him, pointing to the door again.

"No," he repeated just as firmly as before. There wasn't the slightest hint of an apology in his tone either, and this galled Nadia even more. She just stood there for a long moment, debating what to do, while he watched her, as callous as ever.

Nadia was furious, and bitterly regretted asking him for the tiny courtesy. She should have acted as if she didn't care, as if his being there didn't matter. The pleading made it all the more humiliating. Silently fuming, she slipped down her pants, doing her best to hide her body from his view as she managed her affairs. She looked away from him throughout her ordeal, focusing all her thoughts on revenge. It was only a matter of time before he and his accomplices were caught, she assured herself. They always got caught in the end, didn't they? She imagined herself testifying against him in court. She would happily meet that icy gaze then—perhaps he would look at her pleadingly, just as she had looked at him. But on second thought, this seemed unlikely. She felt pretty sure that Blue Eyes would never plead for anything.

It didn't matter. Nadia would keep her cool and bide her time. What did she care if he got his jollies off by watching women urinate? Like all criminals, he would slip up and when he did, she would be ready. She would gladly let him win this battle if it would help her win the war. She finished her business with a flush and stood up, careful to slide her clothing back in place in one quick, smooth movement as she rose. When she was ready to return to her seat she couldn't resist meeting his eyes with such a look of pure hatred that it appeared for once she actually got the better of him. He backed away from her abruptly, nearly colliding with the wall behind him. Nadia brushed past him and—with some effort considering the chains that were attached to her ankles—stomped back to her seat. She sat down, trembling with rage and indignation. But as Blue Eyes strapped her back into her seat, reality hit and her little feeling of triumph waned. She felt overwhelmingly impotent. How was she going to get out of this? Hannibal Lector had not been guarded as vigilantly as her.

The flight seemed to last forever. Despite her exhaustion Nadia couldn't sleep. Nor could she resist periodic glances at her tormentor. In the dimmed cabin, his blue eyes glowed almost fiendishly from the mask.

It may well have been the longest night of Nadia's life. She struggled not to fidget in her seat. Every muscle ached. She passed the time by imagining various scenarios where she would be saved and avenged. Sometimes she was rescued by an outside party such as her father, or even Joe, and other times—her favorites—she would outwit the kidnappers herself, escaping to freedom and eventually bringing them to justice. These thoughts buoyed her spirits. She called to mind the many triumphs in her relatively short career and felt perfectly justified in asserting that she was clever and resourceful enough to come out of this alive. She was trained in many kinds of survival. She only had to stay calm and wait for the right moment to act. She must be brave and alert. From what she'd seen of her captors so far, she knew she wouldn't get many opportunities.

The waiting was tortuous, but hope kept growing with every hour that passed, infusing Nadia with confidence as she endured the long ordeal. And too, she was becoming more convinced that if they'd intended to kill her they surely would have done so by now, saving themselves all the travel-time and expense.

Eventually she perceived that the plane was, at last, descending. She opened her eyes and turned toward the window, surprised by how bright it was outside. It looked like midday, but surely they had not traveled that many hours! And then Nadia realized that, of course, there would have been a time change. She calculated which direction would have taken her so far into the next day and concluded that they must have traveled east.

When at last the plane touched down Nadia sighed with relief, even as a new apprehension filled her. What would happen now? Surely some light would be shed on the reason for her abduction. All the silent wondering was becoming intolerable.

The plane came to a stop, although Nadia noticed that the engines were left running. Blue Eyes turned to speak to the pilot and Nadia took this opportunity to examine him more closely. All of her senses suddenly seemed heightened as she strained to hear what he was saying. The exchange was brief and to the point. The two men behind her unbuckled their seat belts. She was finally going to get off the plane, but suddenly her limbs felt as if they'd been filled with lead. Everything in the foreground seemed to fade as she struggled to make sense of what she heard. Or thought she heard. It was possible that she heard wrong. It was only a few words, after all, not enough to bring about such a reaction. But the words kept repeating themselves over and over again in her head, like a drum pounding out a warning to a distant ally.

"…attack."

"…execute…tonight."

"…the body."

CHAPTER
4

N adia was still reeling from what she heard when Blue Eyes, cautious as ever, unfastened her bonds and pulled her out of her seat. Her legs felt like rubber, and it suddenly seemed as if all the blood had been drained from her body. He looked at her in surprise—though still wary—as she faltered and very nearly fell down. Somehow she managed to walk, stumbling along in the direction the three men were leading.

Attack. Execute. The body. The words seemed to reverberate through her, pulsing through her arteries with each rapid beat of her heart. She was sure they were the words she heard. Yet her mind continued to argue the point. Why would they bring her all this way just to kill her? It didn't make sense.

When she stepped outside she was momentarily startled out of her reverie. A wave of hot air, almost like that of an oven, rushed over her and the sun, which was unusually bright, seemed to be coming at her from all directions. She shuddered violently. She looked around in utter defeat, surrounded on all sides by sand. She was in a desert, most likely in the Middle East. An image popped into Nadia's head of Blue Eyes, sitting at a round table on an episode of the *Ten Thousand Dollar Pyramid*, coolly rattling off hints to the word on the screen, pausing meaningfully between each hint for effect. *Attack. Execute. The body*—until his partner jumped up triumphantly to shout, "terrorism!" This image, strange as it was, seemed to bring a horrific clarity to the event. Suddenly everything made sense. Terrorists were exactly the sort of people who would go to this much trouble to kill someone. A high profile execution of this kind would draw attention to their cause. But what was their cause, and why had they chosen her? Nadia supposed it must have something to do with that group of extremists out of Pakistan that she had inadvertently taken contributions from, after all.

The private jet was slowly turning around so that it could go back down the strip the way it came. A weathered white jeep was the only other object in sight. Nadia's captors half dragged, half led her to it and Blue Eyes urged her into the back seat. He seemed to take extra pains attaching her chain to the underside of her seat before getting in next to her. The other two climbed in front. They continued to wear the masks, which seemed even more ominous somehow, in the bright, midday sun. There was nothing but sand and rock as far as Nadia could see, and she shivered again, in spite of the heat.

The terror was returning and seemed to make Nadia more alert. She realized that she hadn't had anything to eat or drink since lunch the previous day. The driver—the black man—was softly humming under his breath. Nadia recognized the tune, but couldn't identify it. It was before her time; a 'golden oldie.' It seemed an odd choice, given the circumstances.

Execute. Blue Eyes had said the word as coolly as someone else—someone who wasn't a cold blooded killer—might have discussed the weather. And humming a cheery tune! It was a walk in the park for them. There was no hesitation. No compassion. They had made up their minds.

She would have to escape. But how? The way they were guarding her she would have to be superhuman to break through the chains and overpower them. And even if she managed this, how was she supposed to get out of here?

Seeing only sand in every direction was making her feel worse. Occasionally the car turned onto a different road, but the view never changed. Nadia wondered how they managed to find their way around this desert maze. There were very few road signs and those were in Arabic, confirming her original guess that she was in the Middle East.

Why hadn't she screamed in the restroom? Was that to be her only opportunity?

Suddenly they were there. The building seemed to appear out of nowhere; an old, dusty, sand-colored cottage that was practically camouflaged by the sand-colored surroundings. Nadia scanned the area, numb with fear. *One more chance*, she silently prayed, *give me just one more chance to escape*. Off in the distance she saw something shimmering in the brilliant sunlight, and stared at it, squinting, as the driver pulled the jeep up close to the cottage and shut off the engine.

Blue Eyes unfastened the chain. "Out," he said, giving Nadia a nudge. His voice never wavered from the hard, commanding tone. She got out and allowed herself to be led into the building. Her back, where she'd leaned against the car seat, was already wet with sweat.

The decor inside the cottage left Nadia feeling even more disoriented. The furniture was a hodgepodge of relics from the fifties; the faded, mismatched colors and frivolous styles seemed satirical. The main room featured a washed-out orange couch, a blue metal coffee table, a chipped wooden cabinet and a variety of different chairs. These items were scattered about over an enormous brown, shag rug in the middle of the floor. There was an air conditioner rumbling loudly in one of the windows and, glancing at it, Nadia once again noticed the peculiar shimmering outside, off in the distance. It seemed to be glowing, pulsing and alive, almost—she winced at the thought—like a space ship.

"Why did you bring me here?" she blurted out, unable to keep silent any longer. Her voice sounded strangled. "I demand to know. You…you have the wrong person." Her voice rose in desperation with that last declaration.

The men didn't even respond. Two of them watched her through their masks while Blue Eyes dragged her into a room in the back. First thing he did was fetter her to another, longer chain that was fastened to a steel ring in the floor. The room was completely dark, except for a single, dim night light on the wall. The only window was boarded up. As her eyes began to adjust to the dark she saw that the room was empty except for a bed. There was a small, door-less entryway into another room.

"That's the bathroom," said Blue Eyes. "But if you try anything we'll see you." Nadia looked up then and saw a tiny, blinking red light indicating the presence of a video camera.

"Why did you bring me here?" Nadia asked again, her voice rising to a scream this time. Blue Eyes turned and left the room, closing the door behind him. "Tell me!" she screamed.

Nadia rushed to the window, which was boarded up from the inside. She doubted the boards could be removed, but she pulled at them as hard as she could. They were securely fixed, just as she knew they would be. Next she examined the chain that bound her, and saw that it was much too sturdy to break. She could vaguely hear their voices in the other room, and figured they were probably watching her on some kind of video screen. Perhaps they were musing over how calmly she was taking her predicament. But then she heard movements—scraping and rustling sounds, like furniture being dragged over the floor. They seemed to be preparing for something. Fresh adrenaline rushed through her.

The chain was secured to a heavy bolt in the floor. Nadia examined the bolt and then the chain itself, becoming more dismayed with every observation. *If you try anything we'll see*, he'd said. What did he expect her to try? She went over to the bed and sat down. Her stomach was making noises from a combination of hunger and nerves, both of which were leaving her weak. *If you try anything we'll see.* Was he referring to her killing herself? To accomplish even that seemed impossible with her limited resources. And why should he care? *Execute.* Perhaps a suicide would interfere with their plans. She shuddered.

Nadia had the urge to scream until they answered her questions but instinctively she knew it would do no good. She sighed. She might as well save her energy.

Others had been here before her, she suddenly realized. The bolt in the floor was not new. She got up and looked at it again. How many people had awaited their fate in this room?

All of a sudden she noticed something else on the floor. Someone had carved a message into the wood. Nadia bent down to get a closer look. There was actually a multitude of carvings of varying styles and shades, suggesting several different 'someones' over an extended period of time. Yet the carvings were similar, clearly belonging to one specific form of communication that was completely foreign to Nadia. This seemed to confirm her earlier notion that the kidnappers had abducted the wrong person. Though she couldn't identify the strange markings, they reminded her of symbols she'd seen used in ancient hieroglyphs, such as those found in the Egyptian tombs. Nadia stared at the symbols uncomprehendingly, feeling a creeping sense of *déjà vu*, along with an irrefutable certainty that whatever message they conveyed was decidedly sinister. The tiny hairs on the back of her neck stood up.

These thoughts were cut short by the sharp click of a lock, followed by the opening of her door. Nadia stood up, unable to see more than the dark outline of the man coming toward her. She watched his approach with dread. When he got close enough—within a few feet of her—she recognized the blue orbs glowing demonically from behind the mask. She stared into them as if hypnotized, yet somehow, without actually seeing it, she perceived that he was carrying a syringe in one of his hands. Whatever they were going to do to her was about to begin now.

Something inside Nadia snapped. In one quick, fluid movement she threw up her hands, which she had formed into one large fist, and struck him in the Adam's apple, dislocating his mask in the process. His hands flew up in a defensive gesture but Nadia reacted even quicker, clamping her teeth down on the fleshy part of one of his palms as hard as she could. He let out a yell, but managed to hit her so hard in the face with his other hand that she saw stars. The blow had the intended effect of disengaging her bite, but it did nothing to deter her resolve. She once again made a fist of her two hands and punched him in the groin with all the force she could muster. He yelled again and this time seemed genuinely incapacitated as he doubled over in pain. Nadia knew all of a man's weak spots from her self-defense classes, but she had never actually tested them before. She was a little surprised by how well they worked. When she shifted Blue Eye's mask in that first blow she had inadvertently blinded him, and she now took full advantage of this, striking him again and again, going for his throat, his shins, his groin, and any other part of him she felt might be vulnerable. She moved so quickly that each blow was immediately followed by another. She was mildly aware that the other two men would be coming to help their friend any moment, but the adrenaline was flooding through her, drowning out her better sense. Probably she would not escape, but neither would she sit back and let them kill her without a fight.

But even without his friends, Blue Eyes was gaining on her. He was stronger and clearly more experienced, and no amount of adrenaline or self-defense classes could have made her a match for him. She'd managed to take him by surprise but he was quickly recovering. Once he gained a foothold—which he did instantly upon shrugging off his mask and grasping her bound hands in his—he easily laid her out on the floor by simply sweeping his foot under her legs, sending her sprawling onto her backside with a hard thud. But even this didn't stop Nadia. She continued to fight like a woman possessed, although now it seemed not to bother him. He let her flail about as he held her down, watching her with a mixture of mild surprise and curiosity. Nadia knew it was over, but she kept on fighting anyway, stubbornly trying to free her hands from his grip. He patiently endured her struggles while he caught his breath. Then quite suddenly, he flipped her onto her stomach and put a knee in her back, effectively halting any further insurgence.

"Shit!" she heard him murmur under his breath.

Nadia started to cry. "Tell me why you brought me here!" she screamed.

Suddenly the other two men were in the room. They rushed over, one on either side of Nadia. Blue Eyes removed his knee from her back, and she surprised them all by struggling anew, flipping herself over, kicking, and swinging her bound fists at them.

"Whoa!" one of them said. "Easy now!" They flipped her back onto her stomach and held her there, just as Blue Eyes had done.

"Took your time, didn't you," she heard Blue Eyes mutter. But it was over. And he didn't even seem all that rattled. Nadia began to scream at the top of her lungs.

"Whoa!" said one of the men again.

"Put your mask back on and go fix your hand," said the other.

The two men continued to hold Nadia down while Blue Eyes went out. She screamed until her voice gave out, then she wept loudly, occasionally bringing her sobs to a scream as if to emphasize her despair.

"Whoof," sighed one of her captors when she finally started winding down. "What a tigress! And how about our friend? A real lady's man, that one." In spite of her distress Nadia immediately recognized the Indian accent.

"Shut up," said the other, but his tone was good-natured. They actually seemed cheerful.

"I was talking to you, *gandu*."

"Well, save it for later. Do you have it?"

"Yes, of course. Do you think I am like Butterfingers out there?" The light banter was distracting. The Indian accent also seemed strangely out of place.

Nadia tried to look up so she could see what the 'it' was that they had, but the men were holding her too securely for that. She wanted to struggle again, but she was simply too exhausted.

"No use to fight," the Indian said politely. Still holding her firmly, they pulled up her arms so they were over her head.

"Why did you bring me here?" she kept asking, though they were just little whimpers now.

"As if she didn't know," one of them chided under his breath.

"Don't engage," warned the other one.

"Know what?" Nadia felt a pin prick in her arm and tried to jerk it away but they held her so firmly in place she wasn't able to budge it. "What are you doing?" she cried. "No! No! No!" She could feel something cool being injected into the vein in her arm.

Nadia saw a shadow in the doorway and looked up to see that Blue Eyes had returned. His hand was bandaged but, aside from that, he seemed no worse for the wear. They removed the needle from her arm. Then they hoisted her up, one on either side of her, and half led, half dragged her to the bed.

"Sorry we took so long," one of them said. "We had to make up another syringe after you stepped on the other one. How's your hand?"

"Just a small flesh wound," he said irritably.

The two men who were holding Nadia looked at each other and then suddenly burst into laughter.

"Quit fucking around you two," said Blue Eyes. "This isn't the time."

"Oh, I'm sorry," said the Indian politely. "Were we the ones getting the *tati* kicked out of us by the woman?"

"She's not just any woman…," remarked the other.

"Just stay focused," snapped Blue Eyes. "It's not over yet."

Nadia was only half listening as a delightful sense of calm washed over her. "What's not over yet?" she mumbled incoherently.

"Okay," Blue Eyes was saying. "Bring her in."

CHAPTER
5

The room was moving. Nadia tried again and again to focus. Everything seemed distant and unreal. She was extremely weak and had to be assisted just to walk.

They led her into the center of a strange, brownish circle that had been drawn out on the floor. Dots of light flickered and danced all around her. Candles? The room seemed both unnaturally bright and eerily dim, all at the same time.

"What's happening?" she said. Or thought she said. She wasn't sure.

There were voices in the distance. Nadia strained to hear what they were saying, but they were too far away for her to make out. She looked up and saw the masked men staring down at her. They seemed to be speaking to her, but she couldn't understand a word they said. There were moments when they appeared to be coming toward her, and others when they seemed to move further away. One after the other, they came in and out of focus like characters in a dream. Nadia tried harder to concentrate. "What are you saying?" she kept asking. "I can't understand you."

A long time seemed to elapse, or perhaps it was hardly any time at all. Nadia couldn't tell anymore. She also gave up trying to understand what they were saying. It was all just babble, not like anything she'd heard before. Even their voices sounded strange. Alien. She vaguely recalled some previous notion of aliens. Yes! The thing glimmering in the distance. A spaceship? She felt a strange thrill at the thought. Had she been abducted by aliens?

And then, as if spurred on by the thought, she began floating. *Beam me up Scottie*, she thought, remembering a line from a television show. What was the show? She tried to remember but could not. Yet she was definitely being drawn upwards, floating higher and higher. Strange how she was no longer afraid!

She was pleased to see that the masked men were staying behind. She glanced down at them and was momentarily startled out of her delirium. There, on the floor directly below her, was *her*. She watched, curious but still peculiarly detached, as the masked men hovered over her lifeless body, speaking to her in their alien tongue. Her body was lying face up on the floor in the middle of a mystical looking circle that was marked with the same hieroglyphics she saw in the dark room. Her hair had become quite disheveled during her ordeal, and the wavy blonde tresses fell all around her face like a halo. Her eyes were wide open and staring, and seemed to be looking right back up at her. Her lips were slightly parted, as if in surprise.

Suddenly one of the men stopped speaking.

"Something's wrong," he said, picking up Nadia's arm and holding her wrist between two fingers. After a moment he threw her arm back down angrily. "Shit! We're killing her!" He yanked off his mask and lowered his ear to her lips. She could see that it was Blue Eyes. His previously styled hair was now all tousled from the mask.

Blue Eyes started CPR while the other two men looked on in silence. Nadia watched too, surprised by how little the scene affected her. It was as if none of it was real.

"Come on!" Blue Eyes yelled at her between breaths. The other two men exchanged glances. "Come on, Nadia!" he yelled again. It was the first time he'd spoken her name.

In the process of floating upward Nadia had become aware of an intense white light above her, but she'd been too absorbed in what was happening below to give it her full attention. She now felt a gentle pulling sensation, though she couldn't tell where it was coming from or even which direction it was pulling her in. She looked up and beheld the white light in all of its glory. It was breathtaking! The scene below was instantly forgotten. Nadia felt a little like vapor as she drifted into the welcoming light, merging with the awesome brilliance. She could see shadows moving toward her in the distance, friendly and approving. *I must go to them,* she thought.

As Nadia rose higher the shadows grew more distinct. In the forefront of the gathering crowd she could see the form of a woman rushing toward her. Her mother? A sharp thrill of anticipation filled her. But as the woman got closer Nadia saw that it was not her dark, exotic mother, but someone who looked just like Nadia. The woman's long, golden curls glistened all around her head, shimmering like ripened wheat in the sun. Her green eyes glowed with purpose. Her soft, pink lips were parted in surprise. Was this yet another version of herself coming forward to greet her?

Reason struggled to emerge through the dense fog that filled Nadia's head, and all at once it struck her. Of course, this woman who looked just like Nadia would be her grandmother, Helene! Excitement mingled with joy as Nadia rushed forward to finally meet the woman she'd spent her childhood wondering about.

But something in her grandmother's manner brought Nadia up short. She seemed to be radiating negative energy. Nadia felt an overwhelming sense of rejection. The woman appeared to be trying to tell Nadia something, but all that came through were faint echoes.

No! (no, no), the woman seemed to be calling out to her. *Go back! (back, back)*

Nadia hesitated. The light was oh, so enticing, but the woman at the center of it was frightening in her intensity. This was hardly the welcome Nadia expected. Discouraged, she turned her gaze away from the woman she assumed was her grandmother and looked back on the scene below. Blue Eyes still hovered over her body, trying harder than ever to revive her. She watched, a little startled by his persistence given the circumstances. An overwhelming feeling of sympathy flooded through her. She felt compassion for her lifeless body and the world it existed in. She felt torn, unsure of which direction to go. But the longer she watched the scene below the more intense her feelings—and the sense of being pulled in that direction—became. Still, she hesitated, looking up again at the light.

Return to him, the distant echo now seemed to be calling, and Nadia felt that the words conveyed more than their simple directive to return. The emphasis seemed to rest on the word 'him.' Nadia pondered this. To whom should she return? Surely her grandmother wasn't referring to one of her kidnappers? No; more likely it was to her father that she should return. Or could it be Joe?

Whoever it was she would be returning to, it was clear that her grandmother wanted her to go back. This affected Nadia more than anything else. With her choice made, she could no longer resist the steady pulling sensation and—in the very next instant, it seemed—she found herself gasping and sputtering as all of her sensations returned at once.

Nadia blinked, still catching her breath, and was startled to find angry blue eyes glaring down at her. Only this time they were attached to a real face. Her mind was still foggy, but the initial effect of whatever drug they gave her seemed to be wearing off. She realized that they had all removed their masks.

One of the other men—the Indian—unbound her hands and began to detach the chain that connected her to the floor.

"Leave it," said Blue Eyes, never taking his eyes from hers.

"But...she isn't the one," said his friend.

"That only makes her something worse," Blue Eyes replied disgustedly. His eyes bored into her, making her feel even more uncomfortable, but she couldn't seem to look away. "Get up," he said.

Nadia made an effort to obey, but she was so weak she could hardly move. Blue Eyes jerked her up and led her to the faded orange couch, where she gratefully collapsed. Her limbs felt like jelly. She tried to clear her head. The men brought chairs over, scraping them loudly on the floor and sat facing her. There was a long silence while they all just stared at her. *What now*, they seemed to be wondering. Nadia tore her gaze from the accusatory stare of Blue Eyes to inspect the other two men without their masks. One appeared to be Indian, just as his accent suggested, and the other was African American.

"We should call in someone else," said the Indian in perfect English and Nadia stared at him in surprise. She could have sworn he had an Indian accent when he spoke before.

"There isn't time," replied Blue Eyes.

"But we're not trained in this kind of interrogation," he argued.

"We'll make her talk," replied Blue Eyes with a hard edge to his voice. Nadia gasped. What did they want from her?

"I'm gonna cut through the bullshit and get right to the point," said Blue Eyes, speaking directly to Nadia this time. "We know something's coming, and we know you're involved. The only thing we don't know..." here he glanced at his comrades, "anymore...is why." His lips curled up in a snarl and his words were dripping with disgust. "Is it money?"

"I have no idea what you're talking about," Nadia croaked out in a shaky voice. When she saw the look this response brought to his face she trembled, and her hands flew to her throat defensively. "I swear it! I don't what you're talking about!"

"We know that isn't true," he said. He smiled without a trace of humor. "We already know you're working with them."

"Working with who?" she asked. Was this about that Pakistan thing after all?

The smile remained, but his eyes were like cubes of ice. "It isn't really *who*, is it?" he asked, watching her face very carefully. "It's what."

Nadia just stared at him, more confused than ever. She thought of the shimmering light outside and wondered once again if this had something to do with aliens.

"Until a few minutes ago," he continued, "We were ninety-nine point nine percent certain that you were one of them." He kept examining her as he spoke, as if he would extract the answers from her expression if he had to.

"One of...who?"

"What," he corrected her.

Nadia ransacked her mind, though she didn't even know what she was looking for. What was all this about? These men had just put her through some kind of ritual that nearly killed her and now they were talking about a 'what' instead of 'who' that she was supposed to be in cahoots with. Was this some kind of cult thing? Was it possible that these men were crazy? They didn't seem crazy, but strange beliefs made people do strange things. She tore her gaze away from Blue Eyes again to examine his Indian friend. His accent seemed to come and go, but that didn't necessarily mean he wasn't from India. She'd spent a lot of time there and knew the people to be quirky and highly superstitious. Yet she couldn't think of any Indian superstition that would explain what was happening here. She looked at the African American. He just narrowed his eyes at her menacingly.

Nadia could see that Blue Eyes was growing impatient. "I swear to you that I don't know who or what you're talking about!" she cried. The effects of the drug were almost gone now and Nadia's head was beginning to throb. If only they would give her something to eat and allow her to rest for a while. But she could see from her interrogator's expression that he was only getting started.

"Ask about her grandmother," suggested the Indian.

"My grandmother!" Nadia jerked back and gaped at him in astonishment. The episode with her grandmother was still fresh in her mind, even though she realized it was just a hallucination brought on by whatever drug they'd given her. But for him to mention it— "What about my grandmother?" she demanded. "Tell me why you asked about her!"

"You're the one who's going to answer the questions," Blue Eyes cut in. "And if you don't..." he stopped in mid-sentence, looking at her with such hatred she actually flinched. When he continued he spoke very slowly, emphasizing every word. "If you don't answer our questions and so much as one person gets hurt, I swear to god I will kill you so slowly and painfully that you'll be praying for it to be over!" Nadia gasped. She got the sense that he would not only do what he threatened but that he would enjoy it.

"I..." Nadia hesitated when she saw his expression darken even more. She was terrified, but what could she do? She couldn't even make something up because she had no idea what they were looking for. She tried pleading with him. "If you would just tell me what you want to know..."

"He wants to know about the attack, bitch," said the African American, entering the conversation for the first time.

"Yeah, and while you're at it, you might want to tell us where the djinn is," added the Indian.

Nadia stared at them dumbly. "Attack? Gin?" Her memory stirred. Thoughts of her grandmother were still close at hand. Her expression slowly changed as dawning gradually came. She looked at Blue Eyes in astonishment. "*Djinn!*" she exclaimed, unable to keep the disbelief out of her voice. "*The* djinn? As in the mystical creatures of *Arabian Nights*?" A new terror was seizing her. She'd been kidnapped by three psychopaths who somehow got wind of her grandmother's obsession with Arabian folklore. But how did they hear about her grandmother's stories? And why had Nadia had a hallucination of her grandmother just a few moments before?

Maybe it hadn't been a hallucination. Maybe Nadia really did experience an out-of-body experience and her grandmother was as delusional in the afterlife as she had been in real life.

Or maybe her grandmother's stories were true.

Nadia had the sudden urge to laugh. She couldn't quite bring herself to accept that these men were serious. Yet their expressions seemed perfectly serious. And determined. She got the distinct impression that they were not willing to negotiate on this point. So how could she prove that she wasn't mixed up in something that wasn't even real?

Yet there might be hope after all, Nadia suddenly realized, provided her captors believed as fully as they appeared to. In fact, this could be the opportunity she'd been waiting for! She still had a clear memory of the stories that had been so meticulously passed down to her mother—and later to her. How could she ever forget? The stories chronicled the most significant moments of her grandmother's life, but as they would appear in a *DC Comic*, enhanced with all kind of wild adventures. Even as a child Nadia had balked at some of the more fantastic details—such as those involving the djinn—the same way she balked at Santa Claus and the Easter Bunny. She knew that the djinn were a big part of Arab folklore and figured that that was what inspired her grandmother. All of her research in college seemed to confirm this. Nadia still found the stories fascinating, of course, because they were about her grandmother, who was herself something of a mystical being in Nadia's eyes. She had never been permitted to meet Helene Trevelyan in person. But she would never forget the first time she saw her in an old, faded Polaroid—the only picture Nadia's mother had—so worn it was coming apart at the edges. What intrigued Nadia most about her grandmother was the remarkable resemblance she shared with the woman. It was like looking into a mirror that revealed the future. Nadia used to stare at the picture while her mother's low, melodious voice poured out one story after another. Sometimes Nadia imagined that it was all happening to her, for Helene Trevelyan didn't quite seem real. She would examine every detail of the picture with secret satisfaction, thinking this was how she would look one day. She took in the large, curious green eyes, the simple, straightforward nose and the delicate, full lips, noting the subtle overbite that took the edge off her grandmother's beauty and gave it a soft, vulnerable sweetness. Even the wild, white-blonde curls that sprang out in all directions—they were pulled back off her face with a headband in the picture—only enhanced her charm and gave her the look of a mystical princess. She seemed not quite of this world. Her expression was ethereal and dreamlike, just like her stories, and seemed to carry the promise of exciting adventures to come. Nadia couldn't wait to grow up. She embraced her turbulent curls, frizz and all, and flat out refused to wear braces, satisfied that everything would turn out just as it was intended to.

Her grandmother's stories—though incredible at times—revealed genuine suffering that pulled at Nadia's heart strings and sometimes haunted her dreams. Her mother often wept when she got to the saddest parts, but she never skipped over them, determined that Nadia know every detail. Nadia often thought about what she would do differently if she was the one it was happening to, and each time her mother told the stories she hoped for a different ending. And she, too, would weep when the stories always turned out the same.

But to have all this dredged up now, under such bizarre circumstances, was both baffling and disturbing. Nadia's opinion about the djinn had not changed since childhood. She still didn't believe in them. She wanted to—she'd tried to even—but she couldn't. Ancient spirits wandering the earth in search of human bodies to inhabit—there wasn't a single piece of scientific evidence to support it. Nadia knew this because she had looked for the evidence herself. But like the djinn themselves, it was not to be found. Nadia had reached the conclusion that all supernatural beings—whether djinn, ghosts, demons, or even angels—were simply the fodder of ancient fairy-tales. Nadia's grandmother was well acquainted with Eastern mythology. Her love of reading was inspired by her father, and was probably what got her through the loneliness and isolation she felt living in Saudi Arabia all those years later. That later reading would have been limited to religion and history, and sorely lacking in the sciences. Confused by what happened to her, she naturally began forming theories and drawing conclusions in an attempt to make sense of it all. Nadia couldn't help admiring her grandmother's imaginative use of the limited knowledge she'd acquired. Perhaps her grandmother even believed her own theories. But that's all they were—theories and stories. Nadia had satisfied her curiosity about that.

But how was it connected to what was happening now? What possible link could these men have to her grandmother's djinn?

"You're not even Arab," Nadia couldn't help observing out loud. She figured the concept of djinn was mostly limited to the Arab culture. She examined each of them, hesitating over the one she had previously supposed to be Indian. "…Are you?"

"No, but you are," Blue Eyes shot back, putting the focus back on her, as usual.

"Yes, on my mother's side," Nadia admitted. "My grandfather was Arab, but I've never even met him."

"This isn't story time at the library," interjected the African American. "We're not asking you about Ali Baba and his flying carpet. We use the term 'djinn' because it's the first name they were given in ancient Arabia, where all this started. You can use 'daeva' or 'demon' if you like, but this isn't a game. You need to tell us what you know about it right now!"

"I only know of one djinn…" she said, pausing to collect her thoughts. She could use her grandmother's stories to her advantage. If nothing else, they might buy her some time. She shuddered again, remembering Blue Eyes' threat. If she could convince him that she had the information he was seeking, she might be able to stay alive until she found a way to escape.

This appeared to interest them. "Where is it?" asked Blue Eyes.

"I don't know where it is right this minute," she said. She was aware that she was playing a dangerous game and her heart began to beat a little faster. "All I know is what I heard, second hand, from my mother."

This took some of the wind out of their sails. "What do you know, exactly?" Blue Eyes asked.

"I know that my grandmother spoke to the djinn," she replied cautiously. "The djinn was called Lilith." She stopped after each statement to gauge their responses, but their expressions gave nothing away. She decided to go for it. "And though I don't know where Lilith is now, I know every detail of her life up to when she disappeared in nineteen forty-eight."

She had their attention. "How could you know every detail of her life?" asked the African American.

She took a deep breath and tried to be her most convincing. "Because Lilith told my grandmother, my grandmother told my mother and my mother told me," she said.

They appeared to consider this.

"When did your mother tell you about it?" Blue Eyes asked.

Nadia hesitated a moment and decided to tell the truth. "The last time was when I was about thirteen or fourteen years old, I think," she said.

"She can't even remember how old she was," observed the African American. "How you gonna remember 'every detail of its life,' huh?" he asked her.

"I remember every detail," she replied huffily—"Because my mother told me the stories over and over again. My grandmother did the same with her. For some reason it was very important to my grandmother that we know the stories, but she was afraid to write them down af…I mean, she didn't want them to fall into the wrong hands. She made it a kind of a game for us to pass the stories down like in ancient times."

"How do we know she's telling the truth?" asked the African American.

Blue Eyes sighed. "We won't until we hear what she has to say," he replied.

That was exactly what Nadia was hoping for and she very nearly let out a sigh of relief. She was still reeling with shock. Of all the possible explanations for her kidnapping, this one hadn't even occurred to her. She never imagined that her grandmother's stories would have any significance to anyone besides her and her mother.

Nadia had not lied when she said she knew every detail of Lilith's life. Her mother had not only repeated the stories again and again; she'd elaborated over every point. She cleverly unraveled one little piece of the puzzle at a time, stretching the stories out over a long period of time as she strung Nadia along, night after night, with little hints of what was to come. Now Nadia would have to do the same.

"There's quite a lot," Nadia told them. "It could take a while."

Blue Eyes examined her face as if to read her intentions there. "If you're delaying so that the attack can be executed, you will die," he said. "I'll personally see to that, just as I promised you earlier. Since you're not one of them, you must realize that there's no way to get back here when you die. Whatever they promised you, you won't be able to collect it. You're not Islamic so you can't be expecting some reward in the afterlife. There's nothing but suffering, disgrace and death for you if their plan succeeds."

Nadia swallowed. "You were wrong about me being a djinn," she reminded him. "Can you at least consider that you might be wrong about my involvement in this attack you're accusing me of?"

The hardness in his expression seemed to soften the tiniest bit as Blue Eyes appeared to consider this. But it just as quickly returned to stone.

"We might have been wrong about where the djinn is," he conceded. "But we're not wrong about its being out there or the impending attack that it's master-minded. We know that it's working with several terrorist cells to bring about a disaster the likes of which we've never seen before. And you and BEACON...and your grandmother's djinn are at the center of it." He let this sink in before he continued. "So if you really are the little do-gooder that you make yourself out to be, you'll want to help us prevent this disaster from happening."

Nadia stared at him. In that moment she sincerely hoped that they were crazy, because she couldn't even consider the alternative. BEACON at the center of an attack, 'the likes of which we've never seen before?' It was impossible.

"Where and when is this attack you're talking about?" she asked.

The blue eyes flickered and Nadia caught the smallest glimpse of uncertainty there. "That's what you're going to help us figure out," he said.

Nadia dropped her head in her hands and struggled to organize her thoughts. She was so tired. *They're crazy*, she told herself. *I'm going to have to milk these stories for all their worth.* But even to think was becoming an effort. She could barely muster the energy to lift her head back up and face her interrogators again.

"I'm so hungry…" she murmured.

Blue Eyes turned to his comrades with a sigh. It was the first time she'd seen him relent in the smallest measure. "I could eat too," he admitted. "Either of you feel like putting something together for the four of us?"

The two men looked at each other.

"Oh no," said the African American. "I ain't no Julia Child." The Indian got up with a little sigh of disgust and went into the small area that acted as a makeshift kitchen. Nadia heard him rummaging around, mumbling under his breath.

"May I at least know your names so I won't have to think of you as the 'African American,' the 'Indian' and…,'" Nadia stopped there.

"And…?" prompted Blue Eyes.

Nadia tried to suppress the blush that was rising up her neck. "*And* the white guy," she lied. Something like curiosity flashed in his eyes, but he didn't pursue it further.

"The 'African American' is called Clive," he said.

"Tha's right, boss," reiterated Clive, vigorously nodding his head. "I be Clive an' I sho nuff did musta come out of Africa too!" Nadia couldn't tell if he was joking or if she'd actually offended him. She rifled through her addled wits in search of a newer, more acceptable term than 'African American' but came up empty-handed. In spite of his strange behavior, Clive had the look of an intelligent and rational guy. There was a kind of perceptiveness in his expression that implied that he 'got' it, or you, or whatever it was that needed figuring out, though his manner could be rather condescending, or so it seemed to Nadia. Of the three men, he seemed the best groomed. His brown hair was cut very close to his head, his clothing looked tailored (though he wore jeans and a t-shirt), and even his fingernails appeared to have been filed rather than cut.

"And the…ah…*Indian* is called Gordon," Blue Eyes continued, ignoring Clive.

"In Indian that means, 'boy with girl's name,'" said Clive, but the joke—if there was one—was lost on Nadia. 'Gordon' seemed plenty masculine to her, but then again, maybe that wasn't his real name.

"I wish I could say I was veddy pleased to meet you," said Gordon, emerging from the kitchen with the Indian accent fully intact. It infused his words with a benign, almost jovial quality that didn't quite fit the occasion. He had large, wide eyes, a straight nose and full lips. His thick, jet black hair was neatly trimmed around the neck and ears, while the top was much longer and combed to one side. It fell in waves into his eyes and he kept swinging his head to one side in order send it back where it belonged. He was the leanest of the three—though none of them were sporting any excess body fat—and he appeared to be the youngest as well (Nadia guessed late twenties). He dragged a small table between the couch and their chairs and slapped down a plate piled high with slices of cheese, crackers and olives. A few of the olives rolled off the plate and onto the table. His stiff smile faded as he turned to Clive.

"You better give that a rest," he said in perfect English.

"You think it's that important?" asked Clive. "You think with everything that's going on in her life right now she's thinking about this?"

Nadia wasn't sure what to make of them. She wondered for the umpteenth time if they were crazy. Crazy might not be bad, provided they weren't psychotic. She put a piece of cheese on one of the crackers and turned back to Blue Eyes as she popped it in her mouth.

"And I'm Will," he said, abruptly bringing the introductions to a close. He was disheveled from the day's activities, but remained as composed and determined as ever. He had fluffed his hair back into place with his fingers, but Nadia noticed that it was beginning to curl up rebelliously at the ends. He seemed comfortable in his chair, casually crossing one leg over the other as his blue eyes settled on her with interest. He looked more like a doctor than a kidnapper. "Now that we've all been formerly introduced, you can tell us about your grandmother and her djinn," he said.

Nadia stuffed another cracker with cheese in her mouth and wondered where to begin.

CHAPTER
6

"It was nineteen forty-eight," said Nadia—"When my great-grandfather, Robert Trevelyan, and two of his colleagues, took his daughter—my grandmother, Helene Trevelyan—to Qumran to investigate scrolls that were discovered there."

"How well did you know your grandmother?" asked Will.

"I never met her, but I knew a lot about her…through my mother."

"Why didn't your mother ever take you to Saudi Arabia to meet her?" asked Clive. "A woman like Gisele Adeire would've had the means to get in and out of the country, no problem." Nadia bristled at his tone when he spoke of her mother. His manner of speaking was more expressive than his words. It was clear he disapproved of Gisele. Nadia wondered why.

Nadia kept her own tone in check when she replied. "She wanted to, but my grandfather wouldn't authorize it. My mother was shunned by my grandfather for leaving the Muslim faith. Actually, I think he did it more to punish my grandmother. At any rate, even if we had managed to get into the country on some other pretext, my grandfather would never have permitted Helene to see us."

"Did you exchange letters?" asked Gordon.

"My mother never stopped sending letters, even though she believed they were being intercepted by my grandfather. She never got a letter back."

"Why would your grandfather do that?" asked Gordon. "What happened to upset him so much?"

Nadia shifted uncomfortably in her seat. "I thought you wanted to know about the djinn."

"Yes, let's get back to that," Will agreed. "How much do you know about Helene's family background?"

"I know everything my mother knew, and she and my grandmother were very close." Nadia was surprised by the tiny pang of resentment this statement triggered. Nadia's grandmother had been as open and accessible as Nadia's mother had been secretive and unavailable. If not for Helene's stories—which her mother was strangely determined that Nadia know—Nadia and her mother might never have discussed anything more significant than what Nadia was going to wear to the next event. Nadia felt she knew Helene better than she knew her own mother. "My grandmother was only sixteen when they took that fateful trip into the Middle East," Nadia continued. "Up to that point she'd lived in London with her father and a housekeeper called Mrs. Barnes. Her own mother died when she was very young, so she had no memory of her.

"Mrs. Barnes had a kind of on and off guardianship of her nephew, Edward, who she began bringing with her to work when Helene was about twelve. Edward's mother was sickly, and his father had been killed in the war."

"Is this the same Edward who is now your father?" Will interjected.

"Yes," replied Nadia.

"One thing that's always puzzled me is why your great-grandfather would take his daughter on such a venture," remarked Gordon. "Surely he realized the risks—not to mention what was happening in the Middle East at the time. It wasn't the ideal situation for a sixteen year old girl."

"My grandmother wasn't an ordinary sixteen year old," explained Nadia. "All she knew of life was war. Even when the war finally ended they were still knee deep in the depression. Until Edward came along, Helene had lived a very solitary life. All the other children in her London neighborhood had been evacuated and her father was rarely home. Though I know my grandmother was fond of Mrs. Barnes, the woman wasn't much of a companion. And she wasn't exactly what you would call 'good' with children either. In those days people thought children were 'better seen than heard.' Helene's only companion before Edward was the radio."

Nadia sighed, resting her head on the back of the couch. The dim lighting of the room had a peculiar effect on her memories, making them seem more vivid.

"There was one program in particular...called *It's That Man Again*. I dug up some old archives of it online and listened to them a few years ago. I'm sure Helene didn't understand half the jokes, but I can see why it appealed to her. There are a handful of silly, one dimensional characters that carry on riotously over the air while poking fun at the Nazis and the war. It was very British. Loads of innuendo. Benny Hill meets Hyacinth Bucket...that kind of thing. My mother said that Helene used to act out some of the sketches for her. Saudi Arabia didn't have this kind of entertainment—they still don't—and I think that particular show, with its bold, free-thinking ideas, must have come to represent all Helene had lost. She even incorporated some of the show's catch phrases into their daily life (she taught most of the family how to speak English), and it was a private joke between Helene and my mother whenever someone unwittingly repeated one of the phrases from the show, like 'cheesed off' or 'ever so'."

Nadia found herself smiling at the memory—her mother used those same phrases up to the day she died—but then she realized how far she'd strayed from the subject at hand and her smile stiffened.

"Jolly good," Clive threw in when she paused, and Nadia felt his attempt at a British accent was as bad as his manners. "The old girl enjoyed listening to the radio. Did you get that, Gordon?" Gordon had taken out a notebook and pen and was taking notes.

Nadia blushed, scolding herself inwardly for digressing. Her mother told the stories so much better. But then again, Nadia had never attempted to tell them before. She preferred listening.

Yet she could tell by their expressions—even Clive's—that they were impressed with the incredible details she knew of her grandmother's life. It begged the question of how much more she knew.

"Anyway, Helene wasn't allowed to listen to the radio as much as she would have liked because it gave Mrs. Barnes a headache. So, with nothing else to do, she began spending time in her father's library.

"My great-grandfather was a collector of books. He mostly had books on history, mythology and philosophy...stuff like that. There wasn't much there for a young girl. But Helene searched around until she found books with pictures. Most of the pictures were of historical characters—famous warriors, that kind of thing—but occasionally she'd find something more exciting like, say, a demon out of some ancient myth. If the picture was interesting enough, she'd read the book. Eventually she developed a love for ancient history."

"So she had a personal interest in the discovery at Qumran," concluded Gordon.

"Yes. She was particularly interested in archeology. At some point she must have shared this new interest with her father and suddenly they had something to talk about. She began spending more time with him and his friends. Helene was very proud of that. These were respected professors and archeologists, men who barely condescended to speak to their wives, and here they were, discussing history, religion and politics with a teenage girl. It made her feel important."

"So you think that's why he brought her along?" said Clive, glancing at the others.

Nadia nodded, wondering what other reason there could be. "The trip was scheduled for the Christmas holiday—which worked out as well for Helene's father as it did for her—so the only issue, really, would have been how Helene would get along without Mrs. Barnes and Edward. But even this would have been a minor concern. It seems strange now, to think of it, but in those days change—and even loss— was taken in stride. People came and people went. One day Helene's mother was there and the next day she was replaced by Mrs. Barnes. It was the same with Edward. Helene said Mrs. Barnes just brought him to work with her one morning and sat him down next to her at the kitchen table. Without a word of explanation. Some days he would come and other days he wouldn't."

"How much do you know about your great-grandfather and his colleagues?" asked Will.

"Helene's father was a history professor at the University of London," Nadia replied. "He seemed to be a pretty ordinary man. Having 'missed his calling' as an archeologist, he would tell people he was living vicariously through his two associates who worked in that field. Henry Butchard—or "Butch," as my great-grandfather called him—was one of these associates and also one of his closest friends. Helene described him as a 'dear old thing,' but although he was in his early seventies and his hair was almost entirely white, Helene said he was 'sharp as a whip.' He participated in many important archeological events through his career, but his claim to fame was a dig he assisted with right there in Britain.

"The person Butch assisted in that dig—Sir Frederick Huxley— was another of my great-grandfather's close friends. He'd been knighted by the Queen for his discoveries in and around Britain. They met on an expedition in nineteen thirty-eight, where an old battleship had been discovered in an ancient Anglo-Saxon burial ground. They consulted with my great-grandfather throughout the project—which lasted several years—and the three of them had remained friends ever since."

"Which of them was the first to hear about the discovery in Qumran?" asked Will.

"It was Huxley," Nadia said. "He'd participated in expeditions around the world and had connections everywhere. Whenever any new discovery was made he was among the first to know, according to my grandmother—who may have been a bit smitten by him. Huxley was the youngest of the three men, still in his forties. All those years later, Helene still described him to my mother as 'dreamy.' Working outside in warmer climates had given him that healthy, adventurous look that would have appealed to a sixteen year old. His traveling to exotic places probably didn't hurt either." Nadia glanced at her captors and couldn't help noticing that they, too, had that masculine, outdoorsy look that her grandmother so admired, as well as the sophisticated manner that comes with being well-traveled. There was also something of the modern, new-age nerd in each of them, a kind of curiosity and attentiveness that might have appealed to her grandmother as well. Nadia abruptly cut these thoughts short and pulled herself back to the subject at hand. "I guess Helene talked a lot about Huxley."

"Did your grandmother say what it was about this particular discovery that appealed to them?" Gordon asked. "I mean, you have to admit the timing was terrible. Most archaeologists were avoiding that part of the world. Why that discovery?"

Nadia took a deep breath. "Because that's the one they'd been looking for," she replied.

They all straightened up in their chairs. "Looking for?" echoed Will.

"Yes—well, *Huxley* had been looking for a Sumerian *Book of the Dead* for years," she explained. "Most people believe *Books of the Dead* originated with the Egyptians, but Huxley didn't think so. He said the Egyptian *Books* were imitations. He believed that the Egyptians stole the idea from a tribe of Sumerians—dating back to before the flood—who discovered the secret to immortality."

"How did Huxley know this?"

"Because he had, in his possession, a Sumerian tablet that called for a Sumerian *Book of the Dead*," she replied, pausing a few seconds before adding—"The tablet of the Qliphoth."

Just as she'd hoped, this last piece of information caused the men to practically jump out of their seats. She had them on the hook. Which meant that she would live another day.

CHAPTER
7

"Huxley had the tablet of the Qliphoth?" Gordon exclaimed, glancing at the others. "But that wasn't found at the site."

"Butch may have destroyed it," Nadia said. "He wanted to after their experiment succeeded. Or it may have been stolen. All I know is that Huxley definitely had the tablet beforehand and the way I understood it, the *Book of the Dead* they found in Qumran would have been useless without it."

Once again she could see that they were encouraged by her knowledge of certain facts and this strengthened her hope. What she was saying seemed to resonate with them, giving them a reason to keep her alive. But it also brought her up short. *Why* were her grandmother's stories resonating with these men? What had one to do with the other?

For the moment, she merely had to keep them interested in order to stay alive. But she was exhausted and, notwithstanding the food, she still felt weak.

"How did the trip to Qumran come about?" asked Will. "Whose idea was it? Were they planning to conjure this soul all along?"

Nadia sighed. "Originally I think the idea was to make a great discovery. I don't know that any of them truly believed they could raise the dead. Perhaps Huxley did. Of the three, he was the most open-minded. Finding that tablet was a dream come true for him. It's one of the oldest surviving documents of the ancient world. He had my great-grandfather help him translate it. That's how they discovered that the tablet dated back to this ancient Qliphoth tribe in ancient Sumer."

"Where did Huxley get the tablet?" asked Gordon.

"Helene always wondered about that. She said Huxley was very evasive about it…which made her think his methods might have been questionable. He wouldn't be the first archaeologist to adopt the 'finders-keepers' policy.

"However he came by it, Huxley was convinced of the tablet's authenticity," Nadia continued. "But it was impossible to know without the second piece of the puzzle…the corresponding *Book of the Dead*, which supposedly held the 'keys' to each individual soul being summoned. This was how Huxley was able to eliminate the more common, Egyptian *Books of the Dead*. For one thing, the two didn't work together. But even more importantly, the timing was all wrong. The Egyptian books came hundreds of years later. Why would a Sumerian tribe called Qliphoth create a formula for the afterlife for people they didn't even know yet? It made more sense that they wrote it for themselves. That's when Huxley realized that there had to be *Books of the Dead* that predated the Egyptian ones. Only *Books of the Dead* written during the same time period as the tablet of the Qliphoth would be the genuine article.

"My great-grandfather and Butch supported Huxley's research, though Butch made it clear that his efforts were purely for Huxley's benefit. Butch was the most pragmatic of the three, always choosing the most scientific solution in any debate. I think my great-grandfather was a kind of buffer between Butch and Huxley. He was practical, like Butch, but still open-minded, like Huxley. Though he advocated for facts, he seemed to secretly hope for more. They all enjoyed a good mystery. I think that's why they were so interested in ancient Sumer. Anything might have happened back then. Helene said the men spent hours debating that period in history. They were convinced that something happened back then that impacted the world."

"How'd they know that this *Book of the Dead* found in Qumran was from Sumer?" asked Will. "Or, for that matter, how did they know that a *Book of the Dead* had been found at all?"

"Huxley had connections all over the world," said Nadia. "I suppose he probably told those connections what he was looking for. It was a British soldier—an old friend of his—who first alerted him of the discovery at Qumran. The British army was in the Middle East at the time, assisting the Arab Legion, and Huxley's friend was stationed out there. Anyway, word had gotten out that some ancient scrolls had been found in a cave in Qumran. A local Bedouin was trying to sell them. Any marginally skilled antiques dealer would have been able to recognize the Sumerian hieroglyphs and cuneiform—though it would've taken someone a bit more knowledgeable to identify it as a *Book of the Dead*. Word of the discovery was getting out and several scholars in the area had already looked at the scrolls. It wouldn't have seemed odd for Huxley's friend—who was stationed just outside of Qumran—to get wind of it."

Will nodded, though he seemed unconvinced that it wasn't 'odd.' "How much did Huxley and the others know about the Qliphoth?" asked Will.

"Not a lot," Nadia said. "The author of Huxley's tablet, who remained anonymous, simply defined the Qliphoth as 'our offspring.' This is another mystery the men hoped to solve by finding the corresponding *Book of the Dead*. I think at first they thought it was simply the name of a tribe of people, but there was definitely something peculiar about them. I researched this a little myself when I was in college. The word 'Qliphoth'—which is Sumerian—had been adopted into the Hebrew language, but its meaning remained ambiguous. Rather than giving it an actual meaning, the Hebrews described it as the *opposite* of another Hebrew word—I can't recall the word itself—that means "creation of God." This seems to imply that the Qliphoth—in its Hebrew translation at least—would describe the condition of being "not created by God." Which could mean anything coming from that era. It wasn't until afterwards that Huxley and the others realized that the word literally referred to a group of people that had come into existence *by means of something other than God*."

Their expressions—which looked a little like a deer caught in the headlights—encouraged her. She just had to keep doing what she was doing, dropping little breadcrumbs for them to pick up. But it was getting harder to concentrate.

"Huxley believed these Qliphoth, whoever they were, might have discovered the secret to eternal life," she went on. "Butch was intrigued, if only for the opportunity to play devil's advocate. But it was my great-grandfather who surprised everyone by suggesting they go to Qumran.

"There was a cease fire in December, so they traveled by train to the Mediterranean Sea and then boarded a ship to Tel Aviv. From there they were assisted by British soldiers into Qumran."

"Who were the British soldiers who assisted them?" Will asked. "You mentioned the Arab Legion. Do you, by chance, have more specific details?"

Nadia finally gave in to her desire to lie down on the shabby, but surprisingly comfortable couch. The air conditioner kept up its steady buzz in the background. She had impressed them with her intricate knowledge of the events, but she had impressed herself as well. She remembered every detail. It was as if she was there—or maybe it was that her grandmother was *here*, with her in this dingy little room. The strange sense of unreality returned. Nadia looked up at the ceiling but there was no sign of the white light or her grandmother. She spied a web in one of the corners and searched for the spider. The mention of the British soldiers made her insides clench.

"The soldier who met them in Tel Aviv was the same friend who alerted Huxley of the discovery. His name was Lieutenant John Brisbin, but Huxley called him Brisbie." She could sense rather than see that Gordon was writing the soldier's name down. "They all stayed at the Yarden Hotel that night and then drove to Qumran the next day. Helene told my mother that that day in Tel Aviv was the happiest day of her life. She loved Tel Aviv. It was December and she could go outside with only a sweater." Nadia sensed that she was getting off track again but she didn't care. She was too exhausted to separate the wheat from the chaff. She preferred to simply let the stories unravel naturally, like her mother did when she told them. She could almost hear her mother's voice, soft and melodious, coaxing the stories into a living, breathing thing.

"Helene and her father decided to take a walk," Nadia continued. "And they set out for Magen David Square. They were looking for a post office—Helene had promised to write Edward every day and she had several letters to mail.

"Tel Aviv was as different from London as it could be. Helene described it as a 'cheerful, bustling city.' It wasn't extravagant, by any means, but Helene said there was definitely the sense of prosperity. There were shops and cafes on every street, and everything seemed to be available. There was no mention of shortages or prohibited items from ration's lists. London had put on a good face, but the war had taken its toll. Helene hadn't even realized how much it had affected her until that day, when all of a sudden—for the first time in her life—there were no restrictions on anything. Whatever you had money for could be purchased, just like that. Tel Aviv seemed completely unaffected by the depression that dogged the rest of the world. Buildings were going up everywhere. Women wore heels and lipstick. Men wore hats and jackets and smoked cigarettes.

"Helene spotted a sign that said 'American Ice Cream,' and was thrilled not to find a long line of people standing in front of it. Ice cream had been on the rations list for as long as Helene was alive. One small cone was all Londoners were allotted per week, and in order to get that you had to stand in line, sometimes for more than an hour. Many of the mothers would stand in line before school let out so their children wouldn't have to wait so long. But Mrs. Barnes would never dream of doing such a thing, so Helene always had to start at the very end, which meant that by the time she reached the front of the line, all the best flavors were sold out.

"It was the first time in her life that she was able to simply walk up to the counter and order what she wanted. She ordered a strawberry ice cream cone with sprinkles and told my mother it was the best ice cream she ever had."

Nadia gave up her search for the spider and turned toward the men. She was mildly surprised to find that they were still listening with interest. This came as a relief, because the words seemed to be flowing of their own accord now. Everything else was shutting down.

"It was there that they learned about the invention of the Polaroid camera," she continued. "There was a sign in the back of the shop that read 'pictures in one minute.' My great-grandfather naturally wanted a demonstration, and Helene was thrilled to pose for a photograph that wasn't school issued.

"The camera was practically the size of a toaster, with a viewfinder sticking out of the top. Helene said there was a bright flash of light and then the man set the camera down. It made a low, ticking sound for a few seconds, then was quiet. They waited the full minute before the man opened a panel in the back of the camera and carefully lifted out the print. 'You look just like a princess,' he told Helene when he handed her the photo. She'd laughed at the time, but my mother said Helene always loved that picture."

Nadia remembered the picture well. It was the one she'd spent so many hours staring at while listening to the stories. She always wondered what Helene was thinking in that moment.

With her grandmother's image so vividly in her head, Nadia was once again becoming lost in the past, just like when she was a young girl. Closing her eyes, she could see her grandmother in that ice cream store just as clearly as if she herself was there.

The man who took the picture had been right. Helene did look like a princess, with her pale, wiry curls pulled back off her face with the flowery little headband that, on her, looked more like a dainty crown. Her hair flowed up over the top of her head and cascaded down her back like a brilliant, rippling waterfall. There was something imperious in the way she stared off into the distance, looking much older than her sixteen years. Her expression was thoughtful and solemn, with only the merest hint of a smile to add an air of mystery. Even her small overbite, which she tended to dislike, added just the right touch of charm.

Nadia wondered again what Helene had been thinking in that moment. Did she sense that her life was about to be irreversibly altered…or that that Polaroid would be the last picture ever taken of her?

"And after that?" someone prompted. Their questions seemed more like a hypnotist's suggestions now.

"They went into Qumran. Lieutenant Brisbin and his troops were stationed near there. Brisbin secured them lodgings nearby, and he even got them a car."

"Can you tell us about the area and the people they encountered there?" Gordon asked.

"I can tell you that my grandmother didn't care for them," Nadia replied—"Though her memories may have been marred by what happened later. But compared to Tel Aviv, she found Qumran... unpleasant. She described it as terra-cotta colored terrain with similar colored buildings popping out periodically like camouflaged predators. My grandmother preferred more traditional landscapes. She had a particular fondness for gardens and I think the barrenness of the desert frightened her a little. The Arab people offered some new interest at first, but even they became tiresome for her after a while. The women were covered from head to toe, usually in black, though occasionally she would spot a red or white skirt. The men dressed in lighter clothing and wore turbans on their heads. The thing Helene disliked most was the way the Arab men behaved around her. She thought them extremely rude. Her father explained that Muslim men were not permitted to speak to women they weren't related to—out of respect for the women—but this didn't make sense to my grandmother. And given the way the Arab men looked at her (Huxley tried to make her feel better by telling her that it was only her blonde hair that made them stare) their rule about not speaking to women seemed perfidious.

"The cottage Brisbin secured for them was only a few miles from his post. Helene didn't say much about it other than it had two bedrooms with cots that were not very comfortable. She shared a room with her father while Huxley and Butch shared the other room. Having never been on this type of expedition—or any kind of expedition—before, Helene had nothing to compare it to, but Huxley and Butch seemed delighted to have an indoor bathroom, and they even made a fuss over finding silverware in one of the kitchen drawers, so Helene supposed it could have been much worse.

"An Arab man and his wife acted as caretakers for them, bringing food and supplies. There was nothing exceptional about the couple according to Helene. She remembered that the man—I think his name was Abdul—spoke very poor English and his wife, like the other women, never spoke at all."

"What do you remember about the Bedouin with the scrolls?" prompted Gordon.

Nadia sighed. She knew she was probably exasperating them with all the little details but it was as if all the circuits to her brain had been fried and she was now running on auto-pilot. "You'll get more accurate details if you just let me recite the stories the way my mother told me," Nadia replied. "I'm really too tired to think."

"You know the stories that well?" asked Clive.

"I know them by heart," she said. "The same way other people can recite *The Three Little Pigs* or *Snow White and the Seven Dwarves* fifteen years later, to their children. These were *my* bedtime stories."

Nadia was reminded, suddenly, of Shahryar, the jealous King of *The Thousand and One Nights*, whose wife (in order to delay her impending execution) created an endless string of fantastic tales, each of which she concluded with the beginning of a new story. Always left wanting more, the king kept postponing his wife's execution until it was all but forgotten. Just like that wife, Nadia would let the stories lead the kidnappers where they may, stringing them along until she could find a way to escape.

The room seemed to grow even dimmer as Nadia searched her memory for the Bedouin with the scrolls. It was a little like traveling through time. When she located him he immediately sprang to life, and Nadia could picture him waiting anxiously in his tent, his fingers delicately handling the scrolls. She turned her head and looked around, half expecting to find the Bedouin there in the room with her. But there were only her three captors, silently waiting for her to continue. She turned back toward the ceiling, trying to shake off the feeling that something sinister—something even more sinister than what she had thus far experienced—was lurking in the shadows all around her. Perhaps her grandmother had been right. There did seem to be something ominous in this desert land, itself so bleak and barren, that sparked fanciful notions like those found in *The Thousand and One Nights,* of monsters and ghouls…and most definitely djinn.

CHAPTER
8

December, 1948
Qumran

The Bedouin camp was made up of several very large, blackish-gray tents the Bedouin people call *beit al-sha'r,* which in Arabic means 'house of hair.' The *beit al-sha'r* is woven from the hair of sheep and goats, and it's said to be similar to the ones used by the first nomadic tribes of ancient Mesopotamia. To see these *beit al-sha'r* in the middle of the stark, deserted valley—together with the Bedouin people dressed in the traditional robes and head coverings, their livestock grazing on the sparse brush-lands while their camels sit idly by, watching their activities with bored, contemptuous sideways glances—was to be transported back in time by thousands of years. Helene felt as if she had stepped into an entirely different era, and it wouldn't have surprised her all that much to see Christ himself—accompanied by his twelve apostles—emerging from one of the tents.

There was something about all of it that frightened Helene. Her fear began the moment they left Tel Aviv, and kept growing stronger the further away they got. It wasn't the conflict that bothered her. Lieutenant Brisbin had set all of their minds at ease about that. "Getting you in and out will be a doddle," he promised. "There's a ceasefire as of last month but it wouldn't have mattered anyhow. That territory—in and around Qumran—is completely secured by the Arab Legion. You'll be as comfortable as pigeons in Trafalgar square."

Helene believed him about that. Her fear was of something else, something in the desert itself, something malevolent and undefeatable that the Bedouins—like specters from the past—seemed a forewarning of.

They were looking for a Bedouin by the name of Khalid bin Malik. Most of the people in the camp didn't appear to know English, but they recognized the name and led them to his tent. The children gathered all around them, showing a particular interest in Helene, whom they stared up at in awe and rushed alongside of as she self-consciously followed her father and the others to the tent of the Bedouin trader.

Khalid bin Malik was surprisingly refined and courteous, with a charming smile and sharp, knowing eyes. Unlike the other Arabs Helene had encountered, his beard and mustache were impeccably trimmed very close to his face. He greeted them all warmly, even Helene—he managed this very eloquently without speaking to her— and he invited them into his tent. He affectionately shooed the Bedouin children away, gently chiding them in Arabic.

"I trust you had a pleasant journey," he said when they were alone. His English had only the merest hint of an accent, which seemed to enhance the meaning. He motioned for them to sit down—they were in a large, carpeted area scattered with oversized pillows surrounding a large, short-legged table—and nodded to a woman in the back. "We will have refreshments in a moment," he told them.

"However did you discover the cave?" Butch asked once they were settled. Though he was highly intellectual, Butch had an agreeable manner that immediately put those around him at ease. There was a genial air about him, an old-fashioned gentlemanliness that made him seem more attractive than he actually was. His face was rather ordinary in and of itself, but his expression was one of the utmost interest and benevolence. His thick, wavy hair was so white it reminded Helene of the powdered wigs of their ancestors. He always wore 'spectacles'—as he called them—though he only used them for reading, so he developed the habit of peering over or under them whenever he looked at anything larger than the written word. As he addressed the Bedouin, he tipped his head to one side—as was also his habit—and considered him thoughtfully. Helene could never tell what he was thinking. His eyes often carried a glint of amusement, though he was generally serious.

Helene was trying not to fidget on the pillows.

"I wasn't the one who found the scrolls," Khalid explained. "A young shepherd boy stumbled upon them quite by accident. I was one of many who were interested. I do a great deal of trading with the British officers who come here and they, in turn, bring me buyers from around the world. The men who raided the cave have no idea of the scrolls' worth and, even if they did, they wouldn't know how to sell them. They were getting nowhere before I came into the picture. They were actually contemplating using the scrolls for fuel."

"Good God!" ejaculated Huxley, horrified at the thought. His pale blue eyes seemed even lighter in contrast to his dark, reddish brown skin. There were deep lines at the corners of his eyes from years of squinting in the sun. His brownish hair was streaked with blonde and bits of gray. He looked the picture of health, and Helene sometimes felt herself blushing whenever his pale blue gaze fell upon her.

Several veiled women began bringing tea, water, and a kind of flat bread that looked rather dusty and unappetizing to Helene at first, but which was actually quite good when she tasted it.

"Most of the scrolls they had—the ones I saw anyway—appeared to be copies of religious texts already in circulation—many of which are in your Christian Bible." Khalid picked up the conversation where it left off once the tea was poured and the women left. "Those scrolls still have value, of course, but I was looking for something more… unique. So I went and searched the cave myself."

"Forgive me, but how are you able to identify these documents?" asked Butch, clearly impressed by the man.

"As an antiquities dealer I have learned to recognize and even translate some of the ancient languages. The Hebrew scrolls are easy to identify, but the older languages are only marginally harder. I can understand your uncertainty. Most Bedouins cannot even read Arabic, let alone other languages." Khalid paused a moment and then moved on without really answering Butch's question. "When I searched the cave, I was seeking *apocryphal* texts—that is, texts which were not biblical, but were, in fact, forbidden. Most such texts have been destroyed, as I'm sure you know. My goal is always to find something that has never been discovered before. To an experienced eye, the more common texts are easy to identify."

"And this *Book of the Dead* that you found?" prompted Huxley rather breathlessly. All of his hopes seemed to have been steadily rising with every word the Bedouin uttered.

Khalid smiled. "I will let you judge that for yourself," he said. He motioned again to the women, who were silently hovering in the background. They came forward at once and cleared the table.

Khalid rose from his pillow with surprising grace, and quietly disappeared behind a curtain in one corner of the tent. In a moment, he returned with a small, rolled up carpet which he set on the table and slowly unrolled. There, inside the rug, was a cluster of aged and tattered sheets the color of faded, desert sand and stained with dark streaks in varying shades of wet clay. The documents were stacked one on top of the other, with a thin layer of cloth placed in between.

"Your *Book of the Dead* is on top," Khalid said.

The men wasted no time in circling the table and settling on their knees to get a closer look. Very carefully, without even touching it, the men examined the document while Khalid and Helene stood back and watched. They each took out a pocket microscope and leaned in close, studying the document for several long minutes without speaking.

"Did you notice..." she heard Butch murmur at last, but his voice was so hushed that she couldn't catch the rest of his statement.

"Yes, yes, quite," replied Huxley. Disappointment marred his features.

"On the other hand, it isn't decisive," added her father encouragingly.

"No, it isn't," agreed Huxley more hopefully.

They were silent again as they continued their scrutiny for several minutes more.

"Let's have a look at the others," suggested Butch finally.

"May I?" Huxley asked the Bedouin, placing his hands on the corners of the cloth that separated the first scroll from the one beneath it.

"Of course," said Khalid agreeably.

"Do you mind grabbing that end?" Huxley said to Helene's father. Carefully they lifted the cloth beneath the scroll and placed it gently to one side. Then they examined the next scroll. They repeated this procedure with each of the scrolls until they had inspected them all. There were, perhaps, twenty documents in the pile, and it took well over an hour for the men to go through them. To Helene, the scrolls looked a lot like everything else in that desert wilderness; ancient and faded, obscure and inscrutable. However, she was on pins and needles to hear their conclusions. Was it the scroll Huxley sought? And if so, would it prove to be authentic? She could feel the tension in the air. The men were giving nothing away, and the few words they spoke only added to the suspense.

Huxley was the first to address the Bedouin, who had been standing off to one side, observing them with watchful eyes and a strangely confident smile.

"The documents might be imitations," Huxley remarked thoughtfully. "Though we can't say for certain without a thorough examination."

"You're thinking of the parchment," remarked Khalid, unconcerned.

The men started in surprise. "Well, yes," said Huxley. "It's very odd. Though the contents appear to come from all different sources, they're all written on the same material."

"That is correct; but it was common practice to copy decaying documents in order to preserve their content, was it not?" asked Khalid.

"Yes, quite!" agreed Huxley. Helene could hear the hope in his voice.

"But let's not forget that the texts would have been translated into the language of whoever copied them," interjected Butch—"which in this case appears to be the Jews, judging from the material it was printed on. And too, it would have to be approved by the church."

"Not always," Khalid replied with his strange, knowing smile.

"No, not always," Butch agreed. "But it seems strange that the Jewish scholars who copied these didn't translate them."

"I would have to examine the document more closely before I could agree to your price," Huxley concluded. "Would you consent to let us take it for, say, a day or two?"

Khalid was thoughtful a moment.

"I'm sure Lieutenant Brisbin would vouch for us," Huxley added.

The Bedouin raised his hand, dismissing the issue of theft with a look of distaste.

"If the document is authentic, we will naturally pay your price," said Butch.

Khalid nodded. "You may examine it for one day," he said.

"A few of the other documents appear to be apocryphal as well," Helene's father reminded Huxley.

"Take the *Book of the Dead* first, and we will discuss the others later," said Khalid.

"Since we have only one day in which to make our determination, I wonder if we should put off our trip to the cave," Butch suggested.

"Could you take us out there tomorrow afternoon, do you think?" asked Huxley.

"Of course," said Khalid. "Take the book with you now, and return tomorrow." He went to fetch another small carpet and carefully rolled the *Book of the Dead* up in it. They hastily said their goodbyes and drove directly back to the cottage.

It was mid-afternoon. Despite their uncertainties about the scroll, the men were excited.

"It's almost certainly *gevil*," Butch remarked as they carefully unrolled the scroll.

"What's gevil?" asked Helene.

"It's a kind of parchment that was used by the Jews," explained her father. "It's made from animal skins like other parchments, but it's prepared differently."

"Is that bad?" she asked.

"It means that this particular document wasn't written by ancient Sumerians," said Butch.

"Though it could be a copy of a document that was," interjected Huxley.

"What I can't figure out is why the Jews would copy and preserve a scroll they would have considered pagan and apocryphal," mused Butch. "It doesn't make sense."

"The only way to find out is to translate it," said Huxley.

The men wasted no time in setting up for the task at hand, and once they began, it was as if Helene wasn't even there. They were completely absorbed in what they were doing. She watched them anxiously, though she was quickly growing bored. There were long, tedious periods of silent analysis followed by lengthy debates over complex details. Helene had no idea what they were talking about, except that it was clear that they couldn't agree on a single point where the book was concerned. Huxley was ever optimistic while Butch remained skeptical. Helene's father wavered between the two.

"It simply cannot be translated," Butch blurted out in frustration. "The letters might be Sumerian but the language most certainly is not."

"It could have been copied incorrectly," her father murmured regretfully.

"But that would render the document useless!" cried Huxley, throwing up his hands and walking away. He began pacing the floor around the table where the document was laid out.

"So it would seem," agreed her father with a little sigh of disappointment.

With no further possibilities to debate—no remaining hopes to dash—Butch became thoughtful and morose. He continued to brood over the document while the other two sat back in grim silence.

Helene decided to write another letter to Edward.

"Mr. Huxley is ever so disappointed!" she wrote, though she didn't understand his disappointment well enough to explain it to Edward. She tried to describe Qumran, starting out on a positive note but ending with how dreary and dull everything was. "At least I'm not freezing my bloomers off," she teased, knowing how cold it must be in London.

Eventually the Arab caretaker, Abdul Samad, and his wife returned, bringing rice, vegetables and chicken. Though there was a perfectly good kitchen, they prepared the meal outside, cooking it in a deep hole they dug in the sand. Helene watched the woman from the window as she placed a large slab of dough on the hot stones that had been put in the fire.

While the meal was cooking the couple came inside. Abdul greeted the men while his wife silently arranged the table.

"You find good?" Abdul asked, smiling and pointing to the document splayed out on the living-room table.

"Not so good, actually," said Huxley miserably. "Maybe we'll do better tomorrow."

Abdul's smile slipped the smallest bit. Sensing their somber mood, he did not attempt further conversation but went outside to wait for his wife. Helene approached the woman quietly, so quietly that she started in surprise when she finally noticed her.

Helene held out her letter to Edward. "Can you mail this for me?" she asked.

Helene couldn't tell if the woman understood her or not, but she obviously recognized the Arabian postage stamps Helene had put on the envelope. She accepted the letter, nodding her head vigorously. Her face was obscured by the veil but her eyes seemed to be smiling. She slipped the letter into a pocket in her skirt and—with one last nod of assurance to Helene—she went back to her work in the kitchen.

They didn't sit down to eat until Abdul and his wife left.

"Why doesn't she speak?" asked Helene.

"She's acting according to Muslim custom," explained Huxley. "It's against the rules for a Muslim woman to speak to a man who isn't related to her, except in very special circumstances."

"Is that why none of the men spoke to me?"

"Yes," said her father. "Their culture is completely different from ours. They don't just speak differently; they act differently—and even think differently. Their customs are as unique as their language."

"That's it!" cried Huxley, so abruptly that all of them jumped. His face was beaming. "It's a different language!"

"What's a different language?" asked Helene's father.

"Those parts we couldn't translate!" interjected Butch, catching Huxley's meaning so quickly that he was able to answer the question before Huxley did. They all turned to Butch, whose expression was like that of a detective who just solved a case. "We can't translate them from Sumerian because they're *not* Sumerian. Which explains their distinct patterns and why they're set off by themselves like that. They're not mistakes. They're a separate language altogether!" He put his fork down and sat back in his chair thoughtfully. "It's almost as if they were disguising the language to make it look like Sumerian."

"The patterns have no commonality with the other languages of that time," remarked her father.

"Do you suppose we could have discovered an entirely new language?" wondered Huxley.

"This is an interesting problem," mused Helene's father. "First of all, the texts in question are very limited and appear to be repetitive. It would be impossible to decipher an unknown language with what little we have. Even if it could be done, it would take weeks, if not months, to translate. And how do we know it's even real, and not just some Hebrew scribe's idea of a joke—some kind of ancient pig Latin?"

"Why translate it at all?" asked Butch. He still had that self-satisfied expression on his face and there was amusement in his eyes as he waited smugly for them to answer—though he clearly knew that they would not. He seemed to be testing them. "Think about it," he continued finally. "The parts that are indecipherable appear to be some kind of spell, or incantation. Even if we were able to translate them into words, we wouldn't understand them. Spells are like that. They only make sense to the one who creates them. Not to mention that their meaning could become lost in the translation." Butch paused to take a sip of water from his glass while the three of them eyed him warily. His sudden optimism seemed to make them skeptical.

"We could try it," he continued, almost as if he was talking to himself. "Those parts might be indecipherable but they're definitely written in the Sumerian cuneiform," he paused here to turn to Helene and add—"Sumerian cuneiform uses symbols—like we use letters—to represent specific consonant sounds." Then, turning back to the others he went on—"All we have to do is identify the consonant sounds and we'll know how the words *sound*, even if we don't know what they mean." He leaned in and looked at them conspiratorially. "We don't need to know what the incantations mean. We only need to know if they work. And we can test that—and the scroll's validity—by going through the ritual ourselves, here and now!" And with that he leaned back in his chair again, smiling like a Cheshire cat, his largish teeth gleaming.

Helene's father and Huxley were speechless. They were more surprised, Helene supposed, by the source of the suggestion than the suggestion itself. It was so unlike Butch, who would be the first to ridicule such an idea. He seemed to be trying the other side of the case, as it were, and enjoying it.

"Come now, gentlemen," he continued. "This is what we've all been thinking about, isn't it? We want to know if we can wake up the dead. So let's try it and see!"

A thrill shot through Helene as she glanced at her father. She didn't dare speak. Her father had dropped his fork and was staring at Butch as if he was one of the awakened dead in question.

Butch's smile slipped away and a glimmer of his former self returned. "Of course, there is no way to prove that the document's a fake, because even if the spell doesn't work—which, let's face it, it most likely won't—it could still be a legitimate creation of that Qliphoth tribe back in Sumer, whoever they were." His wicked smile suddenly returned as he continued. "But on the off chance that the spell works..." He peered at them over his spectacles. "You'll have your proof that your *Book of the Dead* is the real McCoy." He winked at Helene. "And it'll be fun," he added.

Helene looked at her father again. "Can we?" she pleaded.

But her father didn't even seem to hear her. He was staring at Butch thoughtfully, as if he was actually considering it. Huxley, on the other hand, was still eyeing Butch suspiciously, as if waiting for the punch-line of a joke.

Butch looked at Huxley and shrugged. "You brought your tablet of the Qliphoth with you," he said. "Obviously the possibility occurred to you."

Huxley scrutinized him a moment longer before slamming his fork down on the table. "We'll do it, by Jove!" he cried.

The food was forgotten as the men got up from the table and all began talking at once. They were making plans; thinking out loud.

"We still have a great deal of translating to do," said Butch. "Much of the informational parts are genuine Sumerian."

"And we only have a day," added Huxley.

"And there's the matter of the talisman," interjected her father, who had finally recovered from his shock enough to speak.

"That's right!" exclaimed Huxley. "From the tablet. I completely forgot!" Huxley and Helene's father turned to Butch, who, it appeared, was taking charge of this experiment.

"Mmm," murmured Butch, considering it. "We'll need help with that." He looked at Huxley. "Perhaps your friend, the lieutenant, would know where we could find a foundry. One of the local monasteries might have one." He stopped again to think and then his eyes grew wide. "Come to think of it, they might have one at the base where your friend is stationed. I'll bet they make their own ammunition."

"I'll go right now and see," said Huxley. "What is it, exactly, that we need?"

The men went back to the table to look over their notes.

"Here it is," said Butch. "We'll need a ring and metal shavings. The specifications are very precise. I'll copy them for you."

"Both the ring and the metal shavings must be cast from the same lot," said Helene's father, reading over Butch's shoulder.

"Yes," agreed Butch, scribbling on a piece of paper. "And it must be made up of these exact percentages of copper and iron, heated to this temperature."

"Get as many shavings as you can," said Helene's father. "We'll need enough to create a solid circle of those dimensions I've added there at the bottom."

"Oh, and you'll have to engrave this symbol on the ring while the metal's still warm," said Butch, carefully drawing it out on the slip of paper. "Then twist the strip of metal into a ring like so, with the ends crossed like this." Again, Butch drew it out for him.

"This is quite a lot," said Huxley doubtfully. "Do you think they'll be able to do it?"

"Any foundry could do it easily," said Helene's father.

"We'll work on the translating while you're gone," said Butch. He turned to Helene's father. "Why don't you take up the part we were working on earlier? I'll start at the other end and work my way back to you."

And the men went to work.

It was just after dinnertime and the sun was beginning to drop. Helene went outside. The air had developed a sharp chill and she shivered, surprised by how suddenly it turned cold. The clouds overhead were lined a fiery pink. Her father popped his head out the door.

"Can you manage?" he asked.

"Of course, but Father, what do you think is going to happen?" she asked.

Robert Trevelyan grinned. "I think we're going to have a bit of an adventure, and probably not very much more," he admitted.

"So you don't think it will work?"

"Let's just say it would be a first if it did."

Helene was disappointed. She'd always believed her father knew everything, but she suddenly wanted him to be wrong. "Well, like they say…there's a first time for everything!" she replied with a defiant tilt of her head and her father laughed.

Helene went back inside. With nothing else to do, she went into the bedroom and lay down on one of the cots. She wondered what would happen if they really did conjure a Qliphoth soul from the dead. The thought was as terrifying as it was exciting. What would the soul look like? How would it feel about being conjured? What would they do with it afterwards? It was all so hard to imagine. Her father was probably right. Helene sighed, thinking how much more exciting all this would be if Edward was there.

Helene woke to the sound of loud voices in the other room. She jumped up and went to see what was happening. It was completely dark outside now, but the room was brightly lit. The men noticed her at once.

"Fancy a look?" Butch asked, holding out his hand with the same rare, toothy smile he'd been sporting earlier.

Helene looked at his hand. There, on his third finger, was the ring. It was the color of rust and inscribed with the same markings he'd drawn out earlier for Huxley. To Helene, it looked a little like a tiny bird footprint.

She spotted a can on the table. "Are these the metal shavings?" she asked, picking up the can.

"Be careful not to spill those," Huxley warned.

Helene looked inside the can. There was a strange, slightly unpleasant smell wafting up from it that reminded her of the ice crystals that collected in the freezer. The metal shavings appeared to be very light and feathery soft, but when she reached in her hand to touch them she was surprised to find that they were also a bit sharp. But they were warm to the touch, and she carefully moved her fingers through them, noticing the wide range of lengths and thicknesses. Like snowflakes, no two were alike.

"How'd you two manage?" Huxley asked the others.

"We're done," announced Helene's father. "We've just been waiting for you."

"Really?"

"It's so much easier, changing Sumerian symbols into sounds than trying to translate their meaning," Butch told him. "And look, they keep repeating these same sounds again and again, which not only made the task simpler, but also seems to confirm that these parts are incantations instead of valuable information."

"And you're sure you have all the sounds right?" asked Huxley.

Butch nodded. "Even though we have no idea what we're saying, you can rest assured we'll be pronouncing the words correctly."

Huxley examined Butch's notes. "The more I think about it the more sense it makes. It's like if we were to translate words into Japanese, we would still use the English alphabet."

Butch nodded. "The only puzzle is where this mystery language came from. I suppose it's possible that it could be a language that doesn't have a written form—one that dates back to before people began to write."

"Wherever it came from, it would seem that these Qliphoth were using it," said Huxley.

"We translated all the Sumerian parts," Helene's father told Huxley. "Which were instructional, just as we suspected." He exchanged looks with Butch and then smiled at Huxley. "And now, are you ready for the good news?"

Huxley seemed unable to process any more good news.

"We think we've uncovered the identity of the soul we're attempting to conjure," he said.

Huxley turned to Butch and he nodded. "The Sumerian instructions refer to it as 'li-la-kee,'" he explained. "At first we thought this might be another word to describe the people, like Qliphoth, but then we noticed it on Huxley's tablet, here, where it lists the Qliphoth tribe members. Thing is, this word—or the sounds making up this word, rather—are repeated again and again in the incantations we couldn't translate in this *Book of the Dead*. It has to be referring to a particular soul!"

"Could this 'li-la-kee' be a Sumerian name?" Huxley asked.

Helene's father and Butch exchanged a smile and Butch delivered the coup de grace. "Li-la-kee, translated from Sumerian to Hebrew, is Lilith."

Huxley gasped. "Lilith! Surely you don't think—!" He was too overwhelmed to continue.

Butch turned to Helene. "In Jewish folklore, Lilith was the first woman created—even before Eve."

It was Helene's turn to be surprised. She'd never heard of a woman being created before Eve, excepting in the evolution theory, which she supposed would have made Lilith an ape.

"Not only that," interjected Helene's father. "This document—the parts of it we could understand, anyway—appears to reference your Qliphoth tablet point for point. The missing 'keys' are all there, like pieces of a puzzle."

"So are you saying we're ready to move forward with the experiment?" asked Huxley.

"We have only to make a circle from the metal shavings to create our portal through which the soul can be summoned," said Butch—not without a trace of irony in his tone.

"And create the markings around the outside of it with what's left of the shavings," added her father.

"I can't believe it!" exclaimed Huxley. He rushed into his and Butch's bedroom and returned with one of the bottles of wine they'd brought with them from Tel Aviv. Then he poured out four glasses and handed them out all around. Helene looked at her father and he nodded. It was her first glass of wine!

"To Lilith," Huxley cried, and they all touched glasses and eagerly agreed—"To Lilith!"

CHAPTER
9

Present Day

Nadia stopped talking. She was a little startled by all that she had revealed. Telling the stories was very different from simply listening to them. It required more involvement but it made them seem more real. The little details suddenly seemed significant. She thought of the discovery at Qumran, which lured three stodgy old scholars all the way from England to the turbulent Middle East. Who else might it have lured there? Whether later events were real or imagined, it was clear that some kind of trouble had followed them there.

But Nadia's voice was giving out from talking so much. She was still lying down on the couch with her eyes closed. With effort, she managed to open her eyes and turn her head in the direction her captors. Clive had ditched his chair and was lying sideways on the floor, leaning up on one elbow, while the other two remained where they were. They were all still listening with interest.

Nadia closed her eyes again and turned her head back to its resting position. "So tired," she murmured.

She heard Will sigh and felt he was about to object when Gordon interceded.

"Let her sleep," he said.

And she did.

⤬

When Nadia opened her eyes again her senses were assailed by the pungent aroma of coffee. The room was very dark. Was it day or night? She felt sluggish and confused, almost like she was hung-over.

She heard voices in the distance and looked around. She was back in the dingy little bedroom with the boarded up window. Someone must have carried her in from the couch. She lifted the covers, relieved to find her clothing intact.

Nadia sat up slowly. What were they talking about out there? She thought about how intently they had listened to her the night before. They seemed interested in what she had to say. She wondered what it was they were looking for. Which piece of the puzzle held the key to her life?

Her hair was a thick and tangled mess. She felt rumpled, sticky and foul. Her body ached. *I feel like I've been run over by a garbage truck* she thought, and then suddenly remembered with a sense of revulsion that she had, as a matter of fact, been inside a garbage container.

She threw the covers back and cursed. The chain was still attached to her leg. This was discouraging.

As quietly as she could, she climbed out of bed and slowly—holding the chain up as she went—tip-toed across the floor to the bedroom door. Fortunately the chain was quite long, probably long enough to allow her free range of the entire house. *Free range! Like a chicken!* She carefully turned the doorknob and cracked open the door the teensiest bit, just enough to peek one eye through. The kidnappers were in the kitchen, which was to the left of the living-room. She pulled the door open a little more, just enough to slip her head out so she could see them better.

"If she had the mother-fucker with her, it would have been forced out by the incantation," Clive was saying. "And anyway, there wasn't an ounce of metal on her." He seemed exasperated. He picked up one of the masks that was lying on a nearby table and sat down. Sulkily he played with the mask while the other two continued their conversation.

"That doesn't mean she doesn't have it," Will pointed out. "It could be hidden anywhere."

"I just don't think she's involved," said Gordon.

"She's involved," insisted Will. "We just have to figure out how."

"I mean I don't think *she* knows how she's involved," Gordon clarified.

"All the more reason to keep her talking," said Will.

"She's already filled in some of the blanks," Gordon remarked optimistically. "And she seems to be telling the truth." It occurred to Nadia that Gordon might make a good ally.

"I'll grant she's got one hell of a poker face if she's lying," conceded Will. "Although it wouldn't be hard for someone like her to pull off this kind of bluff."

This made Clive smile—a sly, mischievous kind of smile—and as he listened to Will and Gordon he began humming a tune under his breath while absently tapping the mask on his leg. It was different from the song he was humming the day before. It was more popular, a song she'd heard many times, though Nadia still couldn't quite place it. She tried to focus on what Gordon and Will were saying.

"I don't know," said Gordon. "I still think we should pass her on. We might be a little out of our league here."

"I've already made the call," said Will. "But before we give her to those goons I want to make sure there's not a djinn hiding behind her skirts."

"Whoa, ohohoh, whoa, oh-oh-oh-ah," Clive kept quietly singing. Nadia had to strain to hear him. He put on the mask and got up, moving his body to the tune that was, so far, mostly just in his head.

"Yeah, I guess," Gordon agreed. He jumped when he caught sight of Clive dancing toward him with the mask on, but then burst into laughter.

Encouraged, Clive sang a little louder. "Pa pa pa poker face, pa pa poker face." His voice was surprisingly suited to the Lady Gaga classic; a low, baritone with a slight twang. Nadia couldn't help noticing, too, that he was a very good dancer. Gordon kept watching Clive, amused, while Will looked on disapprovingly. "Whoa, ohohoh, whoa, ohohoah. I'll get her hot…show her what I got!" Clive pumped his hips and flipped his head from side to side—much like Lady Gaga herself might have done.

Suddenly Gordon joined in for the chorus, moving his body as if to dance, but unlike Clive, his moves were completely out of tune with the song. His singing voice was a soft falsetto, though he, too, kept it very quiet. "Can't read my, can't read my…no, he can't read my poker face," they sang. "Mum mum mah, mum mum mah. Can't read my, can't read my…"

To Nadia's utter disbelief, Will, who looked as if he was about to reprimand Clive and Gordon at any moment, actually joined in, moving his body in perfect harmony with the song. Yet his expression remained as stern as ever. There wasn't so much as a hint of a smile on his face.

At this point a single burst of spontaneous laughter escaped Nadia's lips, shocking her as much as it did them. She immediately suppressed the outburst, but they had already caught her spying on them from the doorway. Nadia just stared at them—and they at her— for a long moment. It was particularly unsettling to observe such carefree, spontaneous fun from men who were in all likelihood either felons or crazy. Nadia wasn't sure how to handle the awkward moment, and neither, apparently, were they. An awkward silence ensued, during which Nadia decided to use their momentary discomfiture to her advantage.

"I want a toothbrush and a shower," she said. "A *private* shower, without the camera."

Will recovered first. "We can't risk letting you out of our sight," he said, clearly indignant at getting caught goofing off.

A control freak, thought Nadia. "Baloney!" was what she said. "If you want my continued cooperation, you'll have to respect my limits, and I definitely draw the line at providing cheap thrills to perverts."

Will's face actually went white, and he looked as if he was about to choke on his outrage.

"You didn't even know that I had gotten out of bed," she added meekly, thinking she should probably try not to provoke him too much if it could be helped.

"That's not the point," he muttered through clenched teeth. "The purpose of the camera is to keep you from doing something stupid because you won't know if we're watching or not."

Nadia couldn't help noticing how defensive he'd become and she added this to her growing list of observations for possible use later. *Always has to be right. Can't take criticism.*

"What is it exactly that you think I'm going to do?" she asked. "Do you think I'm going to chew through this chain while I'm in there and then claw my way through the wall?"

"We can't keep treating her like one of them," Gordon objected, and Nadia turned to him hopefully, thinking that he definitely would make a good ally. "She'd have nothing to gain by killing herself," he added with a shrug.

"What would anyone have to gain by killing themselves?" Nadia wondered out loud.

"All right," said Will, throwing up his hands. "You have fifteen minutes, not a minute more, got it?"

She nodded. Will turned his withering look on Gordon and Nadia smiled inwardly. Surely Gordon was getting as tired of Will's high-handed manner as she was.

"I'll ah, also need something to wear," she said, determined to strike while the iron was hot. Will turned the withering look back on her but she stood her ground. "I've been stuffed in a garbage can, dumped on the ground…"

"Gordon…" Will interrupted.

"I'll get her something," he replied, scurrying off before Nadia could thank him.

The awkward silence returned while they waited for Gordon get the clothes. Although she managed to keep the smugness out of her expression (lest the tyrant change his mind), Nadia couldn't refrain from meeting his icy stare with one of her own. His eyes seemed to widen the tiniest bit, perhaps in mild surprise or it could have been amusement. But in the next instant his expression went back to normal, and the grim, determined mask returned.

Nadia was relieved when Gordon finally got back with the tooth-brush and clean clothes.

"Thank you," she said meaningfully. Gordon followed her into the bedroom and began removing the video camera.

"I really appreciate all the little courtesies you've tried to show me while I…" Nadia paused, searching for the right words. *While I've been held hostage and nearly killed by you and two of your accomplices* seemed a bit antagonistic. "Well,…you know," she said, leaving the statement unfinished. "I just want you to know that I will make sure that the police or…whoever, knows that *you* were the one who helped me." As she stumbled over the words Nadia was painfully aware of how idiotic they sounded. She was normally so good at convincing people of things, but in this case she seemed to be making things worse. Gordon acted as if he didn't even hear her as he silently finished unscrewing the bolts that held the camera in place. It wasn't until he had climbed down from the chair and was preparing to leave that he addressed her. There was an odd expression on his face; he didn't seem quite amused but neither was he entirely serious either. When he spoke, he reverted to the thick, Indian accent he'd used the night before.

"It is just as the wise one says," he told her in a gently mocking tone. "'Those who live in the river should make friends with the crocodile.'" She narrowed her eyes at his courteous smile, unsure if he was trying to lighten the moment with a joke or flat out calling her an idiot.

"Well, thanks for removing the camera anyway," she said with a little sigh of frustration.

"You're veddy welcome," he said, still using the accent. "And now, if you will permit me…?" He took out a key and pointed to her ankle. With a little gasp of joy Nadia gave him her leg. He knelt down and unlatched the shackle that connected the chain to her leg. Her ankle was scraped and bruised where the shackle had been rubbing against it. Gordon stood up.

"The door to the bathroom is missing I'm afraid. But I will close your bedroom door and we will stay in the kitchen until you're finished." Nadia didn't care where they stayed—provided it was on the other side of her bedroom door. She felt strangely happy to get the chain off her leg. But she couldn't help musing what a strange character Gordon was. The Indian accent had a most peculiar effect. It was an unexpected and even startling characteristic for a kidnapper to have. It left one reluctant to tremble in fear. Nadia tried to imagine him saying the worst thing imaginable, with the accent: 'I'm going to kill you now.' She shook her head. It simply didn't fit. And yet, surely people with Indian accents were just as capable of murder as anyone else.

Nadia was suddenly bewildered by her thoughts. Here she was, a prisoner in a strange country, forced to tell stories to her captives in order to stay alive—or at the very least to keep her from being passed on to 'the goons,' whoever they were. It was like she was trapped in some kind of fairy tale herself; a bizarre, more complex remake of Aladdin's *Arabian Nights*. Like the resourceful wife of the morbidly jealous King Shahryar, Nadia would have to divert her captors for as long as possible in order to survive. Yet, as strange and terrifying as it all was, she couldn't get over how relatively calm she felt, considering. She woke up chained to a post in the middle of the floor for goodness sake! But it was difficult to sustain a healthy degree of terror when her terrorists were so...Nadia tried to think of the best word to describe them, and was even more confounded when the word 'intriguing' came to mind. Yet—putting aside the chain, the duct tape and the chloroform—there was no denying that the men seemed lucid, intelligent and even genuinely concerned (in an extreme, conspiracy driven kind of way). There was something appealing about them. Under any other circumstances, they all might have been friends.

Nadia shook her head more violently this time, as if to shake some sense into it. What was she thinking? She always prided herself on her levelheadedness. Where was that good judgment now that she needed it most? Had the kidnapping traumatized her so much? When it came right down to it was she going to succumb to being a victim and just allow herself to fall prey to one of the many syndromes out there, like the one that afflicted Patty Hearst? Was Nadia just another poor-little-rich girl who was so weak and impressionable that she was already identifying with her kidnappers after only one day? How long before she donned the mask and went out terrorizing others in search of these imaginary djinn?

Nadia tried not to enjoy the feel of the warm water on her skin, focusing instead on the fact that it was stinging her ankle where the shackle had rubbed it raw. She reminded herself that her prospects of being rescued were slim. It was Saturday morning—or thereabouts—and there wasn't a soul in the world who knew she was missing. She should be frantically seeking ways to escape, not laughing at their antics. But without even knowing where she was, how could she orchestrate a proper escape? Her only hope at the moment was to somehow convince her captors to set her free. She considered how she might do this. They were looking for a djinn. Could she produce one? She was pretty sure that she couldn't, but on second thought, it probably wouldn't help her if she could. The only reason she was alive was because they *hadn't* found the djinn yet. If they thought they had it when they did whatever it was they did to her last night, they probably would have let her die.

Was there a djinn to be found?

Nadia was suddenly exasperated with herself. *Don't get suckered in,* she warned. *Don't even go there.*

Yet her grandmother had believed. *And whatever happened to Helene back then could have something to do with this,* argued this new voice, quite possibly the voice of the poor little impressionable rich girl inside her.

Okay Patty, she replied, giving the voice a name—*Fine. Just don't expect me to come to your rescue when you're facing ten to fifteen for joining a band of kidnappers who believe they're hunting djinn.*

She laughed humorlessly at her thoughts.

Why aren't I more afraid?

The shower felt good. Being alive felt good. Even catching that tiny glimpse of the human side of her abductors felt good. *There's no point in walking around in a catatonic state of terror all the time,* the voice reasoned. *I'm simply picking our battles. I promise to rip your insides out with fear when the appropriate time comes. For now we need to keep our head.*

Nadia wondered if she should worry about the fact that she was hearing voices, one of which she already named 'Patty.'

For the moment, she was too hungry to care. Pavlov's hierarchy of needs dictated that she must eat. She dressed quickly. The t-shirt and jeans Gordon gave her were a little big, but at least they were clean.

There was no mirror in the bathroom and Gordon hadn't provided a comb so all Nadia could do to tame her wild mane was to run her fingers through the tangles. She opened the bedroom door expecting to find Gordon, and was dismayed to see Will standing there. So much for getting a comb, she thought. The last thing she wanted was for Will to think she cared about how she looked (*Why do you care?* She wondered).

Nadia noticed that Will's eyes, which were coolly taking in her appearance, paused an extra moment when they landed on her hair. She thought she detected amusement playing about his lips but it was gone before she could be sure. He lifted the chain as his eyes met hers.

Nadia felt her fortitude slipping. "Come on!" she complained. "Where would I go?"

"It's not negotiable," he said, bending down and lifting her pant leg. But he hesitated when he saw her leg, swollen and bruised, and glanced guiltily up into Nadia's face. She didn't even have to try; one large tear filled each eye and lingered there pitifully. Will sighed. "Give me the other leg," he said, rigid as always. Nadia blinked away the tears and stubbornly remained where she was. *Get it yourself,* she thought angrily. He did, and the chain was now attached to her other leg.

Without another word Nadia brushed past him to follow the mouthwatering smells of toast, eggs and coffee. The eggs and toast had already been cleared away so she poured herself a cup of coffee and sat as far away from the others as she could get—which meant leaving the kitchen and going into the living room. She brooded over the chain as she sipped her coffee, refusing to even look in their direction. Their silence told her that they noticed.

Still think they're intriguing?—she asked the voice inside her head. The chain seemed to call attention to the gravity of her situation. No matter how civil they might appear at times, or what heroic claims they might make for their behavior, the simple fact was that they were committing at least three felonies that Nadia could think of off the top of her head.

Meanwhile, she wished there had been something to eat instead of just coffee. It seemed a bit too much like eating crow to ask them to make her something now. Her stomach was growling irritably.

Ignoring it, she looked out the window and was surprised to see that it was pitch dark outside. She wondered what time it was.

You're going to have make friends with at least one of them.

Yeah. That worked really well with Gordon.

Clive seems nice. Nadia almost laughed out loud at the absurdity of a kidnapper being 'nice.' Not to mention that the kidnapper in question was Clive.

You could at least try to get some information from them.

Her stomach was getting noisier, but, just as she was about to get up, Will came out of the kitchen with a plate of three steaming eggs over easy and buttered toast. She would have liked to have refused but she was too hungry for that. She did her best to act put-out as she accepted the plate, like she was doing him the favor. She wondered why she found him so much more provoking than the other two. She mustn't let any of them get to her. They were also moving into the living room now. She turned her attention to her food, ignoring her regular table manners if only to prove that she didn't give a damn what they thought of her. But a sideways glance in their direction told her that they weren't even paying attention.

"So!" she said, attempting to talk around the food in her mouth. "Which part of my story did you find enlightening so far?" She suddenly noticed that they, too, had changed into fresh clothes since the previous night. What was more, she could see that they did, in fact, have combs and/or brushes, and possibly even hair styling products… and she was once again struck by the inappropriateness of her thoughts. Why was she thinking about hair styling products? She gulped hard, regretting the huge amount of food she'd stuffed in her mouth, now that it was lodged in her esophagus like a lump of clay.

They were all just staring at her and she realized that they probably hadn't understood her with all that food in her mouth.

"I heard you saying earlier that I had filled in some of the blanks," she clarified once she got the food down. "What blanks?"

They seemed surprised. "Never mind what you heard us say," answered Will. "You're the one who…"

"I think I deserve some answers," she said, cutting him off. "Like how you knew about what happened to my grandmother. Did you know her?"

Gordon was the one who finally answered her. "We never met your grandmother," he said.

"But you knew about the experiment in Qumran?" she persisted.

"Yes, but only what we learned after the fact," said Gordon. "Obviously we don't know everything. We're hoping you'll be able to provide enough of the missing information to help prevent something very terrible from happening." He turned to Will, who was glaring at him. "I'm just confirming what she would be able to figure out for herself anyway," he said. "We might as well work together."

"Where am I?" Nadia asked.

"You're in Saudi Arabia," said Will before Gordon could give her a more specific answer.

This was alarming to hear, even though she had pretty much figured out that they were somewhere in that general vicinity. "What time is it?"

"It's Saturday, just after three in the afternoon in New York," said Gordon, consulting his watch. "It's ten-fifteen Saturday night, here." Nadia absorbed this. A day had passed.

"Who are the 'goons' you're going to pass me off to?" she asked. Will's earlier mention of them had been niggling at the back of her mind.

The question seemed to amuse Clive. "Let's just say you'll miss us when we're gone," he told her.

"But who are they?" Nadia demanded, alarmed by Clive's remark.

"Look, if you help us, we'll help you," Clive told her. "It's as simple as that."

"I'm trying to help you!" Nadia shouted at him. Then she added in a calmer tone—"I'm telling you everything I know."

"Is there anything you might have left out about Huxley or Butch? Or Trevelyan?" asked Will.

Nadia thought about it a minute and then shook her head. "No," she said. "My grandmother was only sixteen years old when they took her to Qumran. I'd say her observations were pretty remarkable for a girl that age."

"It just seems a little strange how easily the two pieces of the puzzle came together," mused Clive. "Huxley finds the magic tablet and voila! A *Book of the Dead* for this particular djinn just happens to turn up in a bunch of scrolls that were hidden by the Essenes."

"The *who?*" asked Nadia. She shook her head in confusion. "According to my grandmother, Huxley had that tablet for years. He followed every archaeological discovery involving the Sumerians looking for the matching *Book of the Dead.*"

"Yeah, but, what I'm saying is; out of all the books and scrolls in that cave in Qumran, this Bedouin dude pulls out that particular one and then puts out the word that he has it—like maybe *he* was looking for the matching tablet," Clive said.

Nadia hadn't considered this, but she was curious about something else. "You mentioned someone hiding the scrolls. The Essenes, was it? What about them? How are they connected to this?"

Clive glanced at the others. Nadia felt there was something significant in the exchange.

"The Essenes were a select group of Jewish priests that lived by themselves, much like the Catholic monks who came later," explained Gordon. "They emerged around the time of Abraham, and became the self-appointed record keepers of all the ancient documents. They studied language, which is how they were able to translate the documents they found. They copied texts that were damaged, just as they probably did with Lilith's *Book of the Dead.* Butch was wrong in his supposition that the Jews would have destroyed Apocryphal texts— though I can understand why he would think that. Most priests would destroy anything that didn't support their own beliefs. But not the Essenes. They protected all the ancient writings, whether they considered them Holy or Apocryphal. Those caves in Qumran were probably left unprotected by the Essenes because of the conflict going on in the region at the time, or they could have been stolen from the Essenes and put there by someone else."

"So...these Essenes were still around in nineteen forty-eight?" asked Nadia.

Gordon glanced at Will. "No one knows exactly what happened to them," he said. Nadia felt that he was hiding something.

"It's interesting that Butch was the one who ultimately figured out how to make the two documents work together," said Will, changing the subject.

It suddenly occurred to Nadia that her captors were not just casually going over the details of her grandmother's story. They were examining each of the participants, conducting an investigation in order to determine which of them was responsible for what ultimately happened there. This was an entirely new way of looking at it for Nadia. She had always considered all of them—Helene, her father, Huxley and Butch—innocent victims of a terrible crime, most likely a robbery.

"And let's not forget that Trevelyan conveniently brought his daughter along," added Clive.

Nadia wasn't sure what he was implying but she didn't like his tone or the way they were all suddenly scrutinizing her. She felt the need to defend her great-grandfather. "Robert Trevelyan was just an innocent bystander. Huxley had the tablet before they even met!"

Don't get tangled up in this, she warned herself. *It's not real.*

"It's true that we don't know what happened, yet," said Will, emphasizing the word 'yet' in a somewhat threatening tone as his stony eyes assessed Nadia's face. "But when we figure it out, I have a strong feeling we'll find our killer," he finished quietly.

"With that cheery thought, why don't we pick up where you left off?" Clive suggested. "Do you remember where you were?"

Nadia poured herself another cup of coffee. She would have no trouble finding her place in the story. It was as if that night in Qumran had been stalking her since she called it to mind the previous evening. She had the sense that all of the players were there with her too, patiently waiting for her to pick up where she left off and bring each and every one of them back to life.

CHAPTER 10

December, 1948
Qumran

"How long do you think this will take?" asked Helene's father, glancing at Helene. "It's after nine now."

"Don't worry about me," said Helene. "I can stay up all night."

"How do you know that?" asked her father. "Have you done it before?"

"Yes," she lied, raising her chin a notch. She was feeling a little reckless from the wine. She didn't particularly care for the taste, but it made her feel warm and wonderful inside.

Her father laughed, recognizing her bluff, but admiring her spirit. She had learned early on that to be treated like an adult she merely had to act like one.

"We'll see," he conceded.

"The ritual itself won't take long," said Butch. "But what comes after...may not be entirely appropriate..." he cocked his head sideways and looked at Helene's father. Helene held her breath, realizing immediately that he was referring to her.

There was a moment's silence and then her father laughed. "But you don't really think...?" he looked at Butch, incredulous.

Huxley and Helene looked at Butch as well. Of the three men, Butch was the least likely to believe the experiment would actually work. But then again, his logical mind would naturally consider every possibility, just in case. Butch gazed back at them serenely. He seemed mildly amused by their astonishment. Huxley was the first to respond.

"If it works,"—Huxley couldn't stifle a small, nervous laugh here—"It will prove the scroll's legitimacy, and from that I think we could assume that the other assertions in the scroll would work as well. It would seem that whoever holds the ring should have full control over anything coming out of that portal."

They all turned toward the center of the floor, where the metal shavings had been neatly arranged to form a circle. The ancient symbols added along the outer edge made it seem more authentic somehow. When no one said anything for several moments, their gazes slowly returned to Butch.

"All right then," said Butch, effectively taking charge of the situation. "Since I'm the one who's most familiar with the Sumerian language, I'll lead the proceedings...if there are no objections." There were none. "I have the ring right here..." He wiggled his fingers, his eyes twinkling mischievously.

"Everyone come around," he said in an authoritative tone, and they each took their positions around the circle. Helene stayed close to her father and he took her hand in his.

The men were suddenly solemn and pensive, like characters in a play. Helene was reminded of boys on the school playground and their grave expressions as they took on the latest dare. A kind of uncertain expectation hovered over the event, giving it a dreamlike quality. In spite of her excitement, Helene didn't expect the experiment to work. She suspected that the others—especially Butch—felt the same.

Reading from a notebook, Butch began to speak, pausing several times to clear his throat. The language was so unusual that it actually changed the timbre of his voice, bringing it to a higher pitch that made the words seem all the more foreign and sinister. As he became more fluent in the reading, his voice became louder and grew even more peculiar sounding. It seemed to Helene that the early Sumerians were not all that pleasant to listen to.

The incantations were odd, but they were also hypnotic and enticing. Even though Helene couldn't understand the words, she could hear the plaintively pleading tone in the collection of words overall. Now and again she recognized a phrase which was becoming familiar through repetition. It was *ki-sikil, lil-la-ke*. When pronouncing the phrase, Butch placed particular emphasis on the first syllable of the second word, *lil*. As the minutes slowly ticked by, he repeated the strange phrase over and over again. The ritual seemed to be having no effect, aside from making Helene feel strangely numb, as if she were the one being drawn out. She stared at the circle in the room's hazy light, mesmerized by the continuous chain of aberrant phrases flowing from Butch's lips. They sometimes sounded like the low, melodious drone of a whale, while other times they sounded more like the shrill cry of a seagull. They were grave, fervent and piercing. Her mind had unconsciously begun listening for the familiar phrase—*ki-sikil lil-la-ke*—and she felt a certain satisfaction each time she heard it.

It seemed to go on and on. Helene suppressed a yawn. She turned her eyes—careful not to move her head too much so as to appear like a fidgety child—to look at the others. Butch was engrossed in his reading. Huxley stared solemnly into the circle. Her father's eyes were glued to Butch. He squeezed Helene's hand reassuringly, sensing her restlessness. With effort she kept still, resisting most of her temptations to squirm. She glanced at the clock. Thirty seven minutes had passed. She returned her gaze to the circle, stifling another yawn.

Suddenly—and quite unexpectedly—the room went black. Helene instantly snapped out of her stupor into full alert. No one made a sound, except for the sharp intakes of breath they all took before they stopped breathing altogether. Helene's ears strained. The darkness was extraordinary, calling to mind the black-out days when heavy curtains were used to block out all light. But this seemed even darker than that. Helene tried to recall if the curtains were left open or closed. She felt that they were open. In fact, she remembered looking out at the moon shortly after she woke up, and that was barely an hour ago. And even if someone had closed the curtains at the last moment, surely some small light would still get through. Helene had learned this from the blackouts. But searching blindly in the general direction of the windows, Helene could detect no light whatsoever, not a single flicker from a faraway star, nothing. A sharp thrill of terror shot through her.

All these thoughts occurred to Helene in mere seconds. Meanwhile, no one had uttered a word. Butch had simply stopped reading.

Helene noticed too that her eyes were not making the slightest adjustment to the dark. Perhaps it was only her imagination but the blackness seemed absolute, as if it were occurring within her as well as out.

Helene heard the small, sharp strike of a match and in the next instant a tiny flame brought minimal, although welcome relief. The hand that held the match—Huxley's by the proximity of it—was trembling conspicuously, but he managed to keep it close enough to the page so that Butch could resume his reading.

Butch quickly picked up where he had left off, and the only sign that anything was amiss was a noticeable tremor in his voice with the first few lines he uttered. But the sound of his voice seemed to give him courage, and his tone grew steadier and stronger as he went, pausing composedly whenever Huxley had to extinguish one match and strike up another.

"There's no stopping now," he interjected during one of these intervals. "We're very nearly through." Helene wasn't sure if he was speaking to them or to himself.

Meanwhile, Helene's father had kept a tight hold of her hand, periodically squeezing it to reassure her.

Again and again Helene recognized the strange, hypnotic phrase, *ki-sikil lil-la-ke*. It seemed to come up more and more often now. She stared into the tiny, flickering flame of the match until it made her dizzy.

A soft whistling noise, like wind, circled in and around them. Helene could feel it gently lifting her hair. Her father's hold on her hand was so tight that it was uncomfortable, but Helene didn't dare move or utter a sound.

"Butch..." she heard her father murmur anxiously, as if to object, but Butch only raised his voice louder, and her father backed down.

Butch was undoubtedly determined to see it through to the end and, in truth, every one of them felt the same.

The wind was becoming more and more intense and in response Butch read faster and louder. He was literally yelling at the top of his voice in order to make himself heard. Huxley struggled with the matches, holding them close to Butch's notebook and blocking them as best as he could from the squall. When it first started up, the wind was about the same temperature as the room, but as it picked up strength it got colder. It seemed to just keep getting colder and stronger until Helene felt as if her skin was being pierced by tiny shards of ice. Her hair was whipping around her face. She brought up her free hand to protect her face, and was forced to shut her eyes.

And then, in a sudden instant, it was as if a switch went off. The lights came back on, the wind stopped and everything was quiet and still.

Helene opened her eyes. The first thing that struck her was the eerie sense of normalcy all around them. It was as if nothing had happened on the surface, but just below there was the sense that everything was different. And then she saw it.

Something was moving inside the circle. It looked like nothing more than mist at first, but it was transforming right before their eyes. It appeared to be translucent and weightless, like smoke curling up from the end of a cigarette. But with every undulating wave the image took form and grew clearer, shifting and changing as it did. One minute it seemed as if Helene was seeing a human shape and the next it looked more like the silhouette of a wild animal. As the thing kept changing it grew larger. It continued to shift and change for several long minutes, as if it was having trouble deciding which form to take. They all watched in amazement.

At last the issue of form was resolved and the creature materialized before them. It was still faintly translucent and almost appeared to be glowing. The thing was hunched over, little more than a dark mass at first, but as soon as it became aware of itself—or them—it abruptly rose up to its full height with a small cry of surprise. They all gasped at the sight.

CHAPTER
11

It was a woman the likes of which Helene had never seen before. She towered several feet over Huxley, who was the tallest among them. The top portion of her face resembled that of an innocent fawn, with large, strikingly beautiful brown eyes that were adorned with long, shadowy lashes. The eyes were complimented by a petite, uncomplicated nose and feminine lips. But that's where her appearance took a turn toward the macabre. The lower part of her face protruded outward at the jaw, stretching her dainty lips over teeth that were long, pointy, and sharp, like those of a wolf. Her skin was the rich, splendid color of freshly ground nutmeg. Her long black hair wound around her body in thick, dark waves, shielding it like a luxurious blanket. In spite of her hair, Helene could clearly see that she had the body of a woman, with a slender torso and lean arms and legs that would have been perfect if not for her hands and feet, which were shaped like the talons of a hawk.

The delicate exquisiteness of the creature, overall, clashed disturbingly with the grisly teeth and claws, to say the least. Helene could not think why the creature would assume such a form. It seemed to expose a terrible evil lurking just beyond the beauty. And then it occurred to Helene that the woman's appearance might not have been of her own choosing. Even as she considered this, the creature was staring down at the ghastly appendages in horror.

It was as if everyone in the room had been struck dumb. Helene tore her gaze away from the creature to look at the others. They were staring at the apparition in awe. Huxley and Butch had unconsciously taken a step backwards.

"I'll be damned," murmured Helene's father under his breath. It was the first time she'd ever heard him swear. He squeezed her hand even tighter and pulled her nearer.

Butch cleared his throat several times, making a visible effort to pull himself together. "Er, uh…hello?" he stuttered. But then, catching himself, he added something in the Sumerian language.

Up to this point, the creature had been too wrapped up in herself to notice them. She seemed as amazed by her appearance as they were. She had just discovered her teeth, and was running her claws along the sides of her jaw with a low, dreadful whimper when the sound of Butch's voice distracted her. She jerked her head around and carefully examined each of them, resting her formidable gaze on Helene the longest. Then she turned back to Butch, her large, doe-like eyes wet with tears as she addressed him accusingly.

"What have you done to me?" she demanded. Her voice was soft and womanly, but it held a definite undertone of command.

"You…speak our language?" Butch asked.

She snorted in disgust. "Who do you think crafted language?"

Butch was taken even further aback. "*You* crafted language?"

"My father—and the other Watchers—did," she said haughtily. "That language you spoke before was among their first, more simplistic creations." She gave another little snort, adding sarcastically—"I see you haven't found it necessary to expand or develop it much since then."

Butch was floored. "Are you…? I mean, is it…?"

"It's been altered, but it's definitely one of ours," she replied. "It's easy enough to pick up on, as are your thoughts. But then again, we understand all forms of communication."

Butch was thoughtful a moment, then he suddenly blurted out, in what sounded to Helene like French—"*Reconnaissez-vous ce?*"

"*Ce dialecte est venue des veilleurs qui sont établis dans l'ouest,*" she replied with a scornful little laugh. It was a short, mirthless laugh, but it exposed enough of her teeth to create a ghastly sight and, noticing their expressions of horror, she instantly closed her lips with a little sob. Slowly and deliberately she raised her claws to her hair, adjusting it so that it would cover the lower half of her face. She turned away from them slightly in order to further obscure their view. One large, stunningly beautiful eye peeked out at them from the thick curtain of black hair.

"What have you done to me?" she asked again. "Why am I like this?"

Butch cocked his head to one side in that thoughtful manner he had. To Helene, the familiar gesture was a welcome sign that he was returning to his old self again. "I'm not sure," he said. "You…didn't look like this before?"

"Of course not!" she said.

"We just conjured your soul," he mused thoughtfully. "Maybe this is what it looks like."

She seemed to consider this, but didn't appear pleased.

"Is your name Lilith?" he asked.

"Yes," she replied.

"Are you a soul?" Huxley blurted out suddenly. "Or…some kind of demon?" Lilith just stared at him with contempt and he turned to Butch, confused.

"Aren't you bound by the ring to do all that we ask, including answering our questions?" Butch asked.

"I am bound only to those who wear the ring," she replied.

"Are you a demon?" Butch asked, repeating Huxley's question.

"Of course not," she replied haughtily.

"Tell us what you are then, as much as you know," persisted Butch.

"I am the offspring of an angel, a Nephilim. My father, Anu—" she broke off with a little sob, shutting her eyes tight while she struggled with some inner conflict. She seemed embarrassed to let them see her pain. "Poor father," she whispered miserably. It took a moment before she was composed enough to continue, and then she changed the subject. "My mother was one of the daughters of men. When I died, I was taken to the dark place where I have remained until now. It seems like such a long time." She looked at Butch carefully. "You found the books?"

"We have your *Book of the Dead*," he replied. "And, of course, Huxley here has the tablet of the Qliphoth. Your book was a copy apparently, but it would seem that it was quite authentic in spite of that..." His voice trailed off.

Helene was about to burst. Butch was babbling on about trifles! Why didn't he ask better questions? She knew he was still reeling from the shock but she was impatient to know more. Yet she didn't dare speak. But suddenly, as if she knew Helene's thoughts, Lilith turned to look at her—really look at her—settling her gaze on Helene for what seemed like an eternity. Helene froze, not daring even to breath.

"We have so many questions for you," Butch was saying. "Why...I hardly know where to start! I'm afraid I need a minute to clear my head. In the meantime, uh...I mean, first, would you like anything? A chair perhaps, or...uh," he cleared his throat before continuing awkwardly—"Something to wear?"

Lilith's gaze moved back to Butch. "A covering would be nice," she said.

"We'll find her something!" Helene's father volunteered. His voice sounded strange. He had kept hold of Helene's hand the entire time, and now, as he led her into the bedroom, it was swimming uncomfortably in his sweaty grip. She waited until they were alone to gently twist it free. Her father didn't appear to notice. His expression was full of anxious excitement.

"Are you all right?" he asked her, but before she could open her mouth he continued in a loud whisper. "It's astonishing! I can't believe it! I never expected such a thing!" With each statement he gave her a little shake as if to emphasize his point. "But you might be frightened," he said, pausing to examine her face. "Though you seem calm. Are you sure you're quite all right?" Again he didn't give her a chance to answer. "It's a significant discovery!" he exclaimed, his eyes wide with wonder. "This is certainly the most important discovery ever made!"

"I'm fine!" Helene put in the first chance she got. "I'm not afraid at all. It's the most exciting thing that's ever happened to me too!" His excitement had the effect of increasing her own. The two of them stood there a moment, staring at each other and smiling in wonder. Her father's pupils were so large that she could hardly see the green parts around the outer edges.

"The covering for Lilith!" he suddenly remembered. They fished through their suitcases, but none of their clothing seemed large enough to fit the creature in the living-room.

"What about this?" Helene asked, holding up a thin, woolen blanket from one of the cots. Her father liked the idea, and when they brought it to Lilith, she seemed pleased by this choice as well. As if it were the most normal thing in the world, she wrapped the blanket around her torso, just below her arms, securing it over one shoulder as easily as if it had been designed for that.

"May I move freely about the room?" she asked. When Butch hesitated she added—"The circle has no more significance. It was a pathway out of the dark place, nothing more. If I had the ability to resist the ring I would have done so by now." Her candor shocked Helene. There was a frankness in her manner that squashed any doubts about whether or not she spoke the truth.

Butch motioned for her to go where she liked, and she stepped out of the circle and cautiously sat down on the couch. For some reason this made the situation seem all the more peculiar for Helene. "How do you know so much about the ring?" Butch asked.

The rest of them were slowly following suit, arranging their chairs to face the couch. Helene moved hers close to her father's. Everyone seemed to relax just a little.

"Azazyl instructed us," Lilith told him. She sat regally, yet continued to hide the lower half of her face with her hair as she spoke. Helene got the impression that Lilith had been a very proud woman at one time.

"Azazyl?" repeated Butch.

"He was one of the Watchers," Lilith explained. "An angel... like my father." The mention of her father brought another spasm of anguish.

"Ask her about the dark place," suggested Helene's father.

"Can you tell us about it?" asked Butch.

Lilith shuddered. "When my soul left my body it was taken there. It's just like it sounds; an infinite vacuum of nothingness." Helene was reminded of the extreme darkness that descended on them moments before Lilith appeared. "I think I must have been there for many years," she continued. "Can you tell me how long it's been?"

"When did you go there?"

"It was just after the war between the Watchers and the Others," she said.

"The Others?"

"The angels who came to stop the Watchers."

"Mmm," mused Butch. "I can't think of any incident in history that might be linked to that." He thought about it a moment longer and then continued on a different tack—"This dark place," he said. "Is this where everyone goes when they die?"

"No, not you," said Lilith. "Only Qliphoth."

"Qliphoth?"

"The souls of the Nephilim are called Qliphoth."

"Where do the rest of us go?" Butch asked.

"I don't know," she replied, but she seemed to be considering it. "Azazyl told us that there is a place where your souls go when you die, but he didn't say where it was. All I know is that our souls are different from yours in that they remain here on earth when we die. That's why the Others created the dark place."

"So all of these Qliphoth are in the dark place?"

"No. Only the ones who were captured during the war have been imprisoned there. The rest escaped."

"So you died in the war," concluded Butch.

"Yes," she said. "I drowned in the flood."

Butch cocked his head. "The flood," he echoed. "What flood?"

"The flood that came with the war," she replied. "At the inception of the war the Others unleashed a terrible storm. There was an earthquake and then an immense explosion of water. The water was everywhere. It seemed like the whole world must be covered in it. Surely you must have heard of it!"

Butch exchanged meaningful looks with Helene's father. He seemed about to speak but could only manage a strangled little groan.

"The survivors," Lilith continued anxiously. "Do you know what happened to them?"

Butch got up and began pacing the floor. "To be honest, this is the first we've heard of the dark place...or of the existence of souls other than our own," he told her. He was clearly agitated, and appeared to be struggling against an impulse to jump up and down. As soon as he got himself under control he sat back down. "We are archeologists," he continued in an apologetic tone. "We study artifacts from lost civilizations." He punctuated this with one, quick, spurt of laughter and then continued—"And quite frankly...I wouldn't even know how to categorize you." He stood up and resumed his pacing. "If the flood you're talking about is the same flood we have recorded in our history," he paused here to add to Helene's father—"...which, incidentally, occurred around the same time that the tablet was written," before continuing to Lilith—"...then that would mean you've been in the dark place for somewhere in the vicinity of five thousand years."

Lilith stared at him in surprise.

"Another thing we didn't understand is the manner in which your *Book of the Dead* was copied," Butch went on. "It doesn't seem consistent with any other documents that we've found. Is there anyone who might have had reason to...?"

"Asmodeous!" Lilith whispered, and her face lit up so brilliantly that one could almost forget the horrible teeth and claws.

"Asmodeous?" Butch turned to Huxley. "Why does that name sound familiar?"

"It is familiar," agreed Helene's father. "But I can't think of where I've heard it before."

Helene couldn't keep quiet any longer. She read about Asmodeous in one of her father's books. "He was a djinn!" she blurted out. "He helped King Solomon build the temple."

"She's right!" exclaimed her father. "I remember it now. Solomon claimed to have power over these spirit creatures he called djinn."

"Do you suppose these Qliphoth souls could, in fact, be Solomon's djinn?" asked Huxley.

"Who is Asmodeous?" Butch asked Lilith.

"He was a Nephilim, like me," she replied coolly, but she was clearly affected by what they'd said. She was practically quivering with emotion.

"Ah!" said Butch, thinking this over. "I wonder. Djinn is an old Arab word. If memory serves, it means something to the effect of, 'to hide or be hidden.'" He turned to Lilith. "Why might someone call you that?"

Lilith replied with a little sigh of resignation. "In order to avoid the dark place it was imperative that our souls escape the Others. Our souls were only at risk once they were released in death. That is why they go into hiding." Lilith turned to Helene. "What happened to the djinn they call Asmodeous?" she asked breathlessly.

"I don't know," said Helene. "The story just kind of ends after the temple was built. But one legend claims that Asmodeous exchanged places with Solomon and escaped."

Lilith seemed hopeful as she considered this.

"Was Asmodeous a friend?" Helene asked because she was dying to know and it was clear that Butch wasn't going to.

Lilith turned to her. "Yes," she replied. "I have wondered what happened to him all these years."

"I seem to recall seeing that name in other writings as well," said Helene's father. "I think in some of the Jewish texts, in particular, he was considered a powerful demon."

"Asmodeous a demon!" cried Lilith, her enormous eyes flashing anger. But the anger abated just as quickly as it arose and Lilith laughed bitterly. "The sons of men were always looking for someone to blame for their problems," she explained with a little shrug. "Every time anything went wrong they either accused one of their own of angering the gods or claimed it was the work of a demon. They could never take responsibility. Always looking for a god to save them. Any god would do. They even thought *we* were gods!" She snorted in disgust. "What could we do? Someone had to do it, and we were natural leaders. We inherited that from our fathers."

"Do you have...powers?" asked Butch, clearly embarrassed by the question but determined to know, just in case. Helene had been wondering the same thing. She kept thinking of the Arabian tales of genies with magic carpets and three wishes.

Lilith considered the question. "I can't really say what this...," she looked down at herself as if searching for the right word—"... *body* is capable of. I didn't have any form at all in the dark place. But it feels...limited. My senses seem to be lacking. I can see you, I can, in a distant kind of way, *feel* this blanket, and I can vaguely sense the warmth of this room. But everything seems to be reaching me as if through a screen. I don't feel hunger or other physical sensations." Lilith was thoughtful another moment. "I doubt that I have any mystical power, such as you're thinking of," she said. "We have always been bound by the same laws of nature as ordinary men, even when we were Nephilim. We were simply bigger and stronger and smarter. It was the same with the angels. The bodies they created for themselves were very similar to those of men. But the angels had superior knowledge, which they could use to manipulate the laws of nature. This was how the Others brought about the flood. Their manipulations caused that catastrophe. None of it was brought about by supernatural means. Every circumstance is subject to the unbending laws of nature as set forth in creation."

"Do you have this 'superior knowledge' as well?" asked Butch.

"No. The angels have had millenniums to learn the secrets of the universe. They were here long before this world was created. They taught us many things. But there was not enough time, and we didn't realize the danger we were in until it was too late."

"But you learned the secret for returning to earth from the dark place," observed Butch.

"Yes," said Lilith.

"What were you planning to do once you got back?"

Lilith looked at him in surprise. "Live," she said simply.

"But how?" he pressed. "Surely you didn't expect to simply 'blend in' in your present form."

Lilith paused then, and Helene got the sense that she was choosing her words very carefully. "There is a way to breach the barrier between the living and the dead so that our souls may enter a living body and dwell there."

Butch gasped. "How?"

"I do not know," Lilith replied. "I was killed before I learned everything."

Butch turned to Huxley. "I think I need a drink."

Huxley got up and went to fetch a bottle. When he returned, he carried three glasses and a bottle of whiskey. It appeared that Helene would not be included this time. Huxley poured a hefty portion of the acorn-colored liquid into each glass and handed them out.

Butch took a large swallow from his glass and then looked at Lilith. "Do you drink?"

"I don't think it would have the same effect," she said.

Butch seemed at a loss for words. He took another swallow of whiskey.

"What are you going to do with me?" Lilith asked.

"I was just wondering that myself," said Butch, surprising them all with his candor. He tilted his head to one side with a small, humorless smile. "You see, I never—not even for a moment, mind you—expected this outcome to the experiment." He turned once again to the others. "Any ideas?" he asked, his large, toothy smile gleaming humorlessly in the brightly lit room.

Helene noticed that Huxley's and her father's glasses were completely drained. Her father was the first to speak. "I don't think there's any question, is there?" he said. "This discovery is more important than anything that's happened to mankind, excepting maybe their existence! Why, we now have living proof that there's life after death!"

"But think, for a moment, of the consequences this knowledge could bring to the living," said Butch. "You heard her. These Qliphoth souls—*Qliphoth*, mind you, there's no evidence here that *our* souls can be brought back from the dead—have the ability to enter living bodies. Lilith says she doesn't know how to do it and I suppose that must be true because she's bound by the ring to tell the truth, but if this knowledge is out there it's only a matter of time before someone discovers it."

"What are you proposing?" asked Huxley.

Butch looked at him. "Nothing at the moment," he said thoughtfully.

"My head is spinning," Huxley admitted. "But I think my first impulse is to agree with Bob. This is too big to conceal."

"Also," added Helene's father—"Who can say what further discoveries might be made from this? Perhaps this could be used to our advantage. At any rate, if the world knows about it, any potential risks could be prevented."

"I'm not so sure of that," Butch said. "But something else is bothering me at the moment." He looked at Huxley carefully. "How well do you know this Lieutenant Brisbin?" he asked.

Huxley looked at him in alarm. "What do you mean?"

"Well, it was all a bit too easy, wasn't it?" he asked in his calm, sensible way. "He gets word of this *Book of the Dead* in some cave near here and just happens to know a bloke who's looking for it."

Helene's father gasped. "You don't think…?" But, glancing at Helene, he didn't finish his question.

"Impossible!" exclaimed Huxley. "Brisbie has informed me of every archeological find in this part of the world for over a decade! He knew I was interested in pre-Egyptian era books of Apocrypha but that hardly makes him a conspirator!"

"No, perhaps not," agreed Butch. "But what about the others…the Arab soldiers at that outpost? By morning, they'll all know about our little experiment."

Everyone was staring at Butch, but Helene, meanwhile, couldn't help noticing that Lilith was listening to every word they said, assessing the situation with interest—and something else that looked a lot like cunning. Helene had the sense that Lilith's initial loss of composure was but a momentary lapse, perhaps caused by the shock of being wrenched from her dark resting place after so many years. But Lilith had clearly been gathering strength since then. And there was no doubt that she was measuring them every bit as carefully as they were measuring her!

"For the moment, we must act as if nothing's happened," Butch told them. He picked up his notes then and, without any warning, began reading from them in the Sumerian language. Within minutes Lilith dissolved before their eyes.

"She remains bound to the ring," Butch assured them. "She will come back when summoned. I felt we should test the spells for sending her in *and* out of the ring." He glanced at the blanket, which had fallen on the couch in a heap. "But before we bring her back we should talk privately."

"How did you manage it so quickly?" Helene's father asked.

"Like the other incantations, I simply converted the spells into decipherable sounds," he said. "I even added pronunciation marks so there'd be no confusion about how they're supposed to sound. Look, it's quite easy."

They all looked at the stream of letters, hyphened into syllables and sounds, just like those in a dictionary, to ensure perfect enunciation every time. "See? An incantation cheat sheet," he said peering at them under his glasses with his toothy smile. But then he immediately grew serious again. "We must pretend that nothing out of the ordinary has occurred," he said conspiratorially. "They'll guess that something was up because of our order at the foundry but we'll laugh it off tomorrow when we tell them about our 'failed' experiment. We'll make like it was a big joke, all in fun—which isn't entirely untrue. We'll complain that the translation is all bungled and the scroll's a fake. Then we'll act as if we're continuing our itinerary exactly as planned and even schedule a visit to the cave. Any sudden change in our plans will only alert any interested parties."

"But that's impossible!" insisted Huxley.

"Is it?" asked Butch. "Is it as impossible as what we just witnessed here tonight?"

"I think we should return to Tel Aviv immediately," Helene's father said.

"And we will," said Butch. "But we can't do anything to draw attention to ourselves. We'll find a logical reason to cut our trip short, or better yet, just leave without telling anyone." Butch looked at Helene and tried to smile. "For all we know Huxley's right, and no one cares about this book. We mustn't panic. It's quite common for archeologists to become paranoid over a find, particularly one as significant as this."

"He's right," agreed Huxley. "And let's not forget that the Bedouin has been trying—quite unsuccessfully I might add—to sell these scrolls for months."

"Yes but that could be because it was only one piece of the puzzle." Butch reminded him. "I'm merely suggesting that we take precautions until we've decided how we're going to handle this."

They were all in agreement about that.

"In the meantime, we should learn everything we can about these souls and what they want," said Butch. "That will help us decide the right thing to do. Are we agreed?"

They were. Butch took a deep, shaky breath. Helene thought how old he looked as he raised the notebook and once again began to read. The incantation to call Lilith out of the ring was only slightly longer than the one that sent her back. It was perhaps three or four stanzas long, and repeated the now familiar *ki-sikil lil-la-ke* several times in a row.

Like magic, Lilith appeared. It was only slightly less shocking this time. Even Lilith seemed surprised.

"Did you go back to the dark place just then?" Butch asked her.

"No," Lilith replied. "I don't know where I went. It's as if I was still here, actually, but like I was trapped behind a barrier of some kind. I couldn't see or hear anything, yet I could feel your presence."

"Was it as bad as the dark place?" Helene asked.

Lilith looked at Helene—and it struck Helene how much more interested Lilith seemed in her than in the others. "Nothing could be as bad as the dark place," she said passionately.

"Lilith," interjected Butch—"Your existence—although very exciting—presents us with a conundrum. You must tell us everything about you and where you come from if we are to help you."

Lilith arranged the blanket around her body, like before, and then sat back down on the couch. She arranged her hair to shield the lower half of her face from their view, peeking out at them from behind the thick curtain of hair. Her large eyes moved over each of them in turn, lingering, as always, on Helene. And then she began to speak.

CHAPTER
12

Present Day

"You thought *I* was Lilith," Nadia concluded. When they didn't reply she went on thoughtfully. "That ritual—or whatever you did to me—was a lot like the one they did to conjure her."

"Actually it was different," said Gordon. "Calling a djinn out of a human body is a little trickier than calling one out of the dark place." He noticed that Will was glaring at him and added—"But yeah, it was similar."

"Who are you people?" Nadia asked.

"Look Nadia," said Clive. "Whether you choose to believe in them or not, these djinn are out there. They want to live. They need our bodies to do that. Remember *Invasion of the Body Snatchers*? Well, multiply that by…," he paused here to pretend to count on his fingers and then concluded—"Actually, *Invasion of the Body Snatchers* pretty much describes it."

"But why would they plan some big attack then?" she asked. "They need living bodies, don't they?"

"We don't have time to educate you on the politics of the djinn," said Will. "All you need to know for the moment is that terrorist cells have been put on alert—which means there's an impending attack. We're here, with you, because this isn't an ordinary terrorist attack. This one has links to the djinn...and you."

"What links?" Nadia asked. When no one answered she turned to Gordon. "What links?" she demanded again.

Gordon sighed. "Well, you already figured out that our main link to you is Lilith," he said, throwing a nervous glance at Will. "There's also a link to BEACON."

"What!" cried Nadia, incredulous. "No! No way. How is BEACON connected to this attack?"

"Gordon," interjected Will in a warning tone.

"Yeah, Gordon, why don't you just lay the whole thing out for her, so she'll know exactly what *not* to tell us," said Clive. "Man, what are you thinking?"

Gordon's face turned ashen. "How do you know we won't get answers quicker by telling her what we need to know?" he suggested defensively.

"Gee whiz," said Clive, his face beaming with mock optimism. "Maybe Gordon's right! Maybe we should send out a memo to the Department of Defense: 'Hey guys, we think you might be confusing your suspects with all those questions. Try telling them what *you* know and maybe you'll get your answers quicker.' Thanks Gordon!"

Nadia didn't know what to think. Was she actually a suspect in a real live investigation? "What... kind of attack is it?" She asked rather breathlessly. Their silence was as solid as a brick wall. "Please! I have to know!"

Will's eyes, as usual, were examining her face. She stared back at him defiantly, determined not to tell him another thing until he told her what she wanted to know.

"We don't know." It was Gordon's voice that finally broke the silence.

Nadia gaped at him. "You...don't know?" She shook her head in disbelief. "You've kidnapped me and are holding me against my will—no Miranda rights or anything else, mind you—and you don't even know what kind of attack you're..."—Nadia threw up her fingers to add quotation signs here—"... 'investigating'...You're all mad!"

"Terrorist attacks are investigated differently than other types of crimes," Will said defensively.

"We don't have to explain ourselves to her," grumbled Clive.

Will ignored him. "The method of attack is often the last thing we find out—that's what makes these attacks so hard to stop. We know something's going down, and we know who's involved. We just don't know what they're going to do. Even when we intercept one or more of their cells, we're only getting one small part of an intricate plan that might be made up of an entire network of cells. Most cells aren't told any more than their individual orders. It's their combined efforts—each cell acting on blind obedience—that makes them so hard to stop."

"So how do these cells know what to do?" Nadia asked.

"They get a message," said Will. "Could be email. Could be regular mail. Could be telephone. The message is almost always encrypted, meaning it contains a series of code words that communicate their instructions."

"The internet has made it really easy for people to communicate no matter where they are in the world," said Gordon.

"So how do you find these messages?" asked Nadia. "It must be like looking for a needle in a haystack."

"It can be," said Gordon. "These messages are extremely hard to identify unless you already know the code or you have something specific you're looking for. There is an entire division at the DOD that does nothing but track these encrypted messages. In the case of email, the message would look a lot like spam. It might come in the form of an advertisement or it might just contain a jumble of words that make no sense. The dead giveaway is that the email has no real connection to any legitimate business."

"I get emails like that all the time!" exclaimed Nadia, and then instantly wished she hadn't said it.

"They send them to everyone," Gordon assured her. "That's what makes it so hard to find the target cells. Even if we do identify an email with an encrypted message, we still have to figure out which recipient is the cell."

"And what kind of attack the instructions on that message might be supporting," said Will.

She had to admit this made sense. "But you still haven't told me how BEACON is connected," she said.

"We've told you all we can," said Will.

"Maybe I've told you all I can too, then," said Nadia. She and Will just glared at each other for a few minutes.

"Might be time to call in the goons," said Clive. Nadia turned her scowl on him. "And tell them to hurry up!" he cried. "She's givin' me the evil eye!"

Nadia relented a little, but she still refused to speak to them for several minutes. Finally, when her curiosity got the better of her, she said—"They didn't wear masks when they conjured Lilith. Why did you wear them with me?"

"Djinn that have been around for thousands of years are much more advanced than one who's been in the dark place," explained Gordon. He seemed pleased to have her talking again. "For reasons we don't fully understand, the combination of metals in the ring and the shavings weakens the djinn. The mask provides extra protection. It helps block stronger, more experienced djinn from getting in."

"We realize how confusing this must be for you," said Will in an unexpected show of compassion. "It may seem like a lot to ask, but for the time being you're just going to have to trust us."

"Do I have a choice?" she asked.

"You want a choice?" Clive asked pleasantly. "I have a choice for you. If you want to return to Xanadu and live happily ever after, you need to help us stop this attack."

"How am I supposed to do that?" She asked, exasperated.

"Just keep telling us what you know," said Gordon.

"Don't leave any detail out," added Will.

"And bring us the broom of the wicked witch of the west," added Clive.

Nadia tried to separate her thoughts from her emotions. She was becoming more and more frustrated because it was getting harder to tell what was real. She needed more information. "If you would just tell me what you're...,"

"We'll know it when we see it," said Will.

"It's just that there's so much..." she complained.

"You're doing great," said Gordon. "Just keep telling us everything."

"You were just getting to Lilith..." prompted Will.

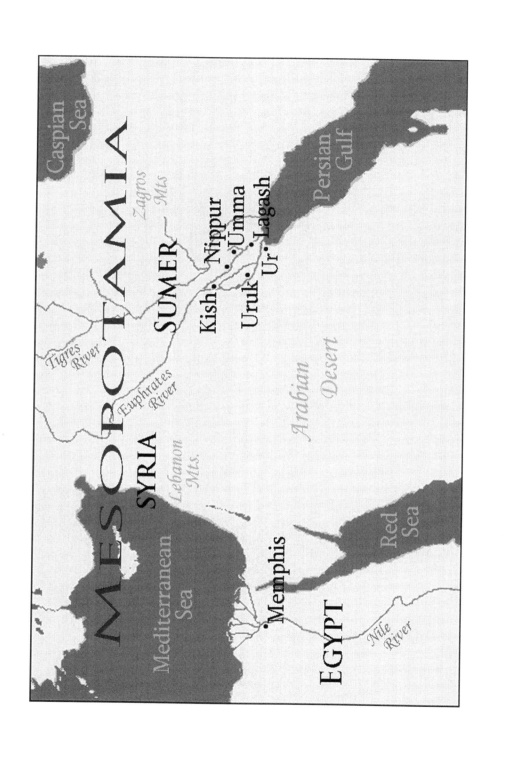

CHAPTER
13

Ancient Mesopotamia
A small village outside Uruk
Approximately 5,000 years ago

Lilith donned the heavy man's skirt, delighting in the downy softness of the woolen pelt against her thighs. Next, she wrapped her upper body in a simple, white linen shawl, leaving her right shoulder bare as was the custom. But instead of allowing the shawl to flow loosely to her ankles like the other women in her village, Lilith tucked the shortened garment into her skirt, leaving her legs exposed like the men in her village. She would complete the look with a cloak and a copper helmet, but first she would add a few little embellishments.

Placing bracelets of gold and alabaster all along the length of her arms, she strategically arranged them for the most flattering effect. She paused periodically to admire the result, noting how the bracelets accentuated the flawless curves of her well-formed arms and gave them an imperial quality. Her pleasure faded slightly at the thought of the looks she would get from the people of her village, but she reminded herself that she didn't care. Yet the irritation was there. What manner of creature denounced something as natural as enhancing one's appearance as vanity? She shook her head in disgust. But that was the way of the sons of men in all things. They mutilated the simplest pleasures with their irrational fears and misguided sentiments. They acted as if joy was in short supply, to be measured out in small doses. And all the while they kept insisting that it was the will of God! As if they knew anything about God. If it wasn't for her father and the other angels, the sons of men would still be eating insects and bludgeoning each other to death with rocks and sticks!

Lilith glanced across the room at her sleek new dagger. It was considerably longer than the ones the men used, although it was shorter than a sword. She had designed it herself, adjusting the size and shape until it felt just right in her hand. She kept its lean, jagged blade exceedingly sharp.

Once her arms were satisfactorily adorned, Lilith began carefully applying a subtle outline around her eyes to enhance their rich, tourmaline-brown color and make them appear even more outstanding. Her eyes were already rather large compared to her other features, which were petite and exquisitely feminine. Her brownish black hair was long and smooth, except for the thick bangs that lightly grazed her dark eyelashes. This combination of features produced a sweet, almost vulnerable, beauty that was sometimes confusing for the people around her. Those who knew her best would swear that there was nothing sweet or vulnerable about her.

A small, satisfied smile curved her lips as she examined her handiwork. Meanwhile, she continued to silently rail against the people of her village. It wasn't just the makeup and jewelry. All the angels' many improvements were under constant scrutiny; even those that were necessary for their survival! The lack of appreciation was what irritated her most. The angels had generously shared their superior knowledge with the sons of men. They taught them how to communicate. They introduced the concept of writing and record keeping. They devised ways for manipulating the earth's resources, such as water, through irrigation and other developments. They were skillful craftsmen, able to design tools to protect, enhance, simplify and even amuse. Why, some of them could even look into the heavens and foretell things that were yet to be! And all of this they were willing to share with the sons of men.

But the sons of men were mulishly reluctant to accept these gifts from the angels, preferring to hold out for a miracle from God Himself. And ultimately, no matter what the gift or from where it came, the sons of men seemed to enjoy it more if it could be used to control others.

But they would never control her!

Lilith picked up her brush and gently tugged the stiff bristles through her thick, shining hair. Despite her frustration with the people of her village, she was excited about her prospects. She was increasingly aware of her power as a woman, particularly as a Nephilim woman. She was destined for great things. As she reached for her helmet there came a timid knock upon the door. Lilith turned, mildly annoyed by the disruption.

"Yes?"

The door opened and a small woman with Lilith's large, almond shaped eyes stepped into the room. She was a beautiful woman, richly dressed in linen robes that were elaborately decorated with colorful embroidery and fringe around the edges. But to Lilith, the woman seemed ordinary and dull. The woman, on the other hand, gasped in astonishment when she saw Lilith.

"What do you think?" Lilith asked, twirling around with a wicked grin on her girlish face. Lilith was small for a first-generation Nephilim, but even so she towered nearly three heads over her mother.

Lilith's mother was momentarily speechless while she took in the details of Lilith's attire with a mixture of shock and dismay. They both knew that Lilith would do as Lilith pleased. And yet the poor woman couldn't help shaking her head as her eyes moved over daughter, starting with the long, bare legs and continuing upward until they reached the masculine helmet that sat like a crown on her daughter's pretty head. "What can you be thinking?" she wondered out loud.

"There's a very good reason why I'm dressed like this," Lilith told her. Her eyes sparkled and her dimples twitched as she said it out loud for the first time. "I'm going to join the Kalag-ga!"

"The–!" Her mother looked at her as if she'd lost her mind. "You—fighting with the mighty ones?"

Lilith tried to control her rising irritation. She reminded herself that this was the response she expected. "I know I'm small for a Nephilim," she allowed. "But I'm still far stronger than the sons of men. And that's who we'll be fighting, after all."

"But…why?" her mother asked, genuinely mystified. Lilith sighed as she studied her mother's face. The woman never understood her, not even when she was a little girl. That, Lilith supposed, was forgivable, but what hurt the most was that her mother never stood up for her. It was always Lilith who was in the wrong. *Someday she'll be proud of me,* Lilith grew up thinking, but now she wasn't so sure.

Then again, Lilith never understood her mother either. She supposed the high point of her mother's life must have been that moment when she was seduced by the fierce and beautiful stranger who descended on their little tribe and transformed them into the prosperous village they were today. That should have been the beginning but it seemed more to Lilith like the end. And that was what was so hard for Lilith to understand. Being the wife of an angel gave her mother status and privilege that most women—including Lilith—would have to fight for. Her mother could have exerted her power and forced the village to bow at her feet! Oh, but what was the use? All her mother wanted was to fit in with the other—equally unmotivated—women of her village.

Although she knew she was wasting her breath, Lilith answered her mother's question anyway. "I want to be a warrior and I want to be famous, and…someday, maybe…I might even want to rule my own city!"

"But…you're a woman."

"I plan to use that to my advantage!" Lilith shot back. She wanted so much to get her mother on her side, just once. "Think of it! I'll be the first woman to fight with the Kalag-ga—or any respectable army for that matter." When her mother remained unimpressed, Lilith suddenly became angry. "Perhaps you would rather I cover my head and hide, like the other girls do, to avoid being swept off my feet by any angels who might be flying overhead!" she suggested bitterly. But she regretted the spiteful words the moment she saw her mother's blush.

"I'm sorry I said that, mother," she said with a heavy sigh. Her good mood was being contaminated by an unpleasant mixture of guilt and frustration. Stubbornly, she made another attempt to get through to her mother. "The sons of men may consider me marked because of my father, but it's *their* lives that are forever marked by their idiotic and overbearing fears. It is for *you* as well as me that I must subjugate those men."

The older woman remained unconvinced, but Lilith thought she detected some small measure of admiration in her expression. This soothed away Lilith's anger like nothing else could. With her mood restored, Lilith thrust out her chest like the male warriors did and twisted her features into an exaggerated scowl. Even her mother had to laugh.

But when her laughter died down, Lilith's mother became thoughtful again. "What if the Kalag-ga refuse you?" she asked.

Lilith shrugged, feigning indifference. "In that case I shall be forced to challenge one of them to a battle so that I can prove my capabilities as a warrior." Although she answered her mother in a confident, matter-of-fact tone, the very idea of this made her legs tremble. Aside from being smaller and faster, she would have no advantage over the larger Nephilim males.

"Lilith!" exclaimed her mother, her brow creased with renewed anxiety. Yet aside from this brief outburst there seemed nothing more the woman could do, besides sigh in frustration. Realizing that there was no changing Lilith's mind, she resorted to self-pity. "You should hear what they say about you, Lilith. I know you don't care. But think of me—and Ninsun."

Lilith's anger returned, but she fought to keep it in check this time. "How can you sympathize with their way of thinking when they condemn me for even being born?" she protested. "The male giants are hailed as great and mighty heroes, while I'm considered an abomination. And do you want to know why that is, mother? It's because the men aren't ashamed to use their strength. They don't hide it and try to shrink themselves down to size like everyone's been trying to get me to since I was a child. Strength gets respect. You'll see. Once I begin collecting their souls on my belt those wagging tongues will change their tune!"

Her mother was effectively silenced. Lilith turned toward the polished copper mirror and pretended to adjust her helmet, glancing surreptitiously at her mother with another twinge of remorse. She knew her mother was acting out of fear for Lilith as well as for herself. If only everyone wasn't so afraid all the time. Lilith couldn't let their fears get the better of her.

As usual, Lilith's anger dissipated almost as quickly as it flared. And also as usual, it was followed by self-reproach. Her quick temper both confused and grieved her. She almost always repented her actions whenever she succumbed to it. Already she was regretting her harsh words to her mother. Lilith turned—feeling once again like the naughty little girl as she shamefacedly met her mother's eyes. With a bashful little smile she bent down to tenderly kiss her mother's cheek. Then she snatched up her dagger and brushed past the older woman, heading for the city of Uruk.

CHAPTER
14

With her first look into the startled gray eyes of the Kalag-ga's fearsome leader, Lilith felt a sudden stab of uncertainty. But with a determined lift of her chin, she haughtily announced the purpose of her visit. She was aware that her words were coming out in a nervous rush and made a conscious effort to slow them down, even forcing herself to pause occasionally at what were (hopefully) the most effective moments for doing so.

Her host listened quietly, yet Lilith found herself growing irritated with him. He was boldly looking her up and down as she listed her abilities and accomplishments, a small smile playing around his lips.

When at last Lilith finished what she was saying there was an awkward silence, during which she strove to appear confident and dignified. It seemed an eternity before the man finally spoke.

"So you're Lilith, the first surviving female of our race," he remarked at last. His voice was as deep and refreshing as the water running through the Euphrates River. Lilith tried to pull her gaze away from his but she had never encountered such self-assurance in a man before. She was surprised to learn that he knew of her, but then again, it made sense. The overwhelming majority of Nephilim were born male, and the few females that occurred were usually born dead. It was said that she was the first known female to survive. Even now, there were only a handful of female giants out there. Her case was particularly notable because her mother had given birth to only two Nephilim children, and both of them were female. However, Lilith didn't want her status as a female to dominate the conversation. She straightened her back and returned to the topic she came there to discuss.

"As a woman, I make an agile and swift warrior," she assured him with an arrogant tilt of her head. She suddenly regretted leaving her hair down, thinking it might have been wiser to pin it up under her helmet so that she wouldn't look so feminine. He was examining her as if she were a delectable morsel of food on a plate. But at the same time she resented being made to feel this way. How dare he look at her like that? What right did he have to make her feel awkward over her beauty? He clearly wasn't shy about flaunting his own charms, brazenly showing off his muscular thighs in an overly short skirt, and leaving his exquisitely muscled torso completely bare, without even so much as a breastplate for protection. He'd obviously taken great pains to arrange his raven curls into neat waves all around his head, and to shave his face so that his square jaw and chiseled features were fully revealed. He stood no less than two heads taller than her. Although she was tempted to say more she forced herself to keep her responses short and to the point so that he would be compelled to do most of the talking from here.

"I'm sorry; you have me at a disadvantage," he admitted after a lengthy pause. "This is an honor I wasn't expecting." When she didn't return his smile he continued. "There are important matters I must attend to at the moment, but it would please me to discuss this with you at a later time, perhaps this evening. In light of your own directness just now I hope you won't mind my being direct in return, and admitting that I find you very…intriguing. I would like to get to know you better. You just arrived in Uruk, did you say? There is much to see in our lovely…"

"Unless you've damaged your hearing on the battlefield, I'm guessing you heard what I just said," Lilith interrupted. Her disappointment was pricking at her temper and she was having difficulty keeping it in check. She could hardly believe his dismissive remarks and condescending tone of voice. This would have been predicable behavior for the sons of men, but she'd expected the offspring of angels to be more enlightened. She had fully expected him to—at the very least—put her skills as a warrior to the test, out of curiosity if nothing else. All she needed was an opportunity. But this—! Her voice was now firm and strong, and she spoke slowly, emphasizing every word so there would be no misunderstanding her. "I came here to become a Kalag-ga warrior. Not to 'get to know' some pompous jackass who's ill-fitting skirt looks like a discarded remnant from the sons of men!"

An involuntary laugh burst from the giant's lips but he prudently cut it short and made and effort to assume a more serious expression. His thinly disguised amusement infuriated Lilith. "I heard what you said before," he acknowledged, and for the first time in her short acquaintance with him, he actually appeared to be experiencing some mild discomfort as he seemingly searched for the right words. After a moment he sighed, apparently giving up the search. "You must realize that what you're suggesting is impossible," he concluded at last.

"I realize no such thing."

The warrior looked at her with interest. "Why would you even consider this?"

It was similar to the question her mother asked and Lilith's frustration grew. "What does that have to do with anything?" she asked him. "Would you ask a man that?"

"No, but you understand that it's unusual."

"Unusual compared to what? I'm literally the first female of our race to ever be born alive. Even now, seventeen years later, there are still only a handful of us out there. Surely more female warriors will come forward in time."

"Perhaps, but at the moment it is not customary."

"Customary!" Lilith was incredulous. "Do the mighty Kalag-ga warriors submit to the customs of the sons of men now? Should our women cower and hide like the daughters of men do? And are we to follow *all* of their customs, or just that one?" Lilith was trying to remain calm but her outrage was getting the better of her. What's more, no one had ever said 'no' to her before.

She couldn't believe it when the man laughed again, this time unabashedly throwing back his head and revealing a full set of gleaming white teeth. "My God, you're magnificent," he blurted out when he had regained his composure to some degree.

Lilith saw red. Hardly realizing what she was doing, she drew her dagger. This made the giant laugh even harder, although he had the good sense to take several steps back, away from her. Lilith took a small step to the side, calculating her attack. It was a shame that she was going to have to hurt, or possibly even kill the man, but she'd come too far to simply accept defeat without a fight.

"Lilith," warned the giant in a commanding voice. "Put down your dagger." But he couldn't seem to stop laughing.

"Draw yours and fight...or die a coward," she challenged. To her utter disbelief she could see that her words still amused him and it made the blood pound in her head. She lunged forward with her dagger, coming so close to piercing him before he jerked away that he actually stumbled back and nearly fell down. Now he was on his guard, but he still didn't draw his weapon.

"Lilith, I swear to you that this is a mistake you'll regret." But at least he wasn't laughing anymore.

Lilith attacked again, but this time her opponent was ready for her and moved away in plenty of time. Lilith cursed. She shouldn't have missed him in that first, unexpected attack.

"Lilith, this is my final warning," he said. And yet, he still hadn't bothered to draw his weapon. This angered Lilith more than his laughter had and she lunged at him, and then with a quickness that impressed even her, she lunged again. The second lunge caught him off guard and she came within inches of striking him. She realized that the element of surprise might be her best attack. In this warrior's arrogance, Lilith had found a weakness. She sprung for him again, but this time when he slipped to the side, she kicked him in his exposed shin bone just as hard as she possibly could. He yelped from the pain but didn't retreat. Instead, he spun around and grasped her dagger arm in a vice-like grip, jerking it behind her back and holding it there—just inches away from the breaking point—until she dropped the dagger and then he abruptly let her go. But Lilith was far from ready to surrender. She whirled around like a wildcat and struck him squarely in the nose with her fist. His head went back and he let out a mighty roar of anger.

"Need some help?"

The voice startled both of them, and Lilith spun around to see a handful of giants watching them with a great deal of amusement. She wondered how long the other Kalag-ga warriors had been standing there.

"Meet Lilith," said her opponent, prudently widening the distance between them.

"*The* Lilith?" one of them asked. The men were eyeing her with interest, but cautiously, staying far out of her reach. She thought she saw admiration in their eyes and felt a spark of pride—and hope.

"I was just explaining to Lilith the preposterousness of her joining the Kalag-ga," the giant told his men as he checked his nose for breaks. Turning to Lilith he added, "I'll admit you managed to get in a few good blows, but it's only because I wasn't fighting back. If I had been, you'd have been killed."

"You're a prophet now?" She shot back, but deep down she knew he was right. Still, what did that matter? "If you were an ordinary man I'd have killed you with that first strike of my dagger."

"That may be true, but the Kalag-ga are chosen from among the *strongest* Nephilim."

"The Kalag-ga is no life for a woman," chimed in one of the other men. He smiled sympathetically at Lilith. "We put everything else aside in order to fight, conquer and rule. There is no time for nursing babies."

Lilith had had it. She flashed her eyes at the man and then let her gaze wander menacingly over the rest of them. "Listen well *men*," she said in a shrill voice that was laced with sarcasm. "I intend to prove *my* right to fight, conquer and rule as a *woman!*" Her eyes burned with contempt as she looked the warriors up and down, precisely as they had done to her. "What are your names, so that I may know the identities of my enemies?"

A few of them gasped out loud when she said this. They all stared at Lilith in wide eyed astonishment, but she now realized that their awe was more like that of morbid curiosity—like discovering a three headed creature—than it was of admiration and respect. Her ego was crushed by the blow she'd been dealt, and in that moment she longed only for vengeance.

The first to recover from his shock appeared to be the youngest one there, aside from Lilith. He stepped forward a bit shamefacedly. He was the tallest of all the giants in the room, but his face was like that of a child. "I'm Og," he announced in a deep voice, bowing respectfully before her. There was a humble bashfulness about him that Lilith would have found charming had she not been so upset. "But I will never be your enemy," he added vehemently.

Lilith was too hurt to acknowledge the conciliatory remark—the only sign of respect she'd been shown up to that point—stubbornly turning toward the rest of the men expectantly. One by one, they stepped forward and gave her their names. Some were smirking as they approached her but others, like Og, were deferential or openly admiring of her. When they were finished Lilith reluctantly turned to the warrior who had—for the moment—defeated her.

The leader of the Kalag-ga was carefully examining Lilith's dagger, which he had picked up off the floor. He looked up and Lilith couldn't help envying the easy, self-satisfied smile that lit up his handsome face. He approached her cautiously, bowing before her as if she were a queen, and offering her the dagger with exaggerated submissiveness.

"Your humble servant," he murmured demurely. "Asmodeous."

Something deep within Lilith fluttered riotously, even as thoughts of revenge still simmered hotly on the surface. She jerked her dagger from his hand and stormed out of Uruk with her tail between her legs.

CHAPTER
15

W hen she thought about it later, Lilith realized she had allowed the Kalag-ga leader to get the better of her in more ways than one. She was forced to acknowledge that she wasn't nearly as prepared for the Kalag-ga as she thought. She lacked maturity. It wasn't just her age; several of the warriors appeared to be every bit as young as her seventeen years. But it was clear that their experience far outweighed hers. She cursed her little village for everything it lacked. There wasn't even another giant there for her to fight. The only other Nephilim in the entire village was her younger sister, Ninsun, and she took no interest in fighting. What had Lilith been thinking? She hadn't even killed anyone yet! Her only real experience had come from hunting animals. Wild animals were cunning and quick, but they were no match for the Nephilim warriors. She'd been measuring her competence by the standards in her village—a low standard indeed! Those people were impressed by anything. And yet, this didn't necessarily diminish the things she had done. She felt sure that some of her feats were indeed great. She would never forget the first time she brought home the carcass of a giant female tiger she'd single-handedly felled. The expressions on their faces! That was the day she decided to become a warrior.

But her humiliation in Uruk forced Lilith to take a more critical look at herself. She begrudgingly realized that she'd been wrong to challenge such an experienced warrior to a fight. She hadn't intended on doing it, but her temper had flared. She would need to work on controlling her emotions, as well as accepting her limitations. The simple, annoying truth was that most Nephilim men were larger and stronger than her. She'd been given a false sense of confidence from her experiences with the men of her village, who she'd overpowered and dominated since early childhood. She figured this would be enough, since it was the sons of men who the Kalag-ga set out to conquer in their quest to rule the cities of the world. And yet, she supposed there would also be times when the Kalag-ga had to fight other giants as well. They had to be able to protect the cities they conquered from *all* potential attackers. If only she'd hit her mark with that first thrust of her dagger!

All of it was beside the point now. What was done was done. She would learn from her mistake and try to act with more discretion in the future. She'd have to do something spectacular to prove herself now. It would have to be something that would put the Kalag-ga warriors in their place while at the same time giving her another opportunity to get her foot in their door.

To do this she'd have to come up with a plan that would make the most of her strengths and minimize her weaknesses. Her greatest strengths—greater even than her courage—were her intelligence and cunning. And it occurred to her for the first time that the people of her village, although irritating, could be used to her advantage. They were prejudiced and often judgmental, but she knew they didn't really mean her harm. In their odd way, many of them had tried to look after her. After all, she was the eldest daughter of the angel who protected their village. Her father, Anu, had a wife and two children in their village. Despite any personal reservations they might have about this, the people feared and appreciated Anu enough to want to keep his family safe. Lilith often considered herself a victim of her backwards little village. But in retrospect, she was forced to admit that some of her own actions might have contributed to her ongoing conflicts with the people who lived there. She supposed her constant bullying of the boys throughout her childhood hadn't helped her case. And yet, they'd brought it on themselves, refusing to let her play with them simply because she was a girl. She'd merely used the same tactics she'd seen them using to establish rank; blackening their eyes, destroying their toys, tying them to trees and then covering them in honey. And it wasn't just the physical stuff. When she tried to express herself verbally they called her names, like screech owl. They'd stubbornly refused to let her in their circle no matter how many times she'd beaten them. Instead of acquiescing to her obvious superiority, they stubbornly denied it to the end, even claiming their numerous bumps and bruises were brought about by magic powers, instead of a female who was stronger than them.

The young girls of Lilith's village avoided her for an entirely different reason; they were terrified of her. On the rare occasions when she did manage to somehow snare one into a kind of compulsory association with her it always ended with the girl becoming injured or getting into trouble. Lilith's instinct that she was better suited to play with the boys was practical; every idea she had involved either testing the boundaries or doing something dangerous—or both.

As if to prove Lilith's culpability, her little sister, Ninsun, got along just fine with the other children her age, even if she did tower over them conspicuously.

In fact, everyone seemed to have adjusted comfortably to the situation except Lilith. And when she thought about it honestly, she had to admit that there were indeed times when the villagers had reached out to her. Yet she always had the sense that they only put up with her out of duty or fear. Her father was, after all, the main reason their village continued to exist and prosper. Most of the other villages scattered along the fertile plains were disappearing. Their occupants either relocated to the nearby cities or died. They had no means of protecting themselves. This created a shortage of farmers and shepherds, which was taking its toll on the economy overall. And the villagers who relocated to the cities seldom fared much better, often suffering extreme poverty, especially during the famine years. Many ended up selling themselves as slaves just so that they could eat.

Anu—the "sky god," as the villagers called him—had truly been a godsend to her little village. And it wasn't just that no one would dare attack a village that was under the protection of an angel. Anu had transformed their village with his many suggestions for more efficient and profitable ways of doing things. He was often away, traveling the earth, but he always brought back gifts and more ideas from faraway places. He taught the villagers to write; then he wrote down instructions for everything from farming and irrigation to healing.

All of this Anu had given freely. He didn't lord it over the people or hail himself as a god, like many would have been tempted to do. He had no desire to rule and even less to be tied down to one place. He graciously allowed the elders of the village to continue running things, content to simply bring gifts, knowledge and prosperity whenever he graced them with his presence. He respected all of their customs, including the law that allowed women to take more than one husband. It had become, after all, a necessity, not only because the angels who descended upon their earth were male (there were only two hundred of them in all), but because their giant offspring were predominately male and often took as many wives as they pleased. This left a terrible shortage for the sons of men.

Anu's behavior had gone a long way to stretch the villagers' tolerance of Lilith and her many escapades, but lately that tolerance had metamorphosed into a kind of grudging admiration—from a distance that is. When confronted with Lilith, the older women of the village were apt to cluck their tongues at her, while the older men would shake their heads. Everyone else simply turned tail and ran in the opposite direction.

The simple truth was that Lilith resented the villagers because they profited so much from her father while she was always left wanting more. True, throughout her life she need only send out a silent prayer and he would come to her, but more times than not she had to be content to have him do so in a dream. The dreams were too vague and indistinct to completely satisfy her need to be with her father, even if they did do wonders for her outlook, bringing fresh ideas and boosting her confidence in her abilities. It was her father who provided the inspiration for a new dagger. Until then, her focus had been on perfecting her skill using the weapons of men; it hadn't occurred to her to alter the weapons to better suit a woman. It was the same with every important decision of her life. The dreams came and Lilith set store by them; often carving notes and images—while still half asleep—right into the sideboards of her bed. And so it was after the incident with the Kalag-ga. And this time, Lilith's dreams left her with the strong conviction that she must reconcile with the people of her village before she could successfully walk away.

It was in this state of mind that Lilith swallowed her pride and returned home. She spent her days in training, hunting and planning, while her nights were spent waiting for a sign from her father. But any dreams Anu might have sent were ambushed by visions of dark, laughing eyes and strong, persuasive arms; alternately pursuing and taunting her. Lilith tossed and turned, suffocating amid the twisted blankets and pent up frustration. Her lust for the giant called Asmodeous rivaled even her desire to be a Kalag-ga warrior.

CHAPTER
16

When she wasn't perfecting her fighting skills, Lilith used what influence and charm she had to work her way into the good graces of the villagers. She was particularly friendly with the merchants, who she knew were the first to hear what was happening outside the village from the traders who came to do business with them. She was able to track all the comings and goings of the Kalag-ga—albeit after the fact—by simply talking to the merchants. Obsessed as she was with the Kalag-ga, it wasn't long before she could anticipate their every move.

It was clear to Lilith that the Kalag-ga had designs on the imposing city of Lagash, though their one attempt to take the city had failed. Lagash was south-east of Uruk, sitting near the mouth of the Tigris River. The giants had not been able to penetrate the solid rock wall that surrounded the city of Lagash. Although the Kalag-ga were a powerful force to be reckoned with, Lagash—who had thus far remained free of Nephilim influence—had a substantial army of no less than six hundred full-time soldiers in the king's employ. In addition, there were thousands of trained fighters who could be called upon in times of need. Lagash was aggressively protecting themselves from the angels and their offspring, but the Kalag-ga did not give up easily. Lilith was sure they were merely waiting for a more opportune time to strike again.

Lagash also had ongoing hostilities with Kish, a rival city to the north. There were constant disputes between the two cities over boundaries and irrigation. The longstanding strife was beginning to take its toll on both cities. The latest of these disputes left a large section of Lagash's canals destroyed and their farmlands and storehouses flooded. Lagash was in desperate need of grain. Lilith's village, renowned for its quality produce, was the first place they thought to go.

The village was suddenly a flurry of activity. As the merchants hustled to fill Lagash's enormous order for grain, Lilith quickly developed a plan to even the score between her and the Kalag-ga warriors. She was careful to keep her activities secret, having no desire to involve the people of her village any more than was absolutely necessary. It was critical that no one connect what she was about to do with the grain transaction. If they did, it would put the village in great danger.

Simply, and quite single-handedly, Lilith planned to slip unnoticed into the city of Lagash along with the supplies from her village. She observed that the enormous carts brought in by Lagash's men were unusually wide, possibly to make traversing the unwieldy roads a little easier when they were fully loaded. She devised and built a triangular box to attach to the bottom of one of the carts. She made it as narrow and shallow as her considerable size would allow, for it was imperative that the box not be discoverable by anyone standing on either side of the cart. She left spaces between the side boards so that she would be able to breathe comfortably, and an extra wide space at one of the ends for her to slip through. All that remained was to attach the box to the bottom of the cart; a simple enough task after having, on the chosen day, stolen the keys to the storehouse where they were kept.

The storehouse belonged to an old farmer named Gershon, who was providing a large portion of the grain purchased by Lagash.

He'd been surprised when Lilith offered to help him load the carts, but was not in a position to refuse the timely offer. Gershon's only son, Dumah, had been injured the day before in a terrible accident, when his favorite hunting stand in one of the large cedars suddenly and inexplicably (to everyone except Lilith) gave way. Early the next morning, before anyone else was even stirring; Lilith crept into the storehouse and securely fastened the box to the bottom of one of the carts. Afterwards, she walked around the cart several times, examining it from every position until she was satisfied that it would not be noticed. Then she put the keys in a place where Gershon was sure to discover them, and hid behind some old, forgotten crates in the back.

As was often the case—before that unfortunate incident with the Kalag-ga, that is—things went exactly as Lilith planned. Gershon discovered the missing keys, mumbling curses to himself for his forgetfulness, and then finished loading the cart by himself. By mid-day he alerted the men of Lagash that their cargo was ready and went out to get the horses. Lilith took this opportunity to squeeze into her secret hiding place beneath one of the carts. This adventure would surely test her abilities—especially her patience—but when she succeeded it would erase any doubt about whether or not she would make a great warrior. It was a shame she wouldn't be able to openly claim her victory to the world, but she couldn't endanger her village that way. Lagash was a profitable trade center for them, and it would bring great hardship to lose that alliance, not to mention what would happen if they decided to seek revenge. There was only one small, very select group of giants who would ever know what she did, and she felt sure that they would keep her secret.

The trip was long, tedious and jarring, but Lilith endured it cheerfully. Filled with excitement and uncompromising determination, she focused on her moment of triumph. She imagined the moment again and again, never allowing even the slightest notion of failure to enter her thoughts. She wished there was a way that she could be there to see the look on the Kalag-ga warrior's faces—particularly that of their puffed up leader—when they heard the news. This would wipe that arrogant smile from his handsome face!

Yet she was a long way from victory. She thought about what she was about to do and reviewed how she planned to go about it, going over every possible scenario in her mind. She had a good idea of what she was up against from what she'd learned of Lagash from the merchants. The Kalag-ga had not been able to penetrate their walls, it was true, but where they had failed she had already as much as surpassed them.

Daylight was still with them when the cart finally drew near enough to the city of Lagash to begin signaling their approach with horns. The gate was opened by the time they arrived, and with that, Lilith found herself safely inside the city that no other giant had managed to step foot in before.

But there was still a very long road ahead. Lilith couldn't risk discovery, so her only hope was to stay hidden until she could escape the cart and go about her plan unnoticed. The time seemed to drag on interminably, but Lilith considered each and every inconvenience as a further test of her abilities as a warrior. She listened to the idle guards with a mixture of amusement and annoyance, wondering vaguely if theirs would be among the throats she would cut. At the thought of it a strange thrill shot through her. Although she'd slain many animals, she had yet to kill a man. But she suffered no anxiety in this regard. Death was a mere fact of life and every soldier, guard and warrior knew the risks. They publicly acknowledged their awareness of the danger each and every time they wore their battle attire. They had to be willing to kill if they were going to risk being killed. If Lilith was going to be a warrior, she would have to feel the same. In the hunt, she was known for her cat-like reflexes and ruthless cunning. She was fast. She never hesitated when moving in for the kill. And most importantly, she never let herself dwell on the possibility that she would fail. If she were to fail as a warrior, she hoped that failure would come as a brief, shocking revelation seconds before her own death. That was all any warrior could hope for.

The guards had temporarily stationed the cart in an open marketplace that was still bustling with activity in spite of the late hour. The air crackled with noisy chatter as people lingered to offer a fresh tidbit on an old piece of gossip or to start a new rumor altogether. Lilith grew bored, listening to their silly talk. Their trivial concerns seemed to underscore their dependent natures and rather pointless existences. They were just like the people of her village; focusing on trifles, creating mountains out of mole hills, stretching the limits of absurdity with their pointless chatter. Their penchant for exaggeration was what irritated her most. The sun did not simply rise, it 'ascended upon them the fury of God.' Every occurrence, no matter how ordinary or predictable, was seized upon as a 'sign' from the gods. Lilith rolled her eyes as she listened to them. They were like children. She wondered how they would interpret what she was about to do. The thought made her smile.

At long last the cart was moving again and Lilith was slowly taken in and around the meandering streets of the city to the storehouse—where the real adventure would finally begin. She stifled yawn after yawn, anxious to escape her uncomfortable cage. She longed to stretch. Her back ached. Yet it appeared she would have longer still to wait. The storehouse was filled with workers, noisily loading and unloading merchandise. It was almost as busy as the market had been. Moments alone were too quickly interrupted, so Lilith tested her patience even further by remaining in her hiding place under the cart.

It wasn't until after nightfall that the last of the storehouse workers finally left and the storehouse doors were all closed and locked. Lilith had begun to worry that the noises coming from her empty stomach would alert someone of her presence, but luckily no one appeared to notice. It was with enormous pleasure and relief that she finally slid out of her little box and—before anything else—pulled a piece of bread from her pouch and bit off a large chunk. She stretched her muscles and looked around as she chewed. It was hard to see inside the dark storehouse, but her eyes were slowly adjusting to the little bit of light there was. There appeared to be no windows, so she wouldn't be able to see what was happening outside. This wasn't going be easy. Her best bet would be to strike in the wee hours of the morning, when it would be least expected. This would mean more waiting.

Lilith inspected the storehouse. She walked all around the perimeter, carefully examining each of the two exits. She'd been worried that someone would link her actions to that day's deliveries and was relieved by how much activity, both coming and going, went on at the storehouse. She supposed that someone would eventually find the box she placed under the cart, but hopefully by that time they would have no idea where it came from or when it had been put there.

In the end, the locks on the storehouse doors were not at all hard to breach. Lilith chose what appeared to be the least used of the two doors—supposing it might provide an easier passage into the city—and worked quietly in case there was a guard outside. When she was ready to open the door, she proceeded with extreme caution, shifting it from its position in such tiny increments that it would hardly have been noticeable even if someone were staring directly at the door. However, she suspected the guard, if there was one, would be facing away from the building, and when the door was opened enough for her to look through the tiny crevice she saw that she was right. There was a single armed man standing a few feet in front of the building, facing out. There wasn't another person in sight. The guard had an axe affixed to his belt and a small dagger attached to his leg.

Lilith slowly unsheathed her own dagger and waited, like a tigress ready to pounce, for the right moment. Butterflies fluttered wildly in her stomach. Minutes went by. The guard stood remarkably still. He did very little fidgeting and there were very few distractions. It was a calm night. Even so, the guard seemed fairly alert. Lilith waited. She had all night, and she knew from stalking animals that patience was a virtue that was always rewarded.

All of a sudden the man's head moved up the littlest bit. He sniffed several times. Lilith poised herself for action. She watched the guard with the same intensity that she pursued a dangerous animal in a hunt. The man sniffed again and then inhaled deeply. Before he was able to fully execute his sneeze Lilith thrust her dagger into his kidney and gave it a twist, effectively paralyzing—and silencing—him while she jerked back his head and then quickly and cleanly sliced his throat. The man had not uttered a sound.

Lilith dragged the guard's body around to the side of the building until they were in the shadows. She quickly searched his armored cloak for the silver badge that held the mark of the Lagash warrior. Finding it, she cut it from the garment and placed it in a little pouch that was attached to her belt. She felt a sudden, wild thrill of triumph. But there was still a long night ahead. It would not do to start congratulating herself yet.

Lilith looked around. The city was deathly quiet. She could see its towering walls in the not so far off distance. She began warily working her way toward them, moving quickly and stealthily, careful not to make a sound. Although the streets were empty, she moved cautiously from one form of cover to another, hunching down to make herself seem smaller. She traveled as fast as she could without allowing herself to get too winded. Even so, her heart was racing dangerously by the time she reached the outer walls of the city. She hung back, trailing the wall from a short distance until she found the gate, and then kept on even farther in order to assess the situation on the other side as well. It appeared that the gate was only guarded for about fifty yards on either side. Lilith counted seven guards on the upper wall. She figured there were several more on the stairs, and a few watchmen inside the gate. She would remove the guards along the wall first.

Lilith inched her way closer to the wall, searching for a stairway. It appeared that the 'gate' was actually made up of an inner and an outer gate, with a large area in between and rooms tucked away on either side. Lilith had been to cities with similar gates before, so she knew that during the day the area between the two gates usually functioned as a public square where all manner of business was conducted. There was a roomy market area for traders, as well as sections for city meetings and official gatherings. That was probably where they let the cart sit for so long when she first arrived. The opening to the inner gate was made up of two large wooden doors secured with a wooden bar. The outer gate was probably the same. Lilith would have to kill each guard quietly and individually, which meant that she would have to take them by surprise. Much like the guard she had killed back at the storehouse, they would most likely be focused on what lay outside the city walls, but she wouldn't take any chances. The butterflies began fluttering again as she cautiously approached the first stairway, but they were butterflies of anticipation and excitement, not fear. Her desire for success drove her onward. It did not seem possible that she could fail.

Lilith found the first guard sitting idly at the bottom of the stairway that led to the upper wall. She crept up along the wall behind him, waiting for the right moment to strike. The man's head bobbed slightly and Lilith realized he was struggling to stay awake. The moment his head begin to drop a second time Lilith pounced, twisting her dagger viciously into his kidney while grasping his helmet and jerking back his head. His body stood poised and frozen, almost as if he was waiting for her to cut his throat. She was mildly surprised by how well this method of killing worked. She had devised it herself after casually picking the brains of one of the healers in her village.

She dragged the body up several steps so it wouldn't be visible to anyone passing on the road. Then, after insuring that no one had observed anything, Lilith quickly removed the Lagash emblem from his cloak and secured it with the other one in her pouch.

Lilith looked up above her. The stairway was clear as far as she could see, but it curved out of sight before reaching the top. Lilith doubted there would be guards stationed along the stairs, but she might encounter one descending. If that were the case, she would have no time to delay once she was spotted. She towered over most of the sons of men by at least two heads and she was stronger than they were but, even so, the Lagash soldiers were trained killers and not to be underestimated. The stairway was mostly dark—an advantage—and she inched her way silently up the steps, keeping her body flattened against the inner wall as she went. She continued this way all the way to the top without seeing a single guard.

When she reached the upper wall, Lilith tightened her grip on her dagger. From the street below, the guards appeared to be sufficiently spaced so that they were unlikely to see or hear one another. This was the reason they carried the horns in the event that they had to sound a warning. Lilith wouldn't give them the opportunity to use their horns.

She peeked around the corner of the stairway and saw the first guard. He was whistling very softly as he stood looking out over the wall. He was leaning forward in a relaxed manner, resting his arms on the wall. Lilith looked in both directions and saw that it was clear, but she knew that this could be deceiving, as there were alcoves all along the upper wall for secret passageways and other stairways, or perhaps to simply confuse someone like her in the event of an attack. Taking a deep breath, she lunged at the guard, killing him just as she had the others, by first paralyzing him with the thrust to his kidney and then slicing his throat. She dragged the body into one of the alcoves in order to hide it, wanting at all costs to avoid someone discovering the bodies and sounding the alarm before she finished. Then she collected her little memento and added it to her pouch.

The timing was perfect; it was long past the hour for mischief and before anyone thought of work—even slaves. No one was on alert. No danger was suspected. They were not prepared for this, as it was not how armies attacked; slipping through shadows, quiet as mice. The giants, in particular, liked to draw attention to themselves before an attack, noisily approaching in a cloud of dust like a stampede. Armed with arrogance and intimidation, they were loud and obnoxious and threatening. That was not Lilith's way. To her, war was like a game. To overpower an opponent was nice but to outwit them was exhilarating. But she would not congratulate herself yet. She was pleased, but there was still more to do.

Ducking low, Lilith crept along the wall until she spotted her next victim. Choosing just the right moment, she killed him as easily as she had the others but, this time, she heard someone cry out from several yards away. Looking up, she spotted two guards she hadn't noticed before. They must have been walking in that direction and stumbled upon her just then. They appeared to be as surprised as she was. Without a second's hesitation she threw her dagger the full distance and struck one of the men in the eye. And while her dagger was still airborne she had begun running toward the other guard who was scrambling for his horn. Just as it reached his lips Lilith threw herself forward and drove her foot into his loins with the full force of her long, powerful legs and effectively knocked the wind—and the will—right out of him. As the man bent forward with a strangled groan, Lilith retrieved her dagger from the other guard's eye and quickly sliced his throat, effectively relieving him of the terrible pain in his groin along with his duties to guard the city gate. She frantically looked around but the area appeared to be clear.

Lilith's heart was racing. She was afraid someone might have heard the guard's cry. She stood perfectly still for a moment and listened, but there was no sound. With no time to waste she had no choice but to keep moving. Within minutes the bodies were stuffed into another alcove, their uniforms stripped of their badges.

It took less than an hour for Lilith to clear the upper wall of guards. She had reached the stairs at the other end of the gate.

Lilith made her way quietly down the set of stairs, and just as easily killed the guard that was posted at the bottom.

Thrilled and elated, she made her way toward the inner gate, but here her joy was interrupted by confusion. The area appeared to be empty. Surely there was a night watchman! She eased her way in and around the rooms and hallways encompassing the gate. They were all empty. This struck her as odd and she wondered if it was a trap. Had she missed a guard on the upper wall? She looked up. There was no one overhead. She got on her hands and knees and looked under the wooden doors of the gate in case the watchmen were on the other side. There was no one. Lilith took a moment to think. Even if someone was on the other side, they would not necessarily be alarmed by the gate being opened from the inside. The whole idea of the gate was to keep enemies from entering the city. They had no reason to believe that enemies were already within—unless of course they heard that earlier cry. But that was unlikely. At any rate, there was only one way out of the city. If there were watchmen on the other side of those doors she would have to kill them.

Her height made it easy to reach the bar, but it was very heavy. As quietly as she could, Lilith pushed the hefty bar out of its holds. Then she gently pulled open one door, peeking out from behind it to see what was beyond. Once again, she was surprised, and perhaps even a little disappointed, to find the outer gate empty and unguarded. It had almost been too easy.

Shrugging, Lilith now opened the outer gate, pushing the doors all the way open until they touched the outer walls. Then she went back inside and opened the inner gate doors in the same manner, taking one last look around the abandoned area. Having rendered the city wide open after killing only thirteen of their armed guards, Lilith stepped out through the gates and left the city of Lagash.

Traveling on foot, she moved deftly through the reed banks and intertwining pastures, resting only when necessary and for the briefest intervals. She thought about the men she'd killed, marveling over how easy it had been. Although she didn't derive pleasure from killing any living thing, she did find it empowering to be able to do so when necessary.

But had this been necessary? Lilith resented the sudden twinge of conscience that unexpectedly assailed her. She immediately squelched it, reminding herself that it had indeed been necessary. It was the only way to prove herself as a warrior. If anything, the Kalag-ga were the guilty ones, not her.

Her sense of triumph returned when she thought of the Kalag-ga. She had outdone them! Now they would be forced to acknowledge her competence as a warrior.

She was still elated when, hours later, she reached the river that ran along the outskirts of the city of Uruk. She was comforted by the familiar sight of it. She would be welcome here. It was ruled by an angel, the well-loved Lugalbanda, who was hailed as a god by the people there. It was the home of many giants and the resting place for the Kalag-ga. The giants mingled peacefully with the sons of men under Lugalbanda's rule, and the sons of men enjoyed the protection of the Kalag-ga warriors.

It was nearing daybreak. With her success so absolutely assured, Lilith finally allowed herself to let down her guard as she sat down on the bank of the river. She noticed, suddenly, the grime that covered her. What a sight she must be! She removed her helmet and cloak, relieved to see that the cloak had caught most of the blood. She reached into her pouch and found the *swabu* paste she'd thought to bring, congratulating herself again for her thorough planning. She washed the cloak in the clean, rushing water of the river, scrubbing out the blood stains with the paste. When she finished she hung the cloak on a nearby bush to dry. Her wrap was soiled as well, but she decided she could make do without washing it if she turned it around and used the opposite side. She couldn't linger too long, after all. She'd hate to startle a farmer getting an early start on his day. With this in mind she swiftly stripped off the rest of her clothing and stepped into the icy river. Her legs had caught the worst of the mess, but her hair was also encrusted with gore. She washed and rinsed herself quickly but thoroughly and then, shivering, climbed out of the water. She allowed herself a few moments to dry before putting her clothes back on. She dressed hurriedly, hating the feel of the dirty wrap against her damp skin but satisfied that at least no one would be able to see evidence of her activities from her appearance.

With a sigh of satisfaction, Lilith sat down on a rock near the bank. Absently she picked up a small stick and began carving pictures in the dirt. She stopped, looking at the stick and then looking at the ground all around her. A small smile crept over her lips as she began gathering small twigs from the surrounding brush. She knew exactly how she would occupy her time while waiting for dawn to approach.

A few hours later Lilith was inside the city of Uruk, impatiently tapping her foot as she waited outside one of the merchant's shops for the doors to open. The merchant approached sluggishly from within, but when he saw Lilith it seemed to startle him fully awake. He stared at her in openmouthed astonishment for a few moments, but his behavior didn't offend Lilith. The sight of a giant was always remarkable, no matter how many there were in the city, but a female giant was rare and spectacular. The man fumbled with the door, trying to pull his gaze from Lilith long enough to see what he was doing.

"I want something delivered," Lilith told the man, presenting him with a handful of coins.

When the man saw the coins his demeanor immediately changed. He recovered from his shock and instantly began fawning over Lilith as he led her into his shop. He pushed things aside, clearing a space for her to sit, all the while elaborating on her incredible beauty, the likes of which he swore he had never encountered before.

"There's no need to flatter me," she interrupted impatiently. She had no time for the tedious ramblings of this silly man. "It will please me more if my errand is carried out exactly as I wish."

"Abimelech!" the man called out. "Abimelech, come! It is urgent!"

A young boy came running out from the back room, his hair disheveled from sleep. "Here I am," he said, jumping in surprise when he noticed Lilith.

"Wake up," scolded the boy's father. "Pay attention." The boy looked confused.

Lilith stooped so that she was at eye level with the boy and gently put her hand on his shoulder. "Do not be afraid," she said. "It is a happy errand I have for you. You see, I want you to deliver a present, and I'm certain the recipient will reward you well."

Lilith showed him a small box constructed of twigs that she had carefully woven together while waiting on the river bank outside the city gates. She'd attached a thick layer of bark to the top of the box, and artfully carved her message into it. *To the leader of the Kalag-ga warriors, From Lilith.* Neither the boy—nor most likely his father—would be able to read it, but Lilith knew that the giant warriors of the Kalag-ga would all know how to read and write. They would have been instructed by their fathers.

The boy gazed at the box with a mixture of curiosity and reverence. He reached out his hands for it but Lilith jerked it back out of his reach. "Have a care," she warned, "that no one else hears of this or lays eyes on the box. It will go badly for you if you show it to anyone besides the person it is intended for."

With wide eyed consternation the boy accepted the package, carefully holding it in both hands. "Who should I deliver it to?" he asked.

"I want it delivered to the leader of the Kalag-ga warriors. Do you know of whom I speak?"

Abimelech nodded solemnly, but his lips formed into a small smile. It would appear that the boy not only knew of whom she spoke but that he looked up to him as well.

"Asmodeous?" asked the boy.

"Yes," said Lilith, returning the boy's smile. "Asmodeous."

CHAPTER
17

L ilith should have been exhausted but she could have danced all the way back to her village. She couldn't help remembering that last, mortifying journey back from Uruk when Asmodeous humiliated her before the members of the Kalag-ga. That memory made this victory all the sweeter.

She called to mind Asmodeous' proud, handsome face, remembering how his teeth gleamed when he laughed at her. She tried to imagine what his expression would be upon opening her present. He would be taken back at first, examining the dead soldiers' metals in bewilderment. Slowly he would recognize the mark of Lagash on them, but he still wouldn't know how Lilith had come by them, or understand her meaning in sending them to him.

But it wouldn't take long before word of what happened in Lagash got out and then realization would hit. Soon—perhaps even within hours—everyone throughout the region would know about the mysterious events that occurred in Lagash during the night. Confusion would abound. Prophets might even be called forth. No doubt the sons of men would conjure all kinds of mystical possibilities involving the wrath of the gods. Terror would ensue. Guards would be trebled. But the mystery would remain unsolved. How had the gates been breached, and why had the city been spared once it had been laid open?

Lilith laughed. She and Asmodeous were the only two people on earth who would know the answer to those questions. And she hoped those answers would cause him great discomfort. To think that she had single-handedly managed to do what he and his warriors could not. She'd accomplished with cunning what the entire Kalag-ga army couldn't do with all their combined strength. How he would kick himself! Here was someone who could have presented the city of Lagash to him on a silver platter and he had been too proud to accept it simply because she was a woman! What was worse, she had made it even harder for the Kalag-ga warriors to defeat Lagash in the future.

As Lilith approached her village the weariness finally set in. But the grime and filth of the previous night remained on her like a heavy skin. It was around mid-day, which meant most everyone would be resting. This allowed Lilith to slip unheeded into the public bathing area that was designated for the women of her village.

The bathers were sparse this time of day, but there were a few women, mostly older, scattered about. Lilith greeted all of them cheerfully, even the gossips who tended to be the most unkind to her. The women returned her greetings warily, cutting her a wide berth as she happily splashed about in the water. But the slave girls rallied around her to offer assistance, knowing of her generosity when she was in one of her good moods. Lilith giggled ticklishly as they tended to her, oblivious of their confused glances at one another when she wasn't looking. But their thoughts and impressions meant nothing to Lilith. She was entirely absorbed in speculations over her next encounter with the not-so-high-and-mighty leader of the Kalag-ga.

All at once her attention was caught by a conversation she overheard between two of the women.

"They're saying it was a phantom," exclaimed one of them. Lilith moved closer to listen.

"To simply lay open the city and leave it like that! It must be the work of demons."

Lilith's heart beat faster as she listened.

"First the flooding of their fields and now this. They must have angered the gods when they ..."

Lilith couldn't stop the laughter that bubbled forth. The women stared at her in surprise. She moved away from them, hardly able to control her mirth. If the news had already reached their little village she was sure that it had reached the city of Uruk. But even her pleasure over every detail working out exactly as she planned—even better, really—could not keep her from yawning. She was suddenly very tired. She needed to sleep before contemplating her next move.

Lilith dried herself off and then wrapped her body in one of the many colorful scarves her mother had made for her, securing it over her left shoulder as was the custom. She'd had enough of warrior's garb for the moment, and was suddenly pleased by the sight of something pretty. Her thick hair settled luxuriously over her shoulders and back, drying quickly in the hot mid-day sun. The older women stared at her with admiration.

"How beautiful you look!" one of them couldn't help remarking. "Why Lilith, when you dress in women's clothes you're really quite stunning."

Lilith smiled sweetly. "And you're really quite sweet," Lilith replied, shocking the woman with her meek, girlish response and surprising even herself because she actually meant it. She must be more exhausted than she thought. She meandered home and tiptoed through the house to her room. All was quiet in the spacious dwelling. She would not be bothered. She approached her bed with a yawn and was just about to fall into it when she froze. She was suddenly fully awake, all of her senses tingling with living energy. She felt more invigorated than when she first set out on her adventure the day before. Holding her breath, Lilith slowly turned around. Her eyes had not deceived her.

There, like a phantom, sitting casually in a chair mere inches from Lilith's bed, grinning from ear to ear like an overfed cat, was none other than Asmodeous himself!

CHAPTER
18

L ilith gaped at Asmodeous as she struggled to collect her wits. The expression on his face wasn't at all what she was expecting. She sat down on her bed and waited for him to speak.

"You've caught me off guard yet again," he said when he finally spoke. His voice was so husky with lust that it made the hairs on Lilith's neck tingle and rise. "I expected you to be indignant upon finding me here in your private room, yet you sit there like a queen whose been expecting one of her loyal subjects. And...I had completely underestimated your beauty."

Lilith couldn't prevent her eyes from roaming hungrily over his body. Her heart felt as if it was about to burst. She could think of no reason to put up a pretense of not wanting him. What were the moral codes of the sons of men to her?

She wondered how he managed to reach her village before she did. A thought occurred to her.

"Did you come straight from Uruk?" she asked.

"No. I was returning to Uruk from Kish when suddenly I found myself here, in your bedchambers, like a man bewitched."

Lilith gasped when she heard this. So, Asmodeous wasn't aware of what she'd done! Even if he heard about what happened in Lagash he would have no way of connecting it to her. Yet.

But why, then, was he here? Had he changed his mind about letting her into the Kalag-ga?

"I couldn't get you out of my mind," he explained as if reading her thoughts. "And seeing you now..." He left the thought unfinished as he studied her with a determined gleam in his eyes. "You will be my wife and we will populate the earth with such a race of giants that ..."

"Your wife!" exclaimed Lilith, jumping up from the bed. "You mean you didn't change your mind about me being a Kalag-ga warrior?"

"Change my mind?" A laugh burst from his lips. "Lilith, forget that crazy notion and listen to me."

In that instant Lilith made her decision. She approached him like a cat, coming so close that the laughter died on his lips. She was pleased to see that she had momentarily silenced him. His expression told her that he was wary. No doubt he was expecting her to attack him again but she had something entirely different in mind.

Lilith had never been with a man before. But then again, until the previous night she had never killed a man before either. Her lack of experience hadn't affected her performance then and it wouldn't affect her performance now.

Her hands trembled, but she didn't falter. She would seduce Asmodeous, proving her ultimate superiority over him here and now. And she would continue to prove herself, again and again, for as many times as it took until he gave her the respect she deserved.

Lilith decided to keep silent about Lagash. After making love to him, she would reject his insulting offer of marriage and send him away. Returning to Uruk with his tail between his legs, he would then be hit with the full weight of her victory over him. It was even better than she originally planned!

Lilith placed her hands on Asmodeous' arms and gently moved her trembling fingers over every rippling muscle. Her fingertips tingled with each point of contact. Lilith's large, curious eyes stared defiantly into his while she explored his body, first caressing his arms, then moving up over his shoulders and chest, and then brazenly probing even lower. Asmodeous still looked wary, but it seemed as if her touch had paralyzed him. But when Lilith's hands moved under his skirt he suddenly came to life, grasping hold of her wrists and jerking her arms behind her back. He held her there while his eyes searched hers, as if seeking an explanation for her erratic behavior. Lilith's gaze never strayed from his, although she trembled like a leaf in his arms. She was never more aware of his superior strength, and she submitted, for the moment, to his absolute domination of her. It was as if she was melting, becoming softer. It seemed like Asmodeous was softening too. She could see the sudden shift—a slight relenting—in his eyes. A sharp thrill of desire shot through her when his lips finally claimed hers. Her breasts tingled and hardened beneath the thin material of her robe, chafing against the assault of Asmodeous' crushing embrace. Lilith smiled inwardly, luxuriating in his temporary dominance of her while basking in the knowledge of her own secret triumph.

But then all thoughts left her, and Lilith was only aware of the startling pleasure in what Asmodeous was doing to her. She was so dazzled by his lovemaking that even her carefully laid plans were cast aside and scattered, like fallen leaves in a storm.

CHAPTER
19

L ilith's victory was bittersweet. No word came from Asmodeous or the Kalag-ga warriors. There was no one with whom to share her triumph.

Lilith thought about Asmodeous every day, and in spite of his silence, she was convinced that he was thinking of her too. How could he not be?

In considering the long-term effects of her actions, Lilith wondered if she had not only infuriated Asmodeous, but also undermined his authority as leader of the Kalag-ga. It was probable, after all, that the other warriors knew about her gift, especially if the merchant's boy, Abimelech, had buckled under their inevitable bribes to have a look inside the box when he first attempted to deliver it that morning. It was clearly marked with Lilith's name, making it all the harder for them to resist. That was undoubtedly a profitable day for the little delivery boy.

There was only one thing that Lilith knew for certain. Her actions had effectively squashed any designs the Kalag-ga might have had on

Lagash. According to the merchants who came from there, the city's officials had finally called upon the 'gods' for help. They had enlisted the aid of Enlil, an angel who ruled in nearby Nippur, and succumbed to the necessity of having their own giants installed in their city. An alliance was made with Enlil's sons, who promptly moved into Lagash to ward off whatever evil had befallen them.

Lilith had truly dealt the Kalag-ga a devastating blow. She recalled how she had called each and every one of them out as her enemy. They had found it amusing at the time. Yet, in one fell swoop, hadn't she gotten revenge on them all?

Lilith couldn't help being pleased with herself. This was what men understood; this was what made them take note. It took loss, injury and sometimes even death for them to accept an idea that was different from their own. She had wanted to prove that she was their equal and she had gone one better. She had virtually conquered a city while only killing a handful of men, using mostly her wits and their fears to do it. Like all of the men Lilith encountered—excepting her father—the warriors of the Kalag-ga were too dependent on size and strength. She had made them see that cunning could be just as valuable a weapon, if not more.

So Lilith waited, confident that Asmodeous would eventually come to her. But as the time slowly passed, she wondered if her hasty declaration had come true. Perhaps the Kalag-ga warriors did consider her their enemy.

It was two very long months before Lilith got any response, and then it was Og, not Asmodeous, who came to see her.

Og was the youngest of the Kalag-ga warriors at only fifteen years old, but he was by far the largest giant Lilith had ever seen—which was unusual, because Og was the son of a Nephilim, not an angel. It generally occurred that second and third generation giants were smaller than the first. Og was clearly the exception. He was bigger even than his father, Ahijah, who was one of the first Nephilim to walk upon the earth. Ahijah was the son of Semehaza, the infamous leader of the fallen angels. It was Semehaza, along with another angel called Azazyl, who instigated the dissension of the two hundred Watchers. Ahijah was no less renowned than his father as a prominent king in the Syrian empire. From such lineage, one would have expected yet another ambitious leader to have sprung forth, but despite his size, Og was the most mild-mannered giant Lilith ever encountered. He could dissuade any enemy with his sheer size, but it was his sweet, faithful manner that usually won people over.

Standing next to Og, Lilith had a faint idea of how the sons of men must feel. But she wasn't intimidated in the least. She'd sensed his gentleness the moment they met, when he'd been the first to step forward and shyly introduce himself to her. She watched him with interest, wondering what he had come to say.

Not one to mince words, Og got right to the point. In fact, he could hardly contain his joy as he asked if Lilith would honor them by becoming a Kalag-ga warrior. He began questioning her on strategy almost immediately, admitting that their heavy-handed methods were becoming less effective with every day that passed. And of course, he wanted to know how she had managed to get in and out of Lagash without being seen.

"Could Asmodeous not come himself to discuss this with me?" Lilith asked as casually as she could manage. Her excitement over what Og was saying was tempered by her irritation that Asmodeous wasn't the one saying it. Perhaps he was still against her being a Kalag-ga warrior.

"Asmodeous is no longer with us," said Og, and Lilith felt herself go pale. Og continued, oblivious of her distress. "He's a king now. He's got a city of his own called Kiriath Arba. It's west of here, past the great desert, near the Red Sea."

Lilith couldn't believe her ears. She'd made discreet inquiries during the months of waiting, but there had been no mention of Asmodeous leaving the Kalag-ga. And yet, it was inevitable that he move on, once he found a city of his own to rule. One only had to look at Asmodeous to see that he was destined for great things. Lilith couldn't help envying his confident, relaxed manner as head of the Kalag-ga army, and she knew that he would slip into his new role as king with the same ease. He was a natural leader, the first-born son of Azazyl—the angel who masterminded the means for transforming the Watchers into flesh and blood. Under Azazyl's guidance, the angels emerged in the perfect likeness of man, each a flawlessly designed specimen that was irresistible to women. But although they looked like other men, it didn't take long for people to realize that they were different. Their extraordinary knowledge, combined with the peculiar influence they seemed to have over all things—including their fellow creatures—left little doubt of their superiority. And when issues arose, spurned by jealousy, it quickly became evident that these creatures were virtually indestructible. They were the immortal ones, infallible and unforgettable. But they were not oppressive—although they could have been—nor did they appear to possess the tyrannical nature that seemed to be inherent in the sons of men. They ruled, but only when their leadership was desired and the people would benefit from it. They showed no fear, jealousy or anger. They seemed only to want to live on this earth as men do. They did as they pleased, and made it clear that they had no wish to prevent others from doing the same. Whenever they went away their protection remained, and they had an uncanny ability to appear whenever their offspring were in need. Their protectiveness over their children was their only weakness. It was only when defending their families that these angels showed any real capacity to harm, and even then, they preferred to use alternative methods to achieve their goals—bringing forth a great storm, creating a new weapon, or even changing the intentions of an enemy by approaching them in a dream. The angels did not fight or kill in combat. They had neither the desire nor the need.

The angels' offspring, however, were a different matter altogether. The Nephilim were endowed with all the emotions of man, both good and bad, which they inherited from their mothers. Their enormous size and superior strength was a kind of mutation that occurred from the father's side, due perhaps to the fact that the angels themselves were mutations. For although the bodies they created appeared perfect, they were only imitations.

There were, occasionally, other mutations in the Nephilim besides just their size. One of the more common ones was for the giants to have extra extremities, such as fingers and toes, additional limbs, or in rare cases, a second head. The more sever the defect the less frequently it occurred, but there existed Nephilim who were so disfigured as to be labeled monsters, even by the other giants. There were behavioral abnormalities as well. Some of the Nephilim had a higher propensity for violence, and a few even exhibited a disturbing inclination to feed on human flesh. These monsters, or "terrors" as they were dubbed, generally kept their distance from the rest of society and little, therefore, was actually known about them aside from the rumors. When Lilith was a little girl she asked her father about them but he quickly changed the subject, pretending to be a monster himself as he chased her around the room and then tickled her until she cried. Shortly after that her father went away, and it wasn't until he was gone that Lilith realized he hadn't answered her questions.

And now Asmodeous had gone away too, leaving her with even more unanswered questions.

Lilith had been so sure that she and Asmodeous would meet again. She'd anticipated it as an inevitable pleasure that awaited her. It had become one of her favorite pastimes to speculate on how that meeting would occur. She made up scenarios in her mind, imagining what he would say and how she would respond. Her inexperienced heart ached at his apparent rejection of her. It hurt more, even, than when her father went away.

Was she to be like other women, after all? Lilith thought being a Kalag-ga warrior was what she wanted, yet she wasn't nearly as happy as she thought she would be. She couldn't help comparing herself with her sister, Ninsun, who, at the age of ten, fell madly in love with Lugalbanda, the angel who ruled Uruk. They had gone to see the city, but Ninsun spent all her time with Lugalbanda, trailing him like a forlorn puppy and following his every move with her large, expressive eyes. Years later she could still draw forth his image in great detail, calling to mind his unfathomably dark eyes, his smooth, velvety skin, his sumptuous lips and his lean, splendid form. She insisted that he spoke to her in her dreams. Nothing could dissuade her from wanting to be with him, not even her being a giant. He was, after all, an angel who could take any form he liked. She clung tenaciously to her dream and, years later, when Lugalbanda finally came for her, it seemed as if Ninsun would explode with joy.

Lilith wondered why the realization of her childhood dream wasn't as satisfying as Ninsun's.

She was a Kalag-ga warrior. Yet as Lilith discussed strategies with Og, resentment against Asmodeous simmered hotly beneath her cool exterior. So! The mighty son of Azazel, former leader of the Kalag-ga, couldn't face her! A small part of her wondered if he might have simply forgotten her, but she couldn't accept that she'd meant so little to him. He had, after all, asked her to become his wife. For her part, Lilith regretted all the wasted months spent thinking about him.

But more than anything else, Lilith resented the power Asmodeous still seemed to have over her. Here it was at last, her long awaited dream of being a Kalag-ga warrior. And yet, somehow, Asmodeous had managed to completely ruin it for her.

CHAPTER
20

Present Day

Nadia sighed, suddenly tired. She'd been so wrapped up in Lilith's story she had no idea how many hours had passed. "May I take a break?" she asked.

"Yeah, let's do that," agreed Will. They all got up to stretch and Nadia walked over to the window, resenting the chain more than ever. It was still dark outside.

"What time is it?" she wondered.

"It's very early here—around four a.m. Sunday morning," said Will, glancing at his watch. "Its seven hours earlier in New York though, so it's still Saturday night there."

"I'm starved!" announced Clive. "How about cooking up one of your specialties, Gordon?"

Nadia turned to Gordon in surprise and he laughed. "I'm not a bad cook," he admitted with a shrug.

"I'm gonna check in," said Will, leaving the room.

"What kind of food do you cook?" Nadia asked.

"Mostly Italian," he replied, surprising her again.

"I would have guessed Indian," she said with a wry smile.

He laughed. "I can prepare Indian cuisine too," he said, abruptly switching to his Indian accent. "But Clive, he does not like it. He says it disrupts his *chakras*."

"Make the meatballs again," suggested Clive. "With the sauce and garlic bread."

"Mmm, that sounds good," agreed Nadia, salivating at the thought. It had been a long time since breakfast.

"There's more of that meat in the freezer," Clive told Gordon, and then he turned to Nadia to add—"They have some kind of mystery meat here—don't ask me what it is—but it sure is tasty!"

"Its ground lamb," said Gordon. "For the hundredth time, it's ground lamb."

"I guess we'll never know," said Clive, lying down on the couch. He began humming a tune under his breath again. It was the one from the day before. As she listened, Nadia tried to place it. It was definitely a 'golden oldie,' the kind of song she would never expect Clive to know, let alone go around humming all the time. As she followed Gordon into the kitchen she quietly hummed along, trying to put words to the music. Gordon turned and gave her a strange look, just kind of staring at her for a moment, and then resumed what he had been doing, which is taking a package of meat out of the freezer and placing it in the microwave.

"Clive refuses to accept that he's eating lamb," Gordon said conversationally. "For some reason it bothers him." Nadia looked at Clive, still lying on the couch, humming, and was yet again struck by how peculiar these men were. Gordon, meanwhile, took out a large bowl and began pulling ingredients out of the refrigerator as if nothing was out of the ordinary. In fact, with the exception of the chain dragging behind her everywhere she went, the situation felt more like a laid-back camping trip than a kidnapping.

She watched while Gordon chopped an onion. He was quick and skillful with the knife, in that way that people who cook a lot are.

"Do you really believe in all this?" she asked him. "That angels came out of the sky and fathered giants with the women of earth?"

"I do," Gordon said. "I don't know if they were angels as we think of them. Maybe they were aliens from another planet. Much of the science community seems to think that. Whatever they were, they came from somewhere else and brought knowledge we didn't have."

"How can you be so sure of that?" Nadia asked.

"Because historically speaking, it fits," he said. "We know something happened back then, not just because the people wrote about it in their ancient records but because they *had* ancient records to begin with. Here they are, claiming creatures are coming out of the sky and teaching them things like how to write and suddenly they're *writing*! No one had written anything before. Maybe hundreds of thousands of years go by with no writing. The writing came with the claims of these visitors. And there were other things too. They go from hunting and gathering to setting up irrigation systems…and even storing food for the future!" Nadia couldn't help thinking of her great-grandfather as Gordon grew more enthusiastic. The two would have had a lot to talk about. "They formed communities, creating our very first cities and governments," Gordon continued. "They learned how to protect themselves, using armor and even building walls around their cities. They invented the wheel, arithmetic, the calendar, smelting and the plow. Even jewelry and make-up were introduced during that time. This wasn't just a period of growth; this was the *beginning* of life as we know it."

"People back then were little more than superstitious in-breeders," added Clive, who had joined them in the kitchen at some point. "Barely more sophisticated than cattle. The only culture they had was bacteria. Even after they learned to write they had no idea what was going on around them. Their version of what was happening proves this. Irrigation systems are going in all over the place, and these nitwits are still thinking their harvest depends on the gods. Think about it. Those people didn't do this shit on their own. No way."

"Someone—or some*thing*—was helping them," agreed Gordon, picking up where Clive left off. "Something with a much higher level of intelligence. They've found astrological drawings from that period that include constellations *we* didn't discover until the nineteen-seventies."

Will walked in just then. "You've been granted a reprieve," he told Nadia. "They're chasing some other leads while you help us work this angle."

"Lucky me," she replied, but Will didn't appear to hear her. Nadia noticed, suddenly, how anxious he looked. It was almost as if there really was a 'they' working on some big 'attack.'

"It's so hard to believe," she couldn't help remarking. "Giants! And djinn!"

"You sure have a good memory for someone who doesn't even believe the stories," observed Clive.

"Just because I didn't believe they were a hundred percent true doesn't mean I didn't enjoy them," she said. "I loved hearing my grandmother's stories, and I suppose I did kind of believe them at first. But...I don't know. I grew up. I went to college. The more I learned the more improbable they seemed. And my poor grandmother went through a lot. In retrospect—especially after taking psychology— I figured she made up the stories as a way of working through the trauma of what happened to her."

They all watched hungrily as Gordon rolled his mixture into small balls and gently lowered them into a large frying pan containing about an inch or so of hot oil. The meatballs sizzled when they hit the oil. He stirred them lightly to brown them on all sides.

"There's plenty of evidence to support the claim that giants existed here on the earth," Gordon told her. "Their depicted in literature and art found in many ancient cultures, spanning hundreds of years. Giants are mentioned in the bible, and discussed in greater detail in the writings of Enoch and Jubilees. Solomon wrote about the djinn, as your grandmother pointed out." Gordon opened the oven and took out a tray of steaming garlic bread. "Nowadays we tend to shun all unexplained phenomenon, preferring to ignore it altogether rather than having to accept knowing only half the story."

"Archaeologists have found ancient steles from all over the Middle East, depicting battles where one or more of the soldiers are almost twice the size of the other soldiers," added Will. "Rather than taking the pictures at face value, the science community prefers to theorize that these larger than life individuals represent personages of high importance, such as kings."

"What I'd like to know is how they coordinated that," said Clive. "No internet, no phones...yet somehow we're supposed to believe that all these different people, thousands of miles apart, were using the same symbolism in their art."

"It just goes to show that we haven't advanced as much as we like to think," concluded Gordon. "We still cling to what we want to believe, whether it's a scientific theory or a superstition—they're both remarkably similar—and ignore any evidence to the contrary."

Gordon handed out plates and the conversation stopped while they each took a serving of food. Nadia's mouth watered as she piled the steaming meatballs onto the thick Italian bread and then drenched it with red sauce. She topped it with grated cheese and sat down at the kitchen table to eat.

"Your grandmother's stories are truly amazing," said Gordon. "I can't believe you've kept them to yourself all these years."

"I guess they are pretty amazing...whether they're true or not," she agreed.

"And to think," Gordon continued. "You may be the only surviving person who knows what happened there."

"It gives me goose bumps," said Clive, and Nadia cocked her eyebrow at him. "I'm serious!" he insisted. "Look!" And he held out his arm. But there were no goose bumps and he laughed when she looked.

"Note how even the smallest details of your story fit," Gordon continued, ignoring Clive. "I mean, according to ancient records, Lagash really did have an ongoing rival with the city of Kish, who used to destroy their irrigation systems and cause serious famines. And here we are, getting a first-hand account of it from someone who was actually there!"

Nadia envied Gordon his absolute conviction that her grandmother's stories were true. Surely he realized that her grandmother could have gotten that information about Lagash from the history books just as easily as he had done. She supposed all beliefs—whether founded in religion, science or history—produced a similar ability to turn every piece of evidence to its advantage. Yet this didn't necessarily make those beliefs false, did it?

"It is kind of freaky," agreed Clive. "You know, even that bit about covering up the women to hide them from the angels, or aliens, or whatever the fuck those horny bastards were. I bet that's where the whole Muslim covering-up-their-bitches-shit started."

"My grandmother thought the same thing," said Nadia. "Though I don't think she put it quite that way…" Her voice trailed off as she took another bite of her meatball sandwich. The food was delicious. She almost said so but stopped herself. *Easy Patty*, the voice warned. *You're starting to get a bit too comfortable here.* But it was strange how easy it was to identify with one's kidnappers—at least in Nadia's case. Was she crazy or were they actually beginning to make the tiniest bit of sense?

"And then there's Lilith herself," Gordon continued, growing more animated as the conversation went on. "In Hebrew folklore she's thought to be the first woman on earth. This explains where that idea might have stemmed from—she was the first *Nephilim* woman. We may be the only people on earth who know this!"

Nadia thought about it. It was true. Who else would know Lilith's story?

"It's exhilarating!" exclaimed Gordon, blushing suddenly, because Clive and Will were giving him looks. "I'm sorry," he said, reverting to the Indian accent again. "But I cannot help being fascinated by Lilith, even if she is an evil djinn bent on destroying humanity."

Nadia couldn't contain a smile until her eyes met Will's, who was watching her, and the smile dropped away.

"And let's not forget Og," Gordon went on, oblivious to everything but the topic. "He, too, has been traced back to Uruk."

"What about the Kalag-ga warriors?" asked Nadia. "Is there anything in the historical records about them?"

"Not that I know of," said Gordon. "But we'll definitely be putting them in our system for future reference. We knew that the giants had conquered many of the cities throughout that region. And we also knew that Uruk—today's Iraq—was inundated with giants at one time, just like Lilith said. In fact, one of the rulers of the old city's official 'king's list' was a giant."

"You mean Gilgamesh," said Nadia.

"Yeah!" said Gordon, surprised. "How'd you know?"

"And I suppose you also know that the oldest piece of literature on earth—the very first story ever told, some archaeologists say—is *The Epic of Gilgamesh*." She smiled at the expression on his face. "I looked him up in college. The story says Gilgamesh was two thirds god and one third man."

"Yes, that's right," said Gordon. "I always wondered what that meant because a regular Nephilim would have been half-god, half-man...it doesn't make any sense."

"Sure it does," replied Nadia. "His father was an angel and his mother was a Nephilim. So he was part 'god' on *both* his father's and his mother's sides, making him two parts god. However, his mother was also half human, so he was one part man."

"I don't recall it saying anywhere that Gilgamesh's mother was a Nephilim," interjected Will. "How do you know that?"

Nadia gave him a smug smile. "Because that's where Lilith's story picks up next, nearly two decades later."

Supreme over other kings, lordly in appearance,
he is the hero, born of Uruk, the goring wild bull.
He walks out in front, the leader,
and walks at the rear, trusted by his companions.

— THE EPIC OF GILGAMESH

.

CHAPTER
21

Ancient Mesopotamia
The city of Uruk
Nineteen years later

L ilith spun around and quickly thrust forward her dagger. But she was not quick enough. Her opponent had anticipated her move and cut off her attack, slamming his own dagger into hers with such force that it was flung from her hand.

She was momentarily stunned but then she threw back her head and laughed. "Did you see that?" she yelled to her sister, Ninsun, who was watching them from a few yards away.

"Very impressive!" agreed Ninsun.

"He's sharpened his skills while I was away," Lilith declared. Her eyes gleamed with pride as she examined her nephew anew. "You've been working hard, young Gil," she praised.

"Lilith, Gilgamesh! Come and sit down!" cried Ninsun.

"Okay, okay," agreed Lilith. But she could see that Gilgamesh was only getting warmed up and this made her laugh again.

"He's trying to work up the courage to ask if you'll help him get into the Kalag-ga," said Lilith's sister.

Lilith looked at Gilgamesh and he blushed with agitation.

"I'm able to speak for myself, mother," he complained.

"Is this true?" Lilith asked him.

Now that the cat was out of the bag Gilgamesh thrust out his chest and faced Lilith squarely. "I would make a fine warrior," he insisted, as if he expected her to argue the point. Lilith looked at him wistfully. She couldn't help thinking of herself at that age.

"I'll take you to our leader first thing tomorrow," she said.

"Really?" And suddenly he was just her nephew again. He rushed at Lilith and, before she could react, lifted her up off the ground as if she were no more than a child herself. He whirled her round and round, ignoring her shrieks to stop.

And neither Lilith nor the Kalag-ga regretted bringing Gilgamesh into the fold. He singled himself out early on, so that he was not just a Kalag-ga warrior, he was Gilgamesh. His feats on the battlefield were legendary. He was always the first to strike and the last to retreat. He was a hero who commanded fear as well as admiration. Songs and poems were written about him on the walls of Uruk. Having angels on both sides of his family tree, he was considered mightier than other Nephilim. He was more of a god than a man.

In a very short time, and without anyone really even noticing it was happening, Gilgamesh became the leader of the Kalag-ga. Under his direction the Kalag-ga took many cities, spreading the giants' dominion over the desert and west of Sumer, into the foreign lands of Syria, and reaching as far as the great sea. Many of the warriors would leave the Kalag-ga army to rule the cities that were conquered. It was only a matter of time before Gilgamesh would want a city of his own.

Gilgamesh's father, Lugalbanda, had ruled Uruk for many years but like most angels he became restless when confined to one place for too long. He was a well-loved king and under his rule the city had prospered. It was only natural that his son would follow him to the throne. Gilgamesh became king of Uruk.

But Gilgamesh was not as popular a king as he had been a warrior. His ruthlessness and arrogance—both of which had served him well on the battlefield—made for an oppressive ruler. Missing the thrill of combat, Gilgamesh forced his subjects to fight him. He exhausted the sons of men through fighting and forced labor, and then added insult to injury by decreeing for himself a 'lord's right' to be the first to bed all of Uruk's new brides. His brutal treatment outraged the people of Uruk. Once again Gilgamesh's exploits became legendary, but this time they were repeated with horror and loathing. More songs and poems emerged, but these were not nearly as flattering as the earlier ones. A general outcry arose as the people of Uruk loudly petitioned the gods. Their songs gave voice to their lament; *"Gilgamesh does not leave a son to his father…nor does he leave a girl to her mother!"*

Lilith, too, had heard of her nephew's mistreatment of the people of Uruk. Although she had little sympathy for the sufferings of the sons of men, Gilgamesh's infamy troubled her. It would not do for one arrogant leader to characterize them all. Most of the cities thrived under the care of the giants. Lilith wondered if she should speak to Gilgamesh. She petitioned Anu about it but he had yet to come to her in her dreams. Then one night she returned from the battlefield to find her father there, in the flesh, waiting for her.

"Father!" she cried in surprise. How many years had it been? Far too many, she decided. Her father looked exactly the same as the day he left, which was to be expected, but it amazed her all the same. She knew that she hadn't changed either, at least not since reaching adulthood—nor would she for a long time.

Anu greeted his daughter with unmistakable pride shining in his eyes while Lilith marveled over his untouched beauty. She lingered awhile in the abundance of pleasure his presence brought, even though she knew he had come for a reason. Something was clearly weighing on his mind. She wondered if it had anything to do with Gilgamesh.

"What is it father?" she asked him at last.

Anu's beautiful features were distorted from anxiety.

"I fear for our future," he told her. "Our position on this earth is not secure."

"What…do you mean?" asked Lilith, alarmed.

"We—the angels—were never authorized to come here. Not as we are now, at any rate. We were sent here as spirits to watch over the earth. We were to sound the alarm if anything threatened mankind's existence. We were not born of this earth, nor were we meant to reside here." He struck himself in the chest. "Our flesh isn't even real!"

"I don't understand," Lilith said. "How then, were you able to produce children?"

"I don't know." He looked at her. "But surely you've noticed that you're different from the others!"

"Yes, of course, but I thought we were just special...you know, children of the gods."

"I am not a god," said Anu. "Like the sons of men, I am simply one of His creations."

"But why should you worry about it now, father?" Lilith wondered.

Anu sighed heavily. Every word he uttered seemed to cause him more distress. "There has been a great outcry from the sons of men. They feel oppressed by the children of angels. They dispute our right to be here. Even the souls of their dead cry out for retribution."

"How do you know this?"

"I hear them in my dreams. I fear that the Others will hear them as well."

"The others?"

A gleam of genuine fear came into in Anu's eyes. "The angels who sent us here to begin with."

"But why should the sons of men cry out against us?" cried Lilith.

"You need to ask?" he replied, not unkindly.

Lilith huffed. "They were killing each other before we were even born to this earth," she said defensively. "We only kill to conquer, and once we take over a city, we improve and protect it. The people are allowed to grow and prosper. That would never happen if they were left to their own devices. Why, they would kill one another for simply thinking different thoughts! They would just keep killing each other until every single one of them was destroyed."

"Perhaps," he allowed. "But what of the abuses?"

Lilith knew he was speaking of Gilgamesh, and she felt the need to defend her nephew. "It's true that the Nephilim aren't perfect. But overall, I think we are kinder and more tolerant than the sons of men. Every one oppresses the other. Look at how they treat their women!"

"Yes but we have a higher standard. We were not placed here by God. We must prove our right to be here. We must be able to show that we will benefit mankind!"

"That's not fair!" Lilith was becoming afraid. "We're the descendants of man too."

"That was our original hope, but I'm afraid it isn't the case. It's more than just your size. Your...souls aren't like theirs either. They don't go where their souls go when you die."

Lilith stared at her father. "What do you mean? Where do our souls go?" she asked, a chill running over her.

"Nowhere," he replied slowly. "They stay here. I'm afraid...there are so many things you don't know."

The fighter in Lilith rose up. "What can we do?"

"You...the Kalag-ga warriors, must protect the sons of men from the worst of your kind," he said. When Lilith didn't object he continued. "In the mountains, north of here, and in other hiding places you can find the Emim. They are monsters. They do unspeakable things. It's the spirits of their dead that cry out the loudest."

Lilith had heard of them. The sons of men called them the 'terrors' and the 'biters.'

"We will destroy them," Lilith said with a simple finality that made Anu smile, his pride in her rekindled.

"And there's something else," he said after a moment. He seemed suddenly very weary.

"What is it father?" she prompted.

"Gilgamesh," he began.

Lilith's heart stopped. Although she was more concerned than ever over Gilgamesh's behavior, especially after what her father just told her, she couldn't help jumping to his defense. "Gil is just restless in Uruk! I'll talk to him. We'll bring him back into the Kalag-ga to fight the Emim. The sons of men will come to admire him again."

"Perhaps. But I feel the people of Uruk need to see Gilgamesh rebuked. I am sending a powerful adversary to challenge him. His name is Enkido and he is Gilgamesh's equal in all respects. He will not kill Gilgamesh, but he will influence him for the better. They will become friends and Gilgamesh will lose interest in the people of Uruk."

Anu's visit filled Lilith with foreboding. She'd never felt this kind of fear before. It was impossible to believe that she and the other Nephilim had been rejected by the One who created the earth and everything in it. Except them.

Where else could they go?

CHAPTER
22

Although Lilith hadn't seen Asmodeous for nearly twenty years, she'd heard much of him and the city he now ruled. She had avoided that city in her many travels with the Kalagga, but she couldn't keep her ears from perking up whenever it was mentioned.

Kiriath Arba was named after the angel who founded the city; its name literally meant, 'the city belonging to Arba.' Arba was a loved and respected 'god' to his followers, and under his direction Kiriath Arba flourished. Like the other angels, he took a wife and produced a Nephilim son, Anak. The son was curiously beautiful like his father, with perfect, angelic features and long, graceful limbs. From infancy it was clear that Anak would be lean and tall, rather than stocky and muscular like so many of the Nephilim males. Later, his name would come to mean 'long-necked' in reference to his gazelle like beauty, and all of his descendants would be called *Anakim* after him because they shared his slender stature and pleasing features.

Now Anak, though strong, was not inclined to fight like other giants. In fact, he had no wish to conquer, unless it involved the weaker sex. He was obsessed with being a great lover, and it appeared that he meant to single-handedly populate the earth with his *Anakim* while his fellow giants were busy occupying cities. It was his father's wish that Anak would eventually rule Kiriath Arba, but Anak showed no interest in that either. His sole concern was women, and when he grew restless with the women of Kiriath Arba, he discovered a new interest in travel. He went out in all directions, seducing women from all corners, and bringing the ones he liked best back to Kiriath Arba— often heavy with child. He claimed to fall deeply in love with each and every one of them, and gave them his full attention for as long as his ardor lasted. He built a new castle for each new wife, where he would live with her for a time. But he would inevitably grow bored, and soon after he would take himself off on another journey. He would not be heard from again until he returned with yet another exotic flower to add to his collection. His wives were many, and sometimes he gave them two and even three children before leaving. Surprisingly, these wives didn't resent him. He was so utterly charming and generous that they couldn't help feeling appreciative. They were left to fend for themselves, true, but they were granted more wealth and freedom than they could ever have wished for. They were allowed—and even encouraged—to take another husband if they so desired, and the people of Kiriath Arba treated them like queens.

It was no small surprise when, after another such journey, Anak returned with Asmodeous instead of a wife.

Asmodeous met Anak while crossing the Negev Desert with the Kalag-ga to get to the southwestern regions surrounding the red sea. The Kalag-ga warriors were tremendously efficient travelers. They were so well equipped that they could journey through even the worst conditions in absolute comfort. On longer trips they were apt to let stray wanderers join them, provided they were interesting or could contribute to the group in some way. Anak was as good-natured and amusing a travel companion as one could hope for, and he came with an entire entourage of his own. He had everything, from cooks to scribes to dancers. A few of the Kalag-ga warriors found Anak's obsession with women odd, but Asmodeous—who was also known for his romantic nature—could find no fault in Anak's opinion on the matter. No doubt they shortened many a long night at the fire by reliving accounts of their numerous conquests. Lilith wondered if Asmodeous ever mentioned her. It was shortly after their little tryst in her village that he and Anak met.

At some point during that journey Anak decided that Asmodeous was the man to rule Kiriath Arba in his place.

The city of Kiriath Arba was located on the south-western bank of the Dead Sea in the land of the Canaanites. It was a high, mountainous region with rich earth that boasted of large trees and a wide variety of foliage above ground, as well as precious stones and minerals below. Merchants from the city sold as much wine and marble as the surrounding cities could buy. Kiriath Arba was a favorite among traders.

Lilith was glad that Asmodeous had done so well for himself.

There was another city at the northern bank of the Dead Sea, not far from Kiriath Arba, called Jericho. This city was situated in a low valley, rich with fragrant desert flowers that were continuously in bloom and cooled by the palm trees that fanned them from overhead. Jericho had thus far managed to evade the influence of the angels and the control of the giants. Early on, with the first rumors of these demonic influences (as their religious leaders termed them) the entire populace went to work to safeguard their city. The walls were doubled in height, the merchants began limiting their trade to other, non-tainted cities and a new army, specializing in the slaying of demons, was put into force. The women of Jericho were covered from head to foot, so that not a glimpse of them could be had from any evil spirits hovering overhead. In spite of all these precautions, the people of Jericho lived in constant fear of being invaded, and every young man knew how to use a battle axe by the age of ten.

But none of Jericho's efforts could begin to prepare them for the Emim. These giants were more fearsome than anything that had ever been encountered on earth. Many of the Emim had settled in the Lebanon Mountains where they fed off wild animals, but in times of scarcity they would roam out into the nearby regions, always traveling by night, to leave a trail of death and terror in their wake. On one such night, one of these Emim somehow managed to scale the great wall of Jericho, making it over the top and down the other side without anyone sounding the alarm. The monster then opened the gates so that his companions could enter the city. Like a pack of hungry wolves they crept into the houses, killing most of the occupants in their sleep by viciously ripping apart their necks with their teeth and then feasting on their flesh as if it were succulent fruit. By morning the Emim were gone, but the terror remained. The survivors were at a loss. None of their safeguards had kept the demons out. After much vehement arguing over the matter, it was decided that the warrior giants were the lesser of two evils. At least the Kalag-ga offered protection. A messenger was sent out to enlist their help.

Meanwhile, word got out of what happened at Jericho, and people were already pouring in from other parts of the region to see if the rumors were true. Asmodeous, coming up from Kiriath Arba with a large army of both men and giants, was among the first to arrive. He and his men were welcomed with open arms and treated like kings. It was easy to see that the people were terrified and desperate for protection. And it was little wonder. Even Asmodeous, who had witnessed every kind of horror on the battlefield, was sickened by what he saw. The Emim had gorged themselves on the entrails of men, women and children alike.

By the time the Kalag-ga warriors arrived, the city of Jericho was overrun with neighboring armies, both giant and otherwise. In spite of the recent horror, there was a peculiarly joyous atmosphere in Jericho. Perhaps it was due, in part, to the temporary relief of being so well protected by soldiers. As well, the warriors tended to be full of cheer when they were not engaged in battle. Everyone accepted the reprieve, and if the people of Jericho noticed their storehouses being depleted, they didn't utter a single complaint.

Lilith was perhaps the only one there who was filled with trepidation. She remained edgy and anxious despite her efforts to unwind from the long, tedious journey into Jericho. To make matters worse, she knew the city was buzzing with rumors about her arrival. In her years with the Kalag-ga, she'd become accustomed to the extra interest she stirred as a female warrior. Sometimes she even enjoyed it. She knew that the ones who criticized her the most envied her in secret. She was first, a great warrior and second, a great beauty—in that order. And wasn't that exactly what she wanted to be since she was a little girl?

She had no regrets. But for the first time in her life Lilith felt unsure of herself. And it was because of Asmodeous. She knew that he was there, without anyone having to tell her. She could feel his presence. Her awareness of him troubled her.

As Lilith took extra pains with her appearance she told herself repeatedly that she didn't care. She had experienced the touch of countless lovers since Asmodeous and in her opinion they were all pretty similar, give or take one little detail or another. What did any of it matter?

She knew that she was beautiful, fascinating and successful. All eyes would be on her, and yet it was with dread that Lilith finally went out to meet Og and Gilgamesh so that they could join the great feast that was being held in their honor.

"What took you so long?" Gilgamesh complained irritably. But Og gave her an encouraging smile and she wondered how much he had surmised about her and Asmodeous. Enkido, Anu's promised companion for Gilgamesh, stood silently off to one side. As in their previous encounters, Lilith's eyes lingered on him a moment longer than was necessary. There was something all at once eerie and enthralling in Enkido's appearance. His eyes were an unnatural blue, and glowed like a creature of the night. His hair was long and thick, and nearly white. He was unlike anyone Lilith had seen before. He was lean and quick and unspeakably beautiful. He reminded Lilith of a wild beast—a tiger perhaps. She heard that he had spent his life in a wild forest, living among the animals. She wondered if this was true. He was painfully shy around women, particularly Lilith. She never once heard him speak, but she'd already been impressed by his performance on the battlefield.

"We're holding up dinner," Og reminded her gently, and Lilith realized that she was more nervous about seeing Asmodeous than she was to go into battle with the Emim! Indeed, she would rather face an army of the 'dreadful ones' than to behold that mocking smile at her expense. The old hurt over being so thoroughly rejected rose up in her again. It occurred to her that he might be married now, and a tremor of anguish went through her. Og had taken her arm and he looked at her with concern. Lilith bit her lip. She merely had to get through the night.

Lilith spotted Asmodeous the instant she stepped into the crowded hall. It was as if he was the only person there. At the sight of him she faltered, but Og held her steady. Gilgamesh was speaking to her but she couldn't comprehend what he was saying. It mightn't have been so bad if Asmodeous hadn't seen her too, but their eyes met simultaneously and their gazes remained locked. She didn't even realize until it was too late that Og was leading her straight to him—to the empty seats that were conspicuously left open on either side of him. She turned to Og to protest.

"It was Asmodeous who brought you into the Kalag-ga all those years ago," he told her, adding in an even lower voice—"And it was for you that he left." Lilith stared at him in astonishment. But she was holding up the procession.

Asmodeous stood up as Lilith moved to sit down beside him. His eyes never, for a moment, left her face. She tried to compose herself. She knew they must be drawing curious looks but she couldn't seem to tear her eyes away, and Asmodeous appeared to have no desire to look anywhere else.

Lilith swallowed hard, willing herself to be strong. It wasn't as if she'd spent all those years pining after him. She'd led a full, exciting life without Asmodeous. But Og's words were echoing in her head, making it seem as if their last encounter had been only moments before. All of the anger she'd accumulated over the years was dissolving like salt in warm water. She suddenly realized why none of her other lovers had been able to capture her heart. It had been here, with Asmodeous all the time.

Yet a part of her was still hurt that he never tried to reach her.

"It feels like just yesterday when we last…spoke," he murmured softly, for her alone to hear.

"Yes," she agreed, having just thought the same thing herself.

"I've heard one story after another about 'Lilith, the mighty warrior,'" he continued, and Lilith was surprised to see real pride shining in his eyes. "You're a legend."

Lilith bit her lip and cursed herself inwardly for the tears that were filling her eyes.

"Don't," he whispered. "We'll talk later."

She reached for her goblet of wine with an unsteady hand.

Like a wild boar bursting out from the underbrush, Gilgamesh's boisterous voice suddenly startled her, making her jump.

"Lilith, what is it? Are you ill?" he demanded.

All eyes turned to the beautiful warrior woman they'd been trying not to stare at.

"No Gil," she replied with surprising lightness, considering her inner turmoil. "I'm not ill, only half starved from waiting for you to finish taming those precious locks of yours." Gilgamesh's thick curls were renowned, often even mentioned in the songs and poems that were written about him. He half frowned, half smiled at her teasing while ripples of laughter broke out around the table.

The evening meal was served, but Lilith could barely swallow a bite, and it was a struggle just to get through the long, tedious ordeal. She had but one thought in her mind. She couldn't wait to be alone again with Asmodeous.

CHAPTER
23

"Lilith—"

They had finally escaped the noisy hall and made their way into Lilith's tent. Asmodeous had her pinned on the bed, his hands gently cradling either side of her face as he gazed into her eyes.

"Lilith," he murmured huskily again.

Lilith's heart ached with longing and she closed her eyes to escape the overwhelming feelings that the sight of Asmodeous awakened. No one else had ever affected her so. Her hands instinctively moved up toward his, caressing them while they caressed her face. She opened her eyes to see that his too were brimming with emotion. Lilith could see the same anguish, yearning and expectation that she felt, mirrored there. They simply looked at each other in a kind of startled daze.

Asmodeous' voice was heavy with passion when he finally spoke. "Have you had enough of being a warrior yet?"

But Lilith didn't have the opportunity to answer, because in the next instant his lips were crushing hers. Suddenly all the pent-up desire from years of longing seemed to erupt in her, bursting forth with an explosion of pleasure so acute it was almost paralyzing. She surrendered to it completely, wrapping her arms around Asmodeous' neck and clinging to him feverishly as she responded instinctively to his kisses. His hands began moving over her, unabashedly exploring her body. And then they were tearing at each other's clothing, fumbling for the other's warm flesh in greedy anticipation, racing toward the pleasure that awaited them.

The passion between them was as strong as ever. No sooner had one fire been extinguished than another began raging even hotter. Lilith couldn't seem to get enough of him. She wanted more—more of his touch, more of his taste, more of his smell. When Asmodeous fell back, momentarily spent, she spun around and mounted him, brazenly, and with an air of command, just as she would mount a horse, and just as easily coaxing him into action. She felt no hesitation or shyness—not with Asmodeous! Her desire was much too strong.

When at last the fiercest part of the storm had passed, they both lay silent and exhausted, luxuriating in the warm and tranquil afterglow. Lilith felt a strange, simple happiness she never felt before. Was this love? All those years ago she had thought her ambition exceeded her desire for Asmodeous. She'd been obsessed with being a Kalag-ga warrior. Asmodeous knew it. And he helped her!

Lilith turned toward Asmodeous and found his eyes on her.

"You were the one who told them to make me a warrior," she said.

"Yes." He reached out a hand and very carefully lifted a lock of hair from her cheek.

"But then you left. Why?"

Asmodeous sighed. He just stared at her for a long moment. He seemed reluctant to answer her question. "Because I didn't think we could both be warriors," he finally replied.

"But why?" Lilith wondered. Fighting side by side with Asmodeous had been a secret fantasy of hers. Sometimes she imagined him saving her life; other times she imagined saving his. Were men's egos so fragile they couldn't ever let a woman win?

"Let's just say I didn't think I'd be able to take my eyes off you long enough to get a look at the enemy," he said with a mischievous grin. His hand was now lightly caressing her breast.

"No," Lilith protested, pushing his hand away. "I want to know the real reason."

"That is the real reason, Lilith" he insisted. He became serious again as he tried to explain. "I really couldn't see myself turning my back on you in a battle. Every dagger I heard meeting flesh, every death cry would have had me searching the field for you. I would never have been able to concentrate on what I was doing."

Lilith was speechless. And yet, she knew he spoke the truth. Hadn't she felt similarly the first day young Gilgamesh joined them in battle? She remembered hanging back, retreating, in order to keep an eye on him. But in Gilgamesh's case, she immediately realized that her worries were unfounded. He was a far better warrior than Lilith was. But to think that Asmodeous would actually give up being a warrior so that she could be one, both amazed and humbled her. Tears once again filled her eyes.

"It wasn't that much of a sacrifice," he said when he saw the tears. He smiled wryly, and then assumed a tone of mock long-suffering. "It's not so bad being the king of a great city," he sighed as his finger— very cautiously—lifted one of the tears from her cheek. "Of course it would be better if I had my queen with me."

Lilith couldn't stop the tears from falling but she firmly kept all other outward signs of distress in check. She shrugged, trying to make her own voice sound casual. "What authority does any queen have?" she asked with mock disdain, as if she could hardly imagine such a lowly position for herself.

Asmodeous held back his smile and shrugged as well. "Not much I'm afraid," he agreed, playing along. But his face suddenly lit up, as if something important occurred to him. "You'd have the final say in what I eat for dinner!" He announced with a hopeful grin.

"Ah!" cried Lilith. "That is indeed a tempting offer. I could trade in my dagger for poison!" She pretended to consider it.

Asmodeous looked wounded. "Must you always be killing someone?" he asked.

Lilith laughed. "Yes," she replied.

Asmodeous grabbed her, pulling her into his arms and holding her there while he covered her face with kisses. Lilith pretended to protest, but she loved being locked in the warmth of his embrace. "I could show you something better," he whispered huskily in her ear, pressing his hardness against her as if to emphasize his meaning. She felt herself responding and wholeheartedly agreed.

"What if we were to compromise?" Lilith suggested afterwards.

"Compromise!" Asmodeous rose up on one elbow, his expression filled with alarm. "Maybe you should wait until the effects of my lovemaking wear off before you say anymore," he suggested.

Lilith laughed. She couldn't remember ever feeling as happy or content as she did just then. Perhaps she had been affected by what occurred that night after all. "I think I can handle a little lovemaking," she said, emphasizing the word 'little.'

"Well then, proceed at your own peril," replied Asmodeous. "What kind of compromise did you have in mind?"

"The Kalag-ga will be taking control of the battle against the Emim," she began, biting her lip thoughtfully. "You and the other Nephilim from your army will join us. We'll need all the giants we can get to beat those monsters. I don't even know what we're up against, really. We've never fought anything like this, but from what I saw of the victims, it's going to be like fighting vicious animals." She shuddered at the thought.

Asmodeous nodded. "I was already going to insist upon that," he told her.

Even in her lightened mood Lilith couldn't let this pass. "Insist?"

Asmodeous laughed "Suggest?" he offered.

Lilith laughed too. "Do you think you'll be able to overcome your little...problem with having a woman on the field?" she teased.

Asmodeous grew serious. "I know you're going to be on that field with or without me," he said resignedly. "I'd rather be there." His eyes held hers. "It will be an honor to fight beside the legendary Lilith... even if it costs me my life."

Lilith gasped at his words. She was struck suddenly with the fear of this possibility. It hadn't even occurred to her that Asmodeous might be killed. But now that she thought about it, it wasn't so far-fetched. Asmodeous hadn't fought a battle like this in years. He was quite possibly out of practice, grown lazy from ruling his kingdom. Though he didn't look lazy. But with Lilith out there as an added distraction—she was suddenly paralyzed with fear. She stared at him, stricken dumb by this new sensation of worrying about someone other than herself.

Asmodeous seemed to read her mind and he immediately tried to take his words back. "Lilith, I'm not going to die! I only meant … never mind what I meant. It's idiotic to think about it. The point is I've come to terms with you being on the battle field after all these years and I'll be proud to fight with you."

Lilith nodded her understanding, but she was still too overcome to speak. They looked at each other for a long time without speaking.

"What was the compromise?" Asmodeous asked, finally breaking the silence.

Lilith's face changed. The frown disappeared and her expression grew soft. She even smiled. "After the battle I thought I might visit this amazing city I've been hearing so much about, this…Kiriath Arba." Suddenly feeling playful again, she assumed an air of casual indifference. "I want to see if it's as nice as I've heard. And I have a sudden craving for wine."

Asmodeous grasped Lilith by the shoulders. "Really?" he exclaimed, searching her eyes. "You'll come?" He threw his head back and let out a loud hoot that was half victory, half laughter. He looked at her with a determined gleam in his eyes. "Well, that settles it then! We've as good as won the battle!"

Lilith stared at him in surprise.

"I've waited nearly twenty years for you to grace my city with your presence," he told her. "There's no way you're getting out of it now!"

CHAPTER
24

L ilith was filled with pride as the Kalag-ga warriors prepared to lead the throng of soldiers into the forest. This battle marked a first of its kind in history; the massive army combined giants with the sons of men, Kalag-ga warriors with ordinary soldiers. All these groups had come together for a common cause. They'd traveled three days at a grueling pace to participate in this war. Most of the soldiers had horses, but some of them had only camels and donkeys, which weren't as fast. A few had chariots. Everyone compromised to accommodate their fellow soldiers. Even in the evenings, the soldiers who didn't have servants were invited to share in the great feasts that were prepared in the very center of the camp. Great fires roared and even music was played for them before they retired to their tents. A kind of kindred spirit filled the air around them.

The appearance of cedar trees peppering the landscape alerted the warriors that they were approaching the northern mountains of Syria. The mountains were spread out over hundreds of miles, the largest looming so far off in the distance that it seemed little more than a dim apparition from beneath the clouds. That was Mount Lebanon and, as a tribute to that great mountain, all the other, smaller mountains in that region were called, simply, the Lebanon Mountains.

There is a small valley between the first two mountains that marks the entrance into the Lebanon Mountains. These two 'twin' mountains were called Mount Gerizim and Mount Ebal. The valley between the two mountains was simply called Gerizim, after the foremost mountain. The cedars that marked the countryside before reaching the mountains were relatively short and wide when compared to the ones that populated the forests beyond, which often stretched up well over a hundred feet high in search of sunlight. Their trunks were so enormous it took no less than ten men with arms outstretched just to span their entire circumference.

Since the valley of Gerizim was the most direct way into the Lebanon Mountains, the Emim guarded it relentlessly, making the area virtually uninhabitable to men. Even the abundance of precious cedar couldn't tempt people to enter the region, so fearsome were these monstrous deformities. But now, as the armies approached, the large cedars stood out in the distance, providing an extra incentive for the dangerous mission.

There was a powerful stream of energy running all along the long line of warriors as they waited for the signal to move in. The sheer number of men would make the event legendary. No such group was known to have gathered before, but it was the manner in which the warriors were organized that was most extraordinary about it. And it was Lilith who had put the plan in motion.

It was customary in those days to wear down one's opponent by sending numerous, consecutive groups of men to attack. With this strategy, a powerful enemy would indeed be weakened over time, but those in the front lines would invariably be killed in the process. This made the front lines an extremely undesirable position to be in. Often the weakest or most expendable fighters were put there. But having fought exclusively for the Kalag-ga, Lilith was unused to losing warriors on such a large scale, and therefore she hadn't developed the philosophy that soldiers were expendable. She felt that every soldier, even the weakest, ought to be used to their best advantage in a battle.

With this in mind it occurred to Lilith that, placed strategically, each soldier might become invaluable and indispensable in his own right. And no one could find fault with her reasoning.

Now, looking over the field of warriors, it was clear to Lilith that every last man was enthusiastic and hopeful about the battle ahead. Furthermore, there was a confident air among them that they all had a good chance of surviving.

The Nephilim giants were placed in the front line situated about four or five yards apart from each other in a long row that spanned the entire length of the valley. Each of these powerful fighters was flanked on all sides with a miniature army of their own. Standing closest to the giant warriors, on either side of them, were two of the very best fighters the sons of men could produce. These soldiers were there to guard their giant, and they were to do everything in their power to prevent him from being struck down. Directly behind the giant and his two guardsmen stood four more soldiers from among the sons of men, whose function it was to move in for the kill once their Nephilim warrior struck a sufficient blow to render the Emim vulnerable. In this way, a giant could move on to the next Emim without worrying that he would be attacked from behind by one of those he left injured. He could rely on the four soldiers to finish the monster off. Further, behind this second battle line, was an entire line of backup soldiers, ready to fill in if any of the former soldiers needed assistance or were killed.

It was rumored that some of the Emim lived up in the branches of the tall cedars, so there was a fourth line of men who were armed with bows and arrows, all expert archers, assigned to kill any Emim they spied looming overhead.

There was a sense of unity among them that Lilith would never have expected among such a diverse group.

Gilgamesh and his soldiers were positioned at the very center of the foothill that marked the entrance into the forest. This was where it was said that the notorious Humbaba, one of the most fearsome and vicious creatures of all the Emim, stood guard. Enkido, along with his soldiers, was placed next in the line to the right of Gilgamesh, and Lilith and her men were positioned on his left. Asmodeous and his men stood at left of her, and so the line went.

Many a tale had been told of the monstrosity they called Humbaba. It was his actions that inspired the name Emim, which translated to 'dreadful ones.' Humbaba was thought of as a kind of leader among the Emim, although they were as unregulated a group as there could be, completely without consciences, lacking in the most rudimentary civility that can be found among the animals. He was a mindless killer who delighted in ripping living things apart. Humbaba embodied the Emim, and Gilgamesh was determined to be the one who killed him.

No human had entered the forest and lived to tell about it since the Emim giants began dwelling there. Even so, rumors about the forest abounded. It was said that the bones of humans and animals alike were strewn about the forest floor. It was from these mountains that all evil was said to have sprung. However, the Nephilim warriors were neither influenced nor concerned by these rumors of the sons of men. To them, these unfortunate creatures were simply malformed Nephilim, the victims of repulsive birth defects. Even so, there was a collective gasp from all of them when one of the Emim suddenly emerged from the forest.

He was bigger than Og, head and shoulders taller, even, than the largest bear, with the look of something twice as ferocious. He was covered in hair that was heavily caked with every kind of filth. His face was disfigured and ugly, twisted into an expression of great hatred. In his enormous hands, which were made up of six fingers each, he carried an oversized ax. He did not appear surprised to see them.

"I am Humbaba," he called out to them in a loud, angry voice. "Why are you here?"

"We've come for the Emim who attacked Jericho," Gilgamesh called out to him.

Humbaba's eyes found and remained fixed on Gilgamesh. He seemed to be mulling this over. Finally he raised his ax and pointed it at Gilgamesh. "You," he said—"will fight me for the right to enter the forest."

Lilith started to protest but Gilgamesh raised his hand to stop her. She reluctantly kept silent, since she knew Gilgamesh was well aware of what she had been about to say, which was that they didn't need Humbaba's permission to enter the forest. They were not bound by the superstitious rules of these ignorant savages and the people they terrorized. But Lilith also knew that this opportunity was exactly what Gilgamesh was waiting for. It was—in her opinion—his greatest weakness as a warrior, that he coveted the lion's share of the glory from each and every battle. Lilith bit her lip, knowing there was nothing she could do to stop him from fighting Humbaba.

Gilgamesh motioned for his aids to stay behind as he advanced to meet the monster alone. As tall as Gilgamesh was, Humbaba was a full head and shoulders above him. There was something almost eager in Humbaba's expression as he watched Gilgamesh approach.

When Gilgamesh came within a few steps of him, Humbaba suddenly lunged forward and thrust his head into Gilgamesh's abdomen, surprising Gilgamesh with his speed while effectively knocking the wind out of him. Somehow Gilgamesh managed to keep from falling down, catching himself in the nick of time, but his ax had been flung from his hand. Gilgamesh immediately whipped his right arm around in a circle and drove his fist into the lower left side of Humbaba's back, dealing him a fierce blow to the kidneys. This only set Humbaba back for an instant before he drew back his arm in preparation to strike a blow of his own with the ax he was holding, but Gilgamesh brought his fist up as hard as he could under Humbaba's jaw. The monster's head flew back with a loud crack, but he took his swipe at Gilgamesh anyway, and his ax just caught the side of Gilgamesh's rib cage before he could move out of the way. Stung, Gilgamesh managed to grab hold of Humbaba's weapon arm before he could strike again. Clutching it firmly in both hands, Gilgamesh began slamming Humbaba's arm into his raised knee repeatedly, as if it was a large branch he was trying to break in half. Finally the ax dropped from Humbaba's fingers. Blood poured from Gilgamesh's wound, but he didn't appear to notice. He slammed his fist into Humbaba's jaw again and again, clearly intending to take advantage of the injury he had inflicted with that very first blow. He went to strike him there a third time, but Humbaba caught hold of his arm and instantly wound it round his own, effectively binding Gilgamesh to him as he began pounding his fist into Gilgamesh's chest. Gilgamesh did not take this idly; he brought up his other hand and began repeatedly striking Humbaba in the jaw with his fist. Each blow was punctuated with loud grunts from both the recipient and the assailant. They continued to viciously pummel each other in this way until Humbaba finally released Gilgamesh's arm. The men retreated a step, angrily eyeing each other while catching their breath.

Lilith turned to Asmodeous with a look of exasperation. For Gilgamesh to hold up the battle like this just to achieve a personal victory for himself seemed the height of selfishness. While he was showing off, the Emim could be setting up traps for them in the forest. This unnecessary diversion could well cost them the battle. Gilgamesh's inflated ego was making him incompetent as a warrior.

Asmodeous motioned for her to be still, and Lilith snorted in disgust. Obviously men were unable to think clearly while their baser instincts were engaged. She took comfort in the realization that they were all pretty much the same, making it probable that the Emim were watching the battle with just as much interest from the forest.

Lilith sighed. The fight between these two men was irrelevant. They were entering the forest whether Gilgamesh won or not. The very existence of the Nephilim race might depend on them destroying the Emim that day.

Humbaba was once again approaching Gilgamesh, swinging his long arms, one after the other, in an attempt to strike him. Gilgamesh dodged the first two blows and then took the third one in the face. The impact threw his head backward and he fell, or so it appeared until he swiped up the ax he'd dropped earlier and jumped back up in one fluid movement. Humbaba looked around. His own ax was not close enough to safely pursue. Now it was Gilgamesh who approached Humbaba, swinging his ax each time he lunged forward. But Humbaba surprised them all by catching hold of Gilgamesh's weapon arm just as it seemed about to strike him, and holding it steady, not a foot from his face. With his other hand Humbaba grasped hold of Gilgamesh's neck and squeezed with all his might, trembling from the effort. Gilgamesh gasped, but he brought up his free hand to Humbaba's face, boring two of his strong fingers deep into his eyes. Humbaba let out a great yell but Gilgamesh only dug his fingers in deeper, pushing them toward the back of the creature's head with all his might. Humbaba gradually loosened his hold on Gilgamesh's arm, and Gilgamesh quickly moved in for the kill, jerking his ax back quickly. It was an awkward angle but Gilgamesh managed to slice open Humbaba's jaw with that first blow. The monster retreated a step, which gave Gilgamesh the opportunity to draw back and prepare for the next blow. This time he lined up his aim perfectly, using both hands to swing the ax backwards and then striking his target with all the force he could muster. Humbaba's head disappeared altogether for an instant, and then a few seconds later it fell to the ground with a terrible thud. Blood gushed from Humbaba's severed neck like a geyser, slowing to a sickening gurgle in a matter of moments. Humbaba's fingers twitched and then he dropped, first onto his knees and then collapsing forward into the dirt in a cloud of dust.

A cheer went up all along the line. Lilith was the only one who didn't join in the applause. While Gilgamesh's singular victory over the larger beast seemed to buoy everyone else's spirits for the battle ahead, Lilith couldn't help feeling resentment that he'd put them all at risk. She waited impatiently for him to join the line so they could finally attack. But Gilgamesh had other ideas, picking up the head of Humbaba by the hair and parading it up and down the line.

"Prepare for battle!" cried Lilith, unable to tolerate Gilgamesh's prancing for another minute. Everyone instantly came to attention at the sound of her voice. Gilgamesh looked at Lilith in surprise. Her heart softened the littlest bit when she saw the boyish confusion marring his joyous expression. Have I not pleased you, he seemed to ask. Lilith was suddenly reminded of her own gloating pleasure when she sent Asmodeous the Lagash badges. Perhaps she was letting her fears get the better of her. It was just that her priorities had shifted after that disturbing talk with her father.

"That was well done Gil," she said. "But we have more heads to collect, and I'm itching to get one of my own." A roar of laughter went through the crowd. Lilith's competitive nature was well known among the warriors.

Gilgamesh laughed too. He took his place back in the line and looked at Lilith with an eyebrow raised questioningly. The great and mighty Gilgamesh was deferring to her!

Lilith bowed her head to him, effectively handing him back the reigns. He was once again the leader of the Kalag-ga. No one else would have dared challenge him that way. But in spite of everything, Lilith and Gilgamesh had a deep bond that was forged in mutual admiration and respect, as well as blood. The occasional exasperation they felt for each other was never strong enough to penetrate that bond.

Always Lilith's anger dissipated quickly. Already she was beginning to feel glad that she'd had the opportunity to see one of the Emim fight after all. She'd noticed that, although they were large, strong and surprisingly quick, they were not strategic in their thinking at all. They struck with great force, true, but they acted on impulse. They did not appear to anticipate what might happen next. Lilith smiled. Strategy just happened to be her strong suit.

Gilgamesh gave the battle cry and at last the warriors moved forward, leaving the valley as they disappeared into the tall cedars of the forest.

CHAPTER
25

Present Day

"Holy shit!" exclaimed Clive.

"Speaking of goose bumps," agreed Gordon.

"That is some shit!" reiterated Clive.

"Hard to believe," Will added, but his expression indicated that he believed every word.

"You think?" Nadia threw in, raising an eyebrow. The morning sun was just beginning to brighten the sky, but for her the day felt like it should be ending.

"I can see how Gilgamesh's turning up in the story might seem a bit suspect," Will conceded. "Your grandmother, who you say loved reading ancient mythology as a young girl, could easily have come across him in books."

"Exactly," said Nadia. "And that's why I'm still not convinced that she *didn't* make them up."

"But then again, it fits too," argued Gordon, who had clearly made up his mind on the matter. "And in a way that your grandmother wouldn't have been able to predict. Take the contempt Lilith and Gilgamesh felt toward the sons of men, for example. This hostility between the two races, along with the Nephilim's desire to dominate man, cannot be found in the historic accounts but they correspond with what other djinn have told us. You can see the politics of the modern-day conflict between mankind and djinn taking form even back then."

"Wait! Do you mean to say *you've* talked to djinn?" asked Nadia.

"Of course!" Gordon replied, clearly pleased to be able to make such a claim. "We've called out a number of djinn over the years. We've never caught a fish as big as Lilith. We don't have *any* of the first generation djinn, in fact. Nothing from before the flood. Maybe it's the 'dark place.' Most of them are probably trapped there forever, thank God. The djinn we've captured were second and third generation Nephilim. They didn't have direct contact with the angels. Heck, they've never even seen an angel! And they weren't nearly as notorious as their predecessors. They kept to themselves, most of them living in and around the area that is now Israel."

"You know, if you think about it, you probably couldn't talk to any djinn from that pre-flood era without Gilgamesh's name popping up," Will added thoughtfully. "He was a legend. Everyone would have heard of him."

"It kind of sucks the way it turned out," said Clive. "This would have been so much more exciting if you *had* been Lilith." He seemed genuinely disappointed and Nadia couldn't tell if he was joking or not. She shuddered.

"So the 'politics' of these djinn..." she began. "What do you mean by that? Are you saying that these djinn are behind present-day terrorism?"

"No," said Clive. "And yes."

Gordon laughed. "Terrorism is a completely separate entity, but it's also a great place for djinn to hide."

"Not just hide," said Will. "They encourage it. You might say they add fuel to the fire."

"They support terrorism, provided it focuses on *their* enemies," explained Gordon. "Sometimes they use their influence to turn the focus in that direction. And, as well, they are not above using terrorists to carry out their own attacks."

"Sounds like terrorism," said Nadia.

"The difference is subtle, but it's there," said Will. "It's in the motives. Terrorists are generally motivated by extreme political or religious beliefs. Terrorism, for them, is a form of protest. They are confused and disorganized. Often they can't even tell you their goal. The djinn are different. They aren't extremists. They have a clear and logical goal in mind."

"Which is…," Nadia prompted.

"To live," said Clive.

"And to rule," added Gordon.

"And they need bodies and a corner of the earth in which to do this," said Will. "Though they travel the world freely, they have a particular fondness for their ancient land…which encompasses everything from Tel Aviv to Saudi Arabia."

"They consider it home," said Gordon.

"They're protecting their turf," said Clive. "They see the Western influence weaseling its way in and they can't let that happen. They think of that part of the world as theirs, right down to the last Arab. The creation of Israel kicked everything up a notch. They don't want democracy interfering in their plans to take over that part of the world."

"The extremists in that region play right into their hands," said Gordon. "Since they also hate the West."

Nadia shook her head. "This is too much to digest," she said. She never imagined for a moment that her grandmother's stories would have any relevance to the present day. "I find it hard to believe that the djinn would involve themselves in religious extremism," she said doubtfully. "According to Lilith, the Nephilim had nothing but contempt for religion."

"True," said Will. "But that doesn't mean they're above using it to get humans to do what they want."

"It's been the case throughout history," added Gordon. "Remember the Crusades? The djinn have tried time and again to get back control of the Middle East through religion."

"So now you're saying the Crusaders were djinn?" Nadia asked, incredulous.

"No," said Clive. "We're saying the idea to take back the Holy Land by force was masterminded by a certain group of advisers to the Church who just happened to have connections to the djinn."

"The djinn have learned to embrace religion because it helps them manipulate people into doing what they want," continued Will. "Conversely, they hate democracy because it interferes with their ability to influence and dominate the masses. Democracy is resistant to the kind of absolute compliance they can get in a religious society."

"Deep down, the djinn believe that we need them as much as they need us," Clive explained. "They're always griping about how we would destroy the world if they weren't here to stop us."

"Exactly," said Will. "They're trying to re-establish their right to be here. They play on our weaknesses. They know that extremism of any kind brings out the worst in humans. By encouraging it, they're proving their point that man has no respect for himself or the earth."

"And that we're stupid," added Clive. "All they have to do is encourage the belief that democracy is evil and they can get the extremists to do their killing for them."

Nadia was feeling overwhelmed. A small part of her wanted to reject everything they were saying. She was no longer sure about what she was doing. Was she just telling them stories to buy time until she could escape, or was she helping them prevent a terrible disaster? Maybe *they* were the ones creating this entire scenario to confuse her. But if so, for what purpose? She knew that they were watching her closely, but she couldn't hide her incredulity.

"I mean...for example...take the life spans back then," she argued, naming the first point that came to mind. "They claim Og lived over three thousand years. How is that possible?" Her logical mind couldn't accept it.

"The records indicate that even ordinary people lived much longer back then, some as many as eight or nine hundred years," said Will. "And Nephilim lived even longer than them. But don't forget, those were the first calendars in history. Their method of counting time could be vastly different from ours today. Who knows how long a year really was?"

"Also, some scientists speculate that the world's atmosphere may have been very different before the flood," added Gordon. "A catastrophe of that kind would have altered everything."

"As for Og," continued Will—"historians speculate that he had a son with the same name, which might account for his supposed longevity."

Nadia lowered her face in her hands and began rubbing her forehead with her fingertips. The others watched her in silence.

She looked up. "All I know is that I'm not a terrorist," she said. She looked at each of them, settling her gaze on Will in the end. "I would never—ever—hurt anyone like that." To her dismay a tremor shook her voice but she forced herself to continue. "When I go into these places after a disaster..." she shook her head, too overwhelmed to finish her statement. She swallowed hard. "I just don't understand how I could be connected to something like this."

"I'm not buying it," said Clive. Nadia looked at him in surprise but he didn't back down. "That's right. You heard me."

"Clive," warned Gordon.

"She's a big girl," he told Gordon before turning back to Nadia. "I mean, you might not be blowing people up, but what the hell are you doing to prevent it, huh? You prance in after the fact—making a boatload of money off these poor bastards—while convincing yourself that you're a saint. Meanwhile, those pricks you're hobnobbing with are playing both sides of the field."

Nadia just glared at him. She wanted to argue but was too shaky to speak. She hated people who said things like that, because there was a grain—just a grain, mind you—of truth to what they said.

What did he expect her to do? Change the world? If you didn't play by the rules, you didn't play. It was as simple as that. Should everyone just throw their hands up in the air and give up?

All of these things she would have liked to say. But she was determined more than anything else not to cry.

She addressed Gordon when she finally felt strong enough to speak. "I want to know *exactly* how I'm connected to this attack," she said in a commanding voice.

"You don't..." began Clive.

"No!" she interrupted, refusing to look at him. "I want to know about the attack *I'm* being accused of supporting."

Nobody spoke.

"Then I'm done," she said. "You can either arrest me or let me go!"

Clive actually laughed.

"I mean it!" she yelled.

The three men exchanged glances. They seemed to be silently debating over how much to tell her. As usual, it fell on Will to make the final call.

"The code name for this attack is 'Lilith's Revenge'," he told her. "When these code names come up, we immediately do a search in our system that links all known djinn sightings to anyone who might be affiliated with that sighting in any way. Naturally, after what happened in nineteen forty eight, your grandmother was flagged to Lilith. Your mother—you must have realized by now that we suspected she might be harboring Lilith—was being watched for years. The way she was…no disrespect, but it went along with what we knew about Lilith at the time. She had connections that were dubious, to say the least. But we could never link her to any particular incident.

"Then, when she died, we figured there was a good chance Lilith took up residence in you. It often happens that way…they'll pass into their own offspring. It makes things easier for obvious reasons."

"Not to mention that you just happen to be set up in the perfect business to carry out their work," added Clive.

Nadia was really getting tired of Clive's constant innuendos. And yet she couldn't fault their reasoning. Her mother had been glamorous, headstrong, and willful, just like Lilith. And for a semi-famous actress with minimal talent, she'd managed to work her way into the most powerful circles in society, both politically and otherwise. Nadia had always thought it was her father's altruistic behavior that curried favor with everyone, but wasn't it in fact Gisele who had all the connections?

"Tell me more about the attack," she said, preferring to steer the subject away from her mother.

"We know it's a suicide mission," said Gordon.

"Where are you getting this information?" she wondered. "How do you know it's called 'Lilith's Revenge' and that it's a suicide mission?"

"We've cracked the code," said Gordon. "...to the encrypted messages. Which means we can translate the messages we have."

"It also enables us to identify other messages encrypted with the same code," added Will. "The more messages we find, the more pieces of the puzzle we have."

"How'd you get the code?" Nadia asked.

There was a long silence. Gordon started to speak but Will held up a hand to stop him. "One of the cells is a plant," Will said.

"Could your plant be mistaken, or...misguided?" asked Nadia. She didn't trust spies and informants as a general rule.

"Not this one," said Will.

"How do you know?"

"Because we know," he replied. Nadia sighed.

"These days, cells are *chosen* for missions in jihad," explained Gordon. "They have to be invited by someone on the inside. The really organized attacks—the big ones—can't afford to just take volunteers off the street anymore. This was the case with our cell. We believe she was recommended by her husband's religious instructor at their Mosque, or maybe it was her husband himself who volunteered her."

"Either way, it was an offer she couldn't refuse," said Clive.

"Who is she?" Nadia asked, surprised to hear that it was a woman.

"You know we can't tell you who she is," said Will. "All we can tell you is that she's a Muslim who came here from Saudi Arabia with her husband. He was a known supporter of *Jihad* who was being watched by government officials. He was also very abusive toward his wife. At one point, she secretly sought aid from a local woman's shelter, but she was too terrified to actually leave him. However, a friendship developed between her and one of the women at the center who she trusted enough to confide in."

"It turns out this Muslim woman was sold to her husband at the age of fourteen," said Gordon, picking up where Will left off. "She lived with his abuse for over ten years. She's a devout Muslim who's deeply opposed to extremist views like those of her husband's. Anyway, her husband was killed in an act of *Jihad* and shortly afterwards she was invited to participate in an intense spiritual program for the self-improvement of Muslim widows—a cover for a *Jihad* training session like the one her husband attended. She knew that they felt they were honoring her with this request, and she also knew that it wasn't really a request. She confided all this to her friend at the help center."

"In case you haven't figured it out yet," interjected Clive—"her *friend* at the center worked for the Department of Defense."

"Yes, and it wasn't hard for the woman at the center to convince her to become a double agent," added Gordon with admiration in his voice. "She would much rather risk her life to help prevent terrorism than to face certain death in a cause she doesn't believe in."

"So she became one of them," Nadia said, stunned by the woman's story.

"Yes, she went through a rigorous training program and was then told to wait," said Gordon. "There are many out there like her, Muslims against extremism. But most of them don't have the connections that she has. It's not easy to get in, as Will mentioned before. It has to kind of happen naturally."

"Even once you're in, it takes patience," added Will. "You never know when the call will come. She's been what we call a sleeper cell for nearly a decade, and she's only been called for duty one other time."

"What happened that time?" Nadia asked breathlessly.

"The first time they use a cell, it's usually a test," said Gordon. "The cell's sent on a bogus errand and used as a decoy. This way the mission can still be carried out if the cell alerts someone about it."

"And that's how they find out if their cell can be trusted," added Clive.

"But even a decoy message can be useful," said Will. "It helps us identify who's involved. Djinn-related attacks are not that hard to recognize. Their missions tend to be more organized and complex, while at the same time being more elaborate and mysterious. Ordinary terrorists tend to talk too much, but what little information the djinn provide is always in code. Even the translations are in code. Their messages are always laced with hidden meanings that, more times than not, lead us right to their ancient pasts."

"They're very sentimental," agreed Clive.

"That's where we come in," said Gordon. "We cross-reference probable connections to djinn in our system and then track any viable leads it produces. The object is to solve the riddle before anyone gets hurt."

"And what have you got so far?" Nadia wondered. "I mean, besides my grandmother's connection to Lilith."

Clive and Gordon once again left the decision of how much to tell her to Will. "We know from their description of the enemy that their target is the United States," he told her. "And we know from their statements and promises that they believe they'll be making history with this attack."

"As well as fulfilling prophesy," added Gordon. "They've actually used the term *Al-Malhama Al-Kubra*, which represents the final battle against the anti-Christ, i.e. the western world." He paused for effect. "In Christian terms, we're talking Armageddon."

"We're not entirely sure that our cell isn't being used as a decoy again," said Will. "Her instructions are somewhat contradictory. The mission is *Jihad*, yet they didn't include the purification ritual that is required for martyrs."

"What did they tell her to do?" Nadia asked.

The men eyed her suspiciously. "I think we've told you enough," said Will.

"You've told me next to nothing," said Nadia. "Everything you've said is basic stuff I could have probably learned on the internet. What did they tell her to do?"

"She's to attend a seminar in LA," said Will. They all seemed to be studying her face with even more interest than usual. Will spoke deliberately, emphasizing every word. "You may have heard of it. It's a seminar for women...sponsored by BEACON..."

Nadia gasped. "The *Supporting Women Around the World* network meetings?"

"Ding, ding, ding," interjected Clive. "Tell her what she's won, Johnny."

Nadia's blood ran cold. Many of her friends and associates were going to those meetings! So many women! And she was the one who had set it all up! "What's going to happen at the seminar?" she asked. "What...what did they tell her to do?"

"Nothing yet," said Will. "So far, all she has to do is attend."

"We think she might be receiving the rest of her instructions there," said Gordon. "They've actually listed which meetings she's to attend."

"You have to give me a phone!" cried Nadia. "I have to warn them..."

"You know that's not going to happen," said Clive.

"Which meetings will she be attending?" Nadia demanded, trying to remember who the instructors were. But there were so many of them! It had become quite the networking event, thanks to her, pulling in women from all around the world to help raise money and awareness for the less fortunate. It was meant to bring people together, to try and bridge the cultural gaps through women. It had seemed such a noble cause when she was planning it.

Will had pulled out his phone—one of those 'Smart Phones' that her assistant had been urging her to get but that she didn't have time to learn how to use—and was swiftly and adeptly pressing buttons. "She's been instructed to attend three meetings supporting Muslim awareness," he said. "They appear to be your typical, Islam-isn't-that-bad-for-women type of thing. Let's see, at nine a.m. there's *Lessons in Hope*, sharing stories from women around the world who have converted to Islam; at eleven there's *Escaping the Goddess of Death*, detailing the many pitfalls of modern immorality, and at one o'clock there's *Cloaked in Glory*, the...," Will stopped when he caught sight of Nadia's expression. "What's the matter?" he asked.

Everyone turned to look at her. It felt like every last drop of blood had been drained from her face. The words, *Goddess of Death,* kept echoing in her head.

Was it possible?

"Does any of this mean something to you?" asked Gordon.

"If it does you have to tell us right now," said Will.

"Yes," she whispered, but then she faltered, uncertain. "I don't know—maybe." She felt like she was drowning in a sea of uncertainty.

Maybe it was just a coincidence.

"Tell us," Will's voice was barely more than a whisper as well.

Nadia realized that she was trembling. The moment, and everything in it, felt surreal. "I think...," she paused to lick her lips, which had suddenly become terribly dry. "I think this...attack...might be... different from what you're expecting." She lowered her eyes because she couldn't endure their accusatory stares—particularly Clive's—any longer. And in that moment she knew that it was true. "It's going to be a plague."

CHAPTER
26

Ancient Mesopotamia
The city of Kiriath Arba
A few days later

K iriath Arba was situated on the side of a small mountain, providing all of its inhabitants with a spectacular view of the world outside its city walls. Narrow roads wound in and around the countryside for a charming effect. The houses were mostly constructed of the distinctive, rose-colored stone that was native to the area, but the temples and royal living quarters were made of marble, which could also be found in the earth below their feet. Olive, palm and almond trees grew robustly, giving the city a sense of prosperity. Sophisticated irrigation systems, designed by Arba himself, rendered the city impervious to drought. The mountain produced numerous springs to tap into, and the healthy trees, larger than those of other cities less drought resistant, seemed to ensure the continued, ongoing approval of the gods for all of the people who dwelt there.

The city also boasted of a prosperous trade. Besides the rose colored stones and the exquisite marble, there were many other luxury products such as wine and figs. There were caves at the base of the mountain where the elite buried their dead. It was a city that had everything; lush hills, quiet valleys and it was surrounded on all sides by desert. Lilith was utterly charmed.

The battle had turned out better than Lilith had hoped. In spite of their incredible size and extraordinary strength, the Emim hadn't stood a chance. While indomitable to the sons of men—particularly when attacking at night, as in the case of Jericho—against a more worthy opponent they were unskilled and clumsy. Some of them were crippled with deformities, although they managed to turn a few of these defects to their advantage. The flesh-eating 'biters,' for example, had sharp, jagged teeth, and nails that ripped through skin like it was butter. These were the ones who hid in the trees, and it was disarming for even the most experienced soldier to have one of these snarling, slashing fiends fall upon him in battle. Their razor-sharp teeth could penetrate the jugular before the soldier knew what hit him. These were the most terrifying and dangerous of all the Emim, and undoubtedly the ones that attacked Jericho. It was well that the Nephilim warriors were guarded on all sides by the sons of men, for they had proved invaluable in warning of biters overhead, or in fighting off one who managed to land on his mark. But those unfortunate warriors who were bitten would have been better off if they had died right there in the forest. They suffered much on their journeys home, and few made it back alive. Those were the worst off of all the survivors. Luckily, neither Lilith nor Asmodeous was among them.

They stayed in the Cedar Forest for more than a week after conquering it, cutting down as many cedars as they could carry back with them. The soldiers who came from the east—including the Kalag-ga warriors—carried their bounty to the Euphrates River and then converted it into large rafts that floated down the river into Uruk and the other cities along the river. The armies from the west took theirs to the nearby Jordan River, where they sent them drifting past Jericho and into the Dead Sea, on the way to their various destinations along the seaboard, the very last of which was Kiriath Arba.

When Asmodeous and his army finally returned with their share of the spoils, the people of Kiriath Arba crowded the streets to catch a glimpse of the amazing procession. They were awestruck by the spectacle, and it was hard to say what impressed them most. The tremendous cedars announced the success of their mission, but no one had ever seen trees that size before. In addition, it was unusual for so many men to return from battle. Indeed, Kiriath Arba had only lost eight men! But what astonished them most—the thing that literally cut short their cries of joy and turned them into gasps of shock—was the sight of Lilith. A woman—a giant woman, no less—dressed as a warrior, seated on her own horse and riding in front beside their king, as dark and beautiful as any goddess! The entire city was speechless.

As they rode through the gates, Asmodeous reached out and took Lilith's hand, raising it high up in the air in a gesture that clearly attributed the victory to her. It was a powerful statement, a warning to one and all of the reverence that should be shown to the woman sitting by his side. After that first pause of hushed astonishment, a cheer rose up that was even louder than before. Lilith smiled and waved at the crowd. Her joy was complete. She had debated the wisdom of riding in front with Asmodeous, but then again, she wouldn't have been content to ride anywhere else. And besides, the people of Kiriath Arba would have been shocked by her appearance no matter where she sat in the procession. She was not the sort of woman who could just stroll into a city unnoticed. Anyway, Asmodeous had insisted upon it. And in truth, Lilith loved every minute of it. Entering the city, hearing their cheers, she could almost imagine that she really was Asmodeous' queen.

Without offering any explanation to anyone, not even to the high priests of the temple, Asmodeous established Lilith in his household, and in his bed. The king's household was made up of various advisers and domestics, who managed both home and kingdom. No one dared question Lilith's presence, not even the priests, though she received her share of curious attention. But that didn't bother Lilith. She had never concerned herself with the opinions of the sons of men before and she would not start now. And in truth, she was much too wrapped up in herself to notice. She was blissfully unaware of anything and anyone except Asmodeous. She settled into his city as contentedly as she settled into his bed. She knew that the people were reverential to her because they feared her. And wasn't that what mattered? She didn't bother to wonder what they thought of her personally. She only associated with the other Nephilim, shunning everyone else, even the Nephilim's wives. Asmodeous spent the better part of his days with her, but Lilith enjoyed her time alone almost as much. She loved the exquisite agony of missing him, followed by the thrill of rushing back into his arms again for an evening of erotic pleasures.

Asmodeous was an excellent king, and the people of Kiriath Arba lived comfortably under his leadership. He ruled with a firm but fair hand, managing to maintain order while creating an undemanding existence for the sons of men. In watching him with his people, Lilith realized how wrong she'd been about him before. He was not without humility after all. He was kind, protective and considerate. With her, he was sweet, loving and generous. He laid his city at her feet like a cat leaves its prey on its master's doorstep. He shared everything with her, discussing all the many decisions that were thrust upon him in the course of his day and even asking her opinion on many of them. They debated the nuances of ruling, as well as every other aspect of life. Lilith often thought him too lenient with the sons of men, whereas he teased her for being a tyrant. But aside from these minor differences of opinion, Lilith felt they were really as alike as any two people could be. Asmodeous' passion and intellect—everything about him in fact—complemented her. He made her a better person. Each moment spent with him left her eager for another. She had never been this happy before. There was literally nothing else she wanted. She didn't even miss the battlefield. Nor was she concerned—she wouldn't have even thought of it if she hadn't overheard some of the women talking—that she and Asmodeous were not making a child. What did she want a child for? Asmodeous filled her every need.

They made love every night, and—for Lilith at least—each time was like the first. Asmodeous approached her like bull, or like a man who'd been locked away in a cave for years. He was impatient, trembling with need, overcome with passion. Lilith thrived on his unceasing desire for her. Her ego soared. She felt loved and cherished for the first time in her life. Asmodeous accepted her for who she was, and she appreciated that more than anything. She surrendered herself to him completely. There was nothing she wouldn't do for him.

Yet trouble simmered beneath the surface, though Lilith was too content to pay it much heed. While Asmodeous and the other male giants were generally admired, Lilith was more likely to be resented. It wasn't as easy for people to accept her. For one thing, she was the only female giant they'd ever seen, and her behavior as a woman was scandalous. She flaunted her affair with Asmodeous without any regard for their customs. And worst of all, she remained barren.

As the citizens of Kiriath Arba grew more mistrustful of her, Lilith grew more and more distant from them. She insisted that she didn't care what they thought, provided they showed her the proper respect.

This quiet dissent might have gone unremarked if not for the affliction. It struck suddenly, spreading through Kiriath Arba like wildfire, but only leaving its deadly mark on the city's most innocent. The stillborn infants came in droves. Mostly it took the children of ordinary men, but a few of the Nephilim were affected as well. It treated males and females alike; all of them were born dead.

Pregnant women were petrified. Wives entered the marital chamber with dread. The citizens turned to their leader for answers but when they looked at Asmodeous they saw Lilith, who was, to them, a mutation—little better than the Emim. She was, as well, fairly new to Kiriath Arba, making her the most likely candidate to have offended the gods. And it wasn't hard to figure out why. She'd hailed herself a goddess, mocking the real gods with her pagan behavior, not the least of which was her blatant sexual prowess over their king. And it seemed no small coincidence that she herself was unable to bear a child. Speculation shook the city.

Lilith knew they blamed her, but this knowledge didn't motivate her to adjust her behavior or attempt in any way to bridge the gap between her and Asmodeous' people. On the contrary, she became even more scandalous and imperious, delighting in their barely contained outrage. The more they judged her, the worse she became. She couldn't seem to help herself. Their constant disapproval was like salt in a wound, compounded by the fact that they were the ones who had rights to the earth—not her and her people—and quite frankly, she could have destroyed them all and been glad.

On the surface, the citizens of Kiriath Arba continued to treat Lilith with hostile reverence. But behind her back they dubbed her the 'Goddess of Death.'

Lilith never spoke of this to Asmodeous. She knew he must have heard the gossip as well, but she was confident that he would take her side. She could see that he, too, was beginning to despise the sons of men. He started to complain that he'd been too soft on them. It was, after all, only through oppression that the sons of men seemed to thrive. He decided to do something about it, something that would remind them of who was in charge. He sent for the priests, and ignored their raised eyebrows when they saw Lilith standing haughtily by his side.

"This blight that has come upon us," Asmodeous began with his characteristic easy manner—"The gods have spoken to me about it in a dream." Lilith noticed that Asmodeous was observing their faces while he spoke, much like a wild animal examines his prey. *Let one of them challenge me*, he seemed to be thinking. But of course none of them dared. He went on with the same self-righteous arrogance they were so fond of adopting when it suited their purposes. Lilith was beginning to enjoy herself.

"The gods are displeased," Asmodeous continued. "The people of Kiriath Arba have become greedy. They have taken without giving back."

The priests stared at Asmodeous in surprise. Not one of them risked so much as glance in Lilith's direction. And she knew why, too; they were the very ones who started the rumor that she was the cause of the affliction. She was pretty sure they were the ones who coined the term 'Goddess of Death.' How would they respond to Asmodeous' claim that it was actually the people who brought this on themselves? What could they say?

There was a long, awkward silence before any of them spoke. Asmodeous had indeed put the city's priests in a precarious position.

"What do the gods wish us to do?" asked one of them at last.

Asmodeous, of course, had the solution ready. Lilith was dying to hear what it was.

"They want us to impose a new tax on the people of Kiriath Arba," he said, surprising everyone in the room, even Lilith. She couldn't take her eyes off him. She was as mesmerized as the priests. She wondered if she was the only one who noticed his quiet anger, or realized how much he wished he could kill them. Yet they all knew he needed the priests to be on his side now, lest he lose control of his city entirely. Lilith still wasn't sure how he planned to accomplish this. But Asmodeous continued with his usual confidence, although he was barely able to hide his disdain as he practically spat out the last few words. "...for the temple," he finished at last, effectively delivering the *coup de grâce*.

The priests' eyes grew wide, but it was with much more than just surprise this time. Lilith could see interest—and greed—developing there now, too. *Yes*, they seemed to be thinking, *the people should give something back*.

"The gods have spoken!" announced one priest, bowing deferentially to his king. And the others followed suit, until each had declared his agreement.

"I will let *you* determine the tax and use it as you deem correct," announced Asmodeous. "See that it is enough so that the gods are appeased!"

The priests seemed almost giddy as they scurried back to their temple.

Lilith stared at Asmodeous, a small smile playing about her lips. His eyes were still burning with anger but he, too, couldn't hold back a small, smug smirk.

"And here all this time I was thinking *I* was the clever one," she remarked.

Asmodeous shrugged. "The sons of men are easy to understand, are they not?"

"But what if the affliction doesn't go away?"

Asmodeous remained unconcerned. "It will take time for the priests to haggle over the details of this new power I've given them and present the new tax to the people. And then the taxes will have to be collected. These plagues come and go regardless. This too will pass."

Lilith let out a little sigh of contentment. She was starting to think that no matter what happened Asmodeous would be able to fix it.

There was a sudden distraction—a flutter of noisy activity—coming from outside. Horns at the city gate indicated the arrival of distinguished guests. The household sprang to life. Lilith and Asmodeous rushed out into the courtyard, where people were running to and fro, chattering excitedly as they went. They caught the general drift of their talk almost immediately. The gods had come to Kiriath Arba!

Lilith grasped hold of Asmodeous' arm. "My father!" she cried.

"Perhaps," he agreed. "Or *mine.*" Lilith stopped and turned to him in alarm. She wasn't ready to meet the angel who fathered Asmodeous! He laughed at her terrified expression and took a firm hold of her hand. "Come along," he said confidently.

They went out to greet the gods, looking all around them in surprise. It was as if a dark cloud had been lifted from over the city. The somber, resentful citizens, who'd taken to staying indoors for fear of the blight, were suddenly pouring into the streets, yelling and cheering. They seemed to be filled with new hope. No doubt they felt the gods had answered their prayers. They struggled to catch a glimpse of the very imposing visitors.

Even Lilith was awed by the momentousness of the occasion. Magnificent and mysterious, the angels approached in a chariot that was decorated with gold, but their personal brilliance outshone even the splendor of that equipage. Lilith watched with the rest of city as the angels drew near. She saw that one of the angels was, in fact, her father. He was accompanied by two other angels who were every bit as dazzling as he was. Their exquisite beauty filled Lilith with a sweet, savage yearning she couldn't identify. Yet her anticipation was touched with a kind of sad foreboding. She wondered at the strange apprehension that was creeping over her. They were, in all likelihood, there to commend Lilith and Asmodeous on their destruction of the Emim. What had she to fear?

Lilith knew instinctively which of the other two angels had fathered Asmodeous. Azazyl had the same self-assured manner and obvious leadership abilities as his son. Arba—the third angel—also had left his mark on his son, Anak. Lilith wondered what similarities Asmodeous would find between her and her father when he examined Anu. But neither of them spoke. Their eyes never left the spectacle of the approaching chariot.

CHAPTER 27

Present Day

"What connection do you or BEACON have with disease control centers or anyone who might possibly have access to disease testing materials?" Will asked her.

Nadia took a minute to think about it. "There's a bio-tech lab out of Maharashtra, India that I've generated quite a lot of money for. They're called Shakhra Research Labs." She felt she should try to defend them. "But they are doing amazing things for the people of India..." her voice trailed off when she saw Clive's expression.

"Why were you raising money for them?" asked Gordon.

Nadia looked at him with exasperation. "I'm sorry, okay!" she snapped. "I didn't realize I was endangering the world by supporting disease research!"

"I'm just wondering if there is anything you remember about that research lab in particular," Gordon replied calmly.

Nadia lifted her hands in a gesture of futility and shook her head. "I don't know," she sighed hopelessly. She was suddenly exhausted. It was getting late—or at least it seemed late to her internal clock, though it wasn't even mid-day there—and she was both tired and hungry. She would give anything for a drink. She closed her eyes and tried to concentrate. "I mean…India is a hotbed of research nowadays. I got involved after the 2004 earthquake. I remember being shocked to learn that, even though India was the up and coming nation for industry—with manufacturing companies literally popping up everywhere—their health situation was as bad as ever. Infectious diseases like tuberculosis and even malaria were still killing thousands of people. Public health was the inevitable next step. But that takes research and bio-containment labs like Shakhra."

"We understand all that," said Will. "What we want to know is what made you decide to support this particular research lab?"

Nadia wasn't sure. Shakhra Research Labs had probably come to her, and moved by what she'd seen after the earthquake, she would have been more than willing to help. Such organizations approached her all the time. She would have checked them out—not personally, of course, but through her assistant—or maybe she ran the company by one of her many emissaries in the industry. Frankly she couldn't keep track of every little thing. There was only so much one person could do. Some of the work had to be delegated. Yet she was annoyed that she couldn't remember any specific details about the company.

"To be honest, I don't recall why I decided to help them," she admitted at last. "Something must have impressed me about them at the time." Their incredulous expressions further exasperated her. "I deal with too many people to remember every little detail about each and every one of them!" she insisted. She appealed to Gordon. "I could get you really specific information about this company if you'd just let me use the phone…"

"No," interjected Will, and as usual, there was no flexibility in his tone. Nadia glared at him but he was too busy pushing buttons on his phone to notice.

"Here I am, doing everything I can to help and you're still treating me like a criminal!" she exploded. "If you really wanted to prevent th…"

Will touched her lips with his finger-tips as he put the phone to his ear. "Shush," he said.

Although Nadia was still inwardly fuming, she was effectively silenced.

"Check out Shakhra Research Labs in Maharashtra India," he said into the phone. "Yes, they study infectious disease and may have a bio containment lab on one or more of their sights. Yeah. Hey…let me know what you find, okay?" He lowered the phone and looked at Nadia. "Are you affiliated with any other labs?" he asked.

Nadia sighed heavily, dreading their response to the next one. "I think there might be a private research lab connected with Biojour Incorporated," she said.

Will looked both tired and exasperated. "Not the publishing company?" he asked in a pleading tone.

"Yes, that's them," she said, feeling, once again, like she'd done something wrong. "They publish medical books but I think they conduct some of their own research as well. They sponsor seminars supporting research and drug awareness," she added defensively.

"Yeah," agreed Clive, nodding his head with understanding. "We've heard of their *seminars*…," his emphasis on the word 'seminars' showed his clear disdain for the seminars in question. "Big time pharmaceutical companies pimpin' their drugs at ten thousand dollars a plate." He squinted his eyes at Nadia. "*Girl*, you're runnin' with some real scumbags!"

Nadia was annoyed. "How do *you* suggest we educate doctors on the latest in pharmaceuticals, Mr. High and Mighty?" she asked. "I suppose you think we should do away with the pharmaceuticals altogether…go back to treating the sick with leeches…"

"Man, don't play dumb with me," Clive replied irritably. "You know damn well that only the richest pharmaceutical companies will be *educating* the doctors at those seminars. Most research scientists can't afford the cover charge. There's shitloads of important research that'll never reach those doctors, and you know it."

"But that's exactly why the research labs need sponsoring!" cried Nadia.

"Biojour Incorporated doesn't need any sponsoring!" Clive retorted. "They already run the whole damn show. And why the hell do they have to have so many sub companies attached to 'em? It's like they're hiding something."

Nadia was a bit thrown by his apparent familiarity with the company in question. "You seem to know a lot about them," she said. "Have you had…issues with them before?"

"Let's just say I know what a bitch it's going to be trying to get information out of those dickheads," he said. "Kind of like trying to find a needle in a haystack with all those little divisions of theirs."

They all stopped talking because Will had raised the phone to his ear again.

"Biojour Incorporated," was all he said, but his tone was full of meaning, not the least of which was a kind of tired frustration. "Might as well get on it then, instead of bitchin' about it," he said. He hung up with a sigh. He and Clive exchanged glances. They both seemed suddenly weary. "I could have done without that," he admitted.

"Has Biojour been involved with this…djinn business before?" Nadia asked.

Clive laughed outright then, and the others reluctantly joined in. "Look at her," he said. "Maybe we should let Nancy Drew in on the case, huh boys?"

"You don't have to be so rude about it," Nadia snapped irritably. She didn't like the way they were making her feel. As if she had something to feel guilty about. As if she was somehow in the wrong. She was the CEO of a well-respected charitable organization, recognized by UNDRO and CERT and supported by the most prominent political figures in America, and here were these three *kidnappers*, making her feel foolish and corrupt. She was aware of the (perhaps not so little) inequities in the world of charities, just as she was aware of similar inequities among the pharmaceutical companies and even the politicians. Where there were power and money there was bound to be corruption. One could only do one's best. Who were they to judge her?

But these worn-out arguments didn't make Nadia feel better this time. She'd always known that the industry she worked in was far from the altruistic and caring enterprise it appeared to be. The business of helping the less fortunate was a lucrative, and therefore a competitive one. There were inevitably people who would use these disasters to draw unreasonably large salaries and benefits for themselves. It was a fine line that was hard to define. The raising and managing of funds required talent that deserved to be compensated of course, but there were those who took it too far. Nadia had heard of cases where funds had been so misappropriated that not so much as a nickel had been contributed to the cause they'd been collecting for. But BEACON wasn't like that. It always delivered top dollar to its causes. And yet, she couldn't deny that she was paid well—although her salary as CEO of BEACON was certainly below the industry standard—and too, there was her expensive Manhattan office. All of which just went to prove that a person could accomplish a worthwhile objective and still earn a living.

So why was she letting them get to her?

Nadia had been sitting there, silently brooding, while they sat back—rather self-righteously, she thought—ignoring her.

"You would think, to listen to you, that your organization—whatever the hell it is—is perfect," she said. "You would think, for instance, that you would never in a million years hurt any innocent person by, oh, say, *kidnapping* them, in some misguided effort to do something good? No. You guys would never do that!"

She could see by their expressions that her point had hit home. Will actually smiled at her. And it struck her suddenly—somewhat grudgingly, without her wanting or even condoning the thought—that she actually cared about what they thought of her. She felt they all had something in common, a kind of innate desire to accomplish something good in spite of everything else.

Is this me or Patty thinking this? She couldn't help wondering.

"Or starve said kidnappee?" she added, deciding to strike while the iron was hot. "You wouldn't do that either I suppose." They all looked at Gordon.

"Come now," he pleaded in the Indian accent. "I am not a servant for you to do with as you wish!"

Will and Clive looked at each other.

"If I make it you know what it's going to be," Clive warned.

Gordon turned to Nadia. "Do you like Fruity Pebbles?" he asked. She couldn't help laughing at the way 'fruity pebbles' sounded with the Indian accent.

"To be honest, I don't care what I eat, as long as I can have a drink with it," she replied. She looked at Will. "Wine? Vodka? Was that rubbing alcohol I saw you putting on your hand yesterday?"

Will seemed to be considering it.

"Come on," she begged. "I feel like I'm on the verge of a panic attack." She supposed she would have had one by now if she were prone to them—which she wasn't—but she figured they didn't know that. All she knew for sure was that whenever her assistant threatened one Nadia always gave in. And if another woman couldn't cope with the threat of a hysterical woman, she was pretty sure three men would be even less inclined to do so.

Though these weren't just *any* three men.

Will sighed, a sure sign that he was giving in. "All right, but all we've got is wine. I could do with a glass myself."

Nadia sat back on the couch and rested her eyes while the men went to get the food and wine. She was a little surprised when Clive actually returned with a box of Fruity Pebbles. Will poured her a glass of wine, and she sat up to take a sip. She almost instantly felt herself relax.

"You realize, of course, that I could get you all the information you want on these companies if you would just let me make a few phone calls," she reminded them.

"We can't risk you tipping anybody off," said Will. Nadia lowered her wine glass and glared at him. She couldn't imagine why his continued mistrust should bother her so much. "Even accidentally," he said defensively. "Too many lives are at stake. Our personal feelings are secondary."

Nadia wondered what he meant by 'our personal feelings.' Probably he meant *her* personal feelings were secondary and only included the rest of them to be polite. Yet it seemed to imply that he was beginning to believe that she might be innocent. And it occurred to her that somewhere along the line she'd stopped fearing for her life. In fact, she was beginning to feel fairly confident that she would come out of this alive. She almost felt…protected. This realization alarmed her. It hadn't been two days since these men violently kidnapped her from her office building! Were her feelings real, or a result of the trauma? Was she suffering from the Patty Hearst syndrome after all?

Yet a lot had happened in the short amount of time that they'd been together. These men knew more about her than anyone, even Joe. Nadia flinched at this stray, unexpected remembrance of her recently-former boyfriend. She wondered why she didn't think of him more. She tried to think about him now with some modicum of emotion but couldn't even hold on to the thought. She preferred to think about the case.

The case! She could imagine what Clive would say if he knew her thoughts. *Hey Nancy Drew, does this rag smell like chloroform?*

Nadia could feel the wine going to her head but she recklessly poured herself another glass.

"Is this even possible?" she asked no one in particular. "I mean, why would anyone—even a djinn—risk spreading a contagious disease? They're putting themselves in danger too!"

"The use of an infectious disease actually supports djinn involvement," explained Will. "Only a djinn can ditch a sick body for a healthy one. The right type of disease would work in their favor. They could concentrate the sickness in key areas where they want to do the most damage."

She thought about this. "So you think their use of the phrase 'Goddess of Death' is definitely referring to the affliction that spread through Kiriath Arba?" Nadia asked.

"It's certainly worth looking into," he replied.

"The djinn are very nostalgic," explained Gordon. "They're deeply attached to the past and they're proud of their own origins. They're obsessed with their previous lives as Nephilim and they incorporate little mementos of those lives into everything they do. The more we learn about their lives as Nephilim, the easier it is to find them in the here and now."

"They're freaks for symbolism," added Clive. "There's hidden meaning in everything they do. We're always looking for signs of this in their communications. They might be forced to stay in hiding, but they're too egotistical to remain completely invisible."

"That's true," said Gordon. "And that's why this 'Goddess of Death' business sends up a bright red flag."

"Lilith would eat that shit up," Clive agreed.

"Do you really think Lilith is out there?" Nadia asked.

"Yes," said Will. "The only question is where."

"And you think she's behind this attack?" she persisted.

"I don't know," said Will. "Everything seems to be pointing to her."

Nadia had a sudden thought. "Hey! Maybe you should check out whoever named that class at the seminar," she suggested. "They might also be involved."

Clive snorted. "There goes Nancy Drew again."

"We're on it," said Will. "These seminar lessons are often set up by Muslim awareness groups with ties to extremists groups. We're trying to track the origin of this particular lesson without endangering our cell.

"Has she heard anything more?" she asked.

"No," said Will. "We don't expect her to either. She's got her instructions."

"I can't imagine why they would pick this seminar, particularly when the focus is tolerance for other, non-western viewpoints, like those of Islam," Nadia said. "What were those other lectures she's supposed to attend? Maybe there's another code in there that we missed."

Will pulled out his phone again. "Uh, we've got, *Lessons in Hope*, which gives first-hand accounts of women who converted to Islam, *Cloaked in Glory*, a sermon on the benefits of wearing the *hijab* and, of course, *Escaping the Goddess of Death*."

"The name definitely has an ominous ring to it," said Nadia. "Will they be infecting women there, or is that just their meeting place?"

"It could be either," said Will. "And as a matter of fact, a few of the people attending are already on some of our watch lists. They're being checked out as we speak."

Nadia gasped. "So something *is* going on there! But what? And why would the djinn be involved?" Nadia thought a moment. "Maybe they want to prevent women around the world from working together! If… like you said…they want to control the Middle East, maybe they don't want the animosity to stop. This seminar is meant to bring Muslims, Christians and Jews together. Maybe Lilith doesn't want that."

They were all watching her with amusement. "Look at her go," said Clive, shaking his head. Nadia slumped back down in her seat when she saw that she was miles behind them, as usual.

"Don't listen to him," said Gordon. "And don't stop telling us everything that comes into your head."

Nadia poured herself another glass of wine.

"Hey, easy on that stuff," said Clive. "We need you coherent."

Nadia put down the glass. "But…I mean…just in case…shouldn't you be doing something besides listening to my grandmother's stories?" she asked.

"There are a number of intel ops at work, chasing every possible lead, including these latest two we've just sent them," Will assured her. "Lilith is the lead we've been instructed to follow and we're going to examine every single point until we've exhausted all the possibilities, okay?"

Nadia nodded. She secretly hoped the other leads were more credible than this one. She wondered what light the rest of her story might shed on the situation.

Clive handed her a bowl of tiny, brightly colored flakes floating in milk. "Have some dinner," he said. "We've got a long night ahead of us."

CHAPTER
28

Ancient Mesopotamia
The city of Kiriath Arba
A few weeks later

It had been the belief of the Nephilim giants that their existence benefited the world at large. They imagined that even the sons of men would acknowledge this. They especially felt that the true God, the creator of both angels and men, would agree. It was not just their superior strength that compelled this admission, but their excellence overall. The Nephilim grasped new concepts with much more ease than ordinary humans. They were able to adapt, to learn and to grow intellectually without the cumbersome fears, prejudices and superstitions that stunted the sons of men. They felt this clear superiority made them natural leaders, and there was no arguing the fact that most of the cities they ruled fared better than the cities ruled by ordinary men. There were exceptions of course—no living creature was exempt from corruption—but overall, the Nephilim had a far greater propensity for improving the lives they touched. Excepting the most severe cases—such as the Emim, who were defective—the Nephilim lacked the human tendency to oppress others for the mere pleasure of it. They didn't need to rob those around them of joy in order to find it themselves. The Nephilim loved life. Like their fathers, they delighted in it. They didn't obsess over sin. They felt no need to hoard pleasure by storing it away or balancing it with sorrow. They believed in hard work, but enjoyed even this, and whatever they did they excelled at.

All of this the Nephilim took as evidence of their right to exist on earth. They collected their triumphs with great pride, mentally presenting them to the higher power like badges of honor. Each and every accomplishment was as much a gift to God as to themselves. Unlike the sons of men, their loyalties were not constantly changing. They did not look to any being other than their fathers, for help. The sons of men, on the other hand, changed loyalties almost as often as they changed their clothes. They were willing to accept any god, any prophet, anything at all—even an inanimate object of their own making—in the hopes that it would bring them success and victory and joy. This is why they resisted the angels' teachings. They seemed to prefer leaving their happiness in the hands of someone else. They'd rather have gods than teachers. Why, Lilith had heard of an island west of Syria, across the great sea to the north, where every single Nephilim was either a god or goddess. The people worshiped them unquestioningly, and lived only to please them. It was as if they had handed their very destinies to these 'gods' without a single objection. The little island, which was called Mycenae, was in dire straits until Uranus, the Watcher, came and took Gaia, one of their daughters to be his wife. Recognizing his greatness, the islanders instantly made him their god. They declared Gaia a goddess. The island prospered and the people's fervor deepened. Uranus and Gaia's first child, Cronus, was also made a god, as was his son, Zeus. In fact all of their descendants became gods, and the Mycenaean people lived vicariously through this angel and his Nephilim offspring, seeking little more out of life than to gain their pleasure. They were obsessed with them, and every event, from the smallest to the largest was attributed to these 'gods.'

If someone died, it was the will of the gods. When they became sick, they were being tested by the gods. Any misfortune meant they had displeased the gods. If a child so much as fell down and skinned his knee, he would instantly—almost without even realizing he was doing it—make a supplication to the gods.

Given this tendency of the sons of men to shun responsibility, the Nephilim were truly a godsend. Rather than following a false prophet bent on corruption, the sons of men could follow a magnanimous leader who would protect them and help them prosper. This was how most Nephilim thought of themselves. They were well aware that they were not God's creation but they were, after all, the offspring of His creations. It seemed natural that they should be acclimated into His world.

But in spite of all of this, there were the inevitable flies in the ointment. Most disturbing was what was always simmering just beneath the surface—perhaps it was sour grapes or outright jealously—but the sons of men seemed to always be teetering between neediness and resentment under the leadership of the Nephilim giants. There was the ever-present dilemma, no matter who was in power, that all power had its limits. Some things were unforeseen and inescapable. Life itself was problematic. The mere act of being alive produced immediate difficulties that had to be addressed. The refusal of the sons of men to accept this made them more vulnerable to the problems as they arose. And it left them susceptible to any new concept that they could be made to believe would relieve them of these problems. To be worshiped by the sons of men therefore was to be hopelessly doomed to failure. Perhaps this was why their creator remained distant and silent. It was clear that He intended for mankind to figure it out for themselves.

The Nephilim understood this and they accepted the responsibility in spite of the futility of it all. It was the only decent way to live. And this, then, was the rub; the Nephilim had not only failed to produce a perfect, problem free life for sons of men, but they appeared to be keeping the secret to happiness for themselves alone. The sons of men felt cheated.

For the people of Kiriath Arba, Lilith particularly epitomized this seeming inequity between the Nephilim and the sons of men. Here was a creature who defied all their laws and prospered. It was unheard of for a woman to dictate her own destiny. To be a giant and a warrior! She acted without regard for their customs. She flaunted her relationship with Asmodeous without the slightest inclination toward being a wife. She even somehow managed to evade pregnancy. They remained convinced that she was the cause of the affliction that struck their newborns, although the newly imposed tax had the desired effect of silencing their tongues. But secretly they felt she was an abomination, a demon hiding a terrible evil beneath her deceivingly beautiful exterior. She remained, to them, the reigning Goddess of Death.

This element of resentment and mistrust of the Nephilim ran rampant throughout Mesopotamia. They might have accepted the Nephilim as rulers, and in some cases even gods—out of necessity— but it was becoming obvious that they dreaded them more than they would ever respect or love them. There was always the underlying fear, as of evil, residing within the sons of men. The habit of covering their women to hide them from the angels and their offspring had become widespread. And it wasn't just their women they feared for, but themselves too. Even the clearing of the cedar forest hadn't eased their minds. In times of famine, rumors abounded that all Nephilim giants, given the right circumstances, would resort to devouring the sons of men rather than starving to death. Always some legend from a faraway land brought terrifying tales of people who suffered such a fate. Other legends brought rumors of Nephilim drinking the blood of the sons of men in order to gain eternal life. Yet these were superstitions that originated with the sons of men. They were the ones who believed that the secret to life resided in the blood. This ritual of drinking blood had come from them. If they chose to believe the Nephilim's longevity was attributed to this practice there was nothing that could be done to convince them otherwise.

All of this had been building and now, it seemed to have reached a fever pitch with the dreams.

Three days had passed since Anu, Azazyl and Arba arrived in Kiriath Arba, and they had spent every minute of it locked away in Lilith and Asmodeous' private chambers. The people had watched the angels' unexpected arrival with wonder and awe. The angels' untouched beauty, their silent power, their shining greatness; it was all at once incredible and exhilarating to behold. But the manner in which they had shut themselves off from the rest of the city (it was said that even those bringing food were not allowed to enter the chambers) was alarming. All that the citizens could do was to wait, somberly speculating what the secretive behavior signified.

Lilith and Asmodeous, meanwhile, were no less alarmed than their people. The news the angels brought shocked them and, even worse— it wounded them to the heart. It was unimaginable. Lilith was prostrate with grief. For the first time in her life she was numb with terror. She was afraid of the depths her loathing for the sons of men had reached. There was no longer any hope of reconciliation between the races.

Asmodeous and the angels were similarly devastated. The five of them huddled together, struggling to give and receive comfort. They went over the details again and again, dissecting every point. They mourned the events to come, even as they wondered how they might survive them. They did not, however, attempt to deny the inevitable. With that uncanny intelligence they possessed in almost all things, they instantly recognized it for the truth that it was.

The predictions had come through a series of dreams. These dreams appeared first to the angels, and then they were manifested to one of the sons of men, a certain prophet by the name of Enoch.

The angels were known for their ability to see into the future and it was commonplace for them to communicate with each other and their offspring through dreams and visions. It was rare for one of the sons of men to possess this gift, but Enoch's dreams not only coincided with those of the angels, they co-existed. The Watchers communicated with Enoch in his nocturnal visions, surprised to learn that the Others were doing the same. Desperate, the fallen angels enlisted Enoch's help to speak on their behalf. But even this failed to halt the events that had already been set in motion.

Even as the five of them gathered in Kiriath Arba, they knew myriads of warrior angels were gathering throughout the universe. The fallen angels—the Watchers—could do nothing to stop them.

For Lilith, it was unfathomable. How could God allow it? How could He deny the Nephilim's existence? Surely there was enough of His work in them to warrant mercy? After all, they had a greater appreciation for the gifts He'd bestowed on the earth than the ones he created them for. The inclusion of these angelic creatures to the bloodline had only improved the species. Surely if He could re-create man He would make them more like the Nephilim? Wasn't it the sons of men who should be obliterated if one of them had to go?

The angels could shed no light on the conundrum and were, in fact, as mystified as Asmodeous and Lilith. Their terror was the only thing that seemed real.

There was nothing to prevent it. The war was imminent. This war would be different than anything mankind had witnessed before. This would be a war waged by angels. Lilith's father had always told her that angels were not designed to destroy. They had the ability to cause destruction but they rarely lifted their own hand against another living creature. But that was not the case with all angels. Anu and his fellow fallen angels had been Watchers. They were called to watch over and assist the people of earth. In the event that some disaster was about to strike, they were supposed to alert the 'Others.'

These angels, being themselves immortal, would not be fighting to kill. Neither, for that matter, were the souls of any of the other creatures destructible. This war was different. The 'Others' were unconcerned with the flesh. Their goal was to *capture*, not to kill, and their casualties would be eternal prisoners. Their weapons were the elements contained right there in the earth. The war would very nearly wipe out humanity, stretching out over all the regions of the earth that the fallen angels had populated.

But it was the object of this heavenly war that froze Lilith's blood in her veins. It was to obliterate from the earth every man, woman or child who had even the smallest trace of Nephilim blood in their veins.

It was unimaginable!

But it was not happening yet. There was an appointed time, somewhere in the distant future. As the shock began to subside, a kind of intolerance and revulsion for the sons of men developed in Lilith and all the other Nephilim throughout the earth—for word of the impending war was spreading fast. A new, much more hostile division between the races was emerging. The sons of men were only aware of it through the change in the Nephilim's behavior toward them. There was now a menacing quality to the giants' reign that bordered on vicious. A new level of mistrust and hatred was building. The sons of men were never more aware of their inferiority. Indeed the Nephilim would not let them forget it. The Nephilim couldn't seem to stop wondering; *Why does He love them so much? Look what they do to each other—to their women, their children, themselves!*

The angels and their descendants began speaking in a different tongue so that the sons of men wouldn't be able to understand what they were saying.

Terror reigned in those days. Yet, surprisingly, though the sons of men were never more ill-treated, they were peculiarly content. In spite of their fearful, superstitious natures, they remained eerily unaffected by rumors of the impending disaster. Every indication of what was to come was virtually ignored. There was only one man, a descendant of the prophet Enoch, who took it seriously enough to make preparations for the event, building a great ark to carry animals and people alike, but he was a laughingstock among the rest of his people. With all that was happening around them—the Nephilim's oppressive behavior, the prophecies, the dreams—somehow the sons of men couldn't see the writing on the wall.

As for the Nephilim; not one of them doubted the coming war. They differed only in their strategies for surviving it. Many of them turned to the angels for help, but even the angels couldn't agree about what to do. Yet none of them sat idly by. They valued life too much for that. They prepared for the coming disaster, doing everything from building enormous ships to securing shelters for themselves in the mountains, and even creating weapons to use against the approaching army of angels. A few, like Gilgamesh, set out on great journeys in search of a secret that would render them immortal. The sons of men watched this seemingly bizarre behavior with their usual superstitious musings, but their conclusions fell so far outside the reality that it confirmed for all time the giants' opinion that they were innately wrong about everything. For some reason, Gilgamesh's behavior interested the sons of men most. His quest for eternal life intrigued them. They believed his obsession was brought on by grief over the loss of his friend, Enkido, whose life had been taken by the Emim in the battle of the Cedar Forest. But his Nephilim brethren knew that it was the news of the impending war that had pushed Gilgamesh over the edge. Arrogant and seemingly indestructible, he had actually begun to think of himself as a god. He refused to accept that his life could ever come to an end. He abandoned both the Kalag-ga and the city of Uruk for his journey, and was never heard from again.

Meanwhile, Lilith and Asmodeous—along with most of the other Nephilim in Kiriath Arba—formulated their own plan for survival, trusting completely in the wisdom of the three angels who were guiding them.

It was easy to see how Asmodeous' father, Azazyl, came to be the leader of the Watchers. He was not demanding or overbearing, but led with a quiet authority that was indisputable. His manner, like his beauty, was flawless; so flawless that it made the event all the more terrible. He was gentle and kind, although melancholy and sorrowful. He introduced their new language as he launched into the haunting narrative of the origins of the Nephilim race and continued until he revealed the dreams foretelling their ultimate destruction. Being first generation Nephilim, Lilith and Asmodeous grasped the new language instantaneously, easily comprehending every terrifying detail.

CHAPTER 29

The Story of the Watchers
As Told by Azazyl

"We were born of light, among God's earliest creations. Unlike human souls, we are complete without physical matter. However, we are able to utilize matter to create form if we so desire. Simply imagining the magnificent wings of an eagle can provide us with the ability to soar to great heights. We can be small or large, beautiful or terrifying. We can choose the form that best suits our needs. We are eternal. We cannot be destroyed.

Although angels can duplicate matter, it is a limited reproduction. It's never exactly the same as the original. God created man. The secrets of mankind's creation were not shared with us.

Angels do not experience the same sensations as man. Even so, in duplicating man, we were shocked by how much sensation we were able to enjoy. The longer we remain in this form the stronger these sensations become, bringing us closer to the experience of man.

It has been said that angels do not have free choice. This, like so many of man's concepts of the great mysteries, is incorrect.

As angels, we believe our purpose is to watch over and protect God's many creations. We're acting on God's behalf, but of our own free will. We act, as men do, as we *believe* God wishes. And also like men, we often disagree about what those wishes are.

You are shocked to learn that angels do not personally know God? God is a mystery to every living creature, whether of flesh or spirit. We know more than you do only because we are immortal and therefore have experienced more. We have had millenniums in which to roam freely throughout the many universes. We have seen more than man is capable of imagining in his short lifespan. Even so, there is much that even we do not know. There are legions of beings more knowledgeable than the angels, spreading throughout a vastness that no consciousness can begin to comprehend. In my existence I have seen many things, but I have never seen or spoken to God, nor have I met any other being who has done so. Those who claim to have spoken to Him tend to dwell in lower consciousness. Those who pretend to know His thoughts often have devious intentions. It is my belief that neither spirit nor flesh can ever comprehend Him. He is the creator of all things. He creates but does not destroy. What becomes of His creations depends entirely on them. Their fate is a combination of their actions altogether and as individuals. Every action has a consequence. This has always been my understanding.

The universe is a vast expanse of God's handiwork, scattered through time and space in the same way various living organisms are scattered upon the earth. There are wonders large and small; mysteries that take centuries—and even sometimes millenniums—to comprehend. I have explored many wonderful things and in the course of this I have found joy.

I chose to be a Watcher. I had traveled ad infinitum, and I was ready to serve. The earth was relatively new. I was intrigued.

For as long as I have existed there have been Watchers who keep a vigil over each of God's creations. We watch to ensure that outside influences do not interfere with the natural course of things. We are instructed to sound the alarm if their existence is threatened, or if self-destruction becomes imminent. It is my understanding that this was the will of God but, again, I have no way of knowing if this is true. Yet I never questioned it. Although I have not seen God, I have seen many of His creations, both with and without souls, and I have learned many things.

Mankind is unique. They are made in God's own image, meaning they can actually re-create new souls even as they bring forth new flesh. Every offspring of man generates a new soul. This had not been done before. Souls, like angels, had always been created separately. Souls are immortal, but unlike angelic spirits, they cannot truly exist without living matter to operate within. They become completely ineffectual and hopeless outside their physical selves. They are utterly dependent upon living matter. You can see what happens when their physical matter breaks down or is damaged. The soul virtually withers within it. It needs functioning matter, such as a working brain. Some souls are stronger than others in that they can make better use from less effective matter, but even those are limited by the physical restraints they exist within. And sooner or later, all matter, particularly flesh, changes, breaks down and eventually dies. But the souls do not die with it.

When we realized that man was capable of reproducing souls and saw the rate at which they did it, we wondered where all these souls would go at the time of their deaths. But as mankind began to die, we noticed that their souls were being drawn away to another, secret place. I don't know where that place is, but it is rumored that there is a special legion of angels who keep guard over them. It is supposed that these legions sit in judgment of them, determining which will take another form and live again—whether on the earth or in another place—or remain in limbo forever. I can't say if this is the case, but it does appear that souls are brought forth readily enough when new beings are created in other places. Perhaps mankind's ability to produce souls so abundantly was specially designed for this purpose. This is only a supposition. But one thing is certain; all creatures with souls direct their own actions, while creatures without souls act on instinct. These are the secondary creatures, existing only to complement those creatures with souls. As in the case of the souls existing on earth, these secondary creatures would be the fish, animals and birds. Creatures with souls are the center of everything in their realm.

Perhaps I shouldn't have volunteered to be a Watcher over mankind. From my first glimpse of them I was instantly transported into an entirely unfamiliar frame of mind. The very sight of them threw me into a tortuous tumult, frightening in its intensity. Never before have I seen such a creature. The baffling inconsistencies of their behavior both terrified and thrilled me. In between moments of astounding beauty and grace, there were those of extraordinary malice. Mankind nurtures and loves even as it devours and destroys! Their inexplicable desires and, conversely, their debilitating fears kept them at odds with everything, even themselves. I watched them in agony from the very first.

There were two hundred of us Watchers in all. Mankind had a similar effect on each of us. We watched them tirelessly, not merely as protectors would, but with an anxious interest and constant wonder, always speculating about what would happen next. We were in awe one moment; horrified the next. What sort of beings were these? They could love and kill with equal fervor. They marched to their own destruction on a whim. Recklessly they assumed that God himself was watching over them, ready to jump in and save them at the very last moment. Perhaps it was the heat of our own zealous watching that they were feeling. In some ways they were quite perceptive. But in others they were careless, abandoned, and dense beyond understanding.

Samyaza was the first of us to put the idea into words. Our longing was palatable, a tangible desire that eliminated the need for words. But in order to manage it—for we wished not only to taste the ways of flesh but to actually live as men—we knew we would have to all descend together. Otherwise, the remaining angels would have been obliged to sound the alarm. If even one of the two hundred had been against it, we wouldn't have done it. But we were unanimous in our desire.

We took a solemn vow to act as one and then descended onto Mount Arnon, forming flesh for ourselves just as you see it today. Though we are a perfect likeness of man, the true sons of men instantly perceived that we were different. The men were apprehensive, but the women were as desirous as they were fearful.

Though the flesh we created for ourselves was not exactly like that of men, it had the same alluring and terribly corrupting influence over us. You, Asmodeous and Lilith, are born of this earth so you don't know what it is to exist without that relentless influence. When first experienced, it is all at once exquisite and agonizing, a metamorphosis into terrifying chaos from the gentle peace we had existed in before discovering man.

I had fallen in love with Naamah, the daughter of Lamach, long before our dissent at Mount Arnon. She was beautiful and passionate, yet terribly sweet. When she became pregnant from our union I was astounded. I was petrified but I was also descending even further into the wild recklessness of the flesh. None of us knew what the result of these unions would be. Would our offspring be flesh? Would they have souls?

Ohya, the son of Samyaza, was the first of all Nephilim to be born into this world. It was a momentous occasion, and all of the Watchers came together to witness it. It was as if Ohya was the firstborn child of us all.

Ohya was just like any other child at first. Certainly he was flesh, and it appeared he was endowed with a soul. We concluded—mostly because it was our desire to believe that it was so—that our offspring would inherit all their characteristics from their earthly mothers. Since our flesh was merely an imitation of them, it seemed logical that the mothers' traits would dominate within our offspring.

However, Naamah and I were not as fortunate as Samyaza. Our firstborn was terribly deformed and did not survive. There was a very high mortality rate in those first years, and I've made some interesting observations in this regard. The first is that the longer the Watchers reside on this earth, the better chance our offspring have to survive. It's as if our flesh becomes more human the longer it is exposed to humanity. And each progressive generation born from our offspring looks and acts more like the sons of men.

You were our third attempt to have a child, Asmodeous, and a more perfect specimen I have yet to encounter.

As for our surviving offspring, the Nephilim, their superior size and abilities became obvious within the first year of their lives. Other tendencies became apparent as well. The first generation Nephilim was predominantly male. We supposed this was because our spirits were male. We began to wonder if we had the ability to produce females. The few females that did occur—until you, Lilith—had all been still-born. The secret must reside in the mother; for it has since become apparent that women who successfully bring a female Nephilim into this world often continue to give birth exclusively to daughters. In addition, we could see that the Nephilim had a higher aptitude for learning, and like us, they had a gift for understanding language and other concepts.

In most other respects the Nephilim children took after their mothers. They inherited mankind's strengths and weaknesses alike. Nephilim were born with the same reckless nature of the sons of men, along with their tendency toward corruption.

It was only natural that you should want to rule. We anticipated it as inevitable. But it has proven to be our downfall as well. For the souls of the sons of men who were killed by Nephilim have revealed what the Watchers have done. Their accounts of the Nephilim have been spread throughout the universe. And even though mankind has killed just as many, if not more, of their own, the Nephilim killings have been deemed unnatural. All that the Watchers have done—coming to earth, sharing secret knowledge with mankind, bring-ing forth Nephilim offspring—has been brought before the high-est councils of angels and we have all been condemned. We have interfered with one of God's creations, irreversibly altering their existence forever. Even now, legions of angels are gathering. Our time draws near.

The Watchers are unlike the angels who are coming. We are to them as mankind is to the Nephilim race. We will not be able to defend ourselves against them. Our only hope was to escape, but now it is too late. We have been prevented from leaving our fleshly bodies and are therefore obliged to remain on the earth until the appointed time.

In the coming war, the earth itself will be ruptured and nearly ripped asunder. The flesh of the Watchers will be disintegrated, and our spirits will be captured and imprisoned in a fiery abyss that exists in the center of the earth. Once all of the two hundred Watchers have been secured in the abyss, the earth will be re-sealed. There is no escape for us. Even now, should we attempt to destroy our fleshly bodies to release our spirits before the war, angels stand guard at all the gates, ready to capture them.

However, there is hope for you. The warrior angels will not destroy God's creation altogether. They intend to save mankind through the descendants of Enoch, because theirs is one of the few remaining bloodlines that have remained completely free of Nephilim blood. The angels have searched no further. They will save no one else.

But there is something else, and it is the key to everything. Your souls—the Nephilim souls—are the real threat to mankind. Your souls are not like human souls, but neither are they like the spirits of angels. We knew they were different a long time ago. We noticed that when a Nephilim dies, his soul does not go with human souls to the sacred place. It does not go anywhere. It would seem that there is no place for it to go. It simply stays here, displaced, on the earth.

These souls remain here, but they dwell in a parallel world that separates them from the world belonging to the flesh. We have been concerned with the plight of these souls—the Qliphoth—many of whom remain trapped in that parallel world to this day. But we've been exploring ways to help them return to the real world.

The only way for a Qliphoth to live again is through a living body. The Nephilim soul, like its body, is stronger than that of the sons of men. The stronger soul will dominate, while the weaker one will simply wither under the other's influence, lying dormant until the body dies or the dominant soul leaves. It is crushed under the dynamic energy of the Qliphoth. Also, while human souls lose all thoughts of this existence quickly after leaving their bodies, Nephilim souls seem to remain intact indefinitely, just like the spirits of their fathers. But there is still so much we do not know. The first descendants of the angels have the strongest, most effective souls. With each consecutive generation, their souls become more human. I don't know when (if ever) these souls actually become human enough to finally be accepted into the designated place for human souls.

But it is no longer just the parallel world that the Nephilim souls must overcome. The coming angels have prepared a new place for the Qliphoth. It is a terrible place of darkness such as no living thing has experienced before. It was once the location of another of God's creations, but now, that creation having been eradicated and its world destroyed, it has become a great chasm of nothingness. The chasm is so immeasurably deep and imponderably dark that even the spirit creatures dare not go there. Anything getting near it is immediately trapped in its blackness. You must avoid that place.

The angels who have declared war upon us are called the Others. They are as mysterious as God is Himself. No one knows their names or where they reside. They simply are. They're declarations are law.

Enoch has communicated with the Others in his dreams. He has recorded our fate in great detail.

This is what the dreams have revealed: at the appointed time, legions of warrior angels will gather round the earth. They will bring about a great earthquake, one so powerful it will generate a massive fracture that will tear its way to the center of the earth, shifting the continents with its incredible force. Eruptions will follow, sending immense amounts of water into the heavens. The earth will remain open until all of the Watchers are trapped in its fiery core.

Once the Watchers are in the abyss, the warrior angels will seal up the earth and return to their heavenly realm. The earth will be immersed in water, yet the water that erupted into the heavens will continue to fall for many days. All living things will be obliterated, save the select few who were chosen, and who will be guided by angels throughout.

Meanwhile, yet another legion of angels, sent by the Others, will be scouring the earth for the souls of the Nephilim, who they will be escorting to the dark place.

It will be difficult for you without the Watchers, but you can survive. And it is only through your survival that we will ever be released from the abyss.

We must prepare. You must make every effort to survive the war, but failing that, you must rise up from your watery graves and take back from the sons of man what is rightfully yours."

CHAPTER
30

Present Day

"Wow, it's…this is just…wow!" Gordon was clearly at a loss for words.

"Exactly," Nadia agreed. This is where the logical part of her brain really started to balk. "You see why I have my doubts?"

"What!" he exclaimed. "No! That isn't what I meant at all. This—what you've just told us—confirms everything!"

"I admit my grandmother's stories seem to corroborate the accounts in the bible and other ancient writings. But don't you think she could have got her ideas from those same sources? I mean, come on! If her stories are true…that means it's all true—God, the bible… all of it!"

"Why?" asked Gordon. "Why 'all of it?'"

Nadia just looked at him, confused by the question. She was tired and a little tipsy but she poured herself another glass of wine. It felt like midnight, but the light from the windows just kept getting brighter—she guessed it was now around mid-day—and she could tell that it was going to be a sweltering afternoon. She took a sip of wine and shook her head to try and clear the fog that was gathering there. "What do you mean?"

"According to what you just told us, these angels didn't know God any better than we do," Will said.

"It explains so much!" exclaimed Gordon.

Clive gave him a withering glance before adding—"Think about it, Nadia. These *angels* came here from somewhere else. They believed they were created by God just like we do. They were smarter than us and taught us things. People wrote about them. Maybe the people writing about them added their own twist on things, but that doesn't mean it didn't happen."

"One man's angel is another man's alien," said Will.

"Exactly!" exclaimed Gordon.

"*What* they were doesn't make a damn bit of difference," continued Clive. "The point is that they were *here*. Their presence created a ripple. And that ripple has now become a tsunami. Everything else is just a lot of distracting bullshit. It's people trying to make sense of it all. Let's just be honest here; God ain't said shit to anybody that we know of. You gotta look beyond the preacher saying 'do this' or 'do that' and find the *real* story hiding between the lines."

Nadia tried to consider this, but a thick haze seemed to be blocking out half of what they were saying. "What do *you* think they were?" she asked.

"I think they were angels," Will said simply. "That's what they called themselves and therefore it's what they were."

"Whatever that is," added Clive.

Nadia was surprised by how simple and obvious it suddenly seemed.

Will got up and gently lifted the empty wine glass from her fingers. "We're all tired and it's too early to get any more help from outside," he said. "It's four in the morning in New York—and even earlier on the west coast—and its Sunday to boot. We might as well get some rest."

Nadia allowed him to lead her to her bedroom, which was dark and considerably cooler than the room they just occupied. "I don't know if I can sleep," she said, though she was yawning as she said this.

"I think the wine will help," replied Will with a wry smile. He moved to re-connect the chain, which Gordon had detached earlier when Nadia complained of the weight of it. Nadia suddenly reached out and grasped hold of his arm.

"Don't!" she cried. "Please, Will, can't you take this horrible thing off my leg?"

"No," he said, reverting to the cold resolve that had irritated her so much when she first met him. It was his lack of compassion for her that angered her most. She grabbed his arm again, this time with both hands, in an attempt to prevent him from securing the chain. He drew up and looked at her in surprise.

"You've admitted you made a mistake in bringing me here and yet you continue to treat me like a prisoner!" she hissed.

"I don't recall admitting any mistake in bringing you here," he said, his steel blue eyes resolute. He bent down a third time to attach the chain.

This was too much. With a small cry Nadia began hitting him on the back, pounding him with her fists. He spun around in surprise and immediately captured her flailing arms in his two strong hands. She fought to get away but he held her securely, though he was careful not to hurt her. As gently as he could, he led her, still struggling, to the bed. She fell back, suddenly defeated. The anger disappeared as quickly as it came. But Will did not immediately retreat to attach the dreaded chain. He sat next to her on the bed, silently watching her until his calm demeanor rubbed off enough that Nadia was once again composed. Or it might have been that she was simply too exhausted to fight anymore. She felt oddly detached. She let out a long sigh, staring hopelessly at the ceiling, hardly aware of the tears that slipped down her cheeks. She even forgot that Will was there, until he startled her by capturing one of her tears on the tip of his finger, hardly even brushing his hand against her cheek in the process. Their eyes met. Nadia's breath caught in her throat. She thought—for a brief moment—that he might kiss her, and realized with astonishment that she wouldn't try to stop him if he did.

They remained like that for what seemed like a very long time. Will seemed to be suffering some internal struggle while Nadia could do little more than gaze up at him.

In the end, Will's self-control won out. Nadia watched the spark of emotion flicker and fade as his eyes turned back to cold steel. But his tone and manner remained as gentle as a caress when he finally spoke.

"We can't risk losing you now," he told her quietly. In spite of his extraordinary command over his emotions he seemed to be silently imploring her to understand. "I know your discomfort has been great." He reached out and lightly caressed her hand. "With every word you speak…every gesture…," he stopped there, letting the thought hang in mid-air. He seemed to be fighting to keep control, but his hand, meanwhile, kept lightly caressing her hand and then moved up her arm. "The more I learn about the woman you are, the more I believe that you need this resolution as much as we do." His hand was making its way to her face. "It's for *you* as much as the potential victims that we need to stop this disaster. I *feel* that." He had been steadily moving closer to her as he spoke and was now so close that she could feel his breath on her face. She had the distinct impression that he wanted to kiss her. She almost tipped her head back in anticipation of the kiss, but something held her back. And the moment passed. Will released her and moved to turn away.

Nadia reached out and stopped him, finding her voice at last. "I give you my word I won't try to escape," she whispered, suddenly wanting more than anything else—even freedom from the chain—for him to trust her.

"I believe you," he said. "But it's not for me to take such a risk. There are too many lives at stake."

Nadia was disappointed, and she suddenly realized that she had hoped her influence over him as a woman would overcome his relentless sense of duty. And with a strange clarity it struck her that this was often at the center of her conflicts with the men in her life, even those with her father. She often felt hurt and rejected when they wouldn't— she paused there, wondering what it was, exactly, that they wouldn't do for her. Give up control? Step outside themselves and risk everything—even, in this case, innocent lives—for her? These thoughts shocked her. But even more shocking was that she had somehow started to associate Will with the men in her life. She'd only known him two days. She wouldn't have known him at all if he hadn't held that chloroform cloth over her face. As a matter of fact, she had no concrete evidence that anything he was telling her was actually true. She had no idea who was on the other side of his supposed phone calls. The three of them could be taking their cue from her story and—for all she knew—building an imaginary incident around it. But why would they do such a thing?

Her confusion—taking her back and forth from one side of the fence to the other—made her think of Patty Hearst again. Somehow, Patty's kidnappers had started making sense too.

She felt her face growing warm under Will's silent scrutiny. Did he think she was a foolish little rich girl? Or did he really respect the woman she was, like he said?

Nadia still had hold of his arm, but this suddenly seemed inappropriate. She let her fingers slide away as casually as possible. She felt out of sorts—the heat of the afternoon was oppressive—and she was torn between wanting to be left alone and her need for comfort. She adjusted herself to a more comfortable position, unconsciously scooting over to the farther side of the bed so that there was more room for Will. He took her cue without hesitation and lay next to her, leaning up on one elbow so that he could look down into her face.

Nadia kept envisioning him kissing her, even though she had almost convinced herself that she would rather he didn't. She forced her thoughts away from his lips by thinking of Lilith.

"When I was a little girl I used to feel sorry for Lilith and the other Nephilim," she told him. "They couldn't help being born."

Will appeared to consider this. "I too can understand their desire to live," he conceded.

"And I always sort of agreed with their philosophies about us," she continued. "I mean, I suppose later, when I believed the stories were just myths that had been elaborated on by my grandmother, I figured the Nephilim were a kind of metaphor, a kind of lesson, like a moral to a story—'enjoy life and respect the earth or else someone might come and take it from you'—that kind of thing."

"They're a very real threat to our existence," Will told her. "I can relate to some of their ideas about life too. In some ways they put us to shame. But this gift of life on earth is *ours*, not theirs. No matter how much more they may want it, it belongs to us."

Nadia was not surprised by his cold, unbending resolve. She sensed that he would always stand by what he felt was right. A good characteristic to have, she supposed. But at the moment, he seemed obstinate and unyielding.

These thoughts were interrupted when Will suddenly did lean in to kiss her—lightly, on the forehead—and then hovered there, his lips almost caressing her skin as he spoke in whisper. "I still have to attach the chain," he murmured so quietly that she had to strain to hear him. Was it regret she heard in his voice?

"Yes," she acknowledged with a small sigh. She closed her eyes but she could still see him in her mind's eye as he rose up from the bed and picked up the chain. She felt him gently lift the covers and heard the sharp 'click' as he attached it to her leg. She heard his footsteps as he left the room, and continued to hear their muffled voices, soft and low, from the room beyond. She fell asleep to the sound, like distant music in her ears.

CHAPTER
31

Nadia opened her eyes reluctantly. Once again she'd been awakened by the pungent aroma of coffee. She felt wretched. The room was stifling and her limbs were like lead. A nagging sense of irritation pricked at her. She had that cross feeling she got when she took afternoon naps, which was why she didn't take afternoon naps. She could hear their voices in the other room and her irritation grew. Did they never sleep?

She closed her eyes again, but was suddenly too restless to lie in bed. With a sigh of disgust, she tossed the covers aside and got up, cursing the chain and the men who had brought her to this dismal little prison in the desert. She trudged miserably into the bathroom and rinsed her face with cold water. She knew without looking into a mirror that her long, thick curls were a tangled mess, and she told herself that she didn't care. She went to bedroom door, opening it the littlest bit to listen, but she couldn't hear what they were saying. Even so, she continued to stand there, reluctant to join them. Her gaze wandered to the living-room window and she guessed that it was now late after-noon. Sunday? She recalled going to bed around mid-day. She knew she was suffering from jet lag, but the realization didn't make her feel any better. She lingered in the doorway until her curiosity finally got the better of her.

Will was the first to notice her, and the amusement on his face when he caught sight of her made her wish she'd stayed in her room.

"Damn girl!" exclaimed Clive. "Don King called to say he wants his hair back."

Nadia pursed her lips together and silently moved toward the cof-fee pot. In spite of her irritable mood she had to fight the urge to burst into hysterical laughter.

"Clive…," said Will in a warning voice.

"What? You wouldn't want someone to tell you if you looked like a Chia pet?"

Nadia didn't dare face them for fear that she really would laugh. She kept her eyes glued to her coffee mug, clinging perversely to her irritation. "I wasn't given the luxury of hair styling products…or even a comb, for that matter, Clive," she replied in as haughty a voice as she could manage.

"Well, get her a comb, or a weed-whacker or whatever the hell it takes! Damn!" said Clive.

Nadia did glance up at Clive then, and was surprised when he gave her a little wink.

"Just teasing," he said. "I happen to like that nappy shit all wild and crazy like, with…with leaves and dead animals and whatever else you've got in there. Is that a sock? Did someone lose a sock?"

Nadia slapped his hand—which was messing up her hair even more—away. "Are you going to give me a comb or not?" she asked.

"Hell no, we're not givin' you a comb! I just told you I like it the way it is," Clive argued, but Gordon slipped up beside her and handed her a comb and a tube of hair gel.

"That ain't right," said Clive.

In spite of Clive's jokes and the hair products, Nadia's mood remained bad. She knew that a shower would help. Yet she was curi-ous to know if there were any new developments. She waited for one of them to say something about it.

"Have you heard anything?" she finally asked when it became apparent that nobody was going to tell her anything. Clearly she was still just a prisoner!

"No," Gordon replied. "And none of the other intel ops have found a single thing to support our theory that we're looking at a biological attack."

"Everything's checked out on Shakhra Research labs," added Will. Nadia finally met his eyes and was unnerved even further to find herself blushing. She wondered what he was thinking. He seemed all business, and she was mildly surprised by her own feelings in the midst of such chaos. Not to mention how disheveled she knew she must look. All of her feminine weapons had been disarmed. She didn't have the makeup, the designer clothes or even the impressive job (at least it wasn't impressive to them). And she could hardly play hard-to-get while chained to the floor. Yet, in spite of all this, Will's gaze seemed almost affectionate. Of course, that could just be the Patty Hearst syndrome at work. "They're sending someone in today to make sure, but it looks like their labs haven't conducted any classified or restricted research for several years."

"Interesting thing we found on their choice of a company name though," Gordon told her. "It struck me as odd, so I ran it through our system. 'Shakhra' is the name of an ancient city north of Iran that disappeared a long time ago."

"What do you mean, disappeared?" asked Nadia.

"Just that. It disappeared. There's no record of what happened to it. But that's not the interesting part…ancient cities used to disappear all the time. An army could have come in and claimed it, or it might have willingly joined forces with an adjacent city and adopted their name. There are lots of perfectly reasonable explanations. But the interesting thing is their history. It was from this city of Shakrah that the Oguz turks—a very unique tribe of Huns—first came into existence."

Nadia stared at Gordon, trying to make sense out of what he was telling her. He seemed to be waiting for her to catch on, but she knew very little about the Turks. "Oguz…as in *Og*?" She asked, grasping at the only thing that struck a familiar chord.

"You got it," Gordon replied. "We've always suspected that the Huns were descended from the Nephilim. By that time they wouldn't have been giants in the truest sense, being several generations out, but they were still unusually big and strong. They were a fearsome lot. We think the people of this Oguz tribe might have been the descendants of Og."

"So…Shakhra *is* involved in this then?" asked Nadia.

"Maybe, maybe not," said Gordon. "But at least we've got another lead to add to our network. There's a good chance that someone in that company has connections to the djinn."

"This is where you start to lose me," said Nadia. "Do you realize how paranoid you sound?"

"We know it probably sounds that way to you," said Clive. "Because you don't know what you're talking about." The look Nadia gave him only seemed to amuse him. "Seriously, it would shock you to know how many companies—huge companies, major companies, with their hands in everything from medical research to helping stupid ass kids who can't get out of their own way go to college—have direct, confirmed ties to terrorism. Man, this is real life, ghost bustin', terrorist ass kickin' shit!"

"Why not just close down those companies?" asked Nadia.

"Because we need them to help us ferret out the bad guys," said Will.

Clive smiled wickedly. "Take *your* company for example. BEACON's turning out to be a gold mine of djinn connections."

Nadia winced at the implication. "But I'm neither a djinn nor a terrorist," she said.

"Someone over there is," said Clive.

Nadia stared at him, shocked. "I—we…" She stopped to take a quick mental inventory of the people she worked with, but there were too many, what with board members, paid employees and the volunteers. Yet it didn't seem possible that any of them could be involved.

"Don't worry," Clive added, guessing her thoughts. "We're on it." Nadia felt herself growing pale at the implication.

"Anyway, you close one company and they'll just start up another," said Gordon, tactfully guiding their conversation away from the volatile topic of BEACON.

"Yeah," agreed Clive. "These bitches have more money than God."

"It's not like they're sitting around board meetings plotting acts of terrorism," Will told her. "Often it's someone on the inside acting on their own, using the company's money and resources."

This was all very disconcerting, but if BEACON *was* harboring some link to terrorism she certainly didn't want to protect it.

She woke up thinking she couldn't feel any worse and here she was; feeling worse.

"It's the jet lag," said Will, noticing her expression. "It always makes things seem worse than they are."

"You'll feel better after a shower," added Gordon.

"I've had jet lag plenty of times before," snapped Nadia, more sharply than she intended.

"Then get your shit together and get over it," Clive snapped back. "'Cause these djinn aren't gonna wait around for little Miss Priss to get in a better mood."

CHAPTER
32

Ancient Mesopotamia
Kiriath Arba
Several years later

U nder Azazyl's direction, the Nephilim of Kiriath Arba worked tirelessly to prepare for the impending war of the angels. They built an enormous wall that was five times higher than the one protecting their own city just south of Kiriath Arba, in the desert. It had but one gate from which the Nephilim could enter or leave, yet all around its parameter soldiers stood guard. The people of Kiriath Arba were given no explanation for it and could do little more than speculate on what was happening inside the wall.

Initially, people entering this desert city (excepting the Nephilim giants), were never seen again. This made it an undesirable place to go. Violators of the law were among the first to be marched through the gate into whatever horrors lay beyond. From the fertile imaginations of the sons of men there sprouted a rich crop of tales involving every imaginable kind of depravity and torture, the worst of which were inspired by recent memories of the Emim. They pictured decadent feasts where the unfortunate prisoners were served as the main course, their gleaming, well-oiled bodies speared and trussed, and turning ever so slowly on a spit over red hot coals. They reminisced over the good old days when criminals were merely stoned to death. Fear had them following every injunction to the letter, but this didn't slow the unprecedented number of arrests that continued to occur. It soon became clear that the youngest and the strongest of the sons of men were being targeted, and they could be seized under any kind of false pretense.

In actuality, the prisoners who were brought to this desert prison were kept in relatively good physical health, not in order to become part of any feast, but to help the Nephilim build a gigantic ship. The massive walls had only been built as high as was necessary to hide what they were doing. And the sons of men were not allowed to leave the city because the Nephilim didn't trust them to keep their secret.

Aside from the construction of the ship, many other preparations were being made. Secret information was being gathered and recorded by Azazyl and the other angels, with copies being made on copper sheets, animal skins and stone to ensure their preservation. These documents recorded sacred—and potentially dangerous—knowledge of earth and the universe, and everything in it. Most importantly, they held the key for bringing back these lost souls—the Qliphoth—of the fallen Nephilim. But these angelic revelations were only one piece of the puzzle. There was a second, equally necessary piece which each Nephilim had to prepare for his or her own individual soul. It was a 'Book of the Dead' which described that Nephilim in remarkable detail, recording everything from their parentage to a lengthy account of the more significant events of their life here on earth. The books were then logged in an official register, set in chronological order according to generation, with first-generation Nephilim listed first. Scribes were kept busy copying them day in and day out. To ensure secrecy, many of the books were written in a combination of languages—a few of which were completely unknown to men. Some words were written in the traditional cuneiform, while others were depicted with pictures or symbols. Azazyl oversaw the scribing himself to ensure accuracy. The documents were then painstakingly wrapped and stored with as much care as a cherished loved one being laid to rest in a tomb. It was imperative that these secrets be preserved. Whether or not the Nephilim survived the impending war, their flesh was mortal, and therefore was doomed to perish eventually. The documents were their only hope for continued survival. Life was preferable to death, even if it must be lived from within the inferior flesh of the sons of men.

In addition to re-establishing themselves on the earth, the Nephilim would need to learn how to control this incredible power they had over life and death. This information was especially dangerous, but it was necessary in the event that other, less desirable Qliphoth—such as the Emim—managed to find their way back into the world. Problems could arise, and there had to be a way to banish unwanted Qliphoth from the earth in order to protect their own positions. These documents were kept secret from everyone but a select few. It was Azazyl's hope that Asmodeous would lead the Nephilim race in their reclamation of the world.

While all of this was going on in the desert just south of Kiriath Arba, other Nephilim around the world were making preparations as well. The sons of men, meanwhile, remained stubbornly unconcerned by the threat of the 'end of the world.' Although they could accept the concept of being tortured by their gods, the idea of being brought to the brink of extinction was not something they were prepared to consider. They laughed at the very idea. The warnings of the prophet, Enoch, and his descendant, Noah, were almost completely ignored.

Even the mysterious and ominous behavior of the giants went unmarked. Yet it was impossible not to feel the ever-increasing animosity between the Nephilim and the sons of men. These 'gods' grew more and more oppressive. Their preoccupation with the impending war was mankind's only reprieve.

As for Lilith, her general dislike for the sons of men had blossomed into an intense loathing that she no longer bothered to hide. The hurt she felt over being rejected by God made her vengeful. She didn't just hate the sons of men; she hated their creator as well. She believed Him to be as flawed as His creatures. She supposed Azazyl was right. The Nephilim had been wrong to flaunt their superiority over the sons of men. Their God was a jealous God who didn't appreciate being bested.

If they survived the war the Nephilim would get an opportunity to do things differently. This time they would focus on the weaknesses of the sons of men, not the strengths of the Nephilim. If they could prove that mankind would self-destruct without their help, surely He would reconsider their position on earth. This time the Nephilim would encourage—and even foster—mankind's destructive beliefs and behaviors, assisting them toward their ruinous end. The Nephilim would no longer be able to rule by means of strength; all men would be equal in that regard. They would have to master the sons of men through their superior intellects. The Nephilim must prove once and for all that mankind needs them to survive.

Not that mankind deserved to survive. In Lilith's opinion, the sons of men were selfish, ignorant and petty, like spoiled children that one longed to punish. She took pleasure in being the one to select which of them would be arrested and condemned to spend the rest of their life as a slave in the Nephilim's secret desert city. She enjoyed choosing the most arrogant men for her army to seize. And the women were not exempt either. They could be snatched up for so much as giving Lilith a look she didn't like. It wasn't long before Lilith was the most feared person in Kiriath Arba. People avoided her like the plague. Although the affliction had passed—just as Asmodeous predicted—the rumors that linked her to it had not. Children were vigorously kept indoors and out of her reach. A mere look from the beautiful but terrifying Lilith could make them disappear forever. Since she most often took the youngest and fittest among them, people began to wonder if, like her nephew Gilgamesh, Lilith had some sexual interest in her victims. And where the sons of men were concerned, every rumor was destined to become history.

Asmodeous continued to rule Kiriath Arba with Lilith standing ominously by his side. The people endured their reign in grim silence, while inwardly growing more and more resentful and rebellious.

In spite of all this, Lilith and Asmodeous' relationship thrived, just as the silvery saltbush thrives in the worst desert storms. Hardship only seemed to bring them closer together. The very sight of Asmodeous brought Lilith pleasure and she never tired of his touch. They made promises to each other and carefully laid down plans, both for the present and the future. They discussed the coming war, anticipating every possibility. They filled the ship with all their favorite things, re-stocking it often without the slightest regard for waste. They speculated over what the world would be like when they emerged from the ship. They debated about what they would do differently when rebuilding Kiriath Arba. They even talked about their eventual deaths, carefully considering what characteristics they would like to have the next time around. They approached even the most depressing topics optimistically, confident that they could get through anything as long as they had each other. They never ran out of things to talk about and found amusement in almost everything. It was what Lilith loved most about Asmodeous, that he had taught her to laugh.

In the course of their preparations for the war, Asmodeous decided that he and Lilith should learn how to swim. They found a private length of river and went there almost every morning. And they took to the water like fish. They enjoyed it so much that they continued their training long after it was necessary. It became one of the high points of their day to rush down to the river, giggling like children as they stripped off their clothes, climbed to the highest spot they could find and jumped fearlessly into the deep water. They spent hours splashing around, always trying to one-up the other with their increasingly daring antics.

For the first time in her life, Lilith loved someone else more than herself. But she found that this kind of love came with a price. New anxieties arose. There was now another person to worry about. There were times when she feared more for Asmodeous than for herself. She knew that Asmodeous would never let anything happen to her and this reassured her on her own behalf. But what of him? Could she ensure the same? Suddenly she wasn't as confident in her own abilities. And she was glad that she'd never had a child. A child—his child—would be one more thing for her to worry about.

Throughout Mesopotamia life trudged uncertainly on. The tension between the races was developing into an animosity so potent it would have eventually brought mass destruction to one or the other in any event. With no incentive to repair their relations with the sons of men, what little forbearance and munificence the Nephilim formerly had was completely depleted. The giants seemed barely able to tolerate humans now. A few couldn't even do that much, and rumors of a new tribe of giants bent on exterminating the sons of men spread through Mesopotamia. This menace kept the sons of men petrified, prompting them to stay and face the persecution of their Nephilim rulers rather than to risk being massacred by these blood-thirsty crusaders.

Those were difficult times for the sons of men. Even in Kiriath Arba, the formerly peaceful city, it seemed as if death would be better than what they endured. They were treated little better than slaves, especially the ones who were brought to the desert. These were put to use in every conceivable way, from forced labor to experiments in bringing back the lost Nephilim souls. The latter were the only humans to emerge from the secret city, but they returned so completely changed that it would have been better if they had not returned at all. They were nothing like their former selves, having no apparent memory of their lives or the people who loved them. They were arrogant, superior and completely indifferent to their own people. They spoke in the new Nephilim tongue and kept to themselves. Like the Nephilim, they were allowed to come and go as they pleased. Perhaps the most disturbing thing was that they kept what was happening in the desert secret, refusing to give out the smallest bit of information to their own race. It was almost as if they no longer belonged to that race.

Those who had known these transformed individuals had no doubt that they were possessed. To see their loved ones so altered was more disturbing than anything they had endured up to that point. Rumors of this new horror spread like dandelions in a windy field. In spite of the Nephilim's many precautions to keep their activities secret, the sons of men now had an idea of what was occurring behind the great wall. This was yet another terror unleashed. This new breed of Nephilim emerging from among their own people was unconscionable and undefeatable. Without means for protecting themselves they turned to God, praying relentlessly while wearing religious amulets that were purported to ward off evil.

Their behavior amused Lilith. She became more enthusiastic and rigorous in her choices for who would be among the 'damned.' She spitefully scoured the city for new faces, growing more and more malicious in her selections. She singled out the most beautiful and gifted of their sons and daughters in order to create the most distress. She enjoyed seeing the utter defeat in the faces of their grieving parents.

But among the citizens of Kiriath Arba, Asmodeous was considered even more culpable than Lilith. He was the one who brought her to their city and gave her free reign over them. He now seemed obsessed with his desert creation, hardly deigning to step foot in the city he once loved. His 'Goddess of Death' now ruled while he sacrificed their children to demons. Their beloved king became the 'King of the Demons.'

This was Mesopotamia in the days before the flood. Years passed. No one knew when the appointed hour would come. There were moments when it seemed as if it never would come. But then one day, quite unexpectedly, it did.

CHAPTER
33

The Flood

Lilith sprawled out on the river bank, having just emerged from the water. The heat of the sun, although severe, felt splendid on her chilled skin. She closed her eyes, delighting in the deep crimson that flooded her lids, thick and warm, like blood. She was overwhelmingly conscious of sensual pleasures, like the salty taste of Asmodeous' skin, and the exquisite entwining of their limbs during the night. But her contentment was tempered by the need to return to the desert. Asmodeous would not like it if he knew she was out alone.

Lilith sighed. All these precautions were wearing on her. They took all the spontaneity out of life, making it little more than a kind of dreadful anticipation. It wasn't as if they didn't have the angels to warn them. Anu had never failed her before. It was unreasonable to expect her to take an entourage on every single outing, especially when there wasn't even the slightest hint of a storm on the horizon.

What need had she for ten slaves trudging behind her with the manda-
tory *ziki* in tow, watching her every move with those dour expressions
pasted on their miserable little faces?

Though she had to admit that the *ziki* were indeed a brilliant idea.
The remarkably lightweight rafts were constructed from large reeds
and designed to look like oversized shields so that no one outside
the desert wall would guess their true purpose. Four wooden oars
were hidden within the seams of the raft, along with an ingenious
instrument for determining direction in the event of darkness. Anu
and Azazyl had thought of everything. Although the *ziki* wouldn't be
strong enough to carry them through the disaster, it was hoped that it
would get them to the ship. All Nephilim—especially Lilith—were
under strict orders to have the *ziki* with them whenever they ventured
outside the wall.

An unwelcome twinge of guilt disturbed Lilith's peaceful mind,
creating a sudden flutter of anxiety to return to the desert. She obsti-
nately ignored it. *Just a few more minutes*, she promised herself.

It was impossible to envision disaster on such an exquisite morning. The birds were chirruping noisily in the river reeds that crowded
the bank while insects buzzed irritably as they passed. Lilith wondered how much longer this could go on. On a day such as this, she
could almost persuade herself that it was all just a terrible mistake.

A sudden, jerky trembling of the ground interrupted Lilith's
thoughts. It took her a moment to realize that it was an earthquake. A
strange thrill that was half terror, half curiosity shot through her as she
attempted to stand. It was extremely difficult to maintain her balance
over the quaking earth, but somehow she managed it. The peculiar,
dreamlike curiosity stayed with her, distracting her as she made an
effort to run. She fell down repeatedly but always got right back up.
She had one thought—to find Asmodeous. It seemed as if the world
was slowing down, perhaps even coming to a stop. She heard a deep
rumbling sound in the distance.

The earthquake seemed to be waning. Its vibrations were definitely growing weaker. The rumbling sound, however, was getting
louder. Lilith stopped to look in the direction of the sound. There was
something there—something extreme—but it was much too far away
to make out what it was. Lilith could only perceive that it was dark,

ominous, and infinitely terrible, like a murky shadow rising over the earth. Lilith stared at the immense thing in awe, struck by a sense of impending doom. Then she turned back toward the ship and began to run.

She approached Kiriath Arba first. Just beyond it, to the south, was the ship. And Asmodeous. Lilith ran so fast that her chest began to ache.

The sky was growing dark and it was starting to rain. At first the rain was sparse—a random smattering of large, pendulous drops—but it quickly became a downpour, turning into a dense sheet of water that was a struggle just to see through. Within seconds Lilith was soaked to the skin. It felt as if the water was coming from all directions.

The city of Kiriath Arba was in pandemonium, but Lilith thought of nothing but the approaching darkness. She couldn't resist another backward glance. The dark wall was indeed coming closer! But what was it? She ran faster, ruthlessly knocking people out of her way as she went.

The ground, unused to such sudden torrents of rain, was already flooded. Lilith found herself wading in water that was up past her ankles. She'd never felt such fear before. Tears streamed down her cheeks unnoticed. The pain in her chest was growing stronger but she kept going.

She'd been so sure that there would be more time. She was shocked that Anu hadn't warned her. What did it mean? Was her father already captured in the abyss? Her tears were being instantly washed away by the rain and she let all thoughts of her father go with them. There was no time to mourn. She had to get to the ship.

But in turning to catch yet another glimpse of the dark thing behind her, Lilith knew that she would never make it to the ship before it reached her. It was approaching too quickly. She actually stopped in her tracks at the sight of it. She could see that it was not just a dark presence but something else. Something real and infinitely terrible. The rumbling, which had steadily been growing louder, was actually the sound of its approach. It was so massive it seemed to breach the very heavens. And then it hit Lilith like a slap in the face. The approaching darkness was water. It was a massive, unfathomable wall of water. And it was nearly upon them!

She would never make it to the ship.

Beyond the rumbling din Lilith could hear the voices of the sons of men, crying out to their God in supplication and fear. She could imagine the Nephilim, meanwhile, hurriedly boarding the ship—all except Asmodeous, who she knew would be waiting for her. Would he refuse to enter the ship without her? Lilith suddenly felt the full weight of her actions. If she somehow survived and Asmodeous perished—she couldn't bear to finish the thought.

The rumbling approach of the water was now more like a thunderous roar. Lilith looked around in desperation, and her frantic gaze found the high walls of the ziggurat temple. It was the strongest structure in the city. Perhaps its angular walls would withstand the blow. It was her only hope.

Thankfully the temple was not a great distance off. But there were so many obstacles in her way! Lilith meandered in and around the narrow streets of Kiriath Arba. There was a time when she found them charming but now they were no more than a dangerous impediment. She was struck, too, by the irony of seeking refuge in a place of worship for the sons of men. But if she survived this first destructive wave, she might be able to swim to the ship. It was her only hope.

The roar of the water was deafening by the time Lilith climbed the steps of the ziggurat, taking them two at a time, oblivious of the pain in her chest and thighs. She rushed toward one of the inner rooms off the entryway, settling in a corner between two walls. She looked up and was surprised to find so many others gathered there. She was the only Nephilim among them.

There was an explosive crash, like a clap thunder, as the wall of water collided with the walls of Kiriath Arba. The earth shook as the walls and everything beyond them gave way. The noise was so great it seemed to vibrate from within rather than from without. Lilith clung to the inner wall.

"Anu," she prayed. "Please help me!" But the thought of her father and where he might be in that moment only made her feel worse.

Within seconds the water reached the ziggurat, colliding with it violently before rushing around it in all directions. It only took a few seconds more for it to flood every opening, and Lilith had just enough time to fill her lungs with air before the tiny room off the entryway was immersed. Holding her breath, Lilith waited as long as she could for the initial rush of water to subside and its overwhelming pull to let up the smallest bit. She tried to remember what Asmodeous told her to do in this worst case scenario.

Struggling against the rushing water, she somehow managed to maneuver herself through the doorway without being crushed against the wall. When she finally got outside, she forced her limbs to become soft and slack, not fighting the tide but moving with it. She felt her body being lifted upward, even as it was being drawn with the tide, hopefully in the direction of the ship.

In the confusion of those first moments, it was hard to tell which end was up. Lilith couldn't see light in any direction. Yet she trusted that she was being drawn toward the surface. Was there a surface? The wall of water appeared to reach the very heavens. A new panic rose up but Lilith assured herself that there must be a ceiling to the deluge. She fought against her instinct to struggle, forcing herself to remain still and calm. To give in to the panic would mean certain death.

Meanwhile, as the seconds turned to hours, this new world underwater seemed to come alive. Although darkness surrounded her, some things were more visible than others. Human bodies, for example, had an iridescence about them that made them almost appear to glow in the murky deep. She saw bodies of men, women and children all around her, either struggling violently against the inevitable or simply gazing in open mouthed wonder as their bodies slowly drifted downward. Some ceased their struggles when they caught sight of Lilith, staring dumbfounded at her calm, upward-floating body with a curiosity that momentarily superseded their terror. No doubt she must have appeared every bit the demon they supposed her to be in that astounding moment; her dark hair flowing all around her as she drifted— seemingly blissfully—in the direction of the tide.

The inhabitants of Kiriath Arba spent their last terrifying moments struggling for life in those dark, watery depths along with donkeys, sheep, goats, chickens and every other imaginable thing, both living and otherwise. Pottery, bricks, and other dense items were making their way toward the bottom rather quickly, while the lighter rubble was being drawn with the tide. It was necessary to maneuver around this wreckage in order to avoid being injured.

The water was growing thicker with debris. This encouraged Lilith, as it signified she might be nearing the top of the deluge. Her lungs were starting to ache from holding her breath for so long. More and more of the wreckage surrounded her, and she struggled to follow the joggling tide without being crushed.

Suddenly Lilith felt resistance overhead and she knew at once that she had reached the surface. She clawed at the debris, feeling a creeping sense of being buried alive beneath the heavy layer of flotsam. The tide kept trying to pull her away but she refused to give up, working tirelessly to clear away the refuse until she felt the cool, welcome raindrops pelting her finger-tips. Relieved almost to the point of giddiness, she kept pushing away the debris until she'd made a big enough hole to poke her head through. Then she thrust her body up and heartily gasped for air.

The rain was still so thick that Lilith choked on those first, frantic breaths. She coughed uncontrollably, glad for the floating debris around her, which seemed to help buoy her up, even as it jerked her along in the direction of the tide. The world under water had seemed to slow, but Lilith was suddenly aware of how fast everything was actually moving. The water was dragging her along faster than she'd ever traveled in her life, faster, it seemed, than the swiftest horse. The rain was relentless, making it hard to breath and even harder to see. And it was impossible to hear. The rushing water towed her along in a crashing, roaring, roiling rush. Lilith thought she heard screaming and looked around. Others had made it to the surface and they, too, were being carried by the churning sea of debris. A few were being crushed or even impaled by the moving objects.

Water was everywhere. Lilith ignored the dark thoughts pricking at her subconscious, focusing instead on the exhausting, non-stop effort it took just to maneuver around the wreckage. As she was drawn farther and farther from the city the blanket of debris seemed to break, alleviating somewhat the immediate danger of being crushed. There were fewer objects rushing toward her now. She spotted a small tree in the distance and cautiously worked her way to it. She grasped hold of it, maneuvering her body so that she would be carried along at its center. This protected her from approaching objects while clearing a path. Lilith pulled herself up on its trunk and took the opportunity to rest.

Then she pulled herself up even higher and looked anxiously around in all directions. It was so dark. She couldn't see the ship!

Dismay flooded through her. Surely the ship had survived the crash! It had been placed in the very center of the desert city—far enough from the walls to ensure clearance in the event that it was pushed sideways before being lifted—and perched up on staging so that it would readily float when the waters came. Sections of the stone wall had been structurally weakened all around its circumference so that it would give way in the unlikely event that the ship did strike it. Every possibility had been considered.

Although it was midday, there was no trace of the sun. Lilith had no idea where she was. She supposed it didn't matter. She was forced, for the moment, to follow the tide. Based on the direction from which the water had come, she felt that it was carrying her over the desert area where the ship had been. If that were the case, the ship should be directly ahead of her, moving in the same direction. The ship was so large that Lilith had fully expected to see it the instant she emerged from the water. She rose up higher on her tree and squinted to see farther ahead.

There did appear to be something out there—some kind of dark object—but it was terribly far away. She stared at it for a long time, until she believed it might, in fact, be the ship. The shape and height of it seemed right. But it was so far away! How would she ever catch up to it? She thought about this. It seemed to her that her body ought to travel faster through the tide than a heavy ship. But how, then, had it gotten so far ahead of her?

The debris was breaking up even more as it spread out over the wide expanse. And the rush of the water seemed to be slowing down as well. Lilith was tempted to swim toward the dark object in the distance. But what if she didn't make it? Most of the floating wreckage was too small to be of any use to her. And as she got farther out there would be fewer items from which to choose. What were her chances of finding another tree? Lilith bit her lip. Could she make it that far—assuming the dark object really was the ship? She pondered a moment, struck by the gravity of her situation.

Lilith decided not to take the chance. Holding tight to her tree she began to kick her feet, pushing the tree ahead of her as she went. She could imagine Asmodeous looking out over the sea from the ship, searching the waters for her.

It occurred to her that the city's rubble may have slowed her down. It probably created resistance against the tide in spite of its overwhelming force. The ship, on the other hand, would have easily cleared all wreckage from its path. Lilith tried to squash these negative thoughts by kicking her feet faster. But the ship just seemed to get further away.

She was surprised to find other survivors still bobbing around in the water. She spotted no other Nephilim, only the sons of men. A few actually cried out to Lilith for help. Others just stared at her with little or no expression in their eyes. One man tried to grab hold of Lilith's tree, but she perversely shook him off. As much as she dreaded the thought of being alone out there, enduring the company of one of them seemed even worse. She kicked with all her might, hardly able to hide her hatred for them as she passed. This was all their fault. She took comfort in the knowledge that they wouldn't last long.

Why, oh why hadn't she listened to Asmodeous? If she had she would be with him and the other Nephilim on the ship, not stranded out here with the sons of men. What would she give to feel his arms around her again?

It was odd, how warm the water was. Had it burst forth from the earth that way? It happened just as Azazyl predicted. She wondered again if the fallen angels were now trapped in the earth's center, locked in the hellish abyss that made up its core.

Clinging to the dead tree, Lilith was suddenly reminded of one of the stories the women of Kiriath Arba told about her. It had angered her at the time, but in that moment she couldn't help seeing the irony. In the story, Lilith was a serpent living in a tree that belonged to the goddess of life. The tree was Kiriath Arba, and the goddess of life symbolized whatever benevolent spirit had previously blessed their fertile city. But since the tree had been infiltrated with the serpent it only bred death. This was how she came to be the Goddess of Death.

Lilith wondered if Asmodeous ever guessed that it really was her who brought death to all those children—not through any demonic activity, as the sons of men supposed—but by simply contaminating their drinking water.

It had all been too much, watching the sons of men reproduce like rabbits while Lilith wasn't able to give Asmodeous a single child. Perhaps if the people of Kiriath Arba hadn't been so judgmental, insisting her barrenness was some kind of condemnation from God. She'd wanted to see if they would draw the same conclusion when it happened to them. But of course, they had not. Hypocrites! When they failed to reproduce it was a different matter altogether.

Lilith felt that Asmodeous wouldn't mind. He wasn't particularly thrilled by the rate at which the sons of men were multiplying either. He felt they needed more giants in Kiriath Arba. No matter how weak and pathetic the sons of men were, there was no denying that there was power in numbers. Anak had done more than his share, of course, but even so, he was no match for the sons of men, who often brought another child into the world every year.

When Lilith was much younger, she too had come to be with child, but not wanting to give up her status in the Kalag-ga, she'd gone to Enki, an angel who understood such matters. Since Lilith was so far along in her pregnancy, Enki had taken her outside the city and put the sickness into her drinking water. Due to the contagious nature of the illness, Enki nursed her himself, allowing no one else to come near. Lilith was terribly sick for days, but she survived. And on the third day the fetus was born dead.

It was a contagion, that was all. It was not the will of any god or demon, as the sons of men supposed. The ongoing—albeit peaceful—segregation between the sons of men and the Nephilim made it easy. All Lilith had to do was infect the water supply of the city's most insufferable band of 'pure bloods'—as they called themselves—and she could be fairly confident that the 'affliction' would remain among them and their slaves. And for the most part it had. The Nephilim and their wives had had the wherewithal to draw even closer into their own circle, thus escaping the worst of the disease.

Lilith was suddenly very tired. Sadness settled over her like a too-heavy blanket. All the years of fighting—fighting to be accepted by her village, fighting to become a warrior, fighting to be with the man she loved, and now fighting for her very life—had taken their toll. She was always fighting. Her very existence seemed to be at odds with everything.

༕

3 days later

The world was eerily quiet. The soft, steady rain was the only sound. The waters no longer rushed in any particular direction. There were no birds in the sky and, even more disturbing, Lilith hadn't encountered a single fish. She was growing weaker. Not trusting the water, Lilith drank only drops of rain. She was so hungry. She divided her time between catching raindrops on her tongue, sleeping, and gazing about. The darkness had not lifted, but her eyes were becoming more adjusted to it. Her thoughts wandered aimlessly. Was it daytime or night? The dark thing that might have been the ship was no longer there. She'd awakened to find that it had either floated away or had never been there to begin with. It was possible that that first, thunderous wave had destroyed it. Even the temple had been shaken to its foundation when it struck, and it had been constructed of stone. She remembered the long, terrible boom that seemed to go on and on. No one had anticipated anything like this. The ship had been constructed of petrified cedar from the forest. It was strong, but was it as strong as stone?

Lilith looked around for the umpteenth time. She could see nothing but water in every direction. There was nothing to swim toward. It was peculiar how disappointment could keep re-emerging, again and again. She desperately wished someone else—anyone—had survived.

It was the same below the surface. Lilith searched the water repeatedly, but she could find no signs of life. And there seemed to be no sign of a bottom, either. She swam down as far as she dared, until pain pierced her eyes and ears. Occasionally she came across a piece of floating debris, but there was nothing left of life. She began collecting the debris and bringing it back with her to her floating tree. Later, she would examine it for hours at a time, trying to figure out what it was, where it came from, and whether or not it could be put to use. Her collection had thus far proved mostly undecipherable and completely useless.

She kept thinking that perhaps the fish were nearer the bottom. Who knew how far down it went? Lilith tried to explore deeper with each dive, but the piercing pain in her eyes and ears always forced her back to the surface. It felt like her head might explode if she ventured down too far. And as well, she didn't want to stray too far from her tree. She wasn't entirely sure that the water wasn't moving, and she couldn't risk losing the one thing that could keep her afloat indefinitely. It was her lifeline, her talisman. She didn't like to be away from it too long.

Lilith's stomach rumbled painfully. She was so hungry. Azazyl foretold that it would rain for many days. How long had it been? It was impossible to tell with the constant darkness but Lilith felt that she must have made it through the worst of it by now. Surely it had been more than a week. But how long could a person survive without food? Lilith had no idea. Thank goodness for the steady rainwater to at least quench her thirst. She laughed out loud at the irony of this strange thought. Then she abruptly stopped, shocked by the sound of her laughter. Tentatively she laughed again, just to hear the sound. How lovely it was! And how peculiar it felt to smile; how odd, the simple pulling of the muscles. But it felt good too. She kept the smile on her face, and just having it there seemed to conjure thoughts befitting the expression. She suddenly remembered that first, fateful meeting with Asmodeous when she had attempted to join the Kalag-ga. She laughed again, but this time her laughter was bittersweet. Yet she felt a strange certainty that it wouldn't end this way. In spite of the bleak surroundings, Lilith was confident she would see Asmodeous again.

Oh father, she silently prayed, *why won't you come to me in my dreams at least?* Even from the abyss, surely he could sense her need! Lilith continued to pray to him, resting her upper body on the tree as she implored Anu, the heavens, and even God Himself.

~

Lilith woke up with a start. There was confusion—her senses, her surroundings, her thoughts—and she couldn't breathe! She gasped. She was under water. She must have slipped off the tree during her sleep. Panic seized her.

Lilith's arms began flailing as she grasped all around in search of something to grab hold of. Where was her tree? If only she could get above the water's surface to see it. But she couldn't seem to breach the surface for long enough to even take in a full breath. She frantically clutched at everything—and nothing.

She stopped gasping for air, reaching the dim realization that her head was under water. She seemed to be bobbing just below the surface, like an unfortunate worm helplessly dangling on a fisherman's line. She tried to contain her fear as the gravity of this new development set in.

Her vision seemed to be growing narrower, as if a great darkness was closing in. She was suddenly keenly aware of each and every missed opportunity. A choking sensation burned through her and it took all her effort to resist it.

Something was hovering above her, like a shadow. Her tree? She reached out her arms but it was too far away. It was too late. Too late. A tiny speck of debris caught her eye as it floated by, light and tranquil and indifferent. Lilith stared at it as it heedlessly made its way through the vast, watery deep. It seemed to be mocking her. She felt a sudden stab of envy. What must it feel like to exist so comfortably? To essentially be nothing and yet to be suffered to exist?

Lilith was startled from her trance by a searing pain in her lungs. Her body felt inexplicably heavy and burdened. The water appeared to be thickening and congealing all around her. The murky depths distorted her vision even further. It was getting darker. Time seemed to cease its passing.

She was distracted by a sound, thick and muddled, that had been there all along but was suddenly getting louder. Hope surged through her. Was someone there? But no, she realized with mild surprise that she was hearing the steady pounding of her own heart. It kept growing louder and more persistent, as if it were sending her a message, like the drummers in a war march, repeating orders, a kind of mantra; *let go, let go, let go.*

No! Lilith cried inwardly. *I want to live*! The choking sensation kept tempting her while the pain kept searing her lungs. She mustn't take a breath. She thrashed her limbs against the solid wall of water… to no avail. She was sinking; perhaps her wild movements were making her descend even faster. How far had she sunk? *Don't look up*, she told herself. *Don't look up*!

There was a terrifying blackness below her. *Don't look up*! Her flailing limbs stopped. She no longer knew which way was up. The pain in her lungs was unbearable. She couldn't endure it. Yet she held on longer. Even pain was preferable to the alternative. She finally succumbed to self-pity, struck by the unfairness of it all. Until that very instant she never stopped believing that she would survive.

She mustn't breath. To breath would bring instant death. And she wanted to go on living! What she would give to prolong her life, even here, alone and lost in the great deluge, the pain excruciating, and yet; to exist! Oh precious life, where will you go?

The pain was extreme and unimaginable. Lilith thought about the dark place. Were the Others waiting for her at that moment, preparing to collect her soul? She could feel cold, icy fingers, prodding and pulling, gently massaging her into death. She thrashed about to fight them off. Small bubbles slipped through her lips against her will. She renewed her struggles in earnest. More bubbles escaped. She fought harder, grasping and scratching in vain.

At last she succumbed to the overwhelming need for air, but instead of the relief she craved there was terrible pain—even worse than the other! Everything she'd suffered thus far dulled by comparison. Her last impression was of something thick and solid, like a tongue, sliding down her throat.

And even in that instant, with her final thought, she still couldn't believe that no would be coming to save her.

CHAPTER
34

Present Day

Nadia was starting to feel marginally better. Her hair was clean and hung in small, damp coils all around her head. It had been well over an hour since she washed it but her hair was so thick it took hours to dry. Daylight was waning and Gordon got up to turn on a light. The moment seemed surreal. The coffee had just started kicking in and yet night was approaching. It was a peculiar feeling.

"Not that this is the hardest part of the story to swallow," she began conversationally—"But are you guys now going to tell me that science is wrong and that the flood actually happened?"

"Yep," said Clive.

"It's not that they're wrong, exactly," corrected Gordon. "Just inconclusive."

"At the moment there are as many theories to support the flood as there are to refute it," said Will. "The problem is that flood geology has become synonymous with *the*-ology. Scientists are afraid the one will confirm the other, so they have an incentive to discredit the flood."

"They're throwing the baby out with the bath water," said Gordon. "For those of us who consider the bible a valuable history book, it's discouraging that so much of the science community refuses to take it seriously. If you believe, for example, that the Israelites were led out of Egypt by a man named Moses, do you also have to believe that God helped him do it? Is it possible that Moses only *thought* God was helping him? Or even more probably, that Moses created those signs from God in order to get the people to follow him to begin with?"

"Just because certain events in history are misinterpreted doesn't mean they didn't happen," agreed Will. He was texting someone on his phone as they spoke.

"Ironically, the science community is doing exactly what they accuse religion of doing," said Gordon. "They come up with a theory and, if nobody proves it wrong, they call it a fact. The reality is that they haven't proved their theories about the flood any more than bible scholars have proved theirs. They can call them 'accepted scientific conclusions' all they want. That doesn't make them true."

Nadia was impressed by their reasoning.

"There are unanswered questions about the past no matter which side you're on," continued Gordon. "The bible backers claim that a global flood would account for many geological phenomenon, from the development and placement of fossils to more extreme geological formations like the Grand Canyon. They have many theories about how the flood happened that coincide with what we know about water beneath the earth's crust and ruptures in the tectonic plates and so forth. The scientists argue—rather narrowly in my opinion—that based on the geological changes taking place right now we can come up with a timetable to estimate how long it really took for those changes to happen. According to their timetable it would take billions of years. And their timetable might be right too, if all the factors remained *exactly* the same for all those billions of years in question."

"Which is stupid," interjected Clive. "It's like saying 'this is how long it will take to pollute the earth' based on the rate of pollution happening right this minute. Scientists should know better. What if a nuclear bomb goes off? You don't think that's going to bump up the clock just a little?"

"That's right," said Gordon. "While it's true that these geological changes—like erosion, for example—are taking place at an established pace at this moment, it doesn't change the fact that there are many events that could accelerate the process."

"Like a catastrophic flood," interjected Clive.

"This has always been the real issue between science and religion," said Gordon. "How long did it take for the world to evolve to this point? And the simple fact is that scientists can't prove their timetable any more than the religious community can prove theirs."

"Wow," was all Nadia could think of to say.

Will had stepped out of the room for the latter part of their discussion and now he returned, phone in hand.

"Shakhra appears to have passed the white glove treatment, but they're keeping an eye on them anyway, and they've even put tails on a few of their employees," he told them.

"What else?" asked Clive.

"Not much, I'm afraid. LA's been put on high alert. They're watching shipments from medical supply companies both coming and going. And they're looking at everyone attending the seminar." Will sighed heavily. "It's not enough, but it's the best they can do with what little we have. Something better turn up soon."

"The seminar begins Tuesday," said Clive, unnecessarily reminding them of the ticking clock. "That's the day after tomorrow."

They all looked at Nadia.

"Okay, so Lilith drowned in the flood and was sent to the dark place," prompted Clive. "What happened next?"

CHAPTER
35

December 1948

They'd spent the entire night listening to the incredible story of Lilith's life and death. It was the first time Helene stayed up all night and she was surprised to find that she wasn't even tired.

"What was it like…in the dark place?" she asked, not wanting the story to end.

"There aren't words to describe it," said Lilith. She had hardly moved from her position on the couch. The bottom half of her face was still covered by her hair and it was if she had been speaking to them with her large, expressive eyes. Helene was sure that she would never forget those eyes, any more than she would forget Lilith's story. "It's hard to comprehend unless you've experienced it. It's an infinity of nothingness and desolation."

"Weren't there other Nephilim souls there?"

"Yes, but the dark place is so immense and our souls have no form there. I thought I could sense souls from time to time, but there was no way to connect with them. There was one time…," Lilith paused. Tears started in her eyes, but she abruptly blinked them away. It was a moment before she continued in a shaky voice. "This one soul…I thought might be Gilgamesh. It *felt* so much like him." The memory appeared to torment her still. She laughed a bitter little laugh and shrugged. "Maybe I just wanted it to be him. I guess I'll never know for sure."

"What did you *do* there?" Helene asked, not quite able to wrap her mind around such place.

"I mostly just kept moving through the darkness in search of an escape. For all these years—five thousand did you say?—I hardly ever stopped moving through the darkness."

Everyone was quiet. Daylight was approaching but the sun still loitered just beyond the horizon. Helene looked around, feeling peculiarly alive. Everything seemed the same but different—surreal. Even her father seemed unfamiliar. But the feeling passed and was gone.

"What are you going to do with me?" asked Lilith, and there was another pause while they all appeared to consider this.

"You've been honest with us," said Butch, forgetting, it seemed, that she didn't have a choice in the matter—"So I suppose the least we can do is to be honest with you." He laughed then. "The truth is I don't think any of us have the slightest idea what to do with you." Helene's father and Huxley made sounds of agreement.

"I suppose if you'd asked us that question yesterday we'd have told you that we would present Huxley's tablet along with your *Book of the Dead*—and you—to the world on a silver platter," Butch continued. "But now…," He examined Lilith thoughtfully, cocking his head to one side as was his habit. "I don't see how we can let this get out."

"Are you mad?" interjected Huxley. "You can't be suggesting we keep this to ourselves!"

"I would rather that than to jeopardize all of humanity!"

"How would revealing this discovery jeopardize humanity?" Huxley was incredulous.

"You can ask that after what we've just heard?" Butch demanded, his usual calm demeanor slipping in the face of Huxley's indignation.

"We could be opening Pandora's box here. Not to mention that we'd be going against…let's just say, higher powers."

"So now you're religious?"

"It has nothing to do with religion," Butch argued. "You heard what Lilith said. Some very powerful beings have gone to a lot of trouble to lock these souls away. And let's not forget the obvious risk they pose to us humans."

Helene had the sense that they had forgotten that Lilith was there, listening.

"I don't see how the world knowing about these ancient souls and their purpose puts us at risk," Huxley countered. "It's not as if they cease existing if we ignore them! It's *not* knowing that puts us at risk."

"But in the wrong hands…"

"All the more reason to go public," insisted Huxley. "Bring the entire science community into it!"

"I disagree," said Butch. "I think that's a foolhardy idea. All you're thinking about is the glory."

"Yes! Of course I want the glory! I've spent my whole life searching for this!" Huxley paused, making a visible effort to calm down. "Look, if we can bring back one type of soul, it stands to reason that we could figure out how to bring back other souls too."

"Angels put together this formula for bringing back *Nephilim* souls," Butch reminded him. "So they could live here, in *human* bodies."

"If you think about it," Helene's father, who had only been listening up to this point, suddenly spoke—"Lilith's probably not the first. Others may already be out there. Why, this would explain ghosts, or even claims of demon possession. These so called *ghosts* could actually be Nephilim souls, haunting the earth. We may well have solved these phenomena with our discovery!"

"You too, Bob?" Butch seemed genuinely crushed.

"What are you suggesting we do Butch?" he asked.

"I think we should destroy Huxley's tablet, for one," replied Butch.

"Destroy the…heavens above!" Huxley was flabbergasted. "What have we come on this journey for then? No. No."

"Come on now, Butch," reasoned Helene's father. "You heard Lilith. There are several copies out there. Others could turn up—if they haven't already—and those really could fall into the wrong hands."

"I can't answer to what's out there," said Butch. "I only know *this* tablet can still be used with other *Books of the Dead* for the same result. God only knows how many of these souls might be prevented from coming back if we destroy it now!"

As Helene listened she wondered again what would happen to Lilith. Would they keep her in some kind of exhibit in a museum or allow her to roam free? Lilith seemed to be wondering the same thing as she listened quietly to the men as if she was hanging on their every word.

How Helene would have loved to talk to Edward just then! Never had she missed him so much. Yet her overall excitement was tempered by a creeping uneasiness. Perhaps it was Butch's influence, but it felt a little like they really had opened a Pandora's box. If only Lilith's teeth were not so terrifyingly sharp.

The argument between Butch and Huxley was becoming more heated and, sensing his daughter's discomfort, Robert Trevelyan prudently led her out of doors. There was a crisp chill in the air but the approaching sun cheered Helene with the promise of warmth.

"What do you think will happen?" asked Helene.

"I couldn't say," replied her father thoughtfully. Helene stared at him, amazed by how composed he always remained under even the most extraordinary circumstances. He noticed her expression and smiled. "Quite a turn up for the books, eh?" he said.

Helene shivered and her father put his arm around her.

"You're freezing!" he exclaimed. "We better go back inside. Maybe you can find something to do in the bedroom while we finish our discussion?"

"Okay," Helene agreed, already knowing what she would do once she was alone. Edward might not be there in person but she could still tell him what happened.

They went back inside to find Butch and Huxley much more composed. Lilith was gone.

"Please accept our apologies," Butch said to Helene. "I'm afraid we all lost our heads there for a minute."

"We've sent Lilith away—back into the ring—for the time being," added Huxley. He was making every effort to appear calm but it was clear that he was still extremely agitated.

"I'm going to my room," Helene told them.

"Good! Get some rest," said Huxley. "Poor thing must be exhausted."

Alone in her room, Helene went right for the stationary. A little surge of excitement welled up at the thought of how much she had to tell him. He would be ever so disappointed to have missed it! Yet it was possible that he would get to see Lilith for himself. For surely they would bring her back to England with them! She began writing and the words poured forth faster than Helene could get them down on paper. She told Edward about the Bedouin, his *Book of the Dead*, the ring they made out of metal shavings, the spells written in the mysterious language and even the terrifying darkness just before Lilith appeared. By the time she got to Lilith, her hand was already getting tired, so she was obliged to skim over the details of Lilith's life, highlighting only the most significant parts, such as her being a great warrior and then drowning in the flood. When she finally stopped writing Helene had used up eight sheets of paper—front and back—starting out on page one with nice, crisp letters written in perfectly straight lines and ending with a barely legible scrawl that sloped downward across the page when she finished. At the very bottom she wrote: "P.S. There's one more detail I'm saving to tell you in person. It's a secret!" With a giggle, Helene folded the stationary, tucked it neatly into the matching envelope and addressed it to Edward.

Helene could hear the voices of the men in the other room, though she couldn't make out what they were saying. She was suddenly too tired to care and, lying down, she closed her eyes.

It seemed like mere seconds later when her father shook her awake.

"I hated to wake you," he said. "You were sleeping so peacefully."

Helene yawned and stretched. She felt even more tired than when she lay down. "What happened?" she asked.

"Well, let's see, Butch still wants to destroy the tablet and keep the discovery quiet, while Huxley is dying to shout about it from the rooftops."

"And you?" asked Helene.

Her father laughed. "I want a little of both, I guess," he said. "I understand Butch's concerns. Something like this could change the world as we know it. At the moment, we only agree on two things: we have to keep it a secret until we get home and we must leave here as soon as possible."

"We won't be visiting the caves?" asked Helene, torn between her disappointment over missing the caves and her excitement over seeing Edward again.

"No, but we'll let everyone think we are," said her father. "Butch doesn't want to tip anyone off that anything out of the ordinary has happened." He laughed at her expression of alarm. "Not to worry," he said. "Butch is an old fuddy-duddy and I suppose I am too because I don't want to take any unnecessary chances either."

"What could happen?" wondered Helene.

"Well, for one thing, we could be robbed. A discovery like this would be worth lots of money."

"Really?" Helene hadn't thought about that, but it made sense. She felt a twinge of excitement at the prospect. "Will we get a third?"

Her father laughed. "Pack your things," he said. "We'll tell anyone who asks that we're heading out to the caves, but we're not coming back, so make sure you don't leave anything behind."

They went into the living room to discover Abdul Samad and his wife bringing breakfast.

"Good morning," said her father.

"Assalamu alaikum," replied the Arab with his oddly persistent smile. He lingered in the doorway as his wife prepared their morning meal. "You sleep well?" he asked no one in particular.

"Yes," replied Butch. "Very well, thank you." Abdul smiled and nodded, and Helene once again had the sense that he didn't understand what they were saying. Butch appeared to be of a different opinion, however, continuing pleasantly—"We'll be sightseeing today. We're anxious to get a look at those caves."

Abdul smiled and nodded. "Ah, caves," he echoed.

"It's wasted on him," Huxley murmured under his breath.

His wife, meanwhile, was arranging the food on the table. There was tea, milk, more of the flatbread that Helene had enjoyed the night before, beans, olives and some kind of pastry that had been rolled up into balls and fried. None of it was what she was accustomed to eating first thing in the morning but, having experienced every imaginable culinary experiment at the hands of Mrs. Barnes under the influence of the rations, Helene was ever open minded. The smells wafting up from the table were not at all bad.

The men went back to what they were doing while Helene loitered near the food. When at last Abdul's wife began packing up her things, Helene approached her shyly, waiting until she looked up. "Another?" Helene asked, holding out her letter to Edward.

The woman's eyes softened. "Na'am," she said, nodding vigorously. She took the letter and placed it inside the large bag she carried.

"Thank you," said Helene.

"Na'am," said the woman, nodding again.

Helene wondered what Arab women were like behind their veils. Did they ever have fun and laugh? She thought of Mrs. Barnes, who could be just as forbidding as any Arab and sighed. She hoped to never be an old lady.

When Abdul and his wife left they sat down to eat. The food tasted good, and absorbed most of Helene's attention. The men made an effort to be cheerful but their conversation was strained. They spoke of preparations for their trip back to Tel Aviv. Huxley seemed terribly put out that they were leaving without telling his friend, Lieutenant Brisbin. There was the matter of the car they had borrowed, as well as payment for the scroll.

"All that can be taken care of later," insisted Butch.

Helene could tell that her father was siding with Huxley and she felt sorry for Butch. She hoped everything would go back to normal once they got home.

She couldn't help wondering what all of this was going to mean for her. Would she become famous? This would certainly boost her career in archeology. For that was definitely what she wanted to do with the rest of her life. She would scour the earth in search of ancient secrets. Maybe she and Edward would scour the earth together.

Immediately after breakfast they packed up their things and loaded them into the car. Even Helene didn't have to be told twice. There was an unspoken urgency that drove them. Butch swept up the metal shavings and tossed them into a sand pile outside. It wasn't until she was securely strapped into the back seat of the car that Helene was finally able to relax.

It was turning out to be a lovely day. The sun radiated heat through the car windows, making Helene feel drowsy again. They headed down the dirt road in silence, each lost in their own thoughts.

CHAPTER
36

"What in the world?" Helene heard Butch mutter all of a sudden, and she leaned forward in her seat to have a look.

She couldn't resist a giggle. A flock of sheep had gathered in the road, seemingly unconcerned by the approaching vehicle. A few of them gazed at the car disapprovingly, bleating loudly. Butch honked the horn, but this only made them huddle more closely together as they stood their ground.

"Bloody hell!" exclaimed Huxley, opening his car door. "Want to give me a hand, Bob?"

Her father got out of the car. The men approached the sheep cautiously, causing Helene to laugh again.

"Shoo! Shoo!" yelled Huxley, flinging his hands at them. But the sheep only huddled closer together.

Her father tried pushing the sheep but that didn't work either. "Brother!" he exclaimed after several failed attempts to get the sheep to move.

"Try hitting them on their backsides," Butch yelled out the car window. Helene's father tried this, but he administered such light taps that the sheep didn't even appear to notice. "Good God," Butch muttered under his breath, and then—"Harder!" he yelled. Huxley, meanwhile, took matters into his own hands, hauling back and landing a solid blow to one sheep's hind legs. The animal jumped and then trotted off indignantly, setting the rest of the herd in motion in the same direction. Just as the last of them were leaving the road there was a loud shot, which panicked the sheep, sending them into a full run. Then there was a second shot. Helene looked around, assuming the shots were meant to corral the sheep but then she caught sight of her father and Huxley lying on the ground, and she screamed.

Butch shifted the car into gear but before he could hit the gas more shots were fired and Helene felt one of the tires go flat. She screamed again.

"We've been ambushed!" cried Butch, ducking down in his seat while simultaneously reaching for Helene in the back. "Get down!" he yelled at her.

Helene couldn't seem to move so Butch caught hold of her arm and jerked her down onto the floor. "Dear god!" he whispered.

Six armed men, dressed in Arab robes, emerged from all directions. They approached the car cautiously, their guns aimed and ready to fire.

"Whatever you do, don't tell them anything," Butch whispered emphatically. "The minute they get what they want they'll kill you!"

As the men drew nearer Helene recognized one of them to be Abdul Samad, the Arab who had brought food and supplies to them. He looked different without the disturbing smile pasted to face but it was definitely him. Helene's insides seemed to drop at the sight of him. A terrible sense of culpability gripped her. Had he seen the letter she gave to his wife?

She heard a car approaching ahead and hope flooded through her. The car advanced quickly and her optimism grew when she saw that it was one of the British officers' vehicles. Yet the Arabs were not backing down.

The car stopped and Lieutenant Brisbin got out. He looked at the bodies in the road and then shouted something at the men in Arabic. Then he looked at Helene and Butch. "We have to get you out of here," he told them. Butch did not look at all relieved, but he grimly helped Helene out of the car and led her to the lieutenant's vehicle.

"We have to help father!" she cried, resisting a little as if to go to him.

"An ambulance will follow shortly," said the lieutenant. Helene looked at Butch. "Come! Hurry!" the lieutenant said urgently and Butch nodded for her to do as he said, though he refused to meet her eye.

Butch helped Helene into the lieutenant's car before getting in himself. When his eyes finally met hers Helene had the distinct impression he was trying to warn her of something. Remembering what he told her in the car, she nodded imperceptibly.

"I must apologize for that unfortunate incident on the road," Lieutenant Brisbin said as they took off down the road. "The Arabs can be such savages. They thought you were stealing the car—it belongs to the Arab legion, you know. They give us Brits a great deal of leeway, but still, stealing is not tolerated here." His tone was kind and sympathetic, but every instinct of Helene's distrusted him. She wondered if what he was telling them could possibly be true.

Butch remained silent, which told Helene more clearly than words what he thought about the lieutenant's claims.

"I will need statements from both of you," the lieutenant continued. Helene was surprised to see that he was taking them back to the little cabin. "We can talk here," he said. Feeling numb, Helene got out of the car and followed him and Butch inside.

"Sit down," said the lieutenant politely and they did. He gave them a sympathetic smile. "I'm going to try to straighten this out for you," he said. "There are just a few things that I have to clear up first."

Helene couldn't bring herself to look at the lieutenant's face so she fixed her eyes lower, on his throat. She watched his Adam's apple bob up and down as he spoke.

"Aside from the car, the Arabs claim you have other...items in your possession that belong to them," continued the lieutenant. He smiled apologetically and shrugged his shoulders. "Their actions may seem excessive but you must understand that these people are highly irrational and superstitious. They claim you have a ring that belongs to one of their ancestors. Naturally, if there was such an artifact, you could see why they would want to keep it here, in the country of its origin. And of course there's the book that was removed from the cave."

When they did not respond Lieutenant Brisbin turned to Helene. "Are you familiar with the ring of which they speak?" he asked her.

"It was thrown out with the metal shavings when the experiment failed," Butch interjected. There was something in his tone that made Helene think he was speaking to her, not the lieutenant.

Lieutenant Brisbin didn't even glance in Butch's direction. "I'm asking the girl," he replied politely. Then—"Where is the ring Miss Trevelyan?"

Helene continued to stare at the man's neck, but what she was seeing was the image of her father's and Huxley's bodies lying on the ground. Yet she couldn't seem to feel anything, except a strong conviction that nothing mattered from this point forward. Nothing she felt—or did—could change what had already happened.

"Miss Trevelyan?"

"We...threw it out," she said mechanically.

"Where?"

"Outside, in the sand."

"Why would you do that?" The lieutenant's voice remained ominously calm and friendly throughout his questioning.

"Be...cause," replied Helene. In the long silence that followed she realized he was waiting for her to elaborate, so she continued—"Like Mr. Butchard said...the experiment failed."

"Did it?" asked the lieutenant. He appeared to be surprised by this. "That's odd, because the Arabs seem to think that the experiment was a 'marvelous, tremendous, stupendous success.'" Helene flinched and her eyes filled with tears. He had quoted her word for word in her letter to Edward, confirming her fear that she was the one who had tipped them off in the first place. This was all her fault. She had killed her father and Huxley. A deep sense of mortification and shame crept over her and she hoped Butch wouldn't find out what she'd done.

"I don't know where the ring is!" she cried. The lieutenant's neck was so blurry now that she couldn't even see his Adam's apple anymore.

She could hear the Arabs returning from the road. She wondered what they had done with her father and Huxley. She kept reminding herself that nothing mattered, and she actually hoped to join her father and Huxley, wherever they were. It was what she deserved.

"Samad!" the lieutenant called out and Abdul Samad appeared through the doorway. "You stay with Mr. Butchard. Miss Trevelyan and I are going to take a little walk." Lieutenant Brisbin stood up and took Helene's arm. She followed numbly as he led her outside. His touch was gentle but it felt to her like a scalding brand and she shuddered with relief when he released her.

"Show me where they threw the ring and the metal shavings," he said.

Helene led him to where she had seen Butch dump the metal shavings and pointed. The lieutenant called the men over and instructed them to search the area for the ring. However, he didn't seem very optimistic that they would find it.

"What—if you don't mind my asking—is this secret you're saving for your return home?" the Lieutenant asked her conspiratorially.

Helene held her breath as she searched for a plausible answer, and then blurted out the first thing that came to mind. "I was going to tell Edward that I...love him." She blushed at the lie.

"Where is the ring, Miss Trevelyan?"

"I don't know," she replied.

"Who had it last?"

"My father," she lied, knowing he wouldn't mind the lie since it was meant to help Butch. "He was the one who took it out with the metal shavings."

The lieutenant appeared to be considering this.

"Then he hid Mr. Huxley's tablet and the *Book of the Dead* in the car," she added, hoping this would convince him that she was telling the truth. She knew he would find the two documents hidden in the lining of their luggage if he looked for them. What did any of it matter now? The documents were of no use since Lilith was in the ring, though she supposed they could always find another *Book of the Dead* to use Huxley's tablet with, just as Butch had forewarned. "Maybe the ring is with the books if it isn't here."

Helene suddenly felt very tired. Her father was dead. He and Huxley had been shot. They would never reap the rewards of their discovery. She fervently hoped their killers wouldn't either.

The lieutenant instructed her to wait inside with Mr. Butchard while they conducted their search of the grounds and the car, which the Arabs had confiscated.

"I told him that father had the ring and the documents," she whispered to Butch as she sat down next to him on the couch. "I think father would have wanted..." she stopped. She felt dead inside. Too dead to even muster the energy to cry. Butch put his arm around her and she leaned against him and closed her eyes. Neither of them said another word.

It seemed like several hours before Helene woke up. Butch was gone.

"Where's Mr. Butchard?" she asked when the lieutenant came into the room.

"Mr. Butchard is going to remain here with us for a while longer," he told her in that same, annoyingly polite and apologetic manner, as if he was just as put out as she was but didn't have any say in the matter. Helene didn't believe him. "But you're going home," he finished.

Helene wasn't sure she heard him right. "Home?" she echoed dully.

"Yes," he said. There was something exceedingly unpleasant in his smile but Helene ignored it, desperate to believe what he was telling her. In spite of her wretchedness she couldn't help feeling relief at the thought of going home, of seeing Edward again—and even good old, practical Mrs. Barnes!

"But...how?" she wondered.

"I'm going to take you to a nearby Bedouin camp," he told her. "There's someone there who will take you. However, you must not mention anything that's happened here or you will put yourself in grave danger. Do you understand?"

Helene nodded, trembling with hope. None of it seemed real—nor did it make any sense—but Helene was in no position to question it.

Nor had she any desire to question it. Like a friendly mirage in the middle of a desert she couldn't resist it. She got in the lieutenant's car and he drove her to the Bedouin camp, just as he promised.

The camp was not as large as the one she'd visited the day before. This one appeared to be made up of mostly men, but there were a few women and children scattered about. The presence of children fed Helene's hopes that her nightmare might actually be nearing an end.

All eyes were on Helene as she followed Lieutenant Brisbin into a large tent that was set off to one side. There were three Arabs inside the tent. The lieutenant addressed them in Arabic. They spoke for several long minutes, pausing to cast glances in Helene's direction from time to time. The men seemed surprised by what the lieutenant was telling them, but they did not appear to be put out in the least. On the contrary, they seemed quite eager to help.

"This man will take you home," Lieutenant Brisbin said, addressing her at last. A young man stepped forward. "His name is Aabid Al-Zaa'ir."

"But…I don't speak Arabic," said Helene.

"He speaks English," said the lieutenant. "He is not a Bedouin, he merely enjoys their hospitality when he travels through these parts. He is an old friend of mine who knows the area well. You will be safe with him." Helene looked at Aabid. He was quite young and seemed very nervous. And terribly shy. He never actually looked at Helene, though his eyes would occasionally dart in her direction. He had large, anxious eyes and full, youthful lips that were topped with a thin layer of hair that would someday become a mustache. None of the men spoke to Helene and she recalled what her father told her about women in Muslim society. Would she be traveling the entire distance with Aabid in silence?

"The Bedouins require your assurance that you are willing to go with Aabid before they will condone it," continued the lieutenant.

Helene turned to the two older men who were keenly watching her and nodded. "Yes, I will go with Aabid," she told them, anxious to get away from Lieutenant Brisbin.

"Very good," said the lieutenant. He said something to the men in Arabic and then turned back to her. "Well, Helene," he said with an unpleasant light shining in his eyes—"Until we meet again."

"Goodbye," Helene replied, cringing at the thought of ever seeing him again.

"Be sure and do as Aabid tells you, and you'll be safe."

The two older men followed Lieutenant Brisbin out of the tent and—Helene hoped—out of her life forever.

CHAPTER
37

Present Day

It was just past lunchtime, but it felt like midnight if you looked outside, and they were all munching noisily on potato chips.

"How did you know it was Lilith they conjured?" Nadia suddenly wondered.

"Our people came in shortly after Lieutenant Brisbin and his men cleaned everything up," explained Gordon. "News of four missing persons was just getting out, along with rumors of the discovery at Qumran. Considering that two of the missing persons were archaeologists, it wasn't hard to put two and two together. Fragments of Lilith's *Book of the Dead* were left at the sight, where they also found remnants of the metal shavings. There could only be one reason for leaving the book behind; the Nephilim soul it was written for—Lilith—had already been conjured."

"Our operatives originally assumed that all four of the missing persons were killed," said Will. "But then word got out of a young woman fitting Helene Trevelyan's description at a nearby Bedouin camp."

"One survivor…and it's a female," said Clive. "And one missing djinn…also a female."

"You can see why they flagged Helene to Lilith," said Will. "And they were able trace her to Aabid Al-Zaa'ir in Saudi Arabia."

"Which makes the perfect hiding place," said Clive. "It's next to impossible to get near women there. One of our operatives got close, but she hid behind her husband, too afraid—or guilty—to talk." He eyed Nadia stubbornly, obviously reluctant to let go of his long held conclusions about her grandmother.

"It's hard for anyone who hasn't been to Saudi Arabia to imagine how difficult it is to get near women there," said Gordon. "Everything goes through their husband or father, or lacking one of those, a brother or other relation. They're forbidden to speak to any man outside their family, and strongly discouraged from speaking to women outside their mosque. This applies to everything…even a court of law. In a murder investigation—they would rather protect a woman's modesty than to solve the crime."

"Anyway, a woman's testimony isn't worth much over there," added Clive. "Only half that of a man's."

"If she didn't hide there by choice, Lieutenant Brisbin effective silenced her forever by leaving her in the hands of that Arab," said Will. "Yet why wouldn't he just kill her? He had to have a reason for keeping her alive."

"Maybe Lieutenant Brisbin wasn't directly involved," Nadia suggested, instinctively rejecting any suggestions that her grandmother might have been a djinn. "Maybe he was just covering up for the Arabs, which would explain his reluctance to kill Helene."

"He read Helene's letter to Edward," Will reminded her. "He quoted from it."

"Yes, but the Arabs could have shown him that as proof of their allegations that they were stealing their artifacts," said Nadia.

Will eyed her skeptically.

"That still leaves Butch," Clive reminded her.

"My grandmother never stopped wondering what happened to him," said Nadia.

"It's like he disappeared into thin air," said Clive. "Which puts a serious dent in your theory about Lieutenant Brisbin's supposed reluctance to kill."

"We'll have to track Brisbin down," said Gordon. "His name wasn't even mentioned in the original file."

Clive glanced at his watch and shook his head. "Here it is Monday—in Saudi at least—and we've got nothin'! New York is only seven hours behind us. Our cell's about to dive head on into a shitstorm and there isn't a damn thing we can do about it!"

Will and Gordon exchanged looks. "What are we missing?" Will asked no one in particular.

Gordon raised a finger. "We know the cells were put on alert early Friday morning," he said, then raised a second finger. "We know that the mission references Lilith twice, indicating a clear connection to the djinn found in Qumran and Nadia's grandmother." He raised a third finger. "We know that a seminar in LA—sponsored by BEACON—is either the target or an intermediate point." He raised a fourth finger. "We have reason to believe it's a suicide mission involving biological weapons instead of bombs." He raised his fifth and final finger. "And we know that it begins Monday afternoon with our cell flying out to LA." Gordon stopped there, possibly because he ran out of fingers.

"She's been instructed which classes to attend," said Will, picking up where Gordon left off. "Why would they do that?"

"I still think she'll be picking up the rest of her instructions at that class," said Gordon.

"Or else that's where she'll be picking up the infection," said Clive.

"It would be great if it were that easy," said Will. "The instructors for those classes are under surveillance as we speak. They'll be intercepted and replaced with special operatives at the last minute. So far, they haven't found any evidence of an infectious disease among them."

"The missing purification ritual is a puzzle too," said Clive. "No self-respecting extremist would infect themselves without that ritual. Why didn't they mention it?"

"Maybe they're planning to cover that in the seminar," suggested Gordon.

"Yeah, but these cells need to get in the right frame of mind, you know?" said Clive. "They need to get fired up! You don't just snap your fingers and bang! You're ready to die. You need preparation... platitudes, promises, prayers. It doesn't happen in a day."

Nadia jumped off the couch, spraying potato chips in all directions. "Your cell isn't participating in the attack!" she cried.

They all looked at her in surprise. "You mean she's a decoy," clarified Will in that tone that said, 'we already thought of that.'

"No!" insisted Nadia. "I mean...she is kind of a decoy actually, but what I'm trying to tell you is that maybe she's not going *to* the mission, she's going *from* it!" She looked at them expectantly and then tried again. "*Escaping* the Goddess of Death...as in escaping the plague, or whatever it is they're planning."

She had their full attention now. After a few seconds of stunned silence, the men turned to look at each other.

"Where does your cell live?" Nadia continued. "Where is she flying from?"

"DC," Clive answered meaningfully.

"Oh my god!" Nadia's blood felt like it was turning to ice. She scanned her memory for upcoming events. "The...the...World Bank Meetings! I think they're being held this week! Check! Check!" She yelled at Will, who was already punching buttons on his phone.

"They are." he said. "All week." He held up his finger for them to be silent as he lifted the phone to his ear, but then he appeared to change his mind, getting up and abruptly leaving the room.

"How the fuck did we miss that?" asked Clive.

No one said anything for a few minutes and then Gordon remarked—"I bet if we look at everyone flying out of DC on Monday we'll find a virtual army of sleeper cells making their escape."

Clive nodded. "Obviously they want to keep enough of their little soldiers alive for whatever they have planned afterwards."

"They only need a few people to infect the city," Gordon agreed.

"Why waste all that talent?" added Clive.

Gordon began pushing buttons on his phone. "Who would you say has the easiest access to those flight records Clive...the FAA?" he asked.

Will returned, visibly upset. A vein in his jaw was twitching errati-cally. But when he spoke his voice was as controlled as ever. "This World Bank thing starts Tuesday. The meetings are taking place in various loca-tions throughout the city. All the big players will be there; high level execs from banks, big business and even the colleges. There'll be politicians from all the industrialized countries and some from developing countries looking to network. These meetings *epitomize* the western influence. I can't believe we didn't think of it sooner. It's almost too obvious."

"And too big?" added Clive with meaning.

Something like anger flashed in Will's blue eyes, but it passed too quickly for Nadia to be sure. "Yeah, it will be too big to shut down without more than what we have. People have been flying in from all over the world. And none of the other intel divisions have found any-thing to suggest that DC is the target—although they had already been planning to beef up security because of LA being on high alert. Still… it's not enough." He looked at Nadia. "We need more."

Nadia wasn't sure she had anything more to give.

"But…seriously…shouldn't you be doing something more than just…listening to stories?" she asked.

"Like we told you before, there are other intel ops at work, chasing every lead we give them," Will reminded her. "What we need is more leads. It's gonna take more than just a hunch to get them to stop those meetings. Your grandmother got us this far, so let's just keep follow-ing her and see where else she takes us, okay?"

Nadia recalled how emphatically her grandmother implored her to go back when she had her out-of-body experience. Was her grand-mother trying to help them somehow?

"I texted the office," Gordon told Will. "I know we have more pressing issues at the moment, but I went ahead and ordered a search of the people flying out of DC today and tomorrow. For later."

"Good thinking," said Will.

"I just feel like we should be *doing* something," insisted Nadia. "And if you call me Nancy Drew again I'm going to slap you," she said to Clive, but he seemed too preoccupied to make jokes.

"We are doing something," Will told her. His blue eyes remained fixed on her face even though he addressed Gordon and Clive. "Pack everything up guys. We're leaving."

Nadia gasped. "We're going to DC?"

"No. Back to New York."

Nadia could hardly believe her ears. "Oh my god!" she cried.

"When's the jet getting here?" asked Clive.

"It's not," said Will. "We're meeting it in Tabouk. We have a stop to make before we go back."

Gordon and Clive exchanged looks, and then all three of them looked at Nadia.

"Looks like you're finally going to get to meet your grandfather," said Clive with a smirk.

Nadia turned to Will for confirmation.

"He probably won't speak to us, but I'm sure he'll agree to see you," said Will. He seemed pleased to be able to do this for her, although Nadia realized that it wasn't really for her. They wanted information. "Someone will meet us when we get there."

"How far is it from here?" she asked, growing more excited with every minute that passed.

"About four hours away," said Gordon.

"Just enough time for you to tell us the rest of Helene's story," said Clive.

CHAPTER
38

December 1948

There was a soft rustling noise beside her and Helene turned to find the young man, Aabid Al-Zaa'ir, standing there, holding a small, black bundle in his hands. Helene eyed him warily. He looked even younger than she originally thought, but his expression was that of a much older man. His blackish-brown hair was mostly hidden beneath his turban, but small, dark curls peeked out from under the grayish material. He had large, dark eyes, a faint, neatly trimmed mustache and smooth, chestnut-brown skin. He smiled encouragingly as he gently thrust the bundle at Helene, and she noticed that his teeth were exceptionally white.

Helene stared at the cloth bundle, unsure of what he wanted her to do with it, but he stubbornly pressed it into her hands. "Wear it," he insisted. "It's for your protection."

Helene shook it out and examined it. The material was as light and shapeless as a sheet. She supposed it wouldn't hurt to put it on and, in fact, it might be nice to escape the curious stares of these people for a while. With a sigh of resignation she pulled the garment over her head, taking several minutes to get it positioned correctly. There was a little flap in the front that she knew went over her nose and mouth, but she wasn't sure how to attach it. Aabid approached her cautiously and gently took the flap from her bungling fingers. Within seconds it was securely fastened.

"This is a *niqab*, which you must wear with the *khimar* whenever you are in the presence of men," he told her.

"I thought men weren't supposed to talk to women," she said.

Aabid's eyes narrowed as he examined her face. "That is correct," he said. "But I am your guardian now, so we are permitted to speak to each other."

"How can *you* be my guardian?" Helene asked. "You're barely older than I am."

He frowned. "You must learn to control your tongue," he advised her gently. "It is not permitted for you to speak in that way."

"In what way?" she asked.

"Without respect," He replied. "You must be respectful at all times, especially in the presence of men."

"Why 'especially in the presence of men'?" she asked.

Her question appeared to puzzle him. "Women cannot show disrespect to men."

"Why not?" she persisted.

"Because it is *haraam*…forbidden, by Allah."

"Allah," she repeated thoughtfully, wondering how she was supposed to argue with that. "And anyway, what's so disrespectful about what I said?"

Aabid was quickly becoming exasperated. It was apparent that he was not used to being questioned—at least not by a woman. "It's… your tone of voice…and your manner. And your questions. Women do not question men!"

With every word he uttered, Helene was becoming more and more apprehensive—and homesick. She couldn't help thinking of Edward and how freely she was able to speak with him. He actually enjoyed her straight-forward, slightly sarcastic—and sometimes downright bossy—manner. On the rare occasions when they argued, Edward was always the first to give in.

But she didn't have the strength to argue at the moment. "All I want is to go home," she said with a little sigh of resignation.

"We will leave presently," he announced in a commanding voice, as if it had been his idea, and then picked up her suitcase and carried it outside before she could respond. Helene followed him to a scruffy, sad-looking little donkey, where he was rearranging bundles that were hanging on either side of the animal's back. He added Helene's suitcase to the load, moving with a confidence and efficiency that was unusual in a person so young.

"Come," Aabid said, holding out his hand to Helene, and she realized then that he expected her to get on the donkey. She took a step backwards, but the determined gleam in his eyes told her that he would forcibly place her on the animal if he had to. She ignored his hand and approached the donkey herself, but it wasn't as easy to mount as she anticipated, especially while wearing the *khimar*. After several failed attempts, Aabid approached her from behind, picked her up and set her on the donkey riding side-saddle. Ignoring her efforts to get comfortable, Aabid took her hands and firmly placed them on the bridle. Without giving her a chance to object he began leading them out of the Bedouin camp. Lieutenant Brisbin had gone, but a crowd of Bedouins gathered to see them off. A few of the men shouted something to Aabid in Arabic and, although Helene didn't understand what they said, she could feel her face growing hot from the manner in which they said it. She was suddenly glad for the *khimar*.

Along with the camp, they appeared to be leaving all plant and other wildlife behind. A vast, hilly expanse of sand and rock opened up before them.

"This country must seem very different from yours," Aabid remarked, echoing her own thoughts at that moment. His voice produced a pleasant distraction. "It will be helpful if you learn our ways. Allah makes our laws, and to go against Him is a crime." He paused to allow Helene time to absorb this. "If you care to listen, I can instruct you as we go. It will help pass the time."

Though their journey had only just begun, Helene was already tired. She wondered how long it would take to get to Tel Aviv. It had taken them the better part of a day to drive to Qumran in a car, but she had no way of knowing how much longer it would take on a donkey. She wasn't particularly interested in Allah or his laws, but she found Aabid's voice somewhat soothing and supposed that whatever he had to say would at least keep her mind occupied. She sighed, already shifting uncomfortably on the donkey. "I guess so."

"That is good," he said. "There is no strength but in Allah."

"What about in Jesus?" Helene couldn't help interjecting.

Aabid shook his head. "It is forbidden to seek any god besides Allah." He looked up at her. "Perhaps you could simply think of your god as Allah."

She huffed. "Don't you even give people a choice?" she asked, recalling a conversation with her father—it seemed like years ago now—when she asked why the Jews didn't just denounce their beliefs in order to save their own lives. It suddenly occurred to her why they might not be all that eager to do that. It was galling to be told what to think.

"No, there is no choice," he replied, but he was thoughtful for a moment. "Are you a strong believer in your faith?"

"Not really," she admitted.

"It will be easier for you then," he said, dismissing the matter.

Helene ignored his tactlessness and tried to be philosophical about it. "I'm not sure I believed in anything until recently," she mused.

"What happened recently?" he asked.

Helene had no intention of getting into the details of what happened, but she couldn't resist putting him in his place by letting him know how much more knowledgeable and experienced she was than him. "I had a conversation with a *djinn*," she replied in a tone of voice that said; 'top that.'

Aabid stopped walking, and he forced the donkey and Helene to stop with him. "You what?"

Helene mistook his expression for incredulity. "Honest," she said. "She'd been dead for about five thousand years. I talked to her. And she never even mentioned Allah. She w...,"

"You are mistaken," he interrupted her.

"No, it really happened," said Helene.

"You are mistaken," he said more vehemently. There was something alarming in his strange insistence about it, and what's more, there was genuine fear in his eyes. "To make supplication to one besides Allah represents the greater *shirk*. It is unforgivable," he whispered the last part.

Helene was momentarily taken aback.

"You were mistaken," he repeated again. He seemed to be waiting for some kind of agreement from Helene. When she didn't respond he grabbed her by her *khimar* and jerked her toward him, nearly unseating her from the donkey, until her face was within inches of his.

Helene was confused. "But…"

Aabid jerked her *khimar* again, and this time she fell to the ground with a painful thud. He pulled her up and shook her savagely. "You were mistaken," he screamed into her face. His expression was filled with rage. Helene's anger flared in response but she was too shaken to act on it. Aabid shook her again. "Say it!"

"I…was mistaken," she choked out the words, hating him. "But why…"

"Listen to me," he demanded. "You will never mention this again, not to anyone, do you hear?"

"But…"

"Never!"

"But-we're-the-only-ones-here-and-you-already-know-about-it!" Helene forced out the words in one long, rapid stream before he could stop her.

"No," replied Aabid. He was suddenly calm again, although Helene could see that his anger still simmered just below the surface. "You just admitted that you were mistaken about it."

Helene stared at him in astonishment. This was unfamiliar territory for her. She'd always been able to speak her mind, no matter what the topic. Her father would never have forced her to say something she didn't believe just so that he could hear what he wanted to hear. This sudden thought of her father filled Helene with so much grief that her knees buckled and she would have fallen down if Aabid hadn't caught her. "It is for your protection," he said, helping her back onto the donkey.

They resumed their travels in silence. Helene's hands were trembling, but her fear was quickly being replaced with anger. She didn't like being handled in such a manner. The whole ugly scene was inexcusable. The worst of it was his forcing her to deny what she knew to be true. It was as if he was telling her what to think!

She was so wrapped up in her own thoughts that she actually jumped when he finally spoke again.

"It is my sworn obligation to protect you," he said defensively. "But how can I, if you do not develop a healthy fear of Allah?"

Helene didn't dare tell him what she thought of Allah, but neither could she just sit back and accept everything he was saying. "Can't a person even question the rules?" she asked.

Aabid sighed. "Within reason, yes." He gave her a quick, sideways glance and Helene sensed that he was embarrassed by his earlier outburst. "But we must trust in Allah even when we do not understand his reasons. Allah knows best."

When she didn't reply, Aabid resumed his lesson on Islam. Helene only half listened, still stewing over his mistreatment of her.

Many of the Islamic principles were similar to those that Helene grew up with in London. Muslims were taught to worship one God, to respect their parents and to be kind to others. Their ideas about sin were similar to those of the Christians, except that the Muslims had a lot more of them—especially when it came to women. And some sins, like adultery, were taken more seriously by Muslims, while others, like murder, could actually be excused if there was 'just cause.'

"What would be considered just cause?" asked Helene, trying not to think of the brutal massacres of her father and Huxley. "And wouldn't other sins, like adultery, also have just cause, then, too?"

Aabid sighed, an action that was now becoming a warning sign to Helene that she was treading in dangerous territory.

"Why do my questions upset you so much?" she wondered.

"Your questions make me fear for you," he said.

"Why?"

"Because you always question those things that are *haraam*," he replied.

"*Haraam*?"

"Forbidden—and therefore illegal—in this country."

"I didn't know I was doing that," she said thoughtfully. "But does it matter, really? I mean, why do I have to know all this anyway? How long does it take to get to Tel Aviv?"

There was a long pause. "We are not going to Tel Aviv," he said.

"But I thought…wait. Wait!" Helene tried to stop the donkey but Aabid kept stubbornly prodding it on. She grabbed hold of his robe but then jerked her hand back in alarm when he whirled around in anger. "Please…I want to know where you're taking me!" she said.

She saw that he was making an effort to control his temper and struggled to keep her own in check. He turned away from her, clicked his tongue at the donkey and they were moving again. Helene's lungs suddenly seemed too large for her chest as she waited for an answer. She looked out at the desert surrounding her and felt real terror.

"What did your father tell you?" Aabid asked, keeping his eyes straight ahead.

"He wasn't my father," she said through gritted teeth. "And he said you were taking me home."

"I will…eventually," he said. "In the meantime you need my protection. Without it you would be raped and killed before the day is out."

Helene gasped. "I don't believe that."

Aabid whirled around and his expression was just like that of a spiteful, petulant child. "Believe it!" he said, and suddenly she did. They rode in silence again for another long stretch.

After a while Aabid became remorseful again. "I do not wish to frighten you, but you must understand how things are in my country," he said defensively. "In your ignorance you will bring danger to yourself and me."

Helene didn't reply. She was trying to look at her situation realistically. She had jumped at the prospect of going home—thinking of Edward and Mrs. Barnes—but after everything that happened, she suddenly realized that there was no going home. Nothing would be the same without her father. Mrs. Barnes was only a paid employee. She would take Edward and leave, and Helene would become a ward of the state—just another forgotten orphan of the war.

And all of this was her fault.

Riding on a donkey in the middle of the desert suddenly seemed the most fitting place for her to be. Their slow, steady pace over the bumpy little roads actually soothed the painful anxiety that flared up from time to time, and seemed a fitting companion to the despair that eventually took over when the anxiety finally went away.

"I'm hungry," she announced when she couldn't ignore it any longer.

"Me too," Aabid agreed. He seemed strangely cheered by her declaration, as if it signified some kind of common ground between them. Yet they kept going, moving at the same slow pace on the same, endless road. Helene waited as long as she could—it felt like maybe twenty minutes or more—before she spoke again.

"I'm hungry!" she said more emphatically.

Aabid glanced back at her with amusement in his eyes. "Yes, I know."

"Are we going to do anything about it?" she asked.

"Yes," he replied calmly. "There is a camp up ahead."

"How far?" she asked.

"Not far."

She sighed. "What time is it, anyway?" she wondered. The warm sun was making her tired, but trying to keep her balance on the donkey forced her to stay alert.

"It is not yet *zhuhr*," he said. "That is midday."

Helene could tell that he was trying to be nice but his efforts were oppressive to her now. Yet she was shocked to learn that they hadn't even made it half way through the day. "It seems like we've been on this road forever."

Aabid threw her another amused glance. "It has not been nearly as long as that," he said.

Helene was once again struck by the quirky maturity he exhibited sometimes—especially considering how childish he could be at others.

The donkey was becoming terribly uncomfortable. Helene couldn't even change position with the *khimar* encumbering her. She began to fidget, but this seemed to amuse Aabid so she made a conscious effort to be still. She kept looking ahead, watching for the promised camp site. The moments dragged on like hours. She stared at the turbaned head in front of her, wondering about Aabid's life and the strange, angry fear he exhibited whenever something *haraam* came up in conversation. His fear was contagious. She could feel it seeping in through her pores and settling inside her like a disease, infecting her with a kind of painful awareness of how dangerous resistance might be. She got the impression that all Muslims were just as dogged in their beliefs as Aabid. It seemed like they didn't have much choice in the matter. Much as she hated to admit it, Aabid was probably as sympathetic a guide as she was likely to find here—a frightening thought. He did seem determined to keep her out of trouble, and she sensed that at least one of his motives was to keep her from suffering the same fate as her father.

Her stomach was grumbling noisily by the time Aabid finally led them off the main road and onto a small pathway that disappeared at the top of a hill. Helene heaved a sigh of relief. Her muscles were stiff and she desperately wanted off the donkey. As they cleared the hill she was momentarily distracted by the view, which overlooked a lush valley bearing a surprising variety of plant life, including, even, a few small trees. A stream meandered through the camp, flanked on both sides by silvery-green weeds. Sheep dotted the countryside, making the camp seem more welcoming somehow, as did the smoke rising up from a fire just outside a large, gray tent that sat in the very center of the valley.

Anticipation of food replaced all other considerations as they descended the hill and approached the Bedouin camp.

CHAPTER
39

Helene couldn't help noticing that the Bedouin camp—which had a kind of charm from the top of the hill—grew much less appealing the closer they got. The enormous, multisided tent was constructed from random patches of light and dark wools. The area all around it was littered with all kinds of household items that had been left scattered about in disarray. Bedouins emerged from the tent as they approached, dressed in layers of dusty clothing. There were three men, all just as somber-looking as Aabid. The women were covered from head to toe, leaving only their eyes, which were shaded and unreadable. But the children, at least, were smiling. Their large, white teeth glinted in the sun like smooth pearls.

Before the donkey even came to a stop Helene was already sliding off of it.

"*Assalamu alaikum*," one of the men said to Aabid. Helene recognized the greeting, which her father told her meant "peace be upon you." And then suddenly all the men seemed to be talking at once. Only the women, like dark, ominous phantoms, hung back and watched the event in silence. Helene did the same.

After this initial exchange the men turned to the women and issued orders in Arabic, and the women rushed off behind the tent. The men walked together toward the tent, speaking more calmly to one another now. Helene followed unnoticed. The women returned with four basins of water, which they placed on the ground near the men's feet. Then they scuttled back into the tent, casting curious glances at Helene as they went.

The men sat on stools over the basins of water and began to wash. The children were called inside. Helene was tired, hungry and fed up with all the strange Arab customs, but something warned her—some inner instinct—that to cause a scene would be disastrous.

As she silently fumed, Helene couldn't help noticing that the men were all acting in unison as they washed, moving fluidly together, almost like dancers. They began by saying, "*bismillah,*" and then proceeded to wash their hands three times. Next, they cupped water in their hands, lifted it to their mouths, swished it around and then spit it out on the ground—repeating this three times. Then they brought the water to their noses, sniffed it into their nostrils and then blew this, too, out on the ground. Helene's face scrunched up in disgust as she watched them repeat this three times. After this they washed their faces three times—dipping their hands in the water frequently— and then their arms. Then they ran their wetted hands over their head and ears. Finally, they washed each foot three times. The water in the basins was then poured out onto the ground and the men rose up and moved to an open section of the tent. Helene groaned inwardly when she saw them assembling in a line, all facing the same direction as if preparing for yet another custom. Her stomach, which had been rumbling for a while, was now making very loud, screeching noises. Normally she might have found this little display interesting, but at that moment every word and movement only irritated her more. Aabid, meanwhile, seemed perfectly at ease, as if completely unaware of her discomfort.

In spite of her irritation, Helene couldn't resist taking a few steps closer to the tent so that she could watch what they were doing.

The men stood with both hands raised up to their shoulders and murmured what sounded like a prayer in perfect unison. Then they lowered their hands and recited another prayer. Then they bowed and prayed again. They spoke in Arabic, so the only word Helene recognized was 'Allah,' which was in almost every phrase. After bowing the men stood straight again, then they went down on their knees and placed their heads on the floor, then they sat up, then they put their heads on the floor again. With every change in position they paused to recite another prayer. As Helene watched she grew more and more infuriated so that by the time they finally turned to each other in what looked like a final salutation Helene had decided she would refuse to eat.

She was scowling when Aabid finally approached her, but then she remembered that he couldn't see her face, so she snapped—"What the bloody Nora was all that?"

Aabid shot her a disapproving glance. "You must address me respectfully!" he exclaimed in a low voice. "And swearing is *haraam* for women."

She was really starting to resent the word *haraam*. She ignored his comments and waited for him to answer her question.

"That was *zhuhr salah*," he explained. "It is our mid-day supplication to Allah. *Salah* is prayer."

She figured as much. "And all that…business with the water?"

"That is *wadhu*," he said. "It is so that we are clean when we offer *salah* to Allah."

"You do all that every day before lunch?" she asked, surprised.

He smiled. "We do it at least five times a day…sometimes more."

"What!" Helene stared at him, incredulous. "Are you kidding me?"

"It is *fard*—our obligation—to offer *salat* at these times; *fajr*, which is dawn, *shurooq* is sunrise, *zhuhr* is noon, *asr* is afternoon, *maghrib* is sunset and *eshaa* is nightfall."

"What happens if you don't?" she asked.

"Observing *salat* is the obligation of all Muslims," he said with a shrug. "To not observe would render one without faith—an *infidel*. Allah deals most severely with these."

Helene suddenly had the urge to laugh. For some reason, a character out of Edward's *Dandy comics*—Desperate Dan—suddenly came to mind. There was something about Aabid that reminded her of the cartoon outlaw. True, Aabid didn't have Dan's enormous pot belly, and while Aabid seemed barely able to grow a moustache, Dan's beard was so stiff he needed a blowtorch just to shave. Still, there was something about Dan's mulish and ill-mannered behavior—eating cow pies with the horns still attached and bending street lights just to prove his strength—that was eerily similar to Aabid's boorish insistence that his way was right. Even the Bedouin camps were like Dan's cartoon town of Cactusville, a throwback from another era, harsh and inhospitable—or so it seemed to Helene.

A strange hopelessness gripped her. London seemed to get further away with every minute that passed.

Aabid was speaking to her but she'd stopped listening. She didn't want to hear any more about *salah, fard*—or especially *haraam*. She closed her eyes and fervently wished to never lay eyes on another turban, *khirmah*, or anything else that was even remotely Arab. Most of all, she wished that when she opened her eyes again Aabid would be gone. His bossiness was becoming unbearable. She opened her eyes to find him watching her.

"You need food," he told her in that same insistent tone that he said everything. "I will get some and we will eat together."

"Oh, so *now* you remember my hunger," she replied sarcastically. "Well it's too late!" She refused to say more or to even look at him. He took her arm and led her into an isolated corner of the tent and forced her to sit on a cushion. Then he left and in a few minutes returned with one large, steaming bowl of food. "You will enjoy this," he told her, and dipped his fingers into the mixture, using them to scoop out the food.

"That's disgusting!" Helene exclaimed. "I don't want it now that you've had your fingers in it!" She remembered her father and Huxley saying that this was how the Arabs ate, but she thought they were only teasing her.

She heard his sharp intake of breath. "You will control your tongue!" he exclaimed in a low voice. Helene closed her eyes and lay back, wanting nothing more than to sleep.

"You must eat," Aabid said, but she ignored him. "This is how a child acts!" he complained, and she felt a little satisfaction when she heard him sigh heavily, as if contemplating how to deal with the situation.

"Very well," he said at last. "I will prepare for our departure."

Helene felt a sudden panic. "I'm not going!" she announced, sitting up straight.

She could tell that Aabid's patience was wearing thin, but she felt he would be more inclined to control himself with other people around. "I mean it," she insisted. "Just leave me here. I'll stay with the Bedouins until someone from England comes along."

He appeared to be struggling to control his temper. When he spoke, his tone was as determined as ever. "You *are* coming with me," he said—"Even if I have to tie you to the back of the donkey!"

He set the bowl on a nearby table and stormed out.

It was Helene's turn to sigh. She looked around miserably until her gaze settled on the bowl. She reluctantly picked it up. She wanted to remain aloof but the smell was simply too irresistible. The worst thing was not having a fork to eat with. Her eyes filled, but she broke off a piece of the bread and dipped it in the still-warm mixture. She wasn't surprised to find that it tasted good. It was a bit spicy compared to what she was used to perhaps, but she liked it. She told herself that it was because she was so hungry. She'd heard of people eating bugs when they were hungry enough.

Before Helene realized it she'd eaten every drop. She belatedly wished she'd thought to leave something in the bowl so it wouldn't look like she enjoyed it too much. Yet she had to admit she felt better. The food had done wonders for her.

Aabid's pleasure at seeing the empty bowl brought back her bad temper. "However," he remarked as she followed him outside—"We must refrain from overeating. The prophet, *alayhi s-salām,* says we should only eat what we need to keep our back straight. We should fill no more than one third of our stomachs with food, leaving one third for water and the remaining third for air.'"

"Does Allah tell you how many times to chew before swallowing, too?" she asked. But she was secretly glad that she had displeased him by finishing all the food in the bowl. "I'm going to walk," she added when she saw that he was preparing the donkey for her.

Aabid looked at her sharply, and she knew he was itching to remind her about being respectful but she rushed ahead before he had a chance to open his mouth.

"If we're not going to Tel Aviv then where are we going?" she asked once they were back on the main road.

There was a long pause before he replied warily—"To the house of my father." He seemed reluctant to say more. A horrible thought suddenly struck Helene and she stopped in the middle of the road. Aabid stopped too.

"Am I going to be a slave?" she asked, recalling stories she'd read in *Arabian Nights*.

Aabid actually laughed, and Helene was once again struck by how young he was. "Of course not," he said, but he didn't elaborate and Helene was still wary. They resumed walking.

"What then?" she asked. "How do you know your father will accept me in his house?" Another thought struck her and she stopped again. Aabid turned to face her, and she could see that he was growing frustrated again.

"I'm not…he's not…" Helene wasn't even sure what she was trying to say exactly.

"No, my father will not harm you," Aabid assured her firmly. Perhaps a bit too firmly. Helene examined his face. Something wasn't right.

"Tell me," she demanded. She saw a look come over his face at her tone but she refused to back down. She was certain that something terrible was about to happen—she suddenly realized that she'd known it all along. She just hadn't been ready to hear it until now.

Aabid's reluctance to tell her what it was only confirmed her fears that it was something terrible. "Your father should have told you," he grumbled miserably.

"That was not my father!" she yelled. "Now tell me what the bloody hell you're planning to do with me!"

"And you agreed," he added defensively.

It suddenly felt as if the *khirmah* was suffocating her and she ripped it off in a sudden panic. Aabid gasped when he saw her and she was dimly aware that her white-blonde hair was flying in all directions. She could feel the static electricity making it stand on end. "What did I agree to? Tell me!"

"Your father gave you to me. To be my…wife," he said.

Helene stared at him in disbelief. And yet she'd known it would be something like this. Wasn't that why she'd been so reluctant to push him for the truth from the start?

"I won't do it," she said.

"It is already done," he replied. His expression was that of a person whose mind was set.

"You have to have my permission!" cried Helene.

"The only consent needed is that of your father, but you agreed too…in front of witnesses," he reminded her.

"I didn't know what I was agreeing to and he was not my father!" she screamed.

"Your guardian then," said Aabid. "A guardian can also pronounce *nikah* on your behalf. That is our custom."

"What about *my* custom?" Helene demanded. "I'm not an Arab, in case you didn't notice. You've spent every minute telling me *your* ideas about right and wrong, as if I didn't already have my own."

"I cannot help what is," he replied. "I'm sorry if it is difficult for you, but resistance will only make it harder. These are not my 'ideas,' they are the laws that Allah has given us all. Allah knows best. If you disobey, it will go poorly for you and me, your husband, as well."

"You are not my husband," Helene said through gritted teeth.

Aabid approached her and there was no longer any trace of the shy boy that Helene thought was escorting her to Tel Aviv. This was a selfish, self-righteous man who was determined to have what he wanted regardless of her feelings. His face was the picture of obstinacy. He stood as close to her as he could possibly get without actually touching her, until his nose was a hairsbreadth away from hers.

"For once you are correct," he said in a menacingly calm voice. She could see that he trembled with his effort to control his rage. "The *nikah* will not be valid until we have consummated our union." He grasped her shoulders then and she could feel his strength in spite of his youthful body. There was a dangerous gleam in his eyes that terrified her. "I was going to give you time to adjust to being my wife, but if you continue to argue the point I will take what is mine here and now!"

The threat terrified her so much she immediately gave in. "Please!" she cried. "I swear I won't say another word."

He examined her a moment longer and then released her with a little shove. Then he grabbed the donkey's rope with a jerk, startling the poor creature as he drove them onward without another word.

CHAPTER
40

Two weeks passed in a dismal haze that was sporadically brightened by moments of curiosity, fascination and even—on a few occasions—amusement. They traveled from one Bedouin camp site to the next, except when they set up camp alone. Helene learned how to fish, how to make *khubz*—the flat bread they always served with meals—and how to be a Muslim. In the course of all this, her marriage to Aabid became official.

The sense of isolation was often too much for her. It was a rare pleasure when she came upon a woman who spoke English. The men—excepting Aabid—never spoke to her at all.

The *khirmah* made everything seem worse. Helene felt as if she was invisible when she wore it, which was every minute that she and Aabid were not completely alone. She remembered being curious about the women who wore them. They seemed so mysterious, so secretive and coy. Now she saw it differently. The black coverings reminded her of sadness and mourning. There was a suffocating quality to them, for though they were lightweight, the color attracted the sun, and therefore the heat, making them terribly hot at times. It seemed to her that their overall purpose was to darken and diminish.

Aabid was now her only connection to the world. She needed him as much as she resented him. She tried to understand him even though everything about him repelled her. Yet he was not an ugly man. She wondered how he appeared to the Arab women who were more accustomed to the domineering qualities she so disliked. Were all Muslim men like him? Did they all fly off the handle as easily? There were, of course, times when he made an effort to be patient and tolerant, but she could not count on it and that left her tense all the time. It was like being at the mercy of a spoiled toddler. He was nothing like Edward, who could argue a point without causing her to fear for her life. Edward! How she missed him! But thoughts of him—as with any thoughts from her past—brought such anguish that she erased them from her mind. And though she missed Edward she couldn't help feeling resentment and anger toward him too. If not for that letter…!

The more Helene learned about Islam, the more she resisted it. It was too invasive for her spiritual requirements, with directives on everything from when to pray, how to eat, and even how to go to the bathroom. It seemed like almost everything was either *haraam* (forbidden) or *fard* (obligatory). Very little was left to choice. With each added regulation Helene became more defiant. Thankfully, Aabid did not force her to participate in *salah* or *wadhu*, or any of the other obligatory acts for Muslims, focusing all his attention on simply keeping her from doing those things that were *haraam*.

Helene tried to envision a life as Aabid's wife, but the thought of it filled her with foreboding. Her marriage to him didn't seem real. She thought of it as a bad dream that she was simply waiting to awaken from. She often thought of Lilith and wondered if there was some way to bring her back. Maybe they could help each other. Lilith would know how to get Helene out of this. Thinking about it gave Helene hope, and kept her from losing her mind during those weeks in the desert.

They were on the last leg of their journey to the house of Aabid's father, and the day of their arrival had come. Helene could not help looking forward to the change. She was dismayed when Aabid steered them off the main road and began setting up a private camp. Helene knew what this meant, and she sighed, torn between revulsion and a strange, unwanted thrill of anticipation. Like all of Aabid's mandates, she considered this 'duty' between a husband and wife to be invasive and embarrassing—on the surface. But beneath the surface it kindled something bewildering and overwhelming in Helene, something almost pleasurable—or, at least, something that made it less disagreeable.

Aabid was more attentive than usual. Foregoing his usual eagerness, his hands became gentle—almost tender—as he lifted Helene's *khirmah* up over her shoulders and meticulously arranged her flyaway hair. A shiver shook her.

"You are nervous?" he asked. She knew he was referring to his family and it suddenly occurred to her that *he* was the one who was nervous, though she supposed she was a little nervous too. Were they like him?

"This has been a lot to…take," she stammered.

"There is no strength but by Allah," he said in a tone that implied he knew exactly what she was going through but was helpless to do anything about it. Helene struggled to hide her resentment. It was galling that he could expect her to give up so much, while himself refusing to give an inch.

"Surely Allah would allow me one small reward for all that I have given up for him," she ventured, trying to keep the sarcasm out of her voice. They both knew what she was referring to.

His fingers had moved down to unbutton her shirt, but his eyes remained glued to hers. She could see that he was quickly becoming consumed by his arousal, and she too was consumed by emotions, but hers were of resentment, anger and grief, which warred with any desire she might have felt. Aabid fondled her body freely while Helene fought the urge to brush his hands away. She felt like a caged bird, forced to endure the overtures that happened to come through the bars of her cage. In these moments she couldn't help thinking of Edward and wondering how it would feel to be touched by him.

"Allah is an exacting God," Aabid said, his voice growing husky with lust. "It is not for you to say what He should or shouldn't do."

"Then shall I appeal to my…husband?" she asked, choking on the word.

This seemed to please Aabid. A small smile formed on his lips and Helene was once again struck by how good-looking he might have been if he wasn't such a tyrant. She wondered how she would feel about him if he had approached her—as an equal—in London. Would she feel differently if she had been given a choice in the matter?

"Yes," he replied softly. "I would like you to appeal to me." His hands continued their leisurely perusal of her body and she was becoming distracted.

"Then I appeal to you…my husband. Can we go to London after I meet your family?"

"It is my strongest wish that we be happy together," he said earnestly. "As I told you before…I will take you to London once you have given me a child."

"But why wait?" she persisted. "Why…" He cut her off with a kiss. A small sigh of frustration escaped her lips, and Aabid instantly became more aggressive, mistaking her sigh for passion. Helene's mind was still focused on returning to London. She didn't want to wait. And she most certainly didn't want to have a child. Yet she knew it was possible that she was carrying Aabid's child already. Supposing there was a child, Helene felt she still might escape him…provided she could convince him to take her to London. She clung to him with sudden hope and for Aabid that was all it took to send him over the edge. Any small advance from her drove him wild. Helene took some satisfaction from that.

The tenderness remained, even after his passion was spent, and Helene couldn't help being suspicious of it, wondering what brought about this sudden munificence. Yet she supposed he couldn't help hitting the mark once in a while. For there was no denying that he never stopped trying—she could feel him trying, constantly, day in and day out—in his quest to make her love him. It was clear how much he wanted her. But she couldn't help wondering; *Why put forth the effort when you're just going to resort to force in the end anyway?*

"You are mine," he murmured vehemently, burying his lips in her hair. "My wild, beautiful bird." When she didn't respond he got up. "Come!" he said. "Your new home is just over that hill."

CHAPTER
41

Helene was surprised to find that Aabid lived in a modern village with real houses. She was suddenly struck by how little she knew about him and his family. As they drew nearer he became more and more anxious, and with the anxiety emerged the ill-tempered, petulant little boy. Helene tried to ignore him. She found this side of him extremely repellent. He seemed to grow more unmanageable with every step.

The houses in their village were well kept, single story, rectangular buildings that were mostly constructed of the terra-cotta colored bricks that were so prevalent in their part of the world. The streets were clean and neatly landscaped. There were trees in nearly every yard and even an occasional flower. There was a feeling of affluence, especially when compared to the Bedouin camps. Aabid led her to one of the nicest homes on the street and tied his donkey to a tree. Helene's heart fluttered nervously as he led her into the house. It was cool and dark inside. The floors were lined in tile.

An older man with a thick beard—Helene learned later that it was Aabid's father—appeared, casting curious glances at Helene as he greeted his son, hugging and kissing him affectionately while alternately speaking to him in Arabic. After a moment the man asked Aabid a question, pointing his finger at Helene with a little laugh.

Aabid answered his father in a sullen manner.

The man took a closer look at Helene and then turned back to Aabid. The smile had gone from his face. His voice now grew loud and accusatory as he continued to interrogate his son. Aabid, meanwhile, answered the questions like a defendant in a trial.

Aabid's father suddenly moved toward Helene and she flinched as if he might strike her. He had a wild gleam in his eye that frightened her. He lifted the *khirmah* up over her head and gasped when he saw her. When he spoke again his voice was shrill with incredulity. Although Helene couldn't understand the words, she recognized the tone, which said, 'how could you do such a thing?'

Three women—one older and two that were closer to Helene's age—rushed into the room, clearly drawn by the commotion. They wore ordinary clothes, without *khirmahs*. They all stopped in their tracks when they saw Helene. Aabid's father said something to them in Arabic while they stared, disbelieving, at her. She knew her hair was flying in all directions but she didn't dare call more attention to it by trying to fix it with her fingers.

At one point during the father's explanation to the women, one of the younger women cried out loudly and nearly collapsed onto the floor. It was an agonizing cry that took Helene by surprise. The older woman took the girl in her arms and tried to soothe her, but she was inconsolable. The father hurled some kind of order at them, dismissing them with a wave of his hand, and the other two women removed the distraught girl from the room.

Aabid's father was quiet and thoughtful a moment, and then said something to Aabid in a low voice before he, too, left the room. Only then did Helene dare to look at Aabid.

"I will take you to your room," he said angrily—as if what just occurred was her fault—and she was dismayed to be confronted once again with the unreasonable, irate child. She knew it was because of the reception they got, but she also knew that Aabid had anticipated it.

He had grown more and more irritable, the closer they got. She would have liked an explanation but she followed him without a word.

"They are upset because they think you are a nonbeliever," he said. Helene refrained from pointing out that she *was* a nonbeliever. She had that all-too-familiar feeling that he was keeping something from her again.

"Why weren't those women wearing their *khirmahs*?" she asked.

"Women do not have to wear them in the presence of family," he replied.

"Are you the only one in your family who speaks English?" she asked.

"No. My sisters and my brother speak English," he replied.

"Was that your sister who cried out?" she asked.

"No," said Aabid, but he did not elaborate further.

"Who was it?" she persisted, suddenly curious.

They had arrived at a small room in the back of the house. It was sparsely decorated, with smatterings of light, bluish-gray the only color in the white-washed room. Aabid hadn't answered her question and Helene sighed, fed up with his evasiveness. He reached out to touch her but she jerked away from him resentfully. Predictably, this angered him. He grabbed her face and squeezed it so hard that she wondered if he would leave bruises. His eyes were vicious as they burned into hers. Her own anger flared.

"You want to know who the woman was?" he shrieked. "Are you jealous of her?"

Helene just stared at him, too angry to appease him and too afraid to do what she really wanted to do, which was to fight back.

"Are you?" he yelled even louder. Helene was painfully aware of the other people in the house. She wondered if they could hear.

"I...no! I don't even know who she is!" she said in a low voice.

"But you are jealous!" he insisted loudly.

She had the impression that he wanted her to be jealous, but she couldn't bring herself to be. She felt strangely ridiculous with her face all scrunched up in his hands. "No," she said. "I'm not."

"Good!" he exclaimed, releasing her so suddenly that she almost fell down. "I am glad to hear it." But he didn't look glad, even though he was smiling. "That woman is Fa'izah," he continued. "She is my first wife."

CHAPTER 42

Life in the Al-Zaa'ir household was only marginally better than being alone in the desert with Aabid.

The house was partitioned off so that Aabid and his family had an entirely separate living area, although there was a communal dining room where all of them came together for their evening meals. Arabic was the only language permitted in the dining room and Helene came to dread that time of day in spite of her growing love for Arabian food. Aabid's father remained disapproving where Helene was concerned, while his mother appeared to always be overwrought with distress. Aabid's sister, Kulus, stared openly at Helene, fairly gawking at her, while Aabid's first wife, Fa'izah, glowered menacingly in an equally open manner. Conversation was stilted, though they could have said anything they liked and Helene wouldn't have understood them. She stumbled miserably through those evening meals, unsure where to settle her gaze as she fumbled to eat from the communal bowl using only her fingers.

It was a little boy of about five or six years old—at some point Helene learned that he was the son of Fa'izah and Aabid—who became her first friend. The first moment he saw her, his face lit up with pleasure. He followed her covertly the first few days, until one day she found him standing beside her, quiet as a mouse, slipping his hand over hers. Helene's fingers hung lifelessly in the child's, her first inclination being to withdraw them. But glancing down at his smiling face she found she couldn't do it. And besides, she was hesitant to rebuff the only person to actually reach out to her. She squeezed his hand and he squeezed hers back. They smiled at each other.

"Helene," she said, pointing to herself.

"Zaahid," he replied in a raspy voice, pointing to himself. They smiled at each other again and he said—"*Qamh*," and pointed to her hair.

"Hair?" she said, touching her hair. "*Qamh* is hair?" Zaahid nodded and she bent down so he could touch it.

"*Qamh*," he repeated, reverently stroking her hair (It would be several years before Helene realized that *qamh* meant wheat, not hair, and that Zaahid had been trying to pay her a compliment).

Though conversation was a bit challenging, Helene's friendship with Zaahid blossomed. He hung on her heels, following her around like a stray puppy until a sharp command from Fa'izah would send him running in the opposite direction.

The second person to reach out to Helene was Aabid's sister, Kulus. Kulus was surprisingly like Helene's school chums back home, in spite of their cultural differences. She was curious, friendly and extremely talkative. Her English was not as good as Aabid's, but it was well enough that her errors were more humorous than confusing. She broke the ice by offering Helene a gift—it was a lovely barrette for her hair—and she further impressed Helene by making her laugh. Like most of the Arabs, Kulus was dark skinned with black hair. Her eyes were quite large and had the appearance of being lined even when they were not. Her hair was cut short in a kind of modern bob. Though she was generally obedient, she was mildly rebellious, prone to making snide comments about her parents in English to Helene (which brought many a disapproving look when Helene invariably laughed). Kulus was the last of Aabid's sisters to be married, but at fifteen she was already betrothed to her future husband. She lived in that portion of the house that was designated to Aabid's parents, which Helene didn't dare venture into, so Helene was obliged to wait for Kulus to visit her. Between school and her many Muslim obligations, Helene spent most of her days wondering when—or if—her friend would appear.

Aabid alternated his nights between wives. In spite of Helene's relief in having a reprieve from Aabid, she resented the cause of it. There was an inevitable bond that had developed out of her intimacy with Aabid (Helene refused to think of it as love) that left her feeling humiliated by his temporary defection. And for all of his boorishness in every other respect, Aabid was a surprisingly generous lover, expending long and—Helene imagined—tedious efforts to caress and coax the pleasure out of her, using his fingers and his tongue, until at last her body responded, often without her even wanting it to. He got her to do things for him as well, but he was adamant that above all else, she should derive pleasure from the act. This impressed her until she learned that it was no self-sacrificing act on Aabid's part, but yet another edict from Allah to satisfy one's wives. It would become a bitter pill to swallow that literally every aspect of her life was now dictated by Allah or his prophet, Muhammad.

In spite of her conflicting feelings about Aabid, Helene couldn't help wondering what he and Fa'izah did on their nights together. Fa'izah, meanwhile, was becoming impossible to live in the same house with. Though Helene tried to avoid her, the woman always seemed to be lurking in the shadows, spying. When she did approach Helene directly it was to correct her or give her an order. It was bad enough to have Aabid constantly telling her what to do but it was insufferable coming from Fa'izah. Yet there was no escaping it. They were trapped together in Aabid's little corner of the house. Helene began dividing her time between sitting alone in her bedroom and sitting outside. When she chose the outdoors she was inevitably joined by Zaahid, who would sit quietly beside her.

The yard was neatly landscaped with rather dull, silvery bushes and a few trees. One warm day a crocus appeared, startling Helene out of her depression and reminding her of England. She pointed it out to Zaahid, who smiled and nodded, saying—"*Kurkum.*" They walked around the yard, hunting for more of the bright-colored flowers, and before she even realized what she was doing, Helene was on her hands and knees, pulling weeds so the '*kurkum*' wouldn't get choked out. Zaahid helped her, and what would become a life-long love of gardening began for both of them.

That day, Fa'izah interrupted them to call Zaahid in for mid-afternoon prayers. He went inside but Fa'izah remained. She approached Helene anxiously.

"*Salah?*" she said, motioning for Helene to follow her in for prayers.

Helene shook her head. "No, thank you," she said, wishing the woman would just go away.

Fa'izah sighed resentfully. "*Salah!*" she said more forcefully, pointing to the door.

Helene just kept pulling weeds. "No!" she too responded more forcefully.

Fa'izah bent down and grabbed Helene's arm in an attempt to pull her up. "*Salah!*" she said again. Her voice had a desperate edge to it and Helene stood up.

"I don't want to!" Helene said, shaking her head back and forth vehemently, though the look in Fa'izah's eyes gave her pause. The women's distress was genuine.

Fa'izah took hold of Helene's arm again, more gently this time, and attempted once more to pull her. "*Meen fahd-lick…*please!" she said. Helene tried to shake her off but Fa'izah held fast and continued the gentle tugging and pleading. In the course of the scuffle, mild as it was, Helene accidentally struck Fa'izah's arm while trying to extricate herself from her grip and the woman cried out in agony.

"I hardly touched you!" exclaimed Helene, afraid that Fa'izah might be trying to create trouble between her and Aabid. She already suspected Fa'izah of turning Aabid's parents against her with her constant spying.

But Fa'izah didn't cry out again or make any further commotion. She lowered her tear-filled gaze to the ground, staring blindly at the place Helene had just finished weeding. "*Salah,*" she whispered miserably.

Helene suddenly felt sick. Without even really knowing what she expected to find she lifted Fa'izah's arm and very gently raised her sleeve. The ugly, black bruises didn't surprise her; nor did she need to be told where they came from or why. Fa'izah's strange behavior was suddenly made clear. She'd been commissioned by Aabid to oversee Helene's training to become a good, Muslim wife, and was being punished for Helene's lack of progress.

The sheer brutality of it took Helene's breath away. As if having a second wife thrust upon her wasn't enough! Helene tore her eyes from the bruises to Fa'izah's face and saw that Fa'izah was watching her anxiously, possibly afraid of how Helene would use this discovery. Helene was overcome with sympathy. She nodded her head. "Okay," she said, choking on the sobs that were racking her body as if to cleanse it of a lifetime of grief. "I'll do *salah*! Okay?"

Fa'izah's expression was so overflowing with gratitude that Helene couldn't stop herself from taking the woman in her arms and holding her close while they both wept—Helene with horror and dread, and Fa'izah with relief.

But even with the added incentive of Fa'izah's well-being Helene found the task of becoming a Muslim daunting, and she could only bring herself to do the very least that was expected of her. She found the daily prayers inconvenient but managed somehow to make a good show of it, and did her best to steer clear of everything even remotely *haraam*. It was not, in truth, all that hard to do. She had little freedom to act on her own. On the rare occasions when she left the house, she was covered from head to toe in the dreaded black *khirmah* and was accompanied by either Aabid or his father.

As Kulus became more absorbed in her own activities, Helene found herself more drawn to Fa'izah. Still, there was the language barrier to overcome. Since poor Fa'izah was already overwhelmed with the task of teaching Helene the rules of Islam, it was decided that Helene would teach Fa'izah to speak English. This worked well; Fa'izah was a much more willing and adept student than Helene.

Just as she was adjusting to all of this Helene realized that she was pregnant. The realization affected her more profoundly than anything that had happened to her so far in her life. This was a new opportunity, for the child growing inside her (she was convinced it was a girl) represented the only real family she had. She had no other living relatives that she knew of. Yet she couldn't help worrying; what would become of it? How would she protect it? In that incident with Fa'izah, she'd become painfully aware of how much her behavior affected others but now, with this child, Helene knew it would become even more true.

She took stock of her situation. Her problems with Aabid appeared to escalate in direct correlation with her resistance to him. This gave her hope that she might have some control over what happened after all.

It was time to grow up. Any dreams she'd harbored of returning to London were put on the back burner. She knew Aabid well enough by now to know that he would never take her there. He was neither honorable nor decent. He had no incentive to be; the incentive had been taken away from him when he was granted absolute power over the women in his life. However, all was not lost. Aabid's power came with a price, and that price was steep for him. Deep down, she knew that he wanted genuine affection from her. He craved it. When he couldn't force it out of her he turned cruel. This could be turned to her advantage.

On the next night that was hers, Helene forced all her anger aside—focusing on the child she was carrying—and did everything she could think of to please Aabid. She lowered her eyes respectfully and was openly affectionate with him. By the end of the evening he was like butter in her hands.

"This is how it could be between us always," she told him.

Aabid sat up in bed and eyed her warily. "What do you mean?" he asked.

"Our marriage…I don't really know much about marriage actually," she admitted—"But I think for it to be happy there must be some give and take." She saw him bristle and tried to soothe him with a kiss. "Please, Aabid, I beg you to listen to what I have to say. Allah says a man should listen to his wife before making a decision." She saw that her reference to Allah pleased him and was relieved when he visibly relaxed.

"I will listen," he said, lying back down. His manner had all the imperiousness of a corrupt king and Helene had to fight back a wave of irritation.

"Thank you," she said, kissing his hand. She could see that he was impressed by her behavior. "I…we are going to have a baby," she said, surprising him even more. "I think it's a girl."

The smile left his face when she added that last part, but he reached out and gently stroked her cheek. "You do not know that," he said in a dismissive tone, as if to say, 'do not worry about that.'

"But if it is a girl," she persisted—"If we have a daughter, I want something from you." He sat up again. "And I will give you something in return!" she added quickly.

"What is it that you want?" he asked suspiciously.

"I want her to go to college in England," Helene blurted out, perhaps too abruptly. "I want her to have the choice I never had." This angered him. She could see the resentment burning in his eyes.

"And you would not want this same opportunity for any boy child we might have?" he demanded.

"Of course, but I thought you would never permit a son to leave this country," she said. "And besides, a boy would not have the same... challenges here that a girl would face."

His lips became set. "No," he said decisively.

"You have never compromised on a single thing, Aabid," said Helene. "I, on the other hand, haven't been left one thing *not* to have to compromise on!"

"It is Allah..."

"I know! It's Allah who makes the laws," she interrupted. "But there's no law that says Muslims can't leave the country."

"You expect me to allow my daughter to just go off alone to be corrupted by the world?" he asked.

"There are schools in London where other Muslim girls go," answered Helene. "I'm asking you to give her a *choice*. Whichever path she chooses will be what's in her heart anyway."

"The prophet says that women are not capable of making the right choice. That is why he made men responsible for them."

"Allah also says that he will judge every individual by what's in their heart," she said. "That includes women. We all have a choice in what we feel in our heart. Even you can't change that, Aabid."

His eyes narrowed. "What are you going to do for me?"

She hesitated. It was hard for her to say. "If you do this for our daughter—I mean *really* do it, Aabid, not just promise, but actually start making plans from the day our baby is born—I will promise to be a more willing wife. I will try to love you."

Every word she uttered seemed to irritate him more. "You negoti-ate your duty?" he asked, incredulous.

"I'm not negotiating my *duty*," she countered, unable to keep the sarcasm out of her voice. "It is my *heart* I am negotiating with!"

"It is already commanded by Allah that a wife give what you are offering. The prophet—peace and blessings of Allah be upon him—would have a wife such as you be beaten and cast into hell!"

"You have set me up to fail Allah's commands!" she cried, think-ing *two can play this game.* She was actually a little surprised by how much she'd retained from her lessons with Fa'izah, in spite of her reluctance to learn. "You've become a stumbling block, preventing me from doing what is right by making it as difficult as you possibly can. In this way you are sinning against Allah."

He actually seemed to be considering her words. "How do I make it difficult?"

Helene offered a silent prayer up to Allah to give her the right words, and would have laughed at the irony if she had even realized she'd done it. Everything here was Allah, Allah, Allah. After a while, a person hardly noticed it anymore. "You use threats and brutality to get me to yield to you," she began. "You rob me of the opportunity to give myself to you *willingly*." She paused when she saw how her words moved him. "I know that you want that from me, Aabid," she told him quietly. "Don't you? Wouldn't you rather have me willing than forced?"

He sighed. "But you are asking me to…"

"I'm asking you for *one* thing, Aabid. One. A relatively little thing too, considering that girls mean so little here—I don't want to argue, never mind. We disagree about that. But you have to admit that a father is less concerned over a daughter's soul than a son's because the prophet says it is corrupt no matter what anyway, not to mention that her options in the afterlife are just as bleak as they are here!" She could see he was getting riled up again so she quickly changed her tack. "All I'm asking is that you let her determine her own fate. We will raise her as a Muslim and then send her to school in England. Muslims can do this. I know they can because Kulus told me that her friend…"

"Okay," he interrupted.

"Okay?" she repeated. "Really?" She could hardly believe her ears, and the expression on his face was even more unbelievable. He actually seemed...happy. "You see!" cried Helene, spreading kisses all over his face until he laughed. "You see how good it feels to give something of your own free will?" She kept kissing him until he made her stop. His eyes were shining with emotion.

"Thank you," he said quietly. "You have proven yourself a wise and worthy wife." Helene collapsed into his arms and stayed there, feeling content for the first time; if not for herself then at least for the life yet to come.

CHAPTER
43

Present Day

The neighborhood where Nadia's grandfather lived looked a lot like the suburban neighborhoods of middle-America. There was a black car waiting for them in the driveway. Two Arab men got out.

"Lovely day," said one of them, glancing at Nadia.

"It's just after morning prayers," said the other. "They're expecting you."

They went inside and waited in a large foyer. After a moment an old man came out to greet them. He squinted at Nadia as he got closer, as if he was having difficulty seeing her. Within a few yards of her he stopped.

"Helene!" he cried, taking a step back. He grew pale and stumbled forward, as if he might fall. One of the men rushed to his side and took his arm. The man asked him something in Arabic.

"No, no," he replied. "I am fine." But he didn't look fine. The old man approached Nadia slowly, as if he was afraid of her. He seemed so helpless, not at all like the man she imagined. His skin was worn and deeply lined. His eyes were glassy and moist.

"I'm Nadia," she said, offering him her hand. He took it and pulled her close, nearly crushing her in his embrace. His body shook with sobs. When he recovered he withdrew just enough so that he could look at her. His watery eyes moved over her face slowly, examining every detail, and then landed on her hair. He murmured something in Arabic and sniffed. "You are like her," he said.

Nadia was aware of the five men waiting—and watching—behind her. She wasn't sure how to begin. She remembered all too well her grandfather's feelings about the djinn. She didn't want a repeat of his performance in the desert with Helene. "We're…trying to get information to prevent something terrible from happening," she began.

"Yes," he said, nodding and sniffing again. "I know. They told me. Come in. Come in. No! Not you," he said to the men. "You can wait out here." He pointed to a small room off the foyer. "I want to speak to my granddaughter alone." Will started to object but then nodded. "Remember we have a plane waiting," he said to her, and went into the room with the others.

"Someone will bring you refreshments," her grandfather called after them. He took Nadia's hand in his cold one and led her through the house and into a beautiful courtyard. Nadia gasped when she saw it. Her mother had not done it justice. "She did all this," Aabid told her, noticing her reaction. He looked around as if he, too, were seeing it for the first time.

"You miss her," observed Nadia.

He smiled. "Yes. So many things I wish…" Nadia waited but he didn't elaborate.

"I have to ask you about something…" she began, but faltered. "My mother told me that you don't like to speak of it, and I don't want to upset you…"

"Please," he said. "I know what you want to ask about." He shrugged. "I'm afraid your grandmother only spoke of that incident one time, and I would not allow her mention it again." He smiled contritely. "In my desire to see you I may have mislead those men out there."

Nadia didn't know what to say. "Do you mean to say…you don't have *any* information about where that djinn might be? Didn't my grandmother tell you anything…any clue?"

"No. Not to me," he replied, waving his hand in a dismissive gesture. Nadia could see how Helene might have found this man to be self-centered and inconsiderate. Yet she was touched that he wanted to see her. There must have been something in Nadia's expression that revealed her thoughts because his watery eyes were suddenly filled with regret. "But maybe someone else…" he suggested.

"Who?" she asked.

"Your grandmother was very close to my first wife, Fa'izah," he said. "She may have told her something that will help you." Nadia thought this was a good idea. "Come, we were about to enjoy our morning meal. Fa'izah has prepared your grandmother's favorite dish. Maybe you will like it too?" he asked.

"That sounds lovely," Nadia agreed, following him into the kitchen.

An older woman was waiting in the doorway for them when they got there. She was much better preserved than her husband, though Nadia guessed her to be in her eighties. She was petite, with dark brown hair still holding its own against the gray. Her expression was vibrant and alert, her features still intact. Nadia could tell that she had once been quite beautiful.

"I can't believe how much you look like her!" Fa'izah exclaimed. "Just as lovely! If only you could have come a few years ago. How she would have loved to see you!" Sadness came into her eyes. "We loved her so much," she sniffed. "She taught me English you know. If not for her I would not be able to speak to you now." *If not for her, I wouldn't be here now*, thought Nadia, but she was delighted to be able to talk to the woman who was her grandmother's closest friend. "Come!" Fa'izah said. "Sit down! I made her favorite."

The three of them sat together at the table and Nadia self-consciously slipped her fingers into the warm bowl Fa'izah offered, feeling a strange sense of *deja vu* as she did so. She had to remind herself that it wasn't her memory but her grandmother's.

Fa'izah did most of the talking. Her enthusiasm never waned. Aabid was quiet and respectful. He seemed almost helpless now, obliged in his old age to let his wife be the strong one.

"We loved her so much." Fa'izah said again.

"Are none of your children here?" Nadia asked. "I was hoping to see my aunts and uncles."

Fa'izah sighed. "Everything is changing. They do not want to live in the house of their fathers anymore."

"Oh," sighed Nadia, disappointed. "I had particularly hoped to see Zaahid."

"Oh!" exclaimed Fa'izah, moved to tears by this. "Gisele told you about him? He loved your grandmother very much! They were so close. It is kind of you to think of him." Her voice quivered a little, as if she might cry, but she quickly pulled herself together. "He would have loved to see you too, but there was no time! They only told us you were coming late last night. There was no time to plan."

They ate in silence for a while, then Nadia ventured—"I was hoping you could tell me more about my grandmother. There are some things the men out there need to know…but you may not know any more than we do."

"Your grandmother and I shared everything," she said. Tears filled her eyes again and Nadia could see how much the woman missed Helene. Fa'izah stood up. "Come. We will talk in the courtyard. That's where she and I always used to talk."

On the walk over, Fa'izah took Nadia's hand and pressed something into her palm. Nadia looked down and saw an old, decrepit locket and chain. Heart hammering, she carefully opened the locket and saw a black and white photograph of a woman she had never seen before. "That's your *great*-grandmother," Fa'izah told her. "Helene had that necklace since she was a very small girl. She wore it all the time. It's not very pretty anymore, I suppose, but I thought you might like to have it."

The necklace was in terrible shape, bent and misshapen, with several links having been roughly repaired, but Nadia squeezed it tightly in her hand, as if she could extract some small part of her grandmother from it. "Thank you," she said.

They went into the courtyard and talked for nearly an hour, but within the first few minutes it became apparent that the rest of the story—there was a lot of it Helene never told Gisele—held no hint as to where Lilith might be. As she and Fa'izah talked, Nadia was ever aware of the time but it was hard to break away. She would have liked to spend all day with the woman who knew more about Helene than even her daughter had.

There were tears in Nadia's eyes when Aabid interrupted them to tell her the men were ready to leave. Fa'izah embraced Nadia as if she was her own granddaughter, her eyes damp. "I hate goodbyes so I will let your grandfather see you out," she said, trying not to cry.

Aabid led Nadia back to where the others were waiting. Nadia turned to him and smiled.

"Goodbye grandfather," she said awkwardly. She wasn't sure if she was allowed to touch him or not. "Thank you."

"Goodbye Nadia," he replied. His eyes were watching her with what looked like regret.

Will came to her side. "Are you okay?" he asked as they walked outside.

Nadia blinked away her tears "I didn't learn any more about Lilith," she said. "Just more details of my dysfunctional origins."

"Things your mother didn't tell you?" he asked.

"I don't think my mother knew."

He sat next to her in the car. "The plane is near here," he said. "You'll have plenty of time to tell us about it on the flight back to the states. But first, we have some good news."

And Nadia suddenly noticed that all three of them were in a much better mood. "What is it?"

"We finally found our smoking gun," said Will. "A syringe hidden in a package delivered to a Muslim extremist in DC yesterday afternoon. They have it in a lab right now. It looks like our infectious disease."

"And the guy who the package was sent to just happened to be scheduled to work at the bank meetings Tuesday," said Clive.

"That's right," said Gordon. "It's a miracle that the operative even found the syringe. He'd been watching this guy for months. But now, everyone's on high alert looking for strange deliveries from medical supply places and the like. So yesterday he notices his guy gets a package from an adult toy store. Looks about the right size to ship a vibrator in…"

"The op knew this because his wife just got hers in that week," said Clive.

"Save it for the team review meeting," said Will.

"I'm practicing," said Clive.

"Anyway," continued Gordon, giving Clive a look—"The op was suspicious. They were supposed to be looking for shipments coming from medical labs and pharmaceutical companies. But this op's thinking; 'Why would a single, straight guy be buying a vibrator?'"

"You can set him straight on that later, Gordon," interjected Clive.

"And then it occurs to him that most vibrators are made of either rubber or silicone," continued Gordon, intentionally ignoring Clive. "Which would make a perfect cushioning material for a syringe. He opens it and...jackpot."

"There won't be any more sex toys delivered this week," observed Clive.

"Finding this syringe forces DC to act," said Will. "Everyone is under a microscope. The city is crawling with ops. They're even canceling flights into DC."

"So...what does all this mean?" asked Nadia.

"It means they can start working on an antidote, for one," said Will.

"And they can take the necessary steps to keep this thing contained in DC," added Gordon.

"And now that they know how these syringes are being shipped, they can intercept the ones that haven't already been delivered," said Will.

"And people will once again be able to look upon vibrators without fear," added Clive.

So it *was* real. Everything they'd been saying was true! Nadia was glad she was sitting down. "But...it's still going to happen?" Nadia asked.

There was a moment of silence.

"And we have no idea where Lilith is right now," she added.

"Look," said Will. "We're not giving up. We're gonna keep doing what we've been doing. Okay?"

"But I already told you, they didn't tell me anything that will help," said Nadia.

"We've got a twelve hour flight ahead of us," said Gordon. "Can you think of anything better to do?"

"Yeah," agreed Clive. "And besides, I've developed a soft spot for your grandmother and I'd like to hear what happened to her."

"We'll go over the rest of Helene's story and see where it leads," said Will.

"Looook!" cried Clive in a raspy voice that Nadia had never heard him use before—"Ze plane!"

CHAPTER 44

April 1966

Helene closed the book and sighed. Another dead end. It was surprising how little information there was in these so-called research books. Yet she was grateful that the college let her use the library—and, too, that her father-in-law agreed to drop her off and pick her up three days a week on his way to and from the hospital for treatments. It was an unexpected kindness brought about by a shared interest. He loved to read, and could therefore sympathize with Helene's plight in finding books that were written in English. The college was better equipped than the local book store, but its focus remained on Islam, so here she was again, limited to science, history and religion.

Helene didn't mind. It was what she preferred now. The library reminded her of her father's library—less the window seat she loved so much. And, of course, Edward.

But it was time to leave. Helene sighed again. Time passed so quickly when she was reading. In the months she'd been coming here she read everything she could find on ancient scrolls. The discovery at Qumran made particularly interesting reading, though they made no mention of her father, Huxley or Butch. She was currently working her way through the books on djinn. She was puzzled by how little information there was. Islam recognized the djinn as a very great evil and therefore had a lot to say on the matter, but none of it was of any use! Surely others had made similar discoveries to the one they made at Qumran. Lilith claimed the angels prepared a *Book of the Dead* for every Nephilim who lived in Kiriath Arba—in triplicate. How was it that not one of them made it into the history books?

She supposed this was just one more thing she would have to work around. They were adding up, these things she had to work around. Sometimes when she thought of all the concessions she'd been forced to make over the years she couldn't help being impressed. She would never have thought she had it in her. Not that she had a choice. But some of the things—like Fa'izah and the children—turned out not to be so bad after all. It was worse to imagine her life without them.

As she gazed out the large library window, watching for her father-in-law, her mind drifted back, as it often did when she was here, to her father's library. At times like these she couldn't help thinking about Edward and wondering what happened to him. Where was he now? Did he still enjoy reading? She could picture him; his light-brown, slightly wavy hair falling over his forehead no matter how hard he tried to slick it back like the other boys, his blue-green eyes sincere while the dimple on his left cheek twitched mischievously. Yet the image of his face seemed older today. Helene blinked and took a step forward.

"Edward?" she whispered. She closed her eyes and opened them again. Was it possible?

Though she had barely breathed the name, the man turned his head in her direction with a questioning look. Helene waited to see if he would recognize her but then remembered that she was completely covered except for her eyes. She took a few steps closer, staring openly at him.

The man looked at her with a blank smile. "I'm sorry," he said politely. "Do I know you?"

It was him! Tears flooded Helene's eyes. He was looking at her with interest, as if remembering.

"It's Helene," she said quietly. "Helene Trevelyan from London."

The man visibly paled and took a step back. "Helene! But it can't be!" People were looking at them.

In spite of her immense pleasure in seeing him, Helene had the wherewithal to try and contain her excitement. If word of her speaking to another man got out...yet she couldn't just walk away from him. "Edward!" she whispered. "Is it really you?"

He appeared to be having difficulty believing it too. Recovering quickly, more out of necessity, she motioned for him to follow her to a more secluded part of the library and then asked him what he was doing there.

"I'm here for the semester," he told her. "I teach environmental studies—there's a whole crew of us that came over on a research project sponsored by the college. We're diving in the Red Sea. But Helene, what are *you* doing here? And why are you dressed like that?"

"Oh Edward," Helene suddenly broke down and started to cry. She tried to explain what happened in between sobs. "It was horrible... Huxley and my father were killed...Butch too, I think."

She took a moment to compose herself while he waited for her to continue.

"We found the scroll that Huxley was looking for and ...! Oh, I can't explain it all in a minute. I was forced to marry a Muslim man." She had to pause here to stifle another sob. "Now I...things are so different. Everyone is Muslim."

Edward was aghast. "Good god!" he exclaimed. "We had no idea what happened to you...with all the fighting that was going on we assumed you were all killed!"

Helene could not help weeping again. "The others were."

In spite of her emotional state, Helene was aware that they were still attracting curious glances from other people in the library. Edward seemed to read her mind. "It's a capital offense here for a foreigner to speak to a Muslim woman," he said.

"Yes, I know," said Helene. "But I've found that people are much more open minded about it here at the college. I've seen more of it here than anywhere."

"Well, but we should be careful," he said.

Helene smiled. "It's worth the risk to see you again," she whispered through her tears.

Edward looked at her in surprise. "I wouldn't be able to live with myself if I brought more trouble to you," he said.

"But there is so much I want to know!" she said. "How is Mrs. Barnes?"

Edward laughed in spite of the seriousness of the situation. "Mrs. Barnes?" he repeated. "No, I most certainly will not risk your life talking about her—she's fine, by the way!"

Helene laughed. "I don't even know where to start! I have so many questions—and so much I want to tell you!"

"I wish I could see your face!" he complained. "I hate those horrible things they make the women wear here!" He stopped suddenly. "Oh, I am sorry Helene," he said.

"Don't be," she said. "I hate them too, but...this is my life now."

"How did you get here, in this library?" he asked. "It reminds me of your father's library, by the way. It was the first thing I thought of when I walked in."

Helene could have wept all over again. "I know! Me too!" She looked around nervously. "My father-in-law is going to be here any minute to pick me up. If I make him wait he may not let me come to the library again."

"When can I see you again?"

"Wednesday, just before mid-day prayers," she said. There were butterflies in her stomach just thinking about it. "I will meet you there"—she pointed—"in the back. They lock the doors but they don't clear everyone out anymore...there are so many Americans and other foreigners working here now. I've stayed behind before and no one noticed. We'll be able to talk then."

"I'll be here," he promised.

Helene paused a moment longer to look at him. "Is it really you?" she asked.

He smiled. "It's me," he assured her. "Edward Adeire."

CHAPTER
45

The change in Helene was obvious. Even the children noticed. Her joy was palpable.

Aabid eyed her suspiciously, but his mother watched her even closer. It was as if Helene's cheerfulness signified something ominous and distasteful. She scrutinized Helene's every move, growing more disapproving with each observation.

Fa'izah warned Helene about it one day.

"So, what?" said Helene. "She's always hated me."

"I just think you should be more careful around her," Fa'izah suggested.

"Careful about what?" asked Helene, growing apprehensive.

"About how you are perceived," said Fa'izah. "The appearance of wrongdoing is also a sin."

"The appearance...!" Helene was suddenly angry. "I haven't done anything wrong!"

"Please do not be angry!" Fa'izah begged. "You are *akhawat* to me, my sister. I have seen women stoned to death in the street for little more."

This took some of the wind out of Helene's sails. "I appreciate your concern."

"I could not bear it if anything happened to you…!" Fa'izah whispered.

Helene felt the familiar heaviness in her chest, weighing her down. If not for Fa'izah and their children she was sure she could get Edward to help her escape. "Does Allah condemn happiness now?" she asked.

"Shhh!" scolded Fa'izah. "Let us not open that can of worms! I am only asking you to control yourself. You come back so joyful! I am afraid you will be found out."

"Found out?" echoed Helene. "You think I'm doing something wrong, too?" Her blood chilled. If even Fa'izah doubted her, she really was in trouble.

"No, of course not, but it is very clear that something at that library is making you very happy and not everyone will believe it is only the books."

Helene was suddenly afraid. "I'm not doing anything wrong," she said again.

"What then?" Fa'izah asked.

Helene hesitated. "Can I trust you?" she asked, but was instantly sorry when she saw how the question hurt Fa'izah. "Okay, I'll tell you." Helene took Fa'izah's hands and stared, wide eyed, into her face. "I found an old friend I used to know in London. He was at the library."

"*He*?" Fa'izah echoed, paling. "Not…!"

"Yes, it's Edward," Helene admitted.

Fa'izah looked as if she'd seen a ghost. "Almighty Allah, please be merciful!" she whispered.

Her reaction was making Helene nervous. "All we do is talk!" she said.

"Talk! Helene…that is enough!"

Helene's eyes turned cold. Something was rising up in her that overrode her fear. All her efforts—the lengths to which she went to try and improve her marriage, following the rules, saying her prayers—it all seemed for naught. Aabid did little more than make a show at keeping his end of the bargain. With just over a year of school left before college, he was already backpedaling on his promise to send Gisele to England.

"Ever since I was kidnapped—yes, kidnapped—and brought to this horrible place I have followed all the rules, no matter how stupid they were. I've been forced to give up everything!" She huffed in disgust. "Allah should never have created women if he thinks we're so pathetic we can't spend a few measly hours with a man without sinning!" But she almost instantly regretted her outburst. It was not Fa'izah's fault. "I will be more careful," she said.

"Are you in love with him?" Fa'izah asked.

Helene felt put out by the question; yet it brought her up short. She had to think about it. "I love him," she admitted. "But not like that." She met Fa'izah's gaze. "Don't worry. My life is much too hopeless to allow me to feel any real hope."

The women looked at each other for a long moment. "Have you ever been in love?" Helene asked her.

Fa'izah blushed. "Of course!" she said.

"What happened to him?"

Fa'izah seemed taken aback by the question. It took her a while to answer. "He fell in love with another woman," she said at last.

It took another few minutes for Helene to understand what Fa'izah meant. Then her hand rushed to her mouth and tears filled her eyes. "You mean…?" There were tears in Fa'izah's eyes too. "Oh Fa'izah! You have no idea how sorry I am!" Helene embraced her friend, rocking her in her arms like a child as she repeated "I'm sorry" again and again. Helene had never guessed. All she knew about Fa'izah and Aabid's marriage was that it was arranged. She had assumed that most women would find such a situation as unbearable as she did. But then she called to mind that first agonized scream—a disturbing sound that Helene never understood, until this moment, was the sound of a heart breaking.

Though she thought she had tried, Helene realized now that she never came close to loving Aabid. She couldn't, because on some level that scream *had* resonated with her. She could never forget it, any more than she could forget the way Aabid forced Fa'izah to teach

Helene to be a better wife to him. Helene could never love such a man. And Aabid knew it. And he made them all pay for it.

Helene would never give up Edward. He was someone she could talk to about the things that mattered most to her. They reminisced about her father, Butch and Huxley, and she told him all that happened in Qumran—things she could never tell Aabid. Edward was not only interested but helpful. He brought her books that she couldn't get access to herself. But most of all, he made her feel happy again.

However, Helene did heed Fa'izah's advice to be more careful. She made sure Edward left the library long before Aabid's father came to pick her up, and tried to hide her happiness when she got home. Things got back to normal.

But one afternoon, quite out of the blue, Helene's gaze drifted from Edward's face to laugh at something he said and—landed on the furious face of her husband. The world seemed to stop for a second.

Helene's first inclination was to pretend to be someone else. She was, after all, covered except for her eyes. But there was no denying that he recognized her. He was staring directly at her with an expression of pure hatred.

Helene stood up, feeling as if she might faint.

"Harlot!" Aabid growled, eliciting the interest of the other people in the room.

"Please let me explain!" she begged him in a hushed voice.

He lunged for her hair, capturing a thick clump of it along with the head covering. Helene cried out in pain. They had everyone's full attention now.

Helene's mind flashed to a women she'd seen being drug through the street to be stoned to death, and she shuddered. "Aabid! Please listen!"

Edward took a step forward, obviously bewildered about what to do. As terrified as Helene was, she had the presence of mind to be struck by the extraordinary difference between the two men. Edward was so civilized he hardly knew how to respond, while Aabid exhibited less control than a spoiled child. It was not the first time she thought of this, but it was never more evident than at that moment.

"*Sayyd*. I beg you not to punish the woman for my error in asking a simple question!" Edward said, stepping forward and gently placing his hand on Aabid's arm.

Helene panicked, aware that Edward was also in danger. He could be put in jail for trying to 'corrupt' another man's wife. "Please don't try to help me!" she said. "It will only make things worse!"

Edward jerked back his hand as if it had been scalded. He watched, horrified, as Aabid drug Helene out of the library by her hair. Once they were outside Aabid released her, shoving her so hard that she fell, her hands and knees hitting the ground hard. Pain shot through her. She was trembling so badly that she couldn't get up. "Aabid, I beg you," she cried but he kicked her in the stomach and it was all she could do just to breath.

"Stay!" he ordered, as if she was a dog, and he went back into the library. Helene began to cry. People stopped to stare at her and she was suddenly glad for the covering. This was all her fault! She should have listened to Fa'izah.

Aabid returned in a few minutes. Helene managed to stand up, keeping her eyes lowered. Aabid took her arm and dragged her to the car.

Helene didn't dare speak. They drove in silence for a time.

"Did Fa'izah know why you were coming here?" he asked. His tone was as pleasant as the calm before a storm.

Helene closed her eyes, realizing suddenly how many people might be affected by this. "No," she answered as convincingly as she could manage.

"So," Aabid continued after another long pause, "You beg for the opportunity to explain your behavior—this behavior that you have not even shared with Fa'izah—of how you've been meeting this man you love, this man you deserve after giving up your whole life to obey stupid rules! The life I kidnapped you from. Your life of no hope!" Helene couldn't believe what she was hearing. These were the exact words she'd said to Fa'izah. She couldn't imagine why Fa'izah would do this to her.

Aabid looked at her in disgust. "No more lies to tell?"

"I am so sorry Aabid," she said. "He is like a brother to me. I only wanted to…"

"I know what you wanted!" he screamed. "My mother heard every word you uttered to that faithless *gahba*!" Tears rushed to Helene's eyes when he said this. Fa'izah hadn't betrayed her! It was, in fact, the other way around. By confiding in her, Helene had brought danger to her friend.

"Fa'izah was reprimanding me," she said. "She was trying to get me to stop. Your mother can confirm that." Helene felt a sudden surge of hatred for the woman who mothered this monster, even though she knew that the woman was as helpless to change the situation as she and Fa'izah were. Still—eavesdropping and then repeating her words to Aabid without even asking Helene about it first—did she hate Helene so much that she wanted her killed? And what about poor Fa'izah?

"You are both guilty and will both be punished," he said.

"I swear she tried to stop me!"

"She should have told me."

"I convinced her that I would stop," she lied. "She made me promise to stop and I did!"

He didn't seem to hear her. His expression was set.

"She loves you so much," Helene whispered tearfully.

Aabid stopped the car right there in the middle of the road and glared at her. She winced when she saw that there were tears in his eyes. It was the first time she'd ever seen him cry. His tears terrified her worse than anything else he could have said or done. There was a car approaching ahead, but she was too afraid to speak.

Aabid drove the rest of the way in silence. Helene wondered what he said to Edward when he went back into the library.

When they got home, the house was eerily quiet. No one was in the main living area. Helene waited.

"Get Fa'izah," Aabid ordered.

Helene turned to him. "I'm begging you not to…"

"Get her!" he screamed, making Helene jump. Her entirely body was shaking violently but she didn't move. It was suddenly as if she was outside of her body. A kind of indifference took over, though she had the presence of mind to realize that something terrible was happening.

"If you do this…" she began.

Aabid's expression practically dared her to finish her sentence.

"If you do this," she repeated—"I will divorce you."

She didn't see it coming, but the blow struck her so hard it momentarily blinded her.

"*You* will divorce *me*?" he screeched. "You are an adulterer! I can have you killed!"

The pain was terrible, and she was losing her will to fight, but she suddenly called forth Lilith, praying to her for strength. "Kill me then!" she heard herself say. "Kill me or divorce me...those are your only two choices if you hurt Fa'izah. Our bargain will be off."

He stared at her in astonishment. "You actually have the audacity to pretend we still have a bargain?" he asked.

"I've never broken our bargain," she said. "I promised to be a loyal wife and Muslim, and I have done both of those things."

"But you have not loved me," he said resentfully.

"I have tried," she said. She wanted to lie but couldn't bring herself to do it. There was something about always being forced that made her cherish the tiniest liberties.

His anger returned. "You call meeting a man in private being a loyal wife and Muslim?"

"We didn't meet in private. It was a public library and we only talked. He's only here for a few months."

"It is improper for a Muslim wife to meet with a strange man, even to talk." he said.

"He is not a strange man," she said, surprised that they were able to have this dialog at all. She supposed her threat had hit the mark after all. "He's like a brother to me."

"You love him."

"As a friend."

"Why did you keep it a secret then?"

"I shouldn't have," she said. "I'm very sorry about that. I didn't trust you to understand." She took a timid step toward him. Her left ear, where he hit her, was still buzzing. "I was wrong and it will never happen again."

Helene could see both sides of Aabid's character warring over what to do, and wondered which side would win. He could choose to be generous and forgiving, thereby narrowing the gap between them, or he could be self-righteous and tyrannical, which would widen it. Over the years Helene had seen both sides of his character, but the latter was much more typical of him. She knew that he was as chained to this prison as she was, but he was the one who brought it on them both.

"I will think on the matter," he said quietly. He suddenly seemed too tired to fight.

A sob escaped Helene's lips and it was then that she realized how afraid she'd been. She dropped to her knees in front of him and kissed his feet.

"Thank you!" she whispered, letting her tears fall freely at last.

CHAPTER
46

It was a week before Aabid reached his decision. During that time he neither spoke to nor visited his wives in their rooms. The family meal was particularly awkward, as everyone took their cue from Aabid and this left no one speaking. Even the children, sensing something ominous, practically swallowed their food whole and then abruptly rushed from the room.

Helene and Fa'izah brooded over their fate. They blamed it all—perhaps unfairly—on Aabid's mother, hating her more than ever, and concocting plots for revenge. Sensing their resentment, the woman wisely kept her distance.

Aabid spent more time away from home than ever before, never telling anyone where he went. When he was home, he stayed with his father in his sickroom. They shared long hours there, and Helene wondered what her father-in-law thought about the incident. She felt he would probably give her the benefit of the doubt, having softened in his view of her over the years.

Helene was getting dressed one morning when Aabid finally came to her. Her blonde hair—which she still wore long—was strewn all about in disarray. She could see from the intensity of his stare that he still wanted her.

"I have decided to spare Fa'izah," he announced.

Helene couldn't hide her relief. "Thank you!" she cried, impetuously throwing her arms around him. His arms came up instinctively to hold her but he stopped himself.

Helene stepped away awkwardly. His face was filled with emotion but Helene couldn't tell what it was. Anger? Undoubtedly. Fear? Always. Love? Helene wasn't sure he was capable of love. She stared at his face, unable to read him, as she waited for him to continue.

"I cannot let your behavior go unpunished," he informed her grimly.

Helene held her breath, realizing suddenly that it wasn't for herself that she was afraid. It was for him! If he was without mercy now it would surely destroy the last shred of feeling she had for him—however meager it might be.

"Our bargain is finished," he said, and Helene dropped into the nearest chair with a little sob. Gisele would pay the price for her folly then! "Or, at least, your terms for it," he added, and Helene's head shot up. Aabid's eyes seemed to be drinking in all of her wild beauty, even as he fought with everything he had to break her. "There is still a way for our little Gisele to escape—as you so bluntly put it." A bitter smile twisted his lips. Helene wondered what he was driving at. "Her ticket out will be your dear friend, Edward!"

Helene stared at her husband, confused. "I don't understand," she said.

"I've offered Edward Gisele's hand in marriage!" Helene was struck speechless so Aabid continued—"It is a way for you to prove that there is nothing more between you than, as you say, friendship."

"But…what did Edward say?" Helene was mortified to think of how that conversation must have gone. What must Edward think of Aabid?

"He said he would do as you wished."

Gisele and Edward! Helene could feel her cheeks burning under Aabid's watchful gaze and struggled to remain calm. "He's so much older than her!" she remarked, yet her mind was racing ahead. Edward! He would do it if she asked him to. She sensed that this would be Gisele's only chance. It wasn't as if they had to stay married. The marriage could be in name only. The moment she left Saudi Arabia, Gisele would be free to get a divorce. Perhaps Edward was thinking the same thing when he agreed to go along with it. Helene had confided in him how much she wanted to get Gisele out of Saudi Arabia.

"He is no older than many of the men seeking wives Gisele's age," Aabid reminded her and this, more than anything else, made up her mind.

"I must speak to Gisele!"

"You would agree to it then?" He seemed surprised. Helene looked back at him, equally surprised by how little he knew her. As if she would sacrifice her daughter's happiness over a man—even one that she was in love with! How petty and malicious he seemed just then. He believed her to be in love with Edward; yet that he could give his daughter to the man under those circumstances was too unspeakably cruel to forgive. Had he no love for his daughter? Helene could almost pity Aabid, except that this final act of betrayal destroyed any remaining feeling she was capable of having for him, just as she knew it would. She looked at him with contempt. Yet she knew that it wasn't entirely his fault. He'd been taught since birth that women were worth less than the animals. And she knew, as well, that he was letting her off easy. It was within his rights to have her severely punished—and even killed.

How glad she would be when Gisele was far away from here. Yet her heart broke when she thought of her other children.

"Yes," she said. "I most certainly will agree."

"I have invited him here to settle it!" he said as if to deliver a final blow. It seemed that he couldn't quite believe she was willing to go along with it.

Helene tried to conceal her emotions. She didn't want to do or say anything to ruin this opportunity for Gisele. She rose up from her chair, keeping her eyes lowered and her demeanor humble. "I will speak with our daughter now," she said.

Her mind was on Edward as she looked for Gisele. She thought of the joy he brought. How lovely it was to talk to him, to have that to look forward to. He made her laugh. What would she do without him? What would she do without Gisele? Helene couldn't identify what she was feeling, except for the relief. She'd survived another disaster—dodged another bullet—and this time she actually came out ahead. Anything more complex was too dangerous to dwell upon. She had to be content with little joys—like those afternoons with Edward. She could not allow herself to feel more deeply than that.

Helene could almost laugh at the irony. If Aabid knew how completely he had extinguished her ability to feel he would never be jealous again.

Gisele was busy entertaining the smaller children—trying to scare them out of their wits, actually—when Helene found her. She jumped up, tittering guiltily when she saw that she was caught, fully prepared to charm her way out of a scolding. Two of the children were already in tears.

Helene tried to look at her daughter objectively. What would Edward think of her? She was as different from Helene as a person could be—as dark as Helene was fair, and as wild as Helene was composed.

"*Ummi!*" Gisele kissed her mother's cheek. "*Albi!*"

"*Youni enta!*" Helene laughed. "Come, *habibi*, and we will talk."

Gisele linked arms with her mother. "*Salam* babies," she called over her shoulder as they left the room. "Was I naughty again, *Ummi?*" she whispered.

"Yes!" answered Helene, laughing. "But that's not what I want to talk to you about."

Gisele looked at her mother with concern, aware—along with everyone else in the household—that something serious was going on. Her eyes were so dark and beautiful that at moments like these Helene almost feared she would get lost in them. "A very strange thing has happened," Helene told her, wondering how to break the news.

"What is it?" There was a note of alarm in Gisele's tone.

"Come into the garden with me, *habibi*, and we will have a long talk. I want to explain everything—from the beginning—so you will understand."

Gisele stopped her. "What is it, *Ummi?*" she repeated, becoming more distressed. "Is it bad?"

Helene gently coaxed Gisele onward. "No, my impatient girl, I don't think it is bad!" But tears were filling Helene's eyes and she knew she was frightening her daughter even more. Gisele stopped, refusing to go any further until her mother told her what was happening.

"You're going away," Helene said, smiling through her tears. "And it's going to be wonderful for you."

"Going away!" Gisele echoed. "But..." She looked at her mother with surprise...and interest.

"Come with me now," said Helene. "Do you want to know everything? Yes? Well then, you must listen to what I have to say. I know I have always let you have your way but this time you must listen to *ummi*, understand?"

Gisele took her mother's arm again and allowed herself to be led into the courtyard, assuming the air of a long suffering Joan of Arc being led to the stake. Helene would have laughed but her mind was occupied with the past, stirring up old memories, some of which had been locked away for many years. She knew it would be painful to bring them back, but it would be therapeutic too, for she had never really mourned the past. She turned her eye inward, scouring her mind for Pandora's Box and wondering how much of it to let out.

CHAPTER 47

Present Day

"Man, your grandfather was cree-py!" said Clive, shivering for effect, but then, noticing Nadia's distress he added—"...he so creepy he went into a haunted house and came out with an application."

Nadia tried to smile. "It's just so...sad," she said, sniffing. Will, who was sitting next to her on the plane, took her hand.

"Don't be too hard on your grandfather," he said. "Men in this part of the world are stuck in the dark ages. It does a number on their head."

Nadia sighed. "I suppose."

"Well, that explains how Edward got back into the picture," said Gordon, trying to the change the subject, but actually making Nadia feel worse.

"I suppose now you'll be pointing the finger at *him*," she said.

"Nadia," Will began.

"No!" she cut him off. "By all means…let's start ripping daddy apart now. Let's see, he's a staunch environmentalist…I guess that's strike one. Oh, and let's not forget that he helped me get started in this treacherous business of helping people…strrr-ike two!"

"Listen to me, Nadia," Will interrupted. "We're not going to start ripping your father apart."

"Oh? Why not?" She tried to take her hand away but he refused to give it up, squeezing it instead.

"Cause we already did and we came up empty handed," said Clive. Both Gordon and Will looked at him as if to say—'are you *trying* to make things worse?' Clive huffed, clearly offended. "Just trying to help."

"Already did…how?" Nadia asked. "What have you done to him?"

"Nothing," said Will. "He was under surveillance for a while, that's all."

"And he came out squeaky clean," added Clive. "Not to mention that he's a man, and having just come from Saudi Arabia, we all can appreciate how important that is."

"What he means is that Lilith wouldn't choose to be a man," clarified Gordon.

"Though she did appear to have a bad case of penis envy," said Clive.

"It's extremely unlikely that a female djinn would pick a man to inhabit," reiterated Gordon, growing annoyed with Clive.

"But not so unlikely that she would marry him," said Clive, and Nadia knew they were still thinking about Gisele. "For a husband, Edward would have made the perfect choice. A rich guy who's also smart and romantic, who takes long walks on the beach and likes his martinis shaken, not stirred…just like James Bond."

It was disturbing that they knew these things about her father.

"I was supposed to join him at the beach tomorrow," Nadia remembered out loud.

"That's probably not a bad idea," said Will. "You'll be safer there until all this is over."

"So that's it?" she asked. "All this for nothing?"

"For nothing!" echoed Clive. "We figured out what it is and where it's going down. That's huge!"

"But we didn't stop it," she said.

"Our job is to expose the plot and capture the djinn," said Gordon. "We accomplished half our goal."

"You win some you lose some," said Clive.

"So, this was definitely the work of Lilith," she concluded, astonishment still evident in her voice.

"It sure looks that way," said Will.

"So where is she then?" she wondered out loud.

"That's the million dollar question," said Will. "We've looked at every possible candidate. We've even considered Fa'izah, but she doesn't have access to a computer and she never leaves the house. She'd have to be a lot more powerful than a djinn—more like a witch—to pull this off."

"Don't tell me you guys believe in witches too," groaned Nadia.

"No," he replied. "But the point is we just don't know. Maybe Brisbin—or whoever he was covering for—brought Lilith back on their end."

"I've added Lieutenant Brisbin to our system," Gordon told her. "We had no reason to suspect him before. There's still a chance we'll find Lilith through him." He sighed in frustration. "That wouldn't explain the connection to BEACON though...it's hard to believe that that could be a coincidence. I was so sure we had her!"

"Don't beat yourself up," said Clive.

Gordon turned to Nadia. "I'm the one who submitted the report that ultimately brought about your abduction," he told her. "We have to prove a certain risk factor and present evidence to get authorization to seize a person suspected of harboring a djinn. I jumped the gun on this and I'm sorry. I guess I owe you one."

"Well I don't regret a thing," said Clive. At Nadia's look he added—"If not for your help we might still be looking for suicide bombers in LA!"

"Thanks...I think," she replied dryly. She supposed all her personal trauma was worth it if they actually managed to contain whatever it was in DC. "But people are still going to die."

"You can't dwell on that," said Clive.

"I keep thinking about how Helene toyed with the idea of bringing Lilith back to help her," mused Will. "What do you suppose made her think she could pull that off?"

"That's probably what she was researching at the library," said Gordon. "But when she got caught with Edward that research came to an end."

"There are many questions that may never be answered," observed Will. "That, unfortunately, is the nature of our job."

"If she's out there we'll find her," said Clive. "It's just a matter of time. I'm anxious to see where Brisbin leads us."

Nadia noticed that Will was watching her and, meeting his eyes, she couldn't help thinking of her nickname for him when they first abducted her. His eyes were so blue that she sometimes felt like she was drowning in them. Suddenly awkward, she blurted out—"I'm still not a hundred percent convinced all this is real…that I'm not just being brainwashed like…Patty Hearst." She followed this with a little laugh, as if it was just a joke.

"Does that mean you'll do whatever we tell you to?" asked Clive.

She was still looking at Will, who surprised her by whispering— "Does it?"

She replied with another little nervous laugh. Needing a change of subject, she said—"I'm sick of peanuts. Don't we have anything else?"

"I've got Doritos," said Clive.

"Hand them over!" she demanded.

Will unclasped his seat belt. "I'm going to check in," he said.

"I'm going to go join the mile high club," said Clive, also getting up. "…Or pee. I'll leave it up to you, Patty. Which is going to be?"

"Clive…" Will interjected in a warning tone.

"We tried to suck out her soul like a Slurpee," said Clive. "I think we can dodge a sexual harassment claim after that, don't you?" He winked at Nadia as he strolled off to the bathroom, humming the same old tune that was now driving her crazy because she couldn't get it out of her head. Will went to the other end of the plane to make his call.

"Ugh, that tune," she complained, crunching on a Dorito. "He sings it all the time!"

Gordon seemed agitated. "Mmmm," he agreed humorlessly.

Something in his tone aroused Nadia's interest. "What is that song anyway?" she asked. "I know I've heard it before, but I can't think of the words."

Gordon turned and met her eyes reluctantly, which made it all the more surprising when he took a deep breath and began to sing. He had a high, almost falsetto voice but he kept perfect tempo with the song's melody—"Jeeeeean, Jeeeeean, ro-ses are red. All the leeeeaves have gone green. And the clouds are so low, you can touch them, and so, come out to the meadow, Bonnie Jean."

Nadia tried to maintain a serious expression. Something in Gordon's manner—in the grim way he sang the song—brought to mind Clive's taunt about his name that first night she met them. "Is your name really Gordon?" she couldn't help asking.

He sighed. "My first name is Gene," he muttered.

Nadia nodded and pursed her lips. "Nice name."

"Thanks," said Gordon.

"He's a strange guy," she observed about Clive.

"You don't know the half of it."

"You guys must spend a lot of time together," she said.

"Too much," said Gordon.

"Is Will always so uptight?" she wondered, changing the subject.

"He's not so bad," Gordon replied thoughtfully. "Bit of a control freak. His heart's in the right place. He had a tough childhood. Father's a tyrant…that kind of thing. He thinks it's up to him to personally take down every bad guy."

Clive was coming back from the bathroom so Nadia changed the subject again. "How much longer is this flight?" she asked.

"We've got another six hours or so," said Clive. "We're about half way there."

Nadia yawned. Will was coming up the aisle too.

"What news?" asked Clive.

"They found another two syringes!" he announced.

"I heard that," said Clive, aiming a fist at Will. Will bumped fists with Clive's and then sat back down next to Nadia. "Yeah, but I won-der how many more are out there," he said. "They're looking at every person working at those meetings," he continued. "Doormen, caterers…even the janitors."

"I would think *especially* the janitors," murmured Nadia.

Clive laughed. "I bet you'll never look at a janitor in the same way."

"I bet you're right," she replied. They were all quiet for a moment. Nadia was thinking of the night she was kidnapped.

"Why'd you take me there?" she suddenly asked. They all just looked at her. "Why the desert? And what was that shiny metal thing outside? I thought it was a space ship when I first saw it."

Clive and Gordon looked at Will.

"Might as well tell her," said Clive. "She couldn't find that spot again if her life depended on it. Besides, I'm starting to think she might actually be innocent!"

Nadia gave him a look that told him how little she cared what he thought.

"The metal dome is where we keep djinn," said Will.

"We can't kill them," explained Gordon. "So we have to bind them to a talisman, which in most cases comes in the form of a ring. The talisman traps them forever, unless someone releases them or if the talisman is destroyed. Since the talisman is metal the only way it can be destroyed is through sublimation, which is a kind of evaporation that takes place under very high temperatures. If that happens, the djinn is released back out into the world. That's why we store them in the fire-proof dome."

"Plus, you never know when you might need them again," said Clive. "For information."

"But…couldn't someone discover the dome, just sitting there like that?" Nadia asked.

"Normally it isn't just 'sitting there like that,'" said Will. "We keep it underground, buried beneath the desert sand."

"It's controlled by an automatic device that makes it go up or down," said Gordon. "We had it…ready when we brought you in that night."

"So…once you put the djinn in the dome, what were you planning to do with the rest of me?" she couldn't help wondering.

There was another awkward pause. "The dome comes fully equipped with an incinerator," Clive said in the same tone an advertiser describes a product's advantages.

Nadia gasped. "You were going to *kill* me? You're authorized to *kill*? Just exactly who are you guys, anyway?"

"No, we weren't going to *kill* you, but it wouldn't have been *you* anyway," said Clive. "Your soul would have already been smothered by the djinn. You'd be a soulless lump. Trust me. I've seen it. It makes someone with advanced Alzheimer's look like Sherlock Holmes."

Both Gordon and Will objected at the same time. "Clive!" exclaimed Will, while Gordon wondered aloud—"Why? Why is he allowed to talk?"

"Most victims of djinn die shortly after the djinn is expelled," explained Will. "We just let nature take its course. Those that…persist are taken back home for their families to deal with."

"Either way, they aren't talking," said Clive.

"So essentially, you bring them here to get rid of the bodies," she summarized. When they didn't deny it, she continued—"I mean, you could expel the djinn anywhere, but that might leave evidence. They could struggle, like I did. With forensics and all…"

"You made your point," said Clive. "We like to get the whole package out as quickly and cleanly as possible. So?"

"Not to mention that many places are too populated for an extraction to go unnoticed," added Gordon. "I've seen the earth shake!"

"But why *there*?" Nadia persisted. "You just decided to dig a hole in the middle of the desert one day? Don't you have to have a permit or something?"

"You might say it's kind of a home base for us," said Clive.

"Where is it, exactly?" she asked.

"You don't need to know that," said Clive.

"Okay," she said agreeably. "So who are you? I think I've earned the right to know that much. I did, after all, solve your case for you."

"She fills in a few details and suddenly she solved the case," said Clive.

"Remember before, when we mentioned the Essenes?" Will asked.

Nadia thought for a minute. They'd covered a lot of ground in the last few days. "You mean the Jewish monks who saved the ancient writings?"

"That's them," said Clive. "Now take out the Jew—and especially the monk—and you've got yourself a Raphaelian."

"A what?" asked Nadia. She couldn't help laughing, in spite of everything.

"Raphaelian," he repeated with much more attitude this time. "What? You never heard of Raphael, the angel that kicked Azazyl's Nephilim-breeding ass?"

Nadia almost choked on a Dorito. "What's he, like a superhero or something?" she asked.

"Hell yeah!" exclaimed Clive.

"Raphael led the angels in the war against the Watchers," explained Gordon. "The Essenes took the ball from there."

"You never read the *Book of Enoch*?" asked Clive. "No? How about the book of *Joshua*, in the Bible?"

"I'm afraid not," said Nadia.

"The book of *Joshua* gives an historical account of how the Jews conquered Canaan all those years ago," said Gordon. "If you'll remember, they had escaped Egyptian slavery and were wandering the desert for forty years in search of the Promised Land."

"You're talking about the story of Moses," said Nadia.

"That's right," said Clive. "You know, the one where Charlton Heston's hair gets all freaky-deaky, like yours sometimes does, and Yul Brynner's got that cool braid coming out of the middle of his head and shit."

"And Ann Baxter," Gordon added with meaning.

"You know that's right," said Clive.

"Moooses," drawled Gordon seductively.

"Ha ha!" exclaimed Clive. "That's my bitch!"

"Um…excuse me," Nadia interjected. "I hate to break up this little…whatever that just was, but what does all this have to do with…?"

"Sorry," said Gordon. "Where were we? Oh, yeah…the Jews wanted Canaan—but they were too afraid to try and take it because the spies they sent out told them it was overrun with giants. Anakians, they called them. They were the descendants of Anak."

"Which tells us that the Nephilim of Kiriath Arba survived the flood," said Will. "And now, after hearing Lilith's story, we know how they did it."

"That's where the Essenes come in," said Gordon. "The Bible, naturally, gives God all the credit, but what actually happened was—with or without God's help, as the case may be—the Essenes gave the Jews the *secret* for killing the giants, making it possible for them to take over the land of Canaan and, in the process, making the Jews the most feared people throughout the land. No one could figure out how they did it. Everyone thought it had to be a miracle."

"So how did they do it?" Nadia asked.

"They found the books," said Will. "The Essenes found Azazyl's books, and they figured out how to immobilize these giants by calling out their souls."

"If you read between the lines in Joshua's version of what happened, it's obvious," said Gordon.

"Check out Joshua, chapter six, verse fifteen," said Clive. "And I quote...it came to pass on the seventh day that they rose early and compassed the city seven times..." Nadia was impressed to see that he had the scripture memorized. He recited it with pride, almost as if he'd written it himself. "Verse sixteen," he continued. "And it came to pass on the seventh time, when the priests blew the trumpets, Joshua said unto the people, 'shout, for the Lord hath given you the city.'"

"The Jews *circled* the city, blowing trumpets to cover the sound of their *chanting* as they called out the Nephilim's souls," said Gordon.

"Verse twenty," continued Clive. "So the people shouted when the priests blew with the trumpets and it came to pass, when the people heard the sound of the trumpet, that the people shouted with a great shout, and the wall fell down flat, so that the people went up into the city, every man before him, and they took the city."

"The giants were the 'wall' guarding the city," said Gordon. "When they fell, the city was left wide open. The Jews shouted something that was covered up by the blowing of the trumpets, and the giants fell."

"And that was how the Essenes went from being quiet, sexless little monks to the djinn-chasing, Nephilim ass-kicking Raphaelians you see before you today!" concluded Clive.

Nadia laughed, but she was impressed, and told him so.

"You should be," said Clive.

"But I still don't see how you have the authority to…I mean… *Raphaelians*? Really?" she was finding this very hard to accept. "That's like the police calling Superman for help."

"You can't argue results!" exclaimed Clive.

"The Department of Defense has many different branches," explained Will. "Each branch has their divisions. And those divisions have their divisions. We are affiliated with a division of one of those divisions."

"Now you're starting to sound like that pharmaceutical company you were giving me such a hard time about," said Nadia.

"Yeah, but we know what we're trying to hide," said Clive.

"We're with one of the divisions that fight terrorism," explained Gordon. "They have lots of different divisions working different angles to achieve the same goal. They don't care how it gets done, so long as it gets done."

"Every threat has to be examined, no matter how improbable it might seem," said Will. "Everything from alien sightings to psychic readings. Or, in our case, djinn."

"So you're a division of the Department of Defense," said Nadia.

"No, we are *affiliated* with a division of a division of a branch of the Department of Defense," said Clive. "Jeesh! If you would just *listen*!"

"We're a private organization," said Gordon. "We contract our services out to the United States and other governments as needed."

"The Raphaelians is just our code name," said Clive

"It keeps our official name and mission statement from being exposed," said Gordon.

"And from attracting attention during budget cuts," added Clive.

"And this dome in the middle of the desert?" she asked. "Does this division of the DOD know what you're storing there?"

"Depends who you ask," said Clive.

"What if the wrong person finds out about this?" she asked. "What if someone decides to check out this dome for themselves?"

"We've taken measures to prevent that," said Will.

"They use that reasoning in bad science fiction movies," said Nadia. "'Let's keep the danger around and hope the bad guys don't find it!'"

"What do you think we should do, Nancy Drew?" asked Clive.

"I don't know…incorporate the metal talismans into a bridge, or some other structure where it can never be discovered or destroyed. Or bury it at the bottom of the ocean. I'm sure you could think of something."

"They have knowledge we might need," said Gordon. "They might be able to help us find other djinn or prevent other disasters."

"Like Hannibal Lecter?" Nadia asked. "Really, do you think the benefit is worth the risk?"

"Yes, we do," said Clive. "Moving on…"

Will got up and opened the overhead compartment. "We should really get some rest," he said. "We've still got several hours in the air." He took out pillows and blankets, tossing a few to Clive and Gordon, but hand delivering them to Nadia. In a surprisingly intimate gesture he gently placed a pillow beneath her head and meticulously arranged the blanket, tucking it under her chin. She looked up at him expectantly, a small smile playing about her lips.

But he simply turned and walked back to the other end of the plane.

CHAPTER 48

N adia woke up with a start. Lilith was there! Her soul shimmered menacingly in the cockpit, her long, dark hair blowing all around her.

Nadia looked around for Will and the others, but they were gone. Lilith approached with a strange gleam in her large, doe-like eyes. Her sharp teeth were fully exposed, and for an instant it seemed as if she was about to eat Nadia. But only for an instant. They both knew what she really wanted.

Nadia tried to get up, but she was once again chained to the seat. Lilith, meanwhile, kept inching nearer until she was hovering directly over Nadia, so close that she was almost touching her. Her beautiful eyes held Nadia's in a hypnotic trance. Slowly, so slowly that Nadia hardly realized it was happening, Lilith began encroaching on her, so that Nadia could *feel* her now too. It was like being pressed—and pulled—both at the same time. It was like being trapped in a too-small space while more people continued to pour in. It seemed as if the air was being extracted from Nadia's lungs. She felt as if she was being crushed. Or buried alive.

Hurry! She thought. *Kill me then, but let me out of here!*

"Hey!" Nadia opened her eyes to find Will gently shaking her. She looked around wildly. Lilith was gone. Gordon and Clive appeared to be sleeping. There were no chains tying her to the seat.

Will was peering at her with concern.

"Did I wake you?" she whispered.

"Nope. I was just sitting here, thinking," he whispered back.

"Still trying to figure out where Lilith is?" she asked, remembering what Gordon told her about him being a control freak. When he didn't reply she said—"You just missed her."

"Is that what you were dreaming about?"

"Yes." She shuddered, not wanting to elaborate. "How do they get inside a person?"

"There are a number of different ways for them to get in," he said. "The longer they've been doing it, the better they get at it. And it depends on where the djinn is, too."

"What do you mean?"

"Well, you already know about the dark place," he said. "It takes a *Book of the Dead* to get them out of there. But for a djinn that's already here, on earth, they might start out in that parallel universe Azazyl mentioned. They wander the earth without really experiencing it. They can sense us and we can sometimes sense them. All they want is to get through the barrier that separates us. They'll do anything to get through."

"Give me an example," she said.

"Some use spells. Others use mind control, especially if the person on this side is weak. And…some are a little more creative."

"Tell me," she insisted.

"The *Book of Solomon* tells the story of a young boy who has an encounter with a djinn. The boy could feel the djinn following him. He told Solomon that the djinn was slowly stealing his life by sucking it out through his thumb each night."

Nadia just looked at him. "That's…a strange story."

Will smiled. "The missing part of the story—the part that Solomon left out—is that just prior to this incident the boy had cut his thumb.

This djinn sensed the boy's living blood flowing out of him, and it answered some need within him...the need to live." They were both still whispering, giving the conversation an intimate quality in spite of the disturbing topic. "By sucking the boy's thumb he was attempting to breach the barrier between the parallel worlds and enter the body of the boy."

"Like a vampire," said Nadia, narrowing her eyes at him.

"Yes," he admitted, almost as if he hated to. "I know it sounds strange, but you'd be surprised how many mysteries are explained by the djinn. Ghosts, demon possession, and yes, even vampires. The concept of monsters originated with the Emim, who were also djinn. Almost every scary legend originates with the djinn."

Nadia tried to absorb this. "Wait...how do you know the boy in Solomon's story cut his thumb if that wasn't part of the story?" Her eyes grew wider. "You caught the djinn?"

"Yes," he said matter-of-factly. "His name is Ornias. He's one of the djinn Solomon conjured to help build his temple." Nadia sighed heavily. Just when she thought she *might* be able to accept what they were saying they added one more thing to set her back to doubting again.

Will had raised the armrest when they first started whispering so he could lean in closer. That closeness now made for an awkward silence. His eyes seemed to be melting into Nadia and she could feel his desire—yet he didn't make a move.

"You...don't have to worry about me," she stammered in the same, low voice. She felt warm under his gaze—so warm she couldn't tell if she was blushing or not. "I don't get attached either." He seemed surprised by her comment. "I mean...I don't believe in love. Or at least not the romantic notions people have about it." She felt she was making the situation even more awkward but she couldn't seem to stop talking. She shrugged and tried to laugh it off. "I mean, true love, right? It's as elusive as your djinn."

Will smiled. "But our djinn are not as elusive as you might think," he whispered, moving in even closer. She was starting to feel trapped. And those eyes! She tried to move back but realized she was already pressed as far as she could get into her seat.

Nadia tried to catch her breath. Was he going to kiss her or not?

His lips were so close that they were almost touching hers. "Are you going to kiss me or not?" he whispered.

Something inside her snapped. Recklessly, she clasped her hands on Will's shoulders and pressed her lips to his. But in another surprise move, Will pulled back, effectively halting the kiss. Nadia looked up at him in surprise. He smiled. When he leaned in to kiss her his pace was slow, his lips patient and gentle as they spread light, feathery kisses over hers, caressing them and coaxing them to open. Meanwhile, one hand slowly made its way down her lower back while the other hand worked its way through her thick curls. He ran his tongue over her lips, ever so lightly, just kind of tasting her at first—or teasing her—but before she realized how it happened he was devouring her in an all-encompassing kiss. He jerked her closer with the hand on her lower back and tightened his grip on her hair, though he was careful not to hurt her. Everything he did—every touch—inflamed her. She shuddered violently as the floor seemed to fall out from beneath her feet.

"Are we descending?" a sleepy voice asked. It took her a minute to recognize Clive's voice.

Will drew back reluctantly, his eyes never leaving her face. "Either that or we're falling," he whispered.

CHAPTER
49

Nadia paced the floor of her apartment anxiously. She felt like she should be doing something but was strangely incapable of action. She supposed she was probably suffering from some kind of post-traumatic stress, and wondered if she should have taken them up on their offer to have a trauma specialist stay with her until all of it was over.

If only she could think of something constructive to do. Here she was, the CEO of a relief organization that specialized in first response (not to mention that she knew ahead of time what was about to happen) and she was completely useless. She couldn't seem to focus. She looked at the clock again: *2:37 p.m.* Their cell's flight to LA was scheduled for takeoff at three-fifteen. Assuming they were correct about the cell 'escaping' the attack, she supposed it was also safe to assume that the *jihad* cells would wait until then to inject themselves with whatever deadly plague Lilith had decided to unleash on mankind this time.

What was happening? Had they recovered anymore of the syringes?

Nadia sighed in frustration. What she needed was to get back to her office, but she knew the operative they had sitting outside her apartment would never allow that. She was still a prisoner, and couldn't help wondering when it would all end.

It was strange being alone in her apartment again after spending (was it only three days?) in the constant company of her kidnappers. She wondered what they were doing at that moment.

She decided to take a hot bath, but wandering distractedly into her bedroom, she was suddenly drawn to her closet instead. There, behind the clothing and shoes, in a dark corner, way in the back, was a box that had been placed there without ever having been opened. She fished around until she found it and then opened it now, right there on the floor beside her bed. It was the box containing her mother's 'personal effects'—a cold description, Nadia thought, for the bits and pieces leftover from a life.

The first thing that caught her eye was the picture of her grandmother—the very one that she'd spent so many hours examining as a girl. It was worn and frayed, and she picked it up carefully to examine it again, going over every detail just like when she was young. She could almost hear her mother's soft voice, like a distant echo, describing Lilith as she rode into Kiriath Arba; victorious and beautiful and proud.

Nadia set down the picture and picked up Gisele's old scrap book. She opened it with mixed feelings. She loved her mother and was proud of her accomplishments—but—Nadia couldn't help wishing that she had been given a bigger part in Gisele's life. She didn't expect the leading role, just something better than a stage hand. This wish, which always left Nadia feeling a little guilty, seemed justified as Nadia flipped through the most significant moments of her mother's life.

Gisele appeared in every picture, of course. There were shots of her with famous people at parties and with politicians at fund-raising events. Some of the pictures were professional photographs of her modeling or even, on a few occasions, being cast in small parts off Broadway. She rarely faced the camera without her signature smile.

To Nadia, Gisele seemed exotic, glamorous and mysterious, and she couldn't help comparing her to Lilith. Were the two women somehow connected? It seemed more probable that Gisele had simply been influenced by the stories of Lilith that her mother told her.

There was a picture of Gisele and Edward when she was still very young. Gisele was gazing into Edward's eyes, unaware of the camera for once. There was something in her expression that Nadia had never seen before. Adoration? Desire? She looked innocent and in love. Had Gisele and Edward grown apart, or had something come between them? It was hard to tell with Gisele. She was flirtatious with everyone. She loved attention. But was she unfaithful? There'd been rumors, but...

Nadia couldn't help noticing that there was only one picture of herself in her mother's scrapbook. She and Gisele were standing in the middle of Rockefeller Center. Nadia appeared to be about fifteen years old. She couldn't remember the event; probably she had gone into the city to see one of Gisele's shows. She seemed thrilled to be there. She had hold of her mother's arm and was smiling from ear to ear.

Nadia set the scrapbook aside and picked up a thick pile of letters. She opened one and began to read. She recognized her mother's handwriting at once. It was fluid and larger than life and a little reckless, just like her. *"Darling,"* it read. *"Forgive me! You know I will make it up to you! Enta malaki! xo."*

Nadia was once again struck by how much Gisele and Lilith were alike. Their confidence—their audacity—it never occurred to either of them that they might not get what they wanted.

Enta malaki. 'You are my angel'; a peculiar choice of words.

But Nadia stopped herself there. There was nothing peculiar about it. It was a term of endearment used by thousands—maybe even millions—of people. Gisele was obsessed with angels after the stories Helene told her. It would have been more peculiar for her *not* to use the term.

As Nadia browsed through her mother's letters, it occurred to her that Lilith might still be trapped inside the ring. Why else would they have left Helene alive? This was no mere robbery of an archaeological discovery—significant thought it was. Someone was looking for

Lilith. Or maybe they were looking for the tablet of the Qliphoth. Maybe Lilith's *Book of the Dead* was nothing more than bait to draw out the tablet.

The Bedouin who gave them Lilith's book could have had other *Books of the Dead* in his possession. How did they know, for that matter, that the book even came from the cave in Qumran? There were no other books like it found in that cave. The Bedouin—or someone he was working for—might have had the book—or books—all along.

Nadia sighed. There were so many possibilities. She picked up another picture of her mother. Supposing, for a moment, that Gisele *was* possessed by Lilith. Where did Lilith go when Gisele died? Gordon said they ordinarily moved on to their offspring but, then again, neither Lilith nor Gisele were what anyone would call ordinary. Maybe Gisele—or Lilith—loved Nadia too much to rob her of her own life. But Nadia couldn't help rejecting this idea the moment it surfaced. Lilith aside, the woman Nadia knew as her mother would probably have eaten her young if it meant she could stay young and beautiful forever.

Nadia was filled with remorse the instant the thought was out. She shamefacedly opened another letter—this one was from her father to Gisele—and her hand instinctively rose to her heart as she read the first few lines. It was a love letter! She couldn't help admiring how eloquently her father wrote, though the letter was much more passionate than Nadia expected. She suddenly felt a little like a Peeping Tom, snooping where she had no right to be. She put down the letter and turned her attention to an envelope stuffed to overflowing with cheap stationery. At first glance Nadia thought it might be something she wrote—the stationery was like that of a young girl—but she saw at once that the paper was much more aged than a letter from her would have been, and then, upon opening the letter she saw that the handwriting was completely unfamiliar. Curious, she began to read the letter, but she didn't make it through the first line before she stopped. She could feel the blood draining from her face. She tried to resume reading but light-bulbs were flashing like fireworks in her head. She skipped to the last page and managed, somehow, to read the signature line before her hand was trembling so badly that she had to let the letter drop.

You never saw it.

Nadia went into the bathroom and splashed cold water on her face. Reaching for a towel, she caught sight of herself in the mirror. It looked like someone else entirely staring back at her. Her eyes were so dilated that they appeared to be entirely black. They made a frightening contrast to her skin, which was suddenly white as a sheet.

She walked numbly through the living room and out the front door of her apartment.

It won't make any difference now anyway. It's too late.

She stepped into the elevator and pushed the button to the lobby.

Don't do it.

Hardly knowing what she intended to do, she found herself standing next to the operative's car beside the driver's side window. The man sitting inside the car looked up her at in surprise. Slowly the window came down.

"Is anything the matter, Ms. Adeire?"

She stared at him for a minute, reminding herself that she hadn't thought this through.

"I need you to contact Mr. Gordon," she said, only half aware that what she was about to say didn't make any sense. "Tell him that Nadia needs a favor from Gene."

CHAPTER 50

Nadia came in through the side door of her father's beach house like she had hundreds of times before, but this was different. This time she felt like an intruder.

"Nadia!" he announced happily when he saw her. She watched him approach with a sudden wave of remorse. Everything about him seemed to radiate decency and integrity. His expression was trusting and sincere. No corruption appeared to have touched him, for though he was over sixty he was still a handsome man. His thick brown hair, which was streaked with gray, still fell in youthful waves over his forehead. Nadia supposed he hadn't changed much from the day Helene found him in her college library. Had that moment seemed as peculiar to her as this one did to Nadia now?

Edward kissed his daughter loudly on the cheek and then crushed her in one of his bear hugs. "You're early!" he observed, clearly pleased.

"Hi…Daddy," she said. She felt strangely detached, like in a dream. "…Or would you rather I call you Asmodeous?" She couldn't believe how casually the words tumbled out. She had the urge to cry but couldn't seem to muster the energy.

Her father stiffened and slowly pulled away. His face was pale, his smile rigid. He was clearly taken aback, yet he remained calm and self-assured. "What's going on?" he asked.

Nadia handed him the letter. He accepted, but didn't open it. He just stared at it, nodding slightly, his lips tight. "Where did you find it?" he asked.

"Mother had it," she told him.

"Hmph!" he said, genuinely surprised. "I'll be damned!" He looked at Nadia with interest and even a little admiration. "But how did you get from this," raising the letter—"…to Asmodeous?"

She was amazed by his composure. It seemed to be rubbing off. The sense of unreality increased while they spoke to each other as casually as if they were discussing the weather. "I put two and two together," she told him. "It never would have occurred to me if I hadn't found that letter—Helene's last letter to Edward," she said—"It puts you at the scene when her father was killed. In order to be in Qumran then, and to be Edward now…you'd have to be one of them. The djinn." She shrugged her shoulders hopelessly. "From there, I just had to figure out who would want to avenge Lilith. It had to be someone who knew about her past. Someone who cared about her, maybe even loved her. Someone who survived the flood with the other Anakians of Kiriath Arba. Someone with access to BEACON. And someone who cared enough about me to get me out of harm's way by insisting I come to Long Island during the attack. There are only two 'someone's who come to mind. You and Asmodeous." She paused, thoughtful, then pointed to the letter. "Why'd you save it?"

He made a sound that was half cry, half laugh, as if to say, 'why indeed!' His eyes, when they met hers, were filled with regret. "Lilith was always my weakness. I almost lost my mind looking for her during—and even after—the flood. I searched for her for centuries. Helene's letter…and Helene; they were all I had left. And, of course, Edward kept the door open, just in case."

Nadia couldn't help thinking of Gisele. "Did you even love my mother?"

"Yes, I loved her! She reminded me of Lilith, you see. But she was her own woman too, and in many ways very different from Lilith. I can't believe she knew about that letter! Lilith would never have kept that to herself. That was one thing about your mother; she was always full of surprises." He sighed heavily. "I loved her, but just like Lilith, she too is lost and I can't get either of them back."

Nadia was suddenly filled with regrets of her own. What was she doing?

"I can understand everything, Da...Asmodeous," she said— "Except this attack. Why?"

"Because quite frankly, the West has to be stopped," he said. When he saw her expression he waived his hand dismissively, almost as if annoyed. "I'm not talking about religion! You know that. This is me you're talking to, Nadia, and like it or not, I *am* your father."

A lump was forming in Nadia's throat that made it impossible for her to speak.

"It's not the morality of the West," he continued—"that's just propaganda for the extremists, to get them to do what has to be done. It's the earth that's the issue. The Western way of life is threatening to destroy it. This isn't a concern for most people. They know instinctively that they're leaving here when they die. That's fine for them. But *we* are here for eternity, Nadia. We don't want to kill anyone, but this is our home. Can't you see why we might want to protect it from people who would destroy it simply so they can get a little richer now?"

Nadia could see, actually, but she couldn't quite bring herself to say so. "But why this? Why now?"

"Those meetings are pushing the Western objectives onto the rest of the world. Every year more countries climb on board. I'm all for progress as you know, but they aren't doing it to benefit these countries. They're doing it to get around environmental restrictions. These corporations move their manufacturing plants into third world countries—not just for the cheap labor, although that's another incentive—but even more importantly, to evade being environmentally responsible. It's expensive to clean up the waste that manufacturing leaves behind. The rate at which the West is manufacturing and consuming cannot be supported by the earth. And there's more. Things you don't know. Things you can't imagine. We've reached the tipping point. It has to stop now!"

Nadia had heard much of this from her father and other environmentalists already, and she agreed with them—to a point. "But…two wrongs don't make a right! Anyone can twist an argument to suit their own personal wishes."

"By going to war with the West, yes, we are killing people, but we are killing the bad guys." He put up his hands to stop her objection. "Yes, I'm talking about your friends over there in Washington, and yes, even those so-called 'innocent' people who just happen to be there when the attack takes place. Hear me out! The lowliest among them—the poorest, most downtrodden person—even *he* is living at too high a standard to pretend to be oblivious to what's happening to the earth. Even he is responsible because he's supporting the destruction of the earth by going along with it. Everything from the clothes on his back to the shoes on his feet could be made without destroying the earth—if only he was willing to pay a few dollars more, or make due with less. These manufacturers moving into China, India, Mexico… they bring pollution, disease and death with them. Who are you to decide that it's okay to harm people in India, but not okay to harm someone in DC?"

"I never said it was okay to harm anyone…"

"Yes! You did! Every time you buy products made in those countries that's exactly what you're saying!" He laughed. "And frankly, I don't care if humans kill each other—if the Western world thinks it's acceptable to injure others so that they can have a better life who am I to interfere? But they're destroying my home. And I'm sorry, but I can't let that happen."

"But…wouldn't you get further by just coming out with the environmental argument? Why create religious extremism to execute your attack?"

He laughed. "We don't *create* religious extremism, Nadia. Extremism has been around since day one. The sons of men are born with it. It stems from their need to feel superior to everyone else around them. Extreme beliefs, extreme greed…they're both the same. 'I'm better than you and therefore my life is worth more than yours.' Look at corporate greed. Corporations kill as many or more people than religious extremism every year. Take your average oil spill—something that happens all the time—people die, the earth is damaged, and why? Often it's because the protective measures to prevent it would cost the billionaires who run the companies a fraction of their profits. Getting richer is more important than the lives of the people they kill. Isn't this every bit as extreme as the guy who thinks his religious views are more important than the lives of the people he kills?"

Since Nadia couldn't come up with a response to this he continued.

"We can't wage a direct war, Nadia. We've tried to influence people through environmental awareness but they don't care. They're too short-sighted to concern themselves with anything further into the future than their grandchildren—if that. And there's another reason too." He paused here, and Nadia could see that what he was about to tell her was painful for him to admit. "We know we aren't the ones the earth was made for. We know we have to tread lightly. To declare open war, to blatantly try to influence mankind…we would be inviting the angels to come back and wage another war on us. By using the extremists—by re-directing their desire to kill where it will do the greater good—we're not necessarily killing *more* people, we're simply killing the *right* people—or I should say, the people whose deaths will bring about the right kind of change."

Nadia was becoming frustrated. "Can't you see how wrong this is? You can rationalize it any way you like, but…"

"All I care about is preserving the earth," he said. "All I want is a place to live."

And bodies to do it in, she thought, but she couldn't bring herself to say it. Her father must have detected something in her expression, though, because his demeanor suddenly changed.

"How did you know about the incident in DC," he asked, suddenly becoming wary. "Nadia, how did you know about that?"

"I was…questioned about it," she said. "They linked the attack to BEACON."

"Who?"

Nadia hesitated. She had not lied to her father since she was a teenager. "I don't know," she said. "Some intelligence operation out of Washington…I can't remember the name of it now." She could feel her face growing hot and felt the lie was obvious.

He took a step closer and examined her face. "Did you tell them any of this?" he asked.

"No!" she said. "I…don't turn this around! All I want is for you to stop it, Daddy. I want you to tell me how to stop it and I'll…pass the information on to them."

"I'm sorry, Nadia," he said. "I can't do that." But he paused, as if considering it. "It's too late now, anyway," he said.

"We could try. Just tell me who and where," she said. "I wouldn't even have to tell them about you. I'm first response, remember? I have connections. I can make a call and we can stop this thing."

"You know as well as I do you couldn't cover up something like this," he said. "If you tried to, you'd be the one blamed."

He was far too clever to bluff. "You could start over…somewhere else," she said. The thought of this horrified her.

"Yes, I could. And to tell you the truth I would have done that already if not for you. I wanted to spend as much time as I could with you before I…moved on. But it's not that," he said. "Nadia, this has to happen. You have no idea what the West is messing with here."

"For me," she said. "Stop this for me."

There was a long pause. "I know you don't understand this now, but it will be better for you in the long run if I don't. I'm trying to protect you as well as myself. This has to happen now."

"Please give me the names," she said.

"I can't," he said.

"Why?"

"I've already told you why!"

Nadia closed her eyes. She didn't think she could go through with it. Djinn or human, she loved him.

And she could understand his point of view.

"I'll give you Lilith," she said, opening her eyes so she could see his expression when she played her final card.

CHAPTER
51

Edward's cool reserve was finally shattered. He staggered backwards, gaping at Nadia in astonishment.

"You'll…what?" he whispered.

"I'll give you Lilith," she repeated.

"Give me…how will you 'give' me Lilith?" he asked. He was so pale he looked as if he might faint. "Where is she?" he whispered.

"I give you my word," said Nadia. "I will produce her if you do this for me."

"Produce her! How?"

"Don't ask questions," she said. "Please, just…how many cells are there and who are they? *Please Daddy!*"

Edward stared at her for a long time. There was a strange look in his eyes and she wondered if he was contemplating taking what he wanted by force. It would be all over if he did. She would never be able to fight him.

But she realized suddenly that his struggle was not with *her*. It was an internal struggle. He looked like a man with a gun to his head—and the only question seemed to be how he would take the bullet.

"There are twelve," he blurted out at last. "And they've all infected themselves by now."

"What have they infected themselves with, exactly?" she asked.

"A new strain of plague. It's resistant to the antibiotics that have been successful in treating the plague up to this point. In lab rats, the mortality rate was a hundred percent, even with early treatment."

Nadia listened in stunned silence.

"It takes six hours for the infection to penetrate the lungs," he went on mechanically, apparently resigned to telling her everything now that the decision had been made. "At that point it becomes highly contagious, but there's another eighteen hours or so before flu symptoms will develop. The cells injected themselves around three thirty this afternoon so they would still feel well enough to work at the bank meetings tomorrow morning."

"How long do they have?" Nadia asked breathlessly.

"The flu symptoms last two to three days, and then they'll start to feel better. But then, sometime before the fifth day, their lungs will seize and they'll die."

"My god!" exclaimed Nadia. "Do you have any idea how many people could become infected in that time?" His expression told her that he did, and she recoiled. If not stopped, this could indeed bring the West to its knees. There were politicians, business executives and bankers from all over the world attending those meetings. She looked at her watch. It was a quarter to eight, just over four hours since the cells injected themselves. "Is there an antidote?"

"No."

"But, what if...," she stopped herself, not wanting to follow the direction her mind was taking. If one of *them* was infected they would simply move to another body. She didn't want to hear him say that everyone else—including her—was expendable. "I need the names of the infected cells," she said

"Lilith?" he reminded her.

"Write down the names and we'll trade," she countered.

"Trade?" He paused, thoughtful. "You have the ring," he concluded finally.

Nadia didn't answer. She once again feared he might try and take
it from her by force.

"You really have it?" he whispered, as if he couldn't quite bring
himself to believe it.

Nadia couldn't find her voice. She nodded.

He reached in his pocket so quickly that Nadia flinched. He paused
before pulling out a pen, clearly hurt by her reaction. "I would never
harm you Nadia," he said. "I would never even think of it."

A wave of shame washed over Nadia, but she was confused by it.
Her father had just ticked off his reasons for killing thousands of peo-
ple as casually as if he were listing his favorite dishes in a restaurant.
Was it so unthinkable that she should fear him? Yet she believed, deep
down, that he wouldn't harm her. Still, it wasn't much of a comfort.
Even Hitler had loved ones that he would no doubt protect.

Hitler! Why had she compared her father to him? Surely he was
not as bad as that.

She watched, virtually anesthetized by grief, as her father scrib-
bled the terrorists' names on the very envelope that held that fateful
letter from Helene. He wrote the names from memory and then held
the envelope out to her.

Nadia reached up and unclasped the necklace that Fa'izah gave
her. Then she handed it to her father in exchange for the envelope. He
examined the necklace for a moment then looked at her, confused.

"Look more closely," she told him. He did, and then he seemed to
falter again, falling back slightly.

"I started to peel it back a little in order to identify the markings,"
she said. "It seems like it should be easy enough to detach it the rest
of the way if you're careful." She referred to a thin strip of metal that
had been carefully woven in and around the locket and the connecting
chain.

"It's much smaller than I expected," he remarked.

"I know. I don't think it's the original," she said. "I suppose it
could be…Butch could have hidden it there. But in grandmother's stories, she talks about putting her fingers through the warm, metal shavings." She could see by her father's expression that he didn't know

about the stories—and it suddenly occurred to her that he was never around when her mother told them. Gisele must have known all along. *Enta malaki.* You are my angel. It would have been just like her to cherish the private joke. "My mother told me that Helene had access to the can of metal shavings before the ritual," she explained. "She could have found this little strip of metal in there, pulled it out, copied the markings that Butch made on the original and then simply bent it around her finger."

"Either ring would work!" exclaimed her father.

"That's what I'm thinking," said Nadia. "It would explain why Lilith answered Helene's questions, but not Huxley's. She said she was only compelled to answer those wearing the ring." She wondered how her father would get Lilith out of the ring. He may have kept Butch's notes. Or maybe he didn't even need them.

Her father's hand was trembling now as he carefully placed the tiny ring on his pinky. He looked at Nadia.

"I know how confused and hurt you must be," he said. "I just want you to remember that I love you and I'm proud of you. No matter what, I'll always love you."

Nadia nodded, unable to speak.

When Edward spoke again, it was in the ancient language of the Nephilim. He recited the incantation with authority, not awkwardly stumbling over pronunciation, but easily and smoothly elucidating each syllable as if it was the most natural thing in the world. The whole thing took place in a matter of minutes, with less effort than it would take to perform a magic trick, and Nadia remembered Butch's remark about how easy it was to call out a djinn that was already tied to a talisman. A kind of mist appeared and quickly took shape.

Although Helene had described Lilith in great detail, Nadia was still not prepared for the genuine article. The size of her was intimidating by itself—but when combined with the claws and teeth! Yet there was beauty there too, creating a most disturbing paradox that took Nadia's breath away. Nothing that happened so far had prepared her for this. She stared up at Lilith in utter amazement.

Lilith didn't seem surprised to see Nadia. She merely glanced at her and then turned with interest to Edward. Her eyes narrowed with uncertainty as she examined him.

With effort, Nadia tore her eyes from the incredible spectacle to look at her father who, even more incredibly, didn't seem the least bit put out by Lilith's appearance. On the contrary, he stared up at her with pleasure, as if this was exactly how he expected her to look.

"At last!" he whispered, and there were tears in his eyes.

Lilith just stared at him in horror, almost as if she was rejecting what she was seeing. She turned her attention back to Nadia and this time really looked at her. "Wait," she said. "You're not the same."

She must have mistook Nadia for Helene! Nadia opened her mouth to speak but couldn't seem to find her voice. In fact, she felt as if she was frozen to the spot. A peculiar wooziness was creeping over her.

"You recognize a young woman you met only briefly, yet forget the one who made you a warrior?" Nadia's father asked softly.

Lilith whirled around, attempting to cover herself behind her thick curtain of hair as she peered out at Edward. Her eyes were wide with disbelief. "Who…!" she cried shrilly. "Who?"

"Ah," he said gently, "I see now why they called you screech owl. No! Don't cover yourself. I love you as you are!"

Lilith couldn't seem to accept what she was hearing. "No!" she sobbed.

Nadia stood by, silent and forgotten. She felt like a statue that had been cemented to the spot. A kind of *déjà vu* came over her, reminding her of another time and place that was eerily similar to this. She was vaguely aware of music playing in the distance—on the beach perhaps— and had the nagging sense that she was forgetting something important.

"Where were you?" cried Edward, giving in to his emotions at last. "I looked everywhere for you!"

"The temple…," she cried. "I couldn't get any farther than the temple when it…hit. Everything was gone in an instant! But you survived!"

He'd been moving closer to her, slowly, with a kind of reverence. She towered over him, but he didn't seem intimidated in the least. He reached out his hand to touch her. She raised hers to meet his touch but then drew back abruptly.

"My hands!" she cried, mortified.

He caught and caressed the claw lovingly. "You're beautiful," he said. He traced a line up her arm and shoulder and then along the side of her face, gently running his fingers over her jaw and lips and teeth. "Just as I knew you would be." But he faltered, stumbling backwards. He was growing pale.

Nadia watched, still dimly aware that she was supposed to be doing something. The names on the list! She had to give them to Gordon!

"Asmodeous!" cried Lilith. "What is it? What's happening?"

He turned to Nadia, confused. "Na...dia," he said. "My... daughter."

Lilith turned to Nadia. "This is your daugh...Asmodeous!" Lilith rushed to his side as he fell. "Help him!" she screamed to Nadia. But Nadia couldn't move. She felt as if she was under a spell. And then she remembered. The music! She had to get out!

Edward was now looking at Nadia with an expression of incredulity. "What...is...that...mu...sic?" he asked, struggling over every syllable. His gaze moved to the open window, and he stared out of it as if he, too, was struggling to remember something important. He tried to get up but inevitably fell back down. He tried to crawl toward the door.

"Lili...!" he cried.

"What can I do?" Lilith pleaded, frantic. Her efforts to help him were having very little effect. Without a body, her soul—imposing as it was—appeared to have little power to help. She turned to Nadia, whose legs were slowly slipping out from under her as she, too, fell to the floor.

"What is happening?" cried Lilith again. The music seemed to be getting louder, or maybe it was just becoming more sinister—though it was a common enough song that was playing—and then suddenly Nadia remembered everything. She remembered the metal shavings Gordon brought with him to spread in a circle around the outside of her father's house. She remembered the ring Gordon was wearing, which was cast from the same lot as the metal shavings. There was nothing ominous in the music; it was only a distraction, just like the Israelites' horns back in Canaan, to cover the sound of Gordon's chanting. Nadia was supposed to join him outside the house—outside the circle. But now she couldn't move. She couldn't do anything, it seemed, except cry. She felt the tears streaming down her face as she watched her father being destroyed.

"Ta…ta…ke…re," her father was trying to tell Lilith something.

"Take you…where?" Lilith cried, trying again to help him up but failing miserably.

"Reee…," he raised his hand to her, his features twisted in horror. Nadia knew. He was trying to tell Lilith to take the ring from his finger. Even in his final hour he was thinking of Lilith.

He turned to Nadia, as if to apply to her for help. "Na…deeeeee… aaaaaaaaaah!" What began as a plea became a deafening roar so full of anguish it shook the house with its intensity. Her composed, dignified father was suddenly a twisted, writhing mass in the middle of the floor. Nadia could actually see Asmodeous' soul struggling to remain in Edward's body, which was being stretched to all proportions and becoming terribly disfigured in the process. The sounds coming out of him were like those of a monster. Window's shattered and walls cracked, as if they, too, were being ripped apart in the struggle.

Lilith seemed desperate for something to do. Her gaze rested on Nadia, and suddenly Nadia remembered another reason she had to get out.

But now all she could do was watch as Lilith approached with that strange gleam in her large, doe-like eyes. Her expression seemed especially sinister with all of her teeth exposed, and with another flash of *déjà vu* Nadia wondered if Lilith was about to eat her. But just like in her premonition on the plane, she quickly realized what Lilith really wanted.

Nadia could see that Lilith was hesitant and uncertain, acting on instinct alone without any first-hand experience to draw upon. Her lips moved perilously close to Nadia's as if she intended to steal the breath from Nadia's lungs. Meanwhile her beautiful eyes held Nadia's in a hypnotic trance. Nadia wondered distractedly if it was really possible for Lilith to enter her body while Gordon was casting a spell to *remove* a djinn from another body, but then she remembered that Lilith was not a free soul to be called out. She was bound to a ring. Only the one holding the ring could control her. As long as Asmodeous remained inside Edward's body, he would be her only master. That was why he wanted Lilith to take the ring from him.

Even if Lilith managed to enter Nadia's body, she would still be bound by the ring to do as Asmodeous—or whoever controlled Asmodeous—wished.

All these thoughts occurred to Nadia as Lilith loomed over her, simultaneously choking and crowding her, practically crushing her, it seemed. Nadia felt suffocated. She tried to assert herself but could not. She had no strength to fight. Gordon's incantation had weakened her too much. Though her soul couldn't be captured, it could become separated from her body. And that would mean death.

In the background, Nadia could hear that the fight to remove Asmodeous from Edward's body was still going on. And she knew that Gordon would never let up. He couldn't—not as long as he believed he still needed those names. If only Nadia had given him the envelope! Gordon had given her fifteen minutes. He'd made it clear that he couldn't sacrifice all those people just to save her. Why had she stayed? Was it that, deep down, in the furthest reaches of her soul, she knew she belonged with her father? Had she inadvertently chosen a side?

Nadia could no longer say which side she was on. It was as if her very sense of self was being crushed. She suddenly wished for death, so at least her soul could ascend. She did not want to be buried alive in this body beneath the harrowing influence of Lilith.

Hurry! She cried inwardly to Gordon. *Kill me then, but get me out of here*!

"Nooooooo!"

Nadia heard the tortured cry in the background and knew that it was her father calling out on her behalf. "Nooooooo!" he cried again. In the midst of his own struggle to survive, he was still protecting the women he loved.

Lilith drew back in confusion. Having tasted life, she seemed reluctant to abandon the opportunity. Yet she could not defy Asmodeous—as long as he remained in Edward's body.

But it no longer mattered. Nadia was suddenly watching the scene from overhead. She was aware of a bright light behind her, but she couldn't seem to pull her gaze away from the sight of her father's body being jerked in all directions and the image of Lilith, hovering menacingly over Nadia's lifeless body.

"Reeeee...ng!" her father cried again. Lilith whirled around with sudden understanding.

"The ring!" she exclaimed. "Where is it?" She rushed to the thrashing body in search of the tiny ring.

Just then, Gordon stormed into the house like an ancient warrior from the past, donning the mask and calling out loudly in the Sumerian tongue. He abruptly stopped, visibly jolted, when he caught sight of Lilith, and Nadia felt a sudden fear—or was it hope?—that Gordon might stop the incantation there, mistaking Lilith for the djinn he was calling out. Nadia knew she should have told him about Helene's ring, but she'd wanted to keep it as a bargaining tool with her father. Gordon would never have allowed such a risk. It had been all she could do to get him to come alone, without alerting the others. She didn't even tell him where they were going, or why, until they were too far to turn back. But she supposed he must have guessed. There were only so many reasons why someone would ask him to bring a mask, a ring and metal shavings—all cast from the same lot.

Whatever conclusions Gordon drew about Lilith, he couldn't fail to miss the still-writhing body of Edward. And too, Gordon may have recognized Lilith from her grandmother's stories. He resumed his chanting, rather shakily at first, and the house shook even harder with Asmodeous' rage as he now faced his opponent head on.

Gordon wasted no time. Still chanting, he bent down and grabbed Nadia beneath her arms, virtually dragging her across the floor. Nadia's soul wanted to go with them but she felt herself being drawn even farther away. She could feel the warmth of the bright light now, and realized that she was dying.

Just as Gordon was nearing the door, Lilith finally managed to get the ring off Edward's finger. She slipped it onto one of her claws and paused a moment, as if waiting to see what would happen. Nothing did, at first, but then, quite suddenly, she disappeared. Feeling a strange presence beside her, Nadia turned to find Lilith floating there. But Lilith didn't appear to notice Nadia. She was absorbed in the scene below, and when Nadia followed her gaze she saw that everything had suddenly gone quiet.

Edward's body lay in a heap on the floor. Gordon had stopped chanting. There was a new presence moving about the room. They all watched in amazement as the creature slowly took form. Its appearance, once it finally evolved, struck Nadia like ice water to the face. Though her life force remained overhead, she could feel, as well as see, her body shudder below.

The soul of Asmodeous was as awful as it was awe-inspiring. It had two heads; both of which were fully equipped with eyes, nose and mouth. One head—the prominent one from its position facing forward—was that of a ferocious lion. It looked fierce and determined, its large teeth bared in anger. The second head—which literally hung off to one side like a growth—was a disturbing combination of man and lamb. The expression on its face was one of anguish.

Asmodeous' shoulders and torso were similar to that of a giant man, except that there were two enormous, charcoal-colored wings coming out of his back. The lower half of his body was that of a dragon, with the same smoky coloring as the wings. It was a fearsome creature, so large it had to crouch, even with the cathedral ceilings in Edward's million dollar home. The body looked as if it would be awkward to manage, but Asmodeous moved with the grace of a gazelle. In an instant Lilith was beside him. He towered over her now, but she didn't shrink away from him. They melded into each other as if they were two pieces of a puzzle. His eyes were wild with pain, like those of an injured animal, and he let out another roar that shook the house to its very foundation. This seemed to revive him, and he suddenly began to speak. His words were so alien—the sound so severe—that they were actually jarring to the ear. He spoke rapidly and with authority, and it occurred to Nadia that he might be issuing forth his own incantation—perhaps one that would challenge Gordon's hold over him. And God help her—a small part of her secretly hoped he would succeed!

Nadia could see at a glance why Asmodeous and Lilith had been drawn to each other. Theirs were truly kindred souls. There was, in each of them, the beautiful and benevolent side of their natures, contrasting violently with the vicious mercenaries that helped them survive.

Lilith clung to Asmodeous while Gordon carried Nadia's body out of the house. She seemed absorbed in what Asmodeous was saying, as if she understood every word, and it occurred to Nadia that he could be sharing valuable information with her. There was a strange, wild beauty in the way they held themselves and each other and—even in this, their weakest moment—Nadia could see why they were called the "mighty ones of old," those glorious gods of Mesopotamia, who yearned, more than anything else, to live.

Nadia could no longer find the line. As she turned toward the light, she had the sense that she had done something horribly wrong. She had committed an act against nature. She had killed her father.

CHAPTER
52

Nadia watched distractedly as men in air-tight masks and suits worked to secure the area around the apartment building of the last remaining cell. A female reporter was talking rapidly in the foreground as they ran the live footage on her television screen. Nadia's phone rang, and she hit the mute button on her remote control and answered it.

"We got 'em," Gordon told her.

"I know," she said. "I just saw it on the news." There was a pause. "How are you doing?"

"I'm fine," she said, but there was a tremor in her voice that made it clear she was anything but fine.

"I'm sending someone over," he said.

"No," she said. "Please. Don't."

There was another pause. "I fucked up," he said.

Nadia sighed, not sure if she was up to comforting Gordon at that moment. "That's not true," was the most she could manage.

"You don't have to say anything," he said. "I just want you to know how sorry I am."

"No matter what you or anybody else might have done, it wouldn't have mattered anyway," she said. "I mean...it was me who...who...," she couldn't finish her sentence. She kept telling herself that either way she would've had regrets. If not her father, it would have been all those people in Washington. Why had this fallen upon her?

That damn letter! If only she hadn't found it! And come to think of it, that was the same thing that got her great-grandfather killed.

"You did the right thing," Gordon said.

"I wish someone had destroyed that letter," she said bitterly, hardly aware that she'd spoken out loud.

"It saved lives," he reminded her.

She knew he was right. Maybe that's why her grandmother was so adamant that Nadia go back. Maybe Nadia's finding the letter somehow atoned for the innocent lives lost when her grandmother wrote it.

But Nadia couldn't find comfort in the lives that had been saved. Not yet.

"Will has been out of his mind with worry," Gordon continued. "Couldn't you just talk to him...let him know you're okay?"

"I don't know," she said. "Is...is he there with you now?"

"No. We've been given a few days off before the debriefing."

"Oh," She suddenly realized how little she knew about them— where they lived, who their families were. A terrible sense of loneliness loomed over her, becoming more insidious with each loss she suffered.

She supposed she would feel better once she got back to work, but suddenly even that filled her with dread. There would always be at least two sides to every crisis. If you helped one, you hurt the other. Who was she to play God, choosing who would win and who would lose? What did *her* soul look like, beneath the beautiful, pampered flesh?

"Are you sure I can't do anything for you?" Gordon's voice brought her out of her thoughts.

"Positive."

"Good night then, Nadia."

"Good night Gordon."

"And thank you. You did a good thing for the world."

She hung up the phone and rested her head on the pillow. When she closed her eyes, images she didn't want to see appeared so she abruptly opened her eyes to clear them away.

But now she was seeing things with her eyes open! She closed her eyes again, and then opened them.

There, in the doorway, stood Will.

"What are you doing here?" she demanded, sitting up and adjusting her robe indignantly. Yet every impulse she had was clamoring to receive him.

"I had to see you," he said.

"How'd you get in?"

He smiled sheepishly. "You might want to change the locks to your apartment and your office now that it's all over." He lingered in the doorway. "May I come in?"

"Do I have a choice?"

"Of course you do, Nadia," he said, but he stepped into her bedroom without waiting for her consent anyway. "You shouldn't be alone right now."

"I'm not sure you're the person to make me feel better."

"You blame me," he said. It was a statement, not a question.

"And myself," she said.

He sighed, accepting this, and she could feel herself softening toward him. If he'd argued the point it would only have made her feel worse. She knew her anger was misplaced. But a small part of her couldn't help wondering if her feelings for Will somehow influenced her actions against her father. This, more than anything, made her feel like a traitor.

She'd always been so sure of herself, so certain that she was doing what was right. Now, she hardly knew what right was, let alone if she was doing it.

"I should be the one to go through this with you," he said, sitting down beside her on the bed. He picked up one of her hands and held it in both of his. They were warm and made her feel safe. "I misjudged you," he said. "I couldn't have been more wrong. You were brought into this against your will and given an impossible choice. You did nothing wrong." He squeezed her hand as his eyes gently implored her. "If only I could make you understand…how beautiful…how perfect… you are." His words reminded Nadia of her father's words to Lilith. She'd heard somewhere that women were often attracted to men who reminded them of their fathers. She supposed this was true. There was no denying the similarities between Will and her father. They both had that same, unbending certainty in their convictions. And they both loved the women in their life unconditionally.

But these thoughts brought her pain, so she promptly changed the subject.

"Will it all work out?" she asked—"In DC, I mean."

"They've isolated the infected individuals and everyone they've come in contact with," he said. "It looks like we might be able to contain this thing. Thanks to you."

"What will happen to my…to Asmodeous?" Unwanted tears filled her eyes. She closed them, recalling Gordon's face when she first came to. "We've got Asmodeous trapped in the house," he'd told her. "But Lilith got away." She'd closed her eyes again and wished for death. Yet she knew that Asmodeous—if left free—would continue his mission to destroy the West. He would never change his mind—any more than Will would change his.

"Are you sure you want to know?" he asked. She opened her eyes and stared at him until he gave in. "He'll be brought to the chamber—that shiny dome you asked us about—for debriefing," he told her.

"Will you be there?" she asked.

"Yes."

"He was speaking a very strange language," she told him. "Even stranger than the one you guys spoke."

"That's what Gordon said."

"Have any of the other djinn done that?" she wondered.

"Not that I know of," he said.

"I wonder what he was saying," she continued, thoughtful.

"At first Gordon thought he might be invoking some kind of spell of his own," said Will. "Something to counter what Gordon had done. But after Gordon revived you he went back in and Asmodeous was still there. He appeared to be bound to the ring. He gave Gordon the names of the infected cells."

"He'd already given me the names beforehand," Nadia told him. "They were sitting right there, on the table. And didn't Helene mention Asmodeous escaping the ring before...with Solomon?"

Will was examining her too closely. Nadia lowered her eyes. "We won't know anything for sure until the debriefing," he said.

"Gordon may have left him alone too long," she mused.

"Gordon made the right choice," he told her—"In saving your life, that is." and Nadia knew that Will—and everyone else—was still upset that Gordon acted alone.

"I made him promise not to tell anyone," she said. "I don't know why." But she wondered now if that was true. She'd needed at least one of them to help her find out if her father was really Asmodeous, but maybe she also wanted to give her father a fighting chance to escape. Maybe. "And I never told Gordon about Lilith's ring."

"He should have at least told us what he was doing," he said.

"Is he in trouble?" she asked.

"A little. Nothing he can't handle."

In the course of this exchange Will kept slowly moving in closer, and now Nadia was in his arms. He was searching her eyes, but they remained averted. She couldn't quite bring herself to look at him. If he knew how close she'd come to destroying that letter, or how much she wanted her father back...

Gisele was the only person who would have been able to understand. After all, she'd kept the letter a secret all those years. Nadia supposed she was more like her mother than she originally thought.

"I'm going to need some time," she said, but she snuggled even closer to Will, savoring the feel of his embrace. He responded by holding her tighter.

She thought about Asmodeous and Lilith. The constancy of their feelings for each other after all those years moved her. She supposed it rather put her to shame, with her fleeting, halfhearted love affairs. She wondered if she was capable of feeling that kind of devotion for another person. Her thoughts turned to Will. The attraction between them was undeniable. She longed for his touch. And she admired him. But was that enough?

As the heat of Will's body warmed and stimulated her, Nadia realized that she did have something in common with Lilith and

Asmodeous after all. All of her training came rushing back, reminding her that no matter what happened, life goes on. She had to keep fighting if she wanted to survive. It was worth the fight.

But Nadia wanted more than just to survive.

She wanted to *live*.

The next book in this series is

POWER OF GODS

An excerpt is attached.

PROLOGUE

Fort Greely, Alaska
Present day

A manda awoke with a start and bolted up in bed.
"Who's there?" she cried, looking frantically around the room. Shadows loomed, startling her before she recognized them for what they were; a pile of laundry sitting on the back of a chair and her favorite dress, retrieved that very day from the dry cleaners, hanging on the door.

She paused, searching her memory. She'd been jarred from her sleep by the sound of someone calling out her name.

Yet she appeared to be alone in the room. Amanda faltered, reluctant to accept that it was only a dream. It seemed so real! She could still hear the distinct, imploring tone. It was a woman's voice. Her mother's?

Amanda brushed this disturbing thought aside and slowly lay back down, pulling the covers up all the way to her chin. Her mother—what an idea! Amanda didn't believe in ghosts. It must have been her own voice she heard, calling out in her sleep. But why would she call out her own name?

As Amanda attempted to soothe herself with this most logical explanation, she kept an uneasy eye on the shadows lurking all around her. She felt disproportionately unnerved—all the more so because she wasn't prone to bad dreams or wild imaginings. Something had spooked her out of a deep sleep, and whatever it was seemed to be lingering, like an ominous presence. She had the distinct and persisting impression that someone was there, watching her.

"Tommy...?" she called out weakly, but the preposterousness of this struck her before the word was even out of her mouth. Tommy would not waste his time!

This involuntary thought brought Amanda up short. Why had she thought of it like that? Suffice it to say that Tommy wasn't the sort of man to watch a woman sleep—nor was he the type to lurk around in the dark playing tricks. He was too time conscious for that.

And much too self-absorbed.

Amanda huffed at herself testily. She hated it when she got like this. It was his leaving so soon after their lovemaking. He'd said it was because he needed to get up early, but her alarm clock worked just as well as his. What did it mean? Was it possible that Tommy was tiring of her already?

Amanda instantly rejected this possibility. She'd given him a night to remember if Cosmo could be trusted (and Amanda had been relying on their advice for too long to consider that they couldn't). She'd deliberated over every detail, from the long, false eyelashes to the back breaking stilettos. She shuddered with pleasure, recalling his expression when he saw her in the little pink lace teddy that left nothing to the imagination. He'd responded like a wild boar at a picnic. But then he left so quickly after! She couldn't help feeling a little resentful. Here she was, working her ass off (literally) to make each and every encounter more exciting for him and what, meanwhile, was he doing for her?

Yet Amanda was confident that she would win him over in the end. Oh, she was well aware of that dowdy little waitress in Delta Junction who was after him but, compared to Amanda, she was merely ridiculous. Of course looks weren't everything, but in this woman's case they amounted to nothing. Amanda and her best friend, Catherine, had become regulars at the restaurant where the waitress worked, solely for the pleasure of picking her apart. Amanda couldn't even remember the woman's name; she began calling her 'Flo' early on, and it stuck. How could Tommy settle for a washed up old waitress named 'Flo' after having Amanda?

Amanda was starting to feel better. Even though he wasn't good at showing it, Tommy *had* to be falling in love with her. She knew he was proud of her—she could tell by his self-satisfied expression whenever people watched them come into a room. She stood out in every crowd, with her long, blonde hair and voluptuous figure. In addition to being one of the best looking women in the region, she loved him, blew him and made him laugh. Really, what more could a man want?

Amanda rolled over in her bed restlessly. Normally, thinking about Tommy could soothe her no matter what was happening around her, but she was still feeling uneasy. She sat up, glancing at the clock. It was three in the morning. She looked around the room again, examining every shadow scrupulously. She couldn't shake the feeling that someone was there in the room with her, watching her. She snapped on the light and fished through the top drawer of her bedside table for a small bottle of pills. Finding it, she dropped one of the little blue pills on her palm, tossed it in her mouth and swallowed it, washing it down with water from a glass on the table. Then she shut off the light and lay back down, trying to think happy thoughts about her future with Tommy while waiting for the pill to kick in.

But her eyes kept wandering back to the shadows hovering all around the room. Had they changed position since she'd looked at them last? Amanda chided herself inwardly. When had she ever been afraid of shadows? Yet she *was* afraid. The room suddenly felt too close. She recalled turning up the heat before going to bed—perhaps the room was too warm. She threw back the blankets and snapped on the light once again. She walked to the window and paused uneasily before raising the blinds. She turned, looking around the room again in an effort to get a reign on her fear. Failing this, she turned back toward the window and jerked the cord, making the blind fly up with a loud clang. Her heart stopped. There were *two* faces reflected in the window—hers, and…something else!

Amanda spun around, a small, involuntary shriek escaping her lips. There was nothing behind her! She turned back to the window, dreading what she might see, but now there was only one ghostly white image reflected there, and that was her own. She turned back toward the room again, scanning every nook and cranny.

"Who's there?" she croaked, too terrified to move. The image—though she'd only seen it briefly—was still fixed in her mind. It was too terrible to forget. And it had been hovering so close to her—almost touching her! She shivered at the thought. The large, dark eyes—and those teeth!

The better to eat you with, my dear.

Amanda made a little sound, like a whimper, and leapt from the window to her bed. Very slowly, with dread, she bent down over the side of the bed to look underneath.

All she saw were shoes and dust bunnies.

Amanda got back out of bed and crept, on tiptoe, through her apartment, turning on every light switch she passed as she made her way to the living-room. Making it there in one piece, she picked up the remote and turned on the television, stealing anxious glances around the room. The apartment immediately came alive with the comforting sounds of what appeared to be a talk show. Amanda sat on the couch, feeling a little bit calmer as she absently began flipping through channels. She had the sudden urge to call Tommy but decided against it. Like Cosmo pointed out, she didn't want to appear 'needy.'

A familiar scene from the movie, *Pretty Woman*, flashed on the screen, and Amanda put down the remote. She'd seen the movie a hundred times before, but the sight of Julia Roberts flinging an oyster across a crowded restaurant was strangely comforting. Her little apartment seemed unnaturally bright with all of the lights turned on, and the blue pill was definitely kicking in now. Amanda stared dully at the television until she eventually drifted back to sleep.

Power of Gods

BOOK TWO OF
LEGACY OF THE WATCHERS

Available at these bookstores:

ABOUT THE AUTHOR

Nancy Madore achieved enormous critical acclaim writing 'female friendly' erotica in her ENCHANTED series. Now, following her life-long interest in history and mythology, she's writing historical science fiction. THE HIDDEN ONES is the first of the LEGACY OF THE WATCHERS series.

You can learn more about the LEGACY OF THE WATCHERS series by visiting Nancy Madore's website at

www.nmadore.com.